REVENGE

Revenge

Edited by
KATE SAUNDERS

VIRAGO

Published by VIRAGO PRESS Limited 1990
20–23 Mandela Street, Camden Town, London NW1 0HQ

*A CIP Catalogue record for this book is available
from the British Library*

Typeset by CentraCet, Cambridge
Printed and bound in Great Britain

CONTENTS

ACKNOWLEDGEMENTS

The editor is grateful for advice and suggestions from Richard Dalby.

Acknowledgements are due to the following for permission to include the stories which appear in this book: Lisa St Aubin de Terán for 'The Spider's Web'; Candia McWilliam for 'Being a People Person'; Shena Mackay and Deborah Rogers Ltd for 'Curry at the Laburnums' (from *Babies in Rhinestones*, Heinemann, 1983); Mary Flanagan for 'The Wedding Dress'; Lucy Ellmann for 'Pass the Parcel'; Joanna Briscoe for 'Revenge'; Anne Enright for 'The Portable Virgin'; Muriel Spark and David Higham Associates for 'The Portobello Road' (from *The Go-Away Bird*, Macmillan 1958); Faber & Faber Ltd and The University of Arkansas for Ellen Gilchrist's 'Revenge' (from *The Land of Dreamy Dreams*, Faber & Faber Ltd 1981); Emma Tennant for 'Rigor Beach'; David Higham Associates Ltd and Harcourt Brace Jovanovich Inc. for Alice Walker's 'The Revenge of Hannah Kemhuff' (from *In Love and Trouble*, The Women's Press 1984); Maureen Freely for 'Delia and the Avengers'; the Estate of Elizabeth Bowen and Sidgwick & Jackson Ltd for 'Making Arrangements' (from *Ann Lee's* 1926); Ruth Rendell and Random Century for 'A Glowing Future' (from *The Fever Tree*, Hutchinson 1982).

Every effort has been made to trace copyright holders in all copyright material in this book. The editor regrets if there has been any oversight and suggests the publisher is contacted in any such event.

INTRODUCTION

'It is always a paltry, feeble, tiny mind that takes pleasure in revenge', declared the Roman satirist Juvenal. 'You can deduce it without further evidence than this: that no one delights in revenge more than a woman.'

Wafting off his papyrus is a distinct odour of paranoia. Men have cornered the market in ordinary, bog-standard retaliation; usually hasty and ill-considered stuff, meted out with the first blunt instrument that comes to hand. But for women, revenge is an art form; fine, delicate precision engineering, largely beyond male capabilities. The feminine combination of intense imagination and unlimited patience can transform the whole concept of returning injury for injury into a thing of beauty and a joy for ever. These stories are a celebration of the subtlety, psychological insight and wry wit the female of the species brings to her acts of vengeance. Just like the Mounties, she always gets her man.

Francis Bacon defined revenge as 'a kind of wild justice', and condemned it, because it was beyond the law. This probably explains why it belongs so particularly to women. You cannot have an act of revenge unless a crime has been committed, and the crimes men have visited on women down the ages are traditionally outside the statute books. Even today, a wife has difficulty taking her battered head or drained bank account to court, let alone her broken heart or wasted life. Bacon's 'wild justice' is often the only justice available. Women delight in revenge as a revolutionary tribunal which rights the wrongs the law cannot touch.

A man who betrays or exploits a woman does so because he believes she is weak and powerless. He does not realize that the little dear who has been so sweet to him can turn into a grim, implacable termagant, waiting – for years, if necessary – to pounce where it will hurt most. The subculture of modern legend is full of 'true' anecdotes about the revenge of the woman scorned. There's the old chestnut about the boyfriend's telephone left tuned to the speaking clock in Sydney for an entire weekend. Or his flat being sprinkled with water and mustard-and-cress seeds. Or the classic dog-turd behind the radiator, which has him dismantling the whole house to find the source of the smell – see also under haddock, kipper and small deceased animal.

Tales like these are an unofficial guidebook to what women ought to do, instead of following their usual practice of begging him to stay on any terms. Modern legends spring up as an underground acknowledgement that something in society is wrong – in this case, the position of women. Just as the ancients invented Ulysses and Hercules, men who transcended human weakness and became equal to the gods, so we have invented heroines with harder hearts and cooler heads than ours, to balance those unevenly-weighted scales.

Women cannot thump those who offend them – few husbands wake up in Casualty after their wives have been out drinking – so female revenge requires brains rather than brawn. Which makes it all the more effective. 'There are fates more terrible than death;' wrote Louisa Alcott, 'weapons more keen than poniards, more noiseless than pistols. Women use such, and work out a subtler vengeance than men can conceive.'

Alcott's floridly romantic story 'Pauline's Passion and Punishment' is a prime example of high Victorian tragedy, its brooding emotions rent by lightning-flashes of pure melodrama. The heroine, Pauline, is a volatile young woman who has given herself heart and soul to a thorough bounder. When he marries someone else, Manuel, the fiery South American aristocrat who loves Pauline from afar, asks: 'Shall I kill him?'

> Pauline laughed low to herself, a dreary sound, but answered with a slow darkening of the face that gave her words an ominous significance. 'Why should you? Such revenge is brief and paltry, fit only for mock tragedies or poor souls who have neither the wit to devise, nor the will to execute a better.'

Pauline has both. She agrees to marry Manuel, on the condition that he will help her to carry out a complicated scheme which will cause her faithless lover to fall for her all over again, so that he may taste the bitterness of rejection at first hand. Those who know Louisa May Alcott only as the author of *Little Women* may be surprised by the complexity and intensity she brings to 'Pauline's Passion'. Like her famous character Jo March, Alcott began her career writing penny dreadfuls for popular magazines. These are executed with great professional skill, and something more: an awareness of the darker side of sexual infatuation, which rarely surfaces in her novels.

Pauline is not allowed to take pleasure in her revenge. Although Alcott identifies her motives forcefully and sympathetically, she makes it clear that vengeance can only be a poisoned chalice. It is supposed to hurt the perpetrator more than the victim. As Francis Bacon warned: 'A man that studieth revenge keeps his own wounds green.'

Perhaps. But when you have really suffered, when your wounds refuse to form a healthy layer of scar-tissue, nothing can compare to the barbed thrill of returning that suffering with interest. The Bible orders us to trust it to a higher authority: 'Vengeance is Mine, saith the Lord of Hosts, and I Will Repay'. When you have been wronged, however, you cannot wait for the bureaucracy of eternity to get round to your case. The human race has always had an unquenchable desire to knock the Almighty off his throne, and deal with the vengeance business itself. You want the criminal punished in this world, and you don't care if you end up sharing a bunk with them in hell because of it. It may take years, but as the Italians say, revenge is a dish discerning people prefer to eat cold.

And in most of these stories, it has a delicious flavour. La Rusa, the bedridden madame of an equatorial brothel in Lisa St Aubin de Terán's 'The Spider's Web', explains to her persecuted child protégée:

> Sometimes . . . the only sweetness in life is to remember your scores: those that are settled and those still to be so. I was wrong, Dulce, to let those girls get away with crippling me. I was a coward and I gave in. But we have debts to pay now, so listen . . .

La Rusa turns the tables on her discontented prostitutes in a way that is totally satisfying, and as sound as a good nut. Nobody – surely not even the Lord of Hosts – could deny that it is richly deserved. Lisa St Aubin compellingly captures the emotions fermenting under a glass of sultry heat.

Nearer home, among the rain-washed rhododendrons of 1930s South Kensington, the feminist author of *South Riding* also relishes revenge. Winifred Holtby's 'Why Herbert Killed His Mother' is a vicious, hilarious satire which strikes out at the least pleasing aspects of feminine conditioning. Mrs Wilkins is a frilled monster who drivels so revoltingly about 'mother love' that you would need a heart of granite not to sympathize with Herbert.

Sometimes, the ideal act of revenge is no more than a statement of selfhood, flashed out as a warning to others. Nora, the put-upon eldest daughter of a huge Irish-American family in Mary Flanagan's 'The Wedding Dress', longs to establish her own identity.

> Poor Nora: a mother to her brothers and sisters, a husband to her mother.
> She stops crying. Oh, she thinks, to be alone. Alone in a room with a few nice things; where it's all new and clean and mine. Where ten people and their friends are not continually fighting and needing you to settle their arguments.

Nora finally breaks away to get married, but will her burden be any lighter in her husband's home? Protesting against the image of 'goodness' imposed by others, Nora's revenge involves a dream of a dress.

Clothes, as we all know, are symbols of female power and status. In 'Making Arrangements', the elegant Anglo-Irish writer Elizabeth Bowen concocts a shocking act of vengeance from a wardrobe full of expensive gowns. The personality of an absconding wife is described entirely through her dresses, as they are laid out on the arid marital bed by her deserted husband. When love goes sour, Bowen hints, the nicest people can turn unexpectedly vicious.

However, it would be a mistake to assume that love is always the primary motive for revenge. Alice Walker, Candia McWilliam and Shena Mackay have each, in very different ways, written about revenge that springs from class conflict. McWilliam's 'Being a People Person' delicately probes the scarcely perceptible codes and signals which separate social groups. Her hero, Patrick, is an advertising executive aware that he comes out of a lower drawer than his colleagues. 'Strive to belong, behave as if you belong, and you will belong, he told himself . . . If you wanted something enough, you generally got it, and Patrick wanted to be one of them.' But wanting can be seen as a crime in this tribal system.

The class barrier in Shena Mackay's (literally) blistering 'Curry at the Laburnums' is represented by a ticket barrier at a suburban station. Racial hostilities are painfully exposed when middle-class commuters mutiny during a train strike. And Alice Walker's 'The Revenge of Hannah Kemhuff' is a Black American tragedy, in which an old lady splurges her life savings on witchcraft, to avenge the deaths of her children during the Great Depression. Hannah, in narrative that crackles with bitter rage, remembers making the mistake of wearing decent clothes when she takes her starving children to the foodline.

> 'Well, I want you to know that that little slip of a woman, all big blue eyes and yellow hair, that little *girl*, took my stamps and then took one long look at me and my children . . . and she took my stamps in her hand and looked at them like they was dirty, and then she give them to an old gambler who was next in line behind me! . . . and that little white moppet sort of grinned behind her hands . . . And there me and my children about to keel over from want.'

Hannah cannot forget, much less forgive. She has the long memory and iron will necessary for wreaking perfect revenge.

Sometimes, a woman's determination and sense of injury are so powerful that death itself cannot contain them. The narrator of Muriel Spark's incomparably witty and elegant 'The Portobello Road' only has to stop and greet a friend in Portobello market to strike the terror of death into his soul.

> I stood silently among the people, watching. As you will see, I wasn't in a position to speak to Kathleen . . . but I had a sudden inspiration which caused me to say quietly, 'Hallo, George'.

This simple act of revenge is the only catalyst needed to strip the covers off an unsolved murder.

'A Terrible Vengeance', by the Victorian writer Charlotte Riddell, is a splendidly gut-refrigerating interpretation of revenge-from-beyond-the-grave. Riddell achieves her macabre effects with an unusual blend of quirky detachment and acute observation. The bare bones of her story – arrogant gent and low-born beauty – are familiar enough today. A century ago, they would have been absolute clichés, the stuff of taproom ditties like 'She Was Poor But She Was Honest'. However, Riddell coolly goes beyond cliché and sensation-seeking, to turn up an unexpected seam of poignancy. Lucy Heath is a village adventuress – 'a bewitching girl, an arrant flirt, a scarcely well-behaved coquette'. Paul Murray is an upper-class idler, about to make a lucrative marriage. The story revolves around the question: where was he, the night Lucy died? Her desperation may have failed to impress her betrayer during her life, but it takes on a terrible power after death.

In a world where a woman is still encouraged to build all her aspirations around the getting and keeping of a man, love goes deep, and disappointment can kill. Although female revenge is often muted and subtle, it can occasionally erupt in an explosion of Technicolor rage. In Emma Tennant's 'Rigor Beach', a girl's sunny fantasies turn nasty when her boyfriend refuses to play. And Ruth Rendell, queen of the psychological thriller, administers a short, sharp shock to a man who has found someone else. The wronged woman in 'A Glowing Future' acts in a moment of passion, but neatly adds a timing device which will make her vengeance doubly effective. Rendell has crystallized revenge in its purest form. Swift and cruel, it dwells in the past and acts in a kind of eternal present, from which all thought for the future has been erased. Thinking about the consequences – legal or personal – is, after all, what prevents most of us from taking the revenge we secretly dream about.

However, if you are too sensible to do it, and you fear the darker corners of your imagination too much to invent your own scenarios, then reading about the underrated art of revenge is the next best thing. This book is an encyclopaedia of getting your own back, which covers everything from the best methods to the possible side-effects.

More importantly, it shows women writers tackling the fierce emotions that men consider 'unfeminine' – rage, violence, and a venomous determination to fight back. Even today, our male-dominated literary establishment often regards a woman's fiction as a testimonial for her own lovely nature. A tough or cynical story by a woman can still be dismissed as artistically 'bad', because critics disapprove of naughty ladies who do not seem to care sufficiently about their characters. Not realistic, they say, because 'real' women don't think like that. Or do they? Now read on . . .

LOUISA MAY ALCOTT

Pauline's Passion and Punishment

Chapter 1

To and fro, like a wild creature in its cage, paced that handsome woman, with bent head, locked hands, and restless steps. Some mental storm, swift and sudden as a tempest of the tropics, had swept over her and left its marks behind. As if in anger at the beauty now proved powerless, all ornaments had been flung away, yet still it shone undimmed, and filled her with a passionate regret. A jewel glittered at her feet, leaving the lace rent to shreds on the indignant bosom that had worn it; the wreaths of hair that had crowned her with a woman's most womanly adornment fell disordered upon shoulders that gleamed the fairer for the scarlet of the pomegranate flowers clinging to the bright meshes that had imprisoned them an hour ago; and over the face, once so affluent in youthful bloom, a stern pallor had fallen like a blight, for pride was slowly conquering passion, and despair had murdered hope.

Pausing in her troubled march, she swept away the curtain swaying in the wind and looked out, as if imploring help from Nature, the great mother of us all. A summer moon rode high in a cloudless heaven, and far as eye could reach stretched the green wilderness of a Cuban *cafetal*. No forest, but a tropical orchard, rich in lime, banana, plantain, palm, and orange trees, under whose protective shade grew the evergreen coffee plant, whose dark-red berries are the fortune of their possessor, and the luxury of one-half the world. Wide avenues diverging from the mansion, with its belt of brilliant shrubs and flowers, formed shadowy vistas, along which, on the wings of the wind, came a breath of far-off music, like a wooing voice; for the magic of night and distance lulled the cadence of a Spanish *contradanza* to a trance of sound, soft, subdued, and infinitely sweet. It was a southern scene, but not a southern face that looked out upon it with such unerring glance; there was no southern languor in the figure, stately and erect; no southern swarthiness on fairest cheek and arm; no southern

1

darkness in the shadowy gold of the neglected hair; the light frost of northern snows lurked in the features, delicately cut, yet vividly alive, betraying a temperament ardent, dominant, and subtle. For passion burned in the deep eyes, changing their violet to black. Pride sat on the forehead, with its dark brows; all a woman's sweetest spells touched the lips, whose shape was a smile; and in the spirited carriage of the head appeared the freedom of an intellect ripened under colder skies, the energy of a nature that could wring strength from suffering, and dare to act where feebler souls would only dare desire.

Standing thus, conscious only of the wound that bled in that high heart of hers, and the longing that gradually took shape and deepened to a purpose, an alien presence changed the tragic atmosphere of that still room and woke her from her dangerous mood. A wonderfully winning guise this apparition wore, for youth, hope, and love endowed it with the charm that gives beauty to the plainest, while their reign endures. A boy in any other climate, in this his nineteen years had given him the stature of a man; and Spain, the land of romance, seemed embodied in this figure, full of the lithe slenderness of the whispering palms overhead, the warm coloring of the deep-toned flowers sleeping in the room, the native grace of the tame antelope lifting its human eyes to his as he lingered on the threshold in an attitude eager yet timid, watching that other figure as it looked into the night and found no solace there.

'Pauline!'

She turned as if her thoughts had taken voice and answered her, regarded him a moment, as if hesitating to receive the granted wish, then beckoned with the one word.

'Come!'

Instantly the fear vanished, the ardor deepened, and with an imperious 'Lie down!' to his docile attendant, the young man obeyed with equal docility, looking as wistfully toward his mistress as the brute leaned toward her master, while he waited proudly humble for her commands.

'Manuel, why are you here?'

'Forgive me! I saw Dolores bring a letter; you vanished, an hour passed, I could wait no longer, and I came.'

'I am glad, I needed my one friend. Read that.'

She offered a letter, and with her steady eyes upon him, her purpose strengthening as she looked, stood watching the changes of that expressive countenance. This was the letter:

Pauline
  Six months ago I left you, promising to return and take you home my wife; I loved you, but I deceived you; for though my heart was wholly yours, my hand was not mine to give. This it was that haunted me through all that blissful

summer, this that marred my happiness when you owned you loved me, and this drove me from you, hoping I could break the tie with which I had rashly bound myself. I could not, I am married, and there all ends. Hate me, forget me, solace your pride with the memory that none knew your wrong, assure your peace with the knowledge that mine is destroyed forever, and leave my punishment to remorse and time.

Gilbert

With a gesture of wrathful contempt, Manuel flung the paper from him as he flashed a look at his companion, muttering through his teeth, 'Traitor! Shall I kill him?'

Pauline laughed low to herself, a dreary sound, but answered with a slow darkening of the face that gave her words an ominous significance. 'Why should you? Such revenge is brief and paltry, fit only for mock tragedies or poor souls who have neither the will to devise nor the will to execute a better. There are fates more terrible than death; weapons more keen than poniards, more noiseless than pistols. Women use such, and work out a subtler vengeance than men can conceive. Leave Gilbert to remorse – and me.'

She paused an instant, and by some strong effort banished the black frown from her brow, quenched the baleful fire of her eyes, and left nothing visible but the pale determination that made her beautiful face more eloquent than her words.

'Manuel, in a week I leave the island.'

'Alone, Pauline?'

'No, not alone.'

A moment they looked into each other's eyes, each endeavoring to read the other. Manuel saw some indomitable purpose, bent on conquering all obstacles. Pauline saw doubt, desire, and hope; knew that a word would bring the ally she needed; and, with a courage as native to her as her pride, resolved to utter it.

Seating herself, she beckoned her companion to assume the place beside her, but for the first time he hesitated. Something in the unnatural calmness of her manner troubled him, for his southern temperament was alive to influences whose presence would have been unfelt by one less sensitive. He took the cushion at her feet, saying, half tenderly, half reproachfully, 'Let me keep my old place till I know in what character I am to fill the new. The man you trusted has deserted you; the boy you pitied will prove loyal. Try him, Pauline.'

'I will.'

And with the bitter smile unchanged upon her lips, the low voice unshaken in its tones, the deep eyes unwavering in their gaze, Pauline went on:

'You know my past, happy as a dream till eighteen. Then all was swept

3

away, home, fortune, friends, and I was left, like an unfledged bird, without even the shelter of a cage. For five years I have made my life what I could, humble, honest, but never happy, till I came here, for here I saw Gilbert. In the poor companion of your guardian's daughter he seemed to see the heiress I had been, and treated me as such. This flattered my pride and touched my heart. He was kind, I grateful; then he loved me, and God knows how utterly I loved him! A few months of happiness the purest, then he went to make home ready for me, and I believed him; for where I wholly love I wholly trust. While my own peace was undisturbed, I learned to read the language of your eyes, Manuel, to find the boy grown into the man, the friend warmed into a lover. Your youth had kept me blind too long. Your society had grown dear to me, and I loved you like a sister for your unvarying kindness to the solitary woman who earned her bread and found it bitter. I told you my secret to prevent the utterance of your own. You remember the promise you made me then, keep it still, and bury the knowledge of my lost happiness deep in your pitying heart, as I shall in my proud one. Now the storm is over, and I am ready for my work again, but it must be a new task in a new scene. I hate this house, this room, the faces I must meet, the duties I must perform, for the memory of that traitor haunts them all. I see a future full of interest, a stage whereon I could play a stirring part. I long for it intensely, yet cannot make it mine alone. Manuel, do you love me still?'

Bending suddenly, she brushed back the dark hair that streaked his forehead and searched the face that in an instant answered her. Like a swift rising light, the eloquent blood rushed over swarthy cheek and brow, the slumberous softness of the eyes kindled with a flash, and the lips, sensitive as any woman's, trembled yet broke into a rapturous smile as he cried, with fervent brevity, 'I would die for you!'

A look of triumph swept across her face, for with this boy, as chivalrous as ardent, she knew that words were not mere breath. Still, with her stern purpose uppermost, she changed the bitter smile into one half-timid, half-tender, as she bent still nearer, 'Manuel, in a week I leave the island. Shall I go alone?'

'No, Pauline.'

He understood her now. She saw it in the sudden paleness that fell on him, heard it in the rapid beating of his heart, felt it in the strong grasp that fastened on her hand, and knew that the first step was won. A regretful pang smote her, but the dark mood which had taken possession of her stifled the generous warnings of her better self and drove her on.

'Listen, Manuel. A strange spirit rules me tonight, but I will have no reserves from you, all shall be told; then, if you will come, be it so; if not, I shall go my way as solitary as I came. If you think that this loss has broken my heart, undeceive yourself, for such as I live years in an hour and show no sign. I have shed no tears, uttered no cry, asked no comfort; yet, since I read that letter, I have suffered more than many suffer in a lifetime. I am not one to lament long over any hopeless sorrow. A single paroxysm, sharp and short, and it is over. Contempt has killed my love, I have buried it, and no power can make it live again, except as a pale ghost that will not rest till Gilbert shall pass through an hour as bitter as the last.'

'Is that the task you give yourself, Pauline?'

The savage element that lurks in southern blood leaped up in the boy's heart as he listened, glittered in his eye, and involuntarily found expression in the nervous grip of the hands that folded a fairer one between them. Alas for Pauline that she had roused the sleeping devil, and was glad to see it!

'Yes, it is weak, wicked, and unwomanly; yet I persist as relentlessly as any Indian on a war trail. See me as I am, not the gay girl you have known, but a revengeful woman with but one tender spot now left in her heart, the place you fill. I have been wronged, and I long to right myself at once. Time is too slow; I cannot wait, for that man must be taught that two can play at the game of hearts, taught soon and sharply. I can do this, can wound as I have been wounded, can sting him with contempt, and prove that I too can forget.'

'Go on, Pauline. Show me how I am to help you.'

'Manuel, I want fortune, rank, splendor, and power; you can give me all these, and a faithful friend beside. I desire to show Gilbert the creature he deserted no longer poor, unknown, unloved, but lifted higher than himself, cherished, honored, applauded, her life one of royal pleasure, herself a happy queen. Beauty, grace, and talent you tell me I possess; wealth gives them luster, rank exalts them, power makes them irresistible. Place these worldly gifts in my hand and that hand is yours. See, I offer it.'

She did so, but it was not taken. Manuel had left his seat and now stood before her, awed by the undertone of strong emotion in her calmly spoken words, bewildered by the proposal so abruptly made, longing to ask the natural question hovering on his lips, yet too generous to utter it. Pauline read his thought, and answered it with no touch of pain or pride in the magical voice that seldom spoke in vain.

'I know your wish; it is as just as your silence is generous, and I reply to it in all sincerity. You would ask, "When I have given all that I possess, what do I receive in return?" This – a wife whose friendship is as warm as many a woman's love; a wife who will give you all the heart still left her, and cherish the hope that time may bring a harvest of real affection to repay you for the faithfulness of years; who, though she takes the retribution of a wrong into her hands and executes it in the face of heaven, never will forget the honorable name you give into her keeping or blemish it by any act of hers. I can promise no more. Will this content you, Manuel?'

Before she ended his face was hidden in his hands, and tears streamed through them as he listened, for like a true child of the south each emotion found free vent and spent itself as swiftly as it rose. The reaction was more than he could bear, for in a moment his life was changed, months of hopeless longing were banished with a word, a blissful yes canceled the hard no that had been accepted as inexorable, and Happiness, lifting her full cup to his lips, bade him drink. A moment he yielded to the natural relief, then dashed his tears away and threw himself at Pauline's feet in that attitude fit only for a race as graceful as impassioned.

'Forgive me! Take all I have – fortune, name, and my poor self; use us as you will, we are proud and happy to be spent for you! No service will be too hard, no trial too long if in the end you learn to love me with one tithe of the affection I have made my life. Do you mean it? Am I to go with you? To be near you always, to call you wife, and know we are each other's until death? What have I ever done to earn a fate like this?'

Fast and fervently he spoke, and very winsome was the glad abandonment of this young lover, half boy, half man, possessing the simplicity of the one, the fervor of the other. Pauline looked and listened with a soothing sense of consolation in the knowledge that this loyal heart was all her own, a sweet foretaste of the devotion which henceforth was to shelter her from poverty, neglect and wrong, and turn life's sunniest side to one who had so long seen only its most bleak and barren. Still at her feet, his arms about her waist, his face flushed and proud, lifted to hers, Manuel saw the cold mask soften, the stern eyes melt with a sudden dew as Pauline watched him, saying, 'Dear Manuel, love me less; I am not worth such ardent and entire faith. Pause and reflect before you take this step. I will not bind you to my fate too soon lest you repent too late. We both stand alone in the world, free to make or mar our future as we will. I have chosen my lot. Recall all it may cost you to share it and be sure the price is not too high a one. Remember I am poor, you the possessor of one princely fortune, the sole heir to another.'

'The knowledge of this burdened me before; now I glory in it because I have the more for you.'

'Remember, I am older than yourself, and may early lose the beauty you love so well, leaving an old wife to burden your youth.'

'What are a few years to me? Women like you grow lovelier with age, and you shall have a strong young husband to lean on all your life.'

'Remember, I am not of your faith, and the priests will shut me out from your heaven.'

'Let them prate as they will. Where you go I will go; Santa Paula shall be my madonna!'

'Remember, I am a deserted woman, and in the world we are going to my name may become the sport of that man's cruel tongue. Could you bear that patiently, and curb your fiery pride if I desired it?'

'Anything for you, Pauline!'

'One thing more. I give you my liberty; for a time give me forbearance in return, and though wed in haste woo me slowly, lest this sore heart of mine find even your light yoke heavy. Can you promise this, and wait till time has healed my wound, and taught me to be meek?'

'I swear to obey you in all things; make me what you will, for soul and body I am wholly yours henceforth.'

'Faithful and true! I knew you would not fail me. Now go, Manuel. Tomorrow do your part resolutely as I shall do mine, and in a week we will begin the new life together. Ours is a strange betrothal, but it shall not lack some touch of tenderness from me. Love, good night.'

Pauline bent till her bright hair mingled with the dark, kissed the boy on lips and forehead as a fond sister might have done, then put him gently from her; and like one in a blessed dream he went away to pace all night beneath her window, longing for the day.

As the echo of his steps died along the corridor, Pauline's eye fell on the paper lying where her lover had flung it. At this sight all the softness vanished, the stern woman reappeared, and, crushing it in her hand with slow significance, she said low to herself, 'This is an old, old story, but it shall have a new ending.'

Chapter 2

'What jewels will the señora wear tonight?'

'None, Dolores. Manuel has gone for flowers – he likes them best. You may go.'

'But the señora's toilette is not finished; the sandals, the gloves, the garland yet remain.'

'Leave them all; I shall not go down. I am tired of this endless folly. Give me that book and go.'

The pretty Creole obeyed; and careless of Dolores' work, Pauline sank into the deep chair with a listless mien, turned the pages for a little, then lost herself in thoughts that seemed to bring no rest.

Silently the young husband entered and, pausing, regarded his wife with mingled pleasure and pain – pain to see her so spiritless, pleasure to see her so fair. She seemed unconscious of his presence till the fragrance of his floral burden betrayed him, and looking up to smile a welcome she met a glance that changed the sad dreamer into an excited actor, for it told her that the object of her search was found. Springing erect, she asked eagerly, 'Manuel, is he here?'

'Yes.'

'Alone?'

'His wife is with him.'

'Is she beautiful?'

'Pretty, petite, and petulant.'

'And he?'

'Unchanged: the same imposing figure and treacherous face, the same restless eye and satanic mouth. Pauline, let me insult him!'

'Not yet. Were they together?'

'Yes. He seemed anxious to leave her, but she called him back imperiously, and he came like one who dared not disobey.'

'Did he see you?'

'The crowd was too dense, and I kept in the shadow.'

'The wife's name? Did you learn it?'

'Barbara St Just.'

'Ah! I knew her once and will again. Manuel, am I beautiful tonight?'

'How can you be otherwise to me?'

'That is not enough. I must look my fairest to others, brilliant and blithe, a happy-hearted bride whose honeymoon is not yet over.'

'For his sake, Pauline?'

'For yours. I want him to envy you your youth, your comeliness, your content; to see the man he once sneered at the husband of the woman he once loved; to recall impotent regret. I know his nature, and can stir him to his heart's core with a look, revenge myself with a word, and read the secrets of his life with a skill he cannot fathom.'

'And when you have done all this, shall you be happier, Pauline?'

'Infinitely; our three weeks' search is ended, and the real interest of the plot begins. I have played the lover for your sake, now play the man of the world for mine. This is the moment we have waited for. Help me to make it successful. Come! Crown me with your garland, give me the bracelets that were your wedding gift – none can be too brilliant for tonight. Now the gloves and fan. Stay, my sandals – you shall play Dolores and tie them on.'

With an air of smiling coquetry he had never seen before, Pauline stretched out a truly Spanish foot and offered him its dainty covering. Won by the animation of her manner, Manuel forgot his misgivings and played his part with boyish spirit, hovering about his stately wife as no assiduous maid had ever done; for every flower was fastened with a word sweeter than itself, the white arms kissed as the ornaments went on, and when the silken knots were deftly accomplished, the lighthearted bridegroom performed a little dance of triumph about his idol, till she arrested him, beckoning as she spoke.

'Manuel, I am waiting to assume the last best ornament you have given me, my handsome husband.' Then, as he came to her laughing with frank pleasure at her praise, she added, 'You, too, must look your best and bravest now, and remember you must enact the man tonight. Before Gilbert wear your stateliest aspect, your tenderest to me, your courtliest to his wife. You possess dramatic skill. Use it for my sake, and come for your reward when this night's work is done.'

The great hotel was swarming with life, ablaze with light, resonant with the tread of feet, the hum of voices, the musical din of the band, and full of the sights and sounds which fill such human hives at a fashionable watering place in the height of the season. As Manuel led his wife along the grand hall thronged with promenaders, his quick ear caught the whispered comments of the passers-by, and the fragmentary rumors concerning themselves amused him infinitely.

'*Mon ami!* There are five bridal couples here tonight, and there is the handsomest, richest, and most enchanting of them all. The groom is not yet twenty, they tell me, and the bride still younger. Behold them!'

Manuel looked down at Pauline with a mirthful glance, but she had not heard.

'See, Belle! Cubans; own half the island between them. Splendid, aren't they? Look at the diamonds on her lovely arms, and his ravishing moustache. Isn't he your ideal of Prince Djalma, in *The Wandering Jew?*'

A pretty girl, forgetting propriety in interest, pointed as they passed. Manuel half-bowed to the audible compliment, and the blushing damsel vanished, but Pauline had not seen.

'Jack, there's the owner of the black span you fell into raptures over. My lord and lady look as highbred as their stud. We'll patronize them!'

Manuel muttered a disdainful '*Impertinente!*' between his teeth as he surveyed a brace of dandies with an air that augured ill for the patronage of Young America, but Pauline was unconscious of both criticism and reproof. A countercurrent held them stationary for a moment, and close behind them sounded a voice saying, confidentially, to some silent listener, 'The Redmonds are here tonight, and I am curious to see how he bears his disappointment. You know he married for money, and was outwitted in the bargain; for his wife's fortune not only proves to be much less than he was led to believe, but is so tied up that he is entirely dependent upon her, and the bachelor debts he sold himself to liquidate still harass him, with a wife's reproaches to augment the affliction. To be ruled by a spoiled child's whim is a fit punishment for a man whom neither pride nor principle could curb before. Let us go and look at the unfortunate.'

Pauline heard now. Manuel felt her start, saw her flush and pale, then her eye lit, and the dark expression he dreaded to see settled on her face as she whispered, like a satanic echo, 'Let us also go and look at this unfortunate.'

A jealous pang smote the young man's heart as he recalled the past.

'You pity him, Pauline, and pity is akin to love.'

9

'I only pity what I respect. Rest content, my husband.'

Steadily her eyes met his, and the hand whose only ornament was a wedding ring went to meet the one folded on his arm with a confiding gesture that made the action a caress.

'I will try to be, yet mine is a hard part,' Manuel answered with a sigh, then silently they both paced on.

Gilbert Redmond lounged behind his wife's chair, looking intensely bored.

'Have you had enough of this folly, Babie?'

'No, we have but just come. Let us dance.'

'Too late; they have begun.'

'Then go about with me. It's very tiresome sitting here.'

'It is too warm to walk in all that crowd, child.'

'You are so indolent! Tell me who people are as they pass. I know no one here.'

'Nor I.'

But his act belied the words, for as they passed his lips he rose erect, with a smothered exclamation and startled face, as if a ghost had suddenly confronted him. The throng had thinned, and as his wife followed the direction of his glance, she saw no uncanny apparition to cause such evident dismay, but a woman fair-haired, violet-eyed, blooming and serene, sweeping down the long hall with noiseless grace. An air of sumptuous life pervaded her, the shimmer of bridal snow surrounded her, bridal gifts shone on neck and arms, and bridal happiness seemed to touch her with its tender charm as she looked up at her companion, as if there were but one human being in the world to her. This companion, a man slender and tall, with a face delicately dark as a fine bronze, looked back at her with eyes as eloquent as her own, while both spoke rapidly and low in the melodious language which seems made for lovers' lips.

'Gilbert, who are they?'

There was no answer, and before she could repeat the question the approaching pair paused before her, and the beautiful woman offered her hand, saying, with inquiring smiles, 'Barbara, have you forgotten your early friend, Pauline?'

Recognition came with the familiar name, and Mrs Redmond welcomed the newcomer with a delight as unrestrained as if she were still the schoolgirl, Babie. Then, recovering herself, she said, with a pretty attempt at dignity, 'Let me present my husband. Gilbert, come and welcome my friend Pauline Valary.'

Scarlet with shame, dumb with conflicting emotions, and utterly deserted by self-possession, Redmond stood with downcast eyes and agitated mien, suffering a year's remorse condensed into a moment. A mute gesture was all the greeting he could offer. Pauline slightly bent her haughty head as she answered, in a voice frostily sweet, 'Your wife mistakes. Pauline Valary died three weeks ago, and Pauline Laroche rose from her ashes. Manuel, my schoolmate, Mrs Redmond; Gilbert you already know.'

With the manly presence he could easily assume and which was henceforth to be his role in public, Manuel bowed courteously to the lady, coldly to the gentleman, and looked only at his wife. Mrs Redmond, though childish, was observant; she glanced from face to face, divined a mystery, and spoke out at once.

'Then you have met before? Gilbert, you have never told me this.'

'It was long ago – in Cuba. I believed they had forgotten me.'

'I never forget.' And Pauline's eye turned on him with a look he dared not meet.

Unsilenced by her husband's frown, Mrs Redmond, intent on pleasing herself, drew her friend to the seat beside her as she said petulantly, 'Gilbert tells me nothing, and I am constantly discovering things which might have given me pleasure had he only chosen to be frank. I've spoken of you often, yet he never betrayed the least knowledge of you, and I take it very ill of him, because I am sure he has not forgotten you. Sit here, Pauline, and let me tease you with questions, as I used to do so long ago. You were always patient with me, and though far more beautiful, your face is still the same kind one that comforted the little child at school. Gilbert, enjoy your friend, and leave us to ourselves until the dance is over.'

Pauline obeyed; but as she chatted, skillfully leading the young wife's conversation to her own affairs, she listened to the two voices behind her, watched the two figures reflected in the mirror before her, and felt a secret pride in Manuel's address, for it was evident that the former positions were renewed.

The timid boy who had feared the sarcastic tongue of his guardian's guest, and shrunk from his presence to conceal the jealousy that was his jest, now stood beside his former rival, serene and self-possessed, by far the manliest man of the two, for no shame daunted him, no fear oppressed him, no dishonorable deed left him at the mercy of another's tongue.

Gilbert Redmond felt this keenly, and cursed the falsehood which had placed him in such an unenviable position. It was vain to assume the old superiority that was forfeited; but too much a man of the world to be long discomforted by any contretemps like this, he rapidly regained his habitual ease of manner, and avoiding the perilous past clung to the safer present, hoping, by some unguarded look or word, to fathom the purpose of his adversary, for such he knew the husband of Pauline must be at heart. But Manuel schooled his features, curbed his tongue, and when his hot blood tempted him to point his smooth speech with a taunt, or offer a silent insult with the eye, he remembered Pauline, looked down on the graceful head below, and forgot all other passions in that of love.

'Gilbert, my shawl. The sea air chills me.'

'I forgot it, Babie.'

'Allow me to supply the want.'

Mindful of his wife's commands, Manuel seized this opportunity to win a glance of commendation from her. And taking the downy mantle that hung upon his arm, he wrapped the frail girl in it with a care that made the act as cordial as courteous. Mrs Redmond felt the charm of his manner with the quickness of a woman, and sent a reproachful glance at Gilbert as she said plaintively, 'Ah! It is evident that my honeymoon is over, and the assiduous lover replaced by the negligent husband. Enjoy your midsummer night's dream while you may, Pauline, and be ready for the awakening that must come.'

'Not to her, madame, for our honeymoon shall last till the golden wedding day comes round. Shall it not, *cariña?*'

'There is no sign of waning yet, Manuel,' and Pauline looked up into her husband's face with a genuine affection which made her own more beautiful and filled his with a visible content. Gilbert read the glance, and in that instant suffered the first pang of regret that Pauline had foretold. He spoke abruptly, longing to be away.

'Babie, we may dance now, if you will.'

'I am going, but not with you – so give me my fan, and entertain Pauline till my return.'

He unclosed his hand, but the delicately carved fan fell at his feet in a shower of ivory shreds – he had crushed it as he watched his first love with the bitter thought 'It might have been!'

'Forgive me, Babie, it was too frail for use; you should choose a stronger.'

'I will next time, and a gentler hand to hold it. Now, Monsieur Laroche, I am ready.'

Mrs Redmond rose in a small bustle of satisfaction, shook out her flounces, glanced at the mirror, then Manuel led her away; and the other pair were left alone. Both felt a secret agitation quicken their breath and thrill along their nerves, but the woman concealed it best. Gilbert's eye wandered restlessly to and fro, while Pauline fixed her own on his as quietly as if he were the statue in the niche behind him. For a moment he tried to seem unconscious of it, then essayed to meet and conquer it, but failed signally and, driven to his last resources by that steady gaze, resolved to speak out and have all over before his wife's return. Assuming the seat beside her, he said, impetuously, 'Pauline, take off your mask as I do mine – we are alone now, and may see each other as we are.'

Leaning deep into the crimson curve of the couch, with the indolent grace habitual to her, yet in strong contrast to the vigilant gleam of her eye, she swept her hand across her face as if obeying him, yet no change followed, as she said with a cold smile, 'It is off; what next?'

'Let me understand you. Did my letter reach your hands?'

'A week before my marriage.'

He drew a long breath of relief, yet a frown gathered as he asked, like one loath and eager to be satisfied, 'Your love died a natural death, then, and its murder does not lie at my door?'

Pointing to the shattered toy upon the ground, she only echoed his own words. 'It was too frail for use – I chose a stronger.'

It wounded, as she meant it should; and the evil spirit to whose guidance she had yielded herself exulted to see his self-love bleed, and pride vainly struggle to conceal the stab. He caught the expression in her averted glance, bent suddenly and fixed a scrutinizing gaze upon her, asking, below his breath, 'Then why are you here to tempt me with the face that tempted me a year ago?'

'I came to see the woman to whom you sold yourself. I have seen her, and am satisfied.'

Such quiet contempt iced her tones, such pitiless satisfaction shone through the long lashes that swept slowly down, after her eye had met and caused his own to fall again, that Gilbert's cheek burned as if the words had been a blow, and mingled shame and anger trembled in his voice.

'Ah, you are quick to read our secret, for you possess the key. Have you no fear that I may read your own, and tell the world you sold your beauty for a name and fortune? Your bargain is a better one than mine, but I know you too well, though your fetters are diamonds and your master a fond boy.'

She had been prepared for this, and knew she had a shield in the real regard she bore her husband, for though sisterly, it was sincere. She felt its value now, for it gave her courage to confront the spirit of retaliation she had roused, and calmness to answer the whispered taunt with an unruffled mien, as lifting her white arm she let its single decoration drop glittering to her lap.

'You see my "fetters" are as loose as they are light, and nothing binds me but my will. Read my heart, if you can. You will find there contempt for a love so poor that it feared poverty; pity for a man who dared not face the world and conquer it, as a girl had done before him, and gratitude that I have found my "master" in a truehearted boy, not a falsehearted man. If I am a slave, I never know it. Can you say as much?'

Her woman's tongue avenged her, and Gilbert owned his defeat. Pain quenched the ire of his glance, remorse subdued his pride, self-condemnation compelled him to ask, imploringly, 'Pauline, when may I hope for pardon?'

'Never.'

The stern utterance of the word dismayed him, and, like one shut out from hope, he rose, as if to leave her, but paused irresolutely, looked back, then sank down again, as if constrained against his will by a longing past control. If she had doubted her power this action set the doubt at rest, as the haughtiest nature she had known confessed it by a bittersweet complaint. Eyeing her wistfully, tenderly, Gilbert murmured, in the voice of long ago, 'Why do I stay to wound and to be wounded by the hand that once caressed me? Why do I find more pleasure in your contempt than in another woman's praise, and feel myself transported into the delights of that irrecoverable past, now grown the sweetest, saddest memory of my life? Send me away, Pauline, before the old charm asserts its power, and I forget that I am not the happy lover of a year ago.'

'Leave me then, Gilbert. Good night.'

Half unconsciously, the former softness stole into her voice as it lingered on his name. The familiar gesture accompanied the words, the old charm did assert itself, and for an instant changed the cold woman into the ardent girl again. Gilbert did not go but, with a hasty glance down the deserted hall behind him, captured and kissed the hand he had lost, passionately whispering, 'Pauline, I love you still, and that look assures me that you have forgiven, forgotten, and kept a place for me in that deep heart of yours. It is too late to deny it. I have seen the tender eyes again, and the sight has made me the proudest, happiest man that walks the world tonight, slave though I am.'

Over cheek and forehead rushed the treacherous blood as the violet eyes filled and fell before his own, and in the glow of mingled pain and fear that stirred her blood, Pauline, for the first time, owned the peril of the task she had set herself, saw the dangerous power she possessed, and felt the buried passion faintly moving in its grave. Indignant at her own weakness, she took refuge in the memory of her wrong, controlled the rebel color, steeled the front she showed him, and with feminine skill mutely conveyed the rebuke she would not trust herself to utter, by stripping the glove from the hand he had touched and dropping it disdainfully as if unworthy of its place. Gilbert had not looked for such an answer, and while it baffled him it excited his man's spirit to rebel against her silent denial. With a bitter laugh he snatched up the glove.

'I read a defiance in your eye as you flung this down. I accept the challenge, and will keep gage until I prove myself the victor. I have asked for pardon. You refuse it. I have confessed my love. You scorn it. I have possessed myself of your secret, yet you deny it. Now we will try our strength together, and leave those children to their play.'

'We are the children, and we play with edge tools. There has been enough of this, there must be no more.' Pauline rose with her haughtiest mien, and the brief command, 'Take me to Manuel.'

Silently Gilbert offered his arm, and silently she rejected it.

'Will you accept nothing from me?'

'Nothing.'

Side by side they passed through the returning throng till Mrs Redmond joined them, looking blithe and bland with the exhilaration of gallantry and motion. Manuel's first glance was at Pauline, his second at her companion; there was a shadow upon the face of each, which seemed instantly to fall upon his own as he claimed his wife with a masterful satisfaction as novel as becoming, and which prompted her to whisper, 'You enact your role to the life, and shall enjoy a foretaste of your reward at once. I want excitement; let us show these graceless, frozen people the true art of dancing, and electrify them with the life and fire of a Cuban valse.'

Manuel kindled at once, and Pauline smiled stealthily as she glanced over her shoulder from the threshold of the dancing hall, for her slightest act, look, and word had their part to play in that night's drama.

'Gilbert, if you are tired I will go now.'

'Thank you, I begin to find it interesting. Let us watch the dancers.'

Mrs Redmond accepted the tardy favor, wondering at his unwonted animation, for never had she seen such eagerness in his countenance, such energy in his manner as he pressed through the crowd and won a place where they could freely witness one of those exhibitions of fashionable figurante which are nightly to be seen at such resorts. Many couples were whirling around the white hall, but among them one pair circled with slowly increasing speed, in perfect time to the inspiring melody of trumpet, flute, and horn, that seemed to sound for them alone. Many paused to watch them, for they gave to the graceful pastime the enchantment which few have skill enough to lend it, and made it a spectacle of life-enjoying youth, to be remembered long after the music ceased and the agile feet were still.

Gilbert's arm was about his little wife to shield her from the pressure of the crowd, and as they stood his hold unconsciously tightened, till, marveling at this unwonted care, she looked up to thank him with a happy glance and discovered that his eye rested on a single pair, kindling as they approached, keenly scanning every gesture as they floated by, following them with untiring vigilance through the many-colored mazes they threaded with such winged steps, while his breath quickened, his hand kept time, and every sense seemed to own the intoxication of the scene. Sorrowfully she too watched this pair, saw their grace, admired their beauty, envied their happiness; for, short as her wedded life had been, the thorns already pierced her through the roses, and with each airy revolution of those figures, dark and bright, her discontent increased, her wonder deepened, her scrutiny grew keener, for she knew no common interest held her husband there, fascinated, flushed, and excited as if his heart beat responsive to the rhythmic rise and fall of that booted foot and satin slipper. The music ended with a crash, the crowd surged across the floor, and the spell was broken. Like one but half disenchanted, Gilbert stood a moment, then remembered his wife, and looking down met brown eyes, full of tears, fastened on his face.

'Tired so soon, Babie? Or in a pet because I cannot change myself into a thistledown and float about with you, like Manuel and Pauline?'

'Neither; I was only wishing that you loved me as he loves her, and hoping he would never tire of her, they are so fond and charming now. How long have you known them – and where?'

'I shall have no peace until I tell you. I passed a single summer with them in a tropical paradise, where we swung half the day in hammocks, under tamarind and almond trees; danced half the night to music, of which this seems but a faint echo; and led a life of luxurious delight in an enchanted climate, where all is so beautiful and brilliant that its memory haunts a life as pressed flowers sweeten the leaves of a dull book.'

'Why did you leave it then?'

'To marry you, child.'

'That was a regretful sigh, as if I were not worth the sacrifice. Let us go back and enjoy it together.'

'If you were dying for it, I would not take you to Cuba. It would be purgatory, not paradise, now.'

'How stern you look, how strangely you speak. Would you not go to save your own life, Gilbert?'

'I would not cross the room to do that, much less the sea.'

'Why do you both love and dread it? Don't frown, but tell me. I have a right to know.'

'Because the bitterest blunder of my life was committed there – a blunder that I never can repair in this world, and may be damned for in the next. Rest satisfied with this, Babie, lest you prove like Bluebeard's wife, and make another skeleton in my closet, which has enough already.'

Strange regret was in his voice, strange gloom fell upon his face; but though rendered doubly curious by the change, Mrs Redmond dared not question further and, standing silent, furtively scanned the troubled countenance beside her. Gilbert spoke first, waking out of his sorrowful reverie with a start.

'Pauline is coming. Say adieu, not au revoir, for tomorrow we must leave this place.'

His words were a command, his aspect one of stern resolve, though the intensest longing mingled with the dark look he cast on the approaching pair. The tone, the glance displeased his willful wife, who loved to use her power and exact obedience where she had failed to win affection, often ruling imperiously when a tender word would have made her happy to submit.

16

'Gilbert, you take no thought for my pleasures though you pursue your own at my expense. Your neglect forces me to find solace and satisfaction where I can, and you have forfeited your right to command or complain. I love Pauline, I am happy with her, therefore I shall stay until we tire of one another. I am a burden to you; go if you will.'

'You know I cannot without you, Babie. I ask it as a favor. For my sake, for your own, I implore you to come away.'

'Gilbert, do you love her?'

She seized his arm and forced an answer by the energy of her sharply whispered question. He saw that it was vain to dissemble, yet replied with averted head, 'I did and still remember it.'

'And she? Did she return your love?'

'I believed so; but she forgot me when I went. She married Manuel and is happy. Babie, let me go!'

'No! you shall stay and feel a little of the pain I feel when I look into your heart and find I have no place there. It is this which has stood between us and made all my efforts vain. I see it now and despise you for the falsehood you have shown me, vowing you loved no one but me until I married you, then letting me so soon discover that I was only an encumbrance to your enjoyment of the fortune I possessed. You treat me like a child, but I suffer like a woman, and you shall share my suffering, because you might have spared me, and you did not. Gilbert, you shall stay.'

'Be it so, but remember I have warned you.'

An exultant expression broke through the gloom of her husband's face as he answered with the grim satisfaction of one who gave restraint to the mind, and stood ready to follow whatever impulse should sway him next. His wife trembled inwardly at what she had done, but was too proud to recall her words and felt a certain bitter pleasure in the excitement of the new position she had taken, the new interest given to her listless life.

Pauline and Manuel found them standing silently together, for a moment had done the work of years and raised a barrier between them never to be swept away.

Mrs Redmond spoke first, and with an air half resentful, half triumphant.

'Pauline, this morose husband of mine says we must leave tomorrow. But in some things I rule; this is one of them. Therefore we remain and go with you to the mountains when we are tired of the gay life here. So smile and submit, Gilbert, else these friends will count your society no favor. Would you not fancy, from the aspect he thinks proper to assume, that I had sentenced him to a punishment, not a pleasure?'

'Perhaps you have unwittingly, Babie. Marriage is said to cancel the follies of the past, but not those of the future, I believe; and, as there are many temptations to an idle man in a place like this, doubtless your husband is wise enough to own that he dares not stay but finds discretion the better part of valor.'

Nothing could be softer than the tone in which these words were uttered, nothing sharper than the hidden taunt conveyed, but Gilbert only laughed a scornful laugh as he fixed his keen eyes full upon her and took her bouquet with the air of one assuming former rights.

'My dear Pauline, discretion is the last virtue I should expect to be accused of by you; but if valor consists in daring all things, I may lay claim to it without its "better part," for temptation is my delight – the stronger the better. Have no fears for me, my friend. I gladly accept Babie's decree and, ignoring the last ten years, intend to begin life anew, having discovered a *sauce piquante* which will give the stalest pleasures a redoubled zest. I am unfortunate tonight, and here is a second wreck; this I can rebuild happily. Allow me to do so, for I remember you once praised my skill in floral architecture.'

With an air of eager gallantry in strange contrast to the malign expression of his countenance, Gilbert knelt to regather the flowers which a careless gesture of his own had scattered from their jeweled holder. His wife turned to speak to Manuel, and, yielding to the unconquerable anxiety his reckless manner awoke, Pauline whispered below her breath as she bent as if to watch the work, 'Gilbert, follow your first impulse, and go tomorrow.'

'Nothing shall induce me to.'

'I warn you harm will come of it.'

'Let it come; I am past fear now.'

'Shun me for Babie's sake, if not for your own.'

'Too late for that; she is headstrong – let her suffer.'

'Have you no power, Gilbert?'

'None over her, much over you.'

'We will prove that!'

'We will!'

Rapidly as words could shape them, these questions and answers fell, and with their utterance the last generous feeling died in Pauline's breast; for as she received the flowers, now changed from a love token to a battle gage, she saw the torn glove still crushed in Gilbert's hand, and silently accepted his challenge to the tournament so often held between man and woman – a tournament where the keen tongue is the lance, pride the shield, passion the fiery steed, and the hardest heart the winner of the prize, which seldom fails to prove a barren honor, ending in remorse.

Chapter 3

For several days the Cubans were almost invisible, appearing only for a daily drive, a twilight saunter on the beach, or a brief visit to the ballroom, there to enjoy the excitement of the pastime in which they both excelled. Their apartments were in the quietest wing of the hotel, and from the moment of their occupancy seemed to acquire all the charms of home. The few guests admitted felt the atmosphere of poetry and peace that pervaded the nest which Love, the worker of miracles, had built himself even under that tumultuous roof. Strollers in the halls or along the breezy verandas often paused to listen to the music of instrument or voice which came floating out from these sequestered rooms. Frequent laughter and the murmur of conversation proved that ennui was unknown, and a touch of romance inevitably enhanced the interest wakened by the beautiful young pair, always together, always happy, never weary of the *dolce far niente* of this summer life.

In a balcony like a hanging garden, sheltered from the sun by blossoming shrubs and vines that curtained the green nook with odorous shade, Pauline lay indolently swinging in a gaily fringed hammock as she had been wont to do in Cuba, then finding only pleasure in the luxury of motion which now failed to quiet her unrest. Manuel had put down the book to which she no longer listened and, leaning his head upon his hand, sat watching her as she swayed to and fro with thoughtful eyes intent upon the sea, whose murmurous voice possessed a charm more powerful than his own. Suddenly he spoke:

'Pauline, I cannot understand you! For three weeks we hurried east and west to find this man, yet when found you shun him and seem content to make my life a heaven upon earth. I sometimes fancy that you have resolved to let the past sleep, but the hope dies as soon as born, for in moments like this I see that, though you devote yourself to me, the old purpose is unchanged, and I marvel why you pause.'

Her eyes came back from their long gaze and settled on him full of an intelligence which deepened his perplexity. 'You have not learned to know me yet; death is not more inexorable or time more tireless than I. This week has seemed one of indolent delight to you. To me it has been one of constant vigilance and labor, for scarcely a look, act, or word of mine has been without effect. At first I secluded myself that Gilbert might contrast our life with his and, believing us all and all to one another, find impotent regret his daily portion. Three days ago accident placed an unexpected weapon in my hand which I have used in silence, lest in spite of promises

19

you should rebel and end his trial too soon. Have you no suspicion of my meaning?'

'None. You are more mysterious than ever, and I shall, in truth, believe you are the enchantress I have so often called you if your spells work invisibly.'

'They do not, and I use no supernatural arts, as I will prove to you. Take my lorgnette that lies behind you, part the leaves where the green grapes hang thickest, look up at the little window in the shadowy angle of the low roof opposite, and tell me what you see.'

'Nothing but a half-drawn curtain.'

'Ah! I must try the ruse that first convinced me. Do not show yourself, but watch, and if you speak, let it be in Spanish.'

Leaving her airy cradle, Pauline bent over the balcony as if to gather the climbing roses that waved their ruddy clusters in the wind. Before the third stem was broken Manuel whispered, 'I see the curtain move; now comes the outline of a head, and now a hand, with some bright object in it. Santo Pablo! It is a man staring at you as coolly as if you were a lady in a balcony. What prying rascal is it?'

'Gilbert.'

'Impossible! He is a gentleman.'

'If gentlemen play the traitor and the spy, then he is one. I am not mistaken; for since the glitter of his glass first arrested me I have watched covertly, and several trials as successful as the present have confirmed the suspicion which Babie's innocent complaints of his long absences aroused. Now do you comprehend why I remained in these rooms with the curtains seldom drawn? Why I swung the hammock here and let you sing and read to me while I played with your hair or leaned upon your shoulder? Why I have been all devotion and made this balcony a little stage for the performance of our version of the honeymoon for one spectator?'

Still mindful of the eager eyes upon her, Pauline had been fastening the roses in her bosom as she spoke, and ended with a silvery laugh that made the silence musical with its heartsome sound. As she paused, Manuel flung down the lorgnette and was striding past her with ireful impetuosity, but the white arms took him captive, adding another figure to the picture framed by the green arch as she whispered decisively, 'No farther! There must be no violence. You promised obedience and I exact it. Do you think detection to a man so lost to honor would wound as deeply as the sights which make his daily watch a torment? Or that a blow would be as hard to bear as the knowledge that his own act has placed you where you are and made him what he is? Silent contempt is the law now, so let this insult pass, unclench your hand and turn that defiant face to me, while I console you for submission with a kiss.'

He yielded to the command enforced by the caress but drew her jealously from sight, and still glanced rebelliously through the leaves, asking with a frown, 'Why show me this if I may not resent it? How long must I bear with this man? Tell me your design, else I shall mar it in some moment when hatred of him conquers love of you.'

'I will, for it is time, because though I have taken the first step you must take the second. I showed you this that you might find action pleasanter than rest, and you must bear with this man a little longer for my sake, but I will give you an amusement to beguile the time. Long ago you told me that Gilbert was a gambler. I would not believe it then, now I can believe anything, and you can convince the world of this vice of his as speedily as you will.'

'Do you wish me to become a gambler that I may prove him one? I also told you that he was suspected of dishonorable play – shall I load the dice and mark the cards to catch him in his own snares?'

Manuel spoke bitterly, for his high spirit chafed at the task assigned him; womanly wiles seemed more degrading than the masculine method of retaliation, in which strength replaces subtlety and speedier vengeance brings speedier satisfaction. But Pauline, fast learning to play upon that mysterious instrument, the human heart, knew when to stimulate and when to soothe.

'Do not reproach me that I point out a safer mode of operation than your own. You would go to Gilbert and by a hot word, a rash act, put your life and my happiness into his hands, for though dueling is forbidden here, he would not hesitate to break all laws, human or divine, if by so doing he could separate us. What would you gain by it? If you kill him he is beyond our reach forever, and a crime remains to be atoned for. If he kills you your blood will be upon my head, and where should I find consolation for the loss of the one heart always true and tender?'

With the inexplicable prescience which sometimes foreshadows coming ills, she clung to him as if a vision of the future dimly swept before her, but he only saw the solicitude it was a sweet surprise to find he had awakened, and in present pleasure forgot past pain.

'You shall not suffer from this man any grief that I can shield you from, rest assured of that, my heart. I will be patient, though your ways are not mine, for the wrong was yours, and the retribution shall be such as you decree.'

'Then hear your task and see the shape into which circumstances have molded my design. I would have you exercise a self-restraint that shall leave Gilbert no hold upon you, accept all invitations like that which you refused when we passed him on the threshold of the billiard room an hour ago, and seem to find in such amusements the same fascination as himself. Your skill in games of chance excels his, as you proved at home where these pastimes lose their disreputable aspect by being openly enjoyed. Therefore

I would have you whet this appetite of his by losing freely at first – he will take a grim delight in lessening the fortune he covets – then exert all your skill till he is deeply in your debt. He has nothing but what is doled out to him by Babie's father, I find; he dare not ask help there for such a purpose; other resources have failed else he would not have married; and if the sum be large enough, it lays him under an obligation which will be a thorn in his flesh, the sharper for your knowledge of his impotence to draw it out. When this is done, or even while it is in progress, I would have you add the pain of a new jealousy to the old. He neglects this young wife of his, and she is eager to recover the affections she believes she once possessed. Help her, and teach Gilbert the value of what he now despises. You are young, comely, accomplished, and possessed of many graces more attractive than you are conscious of; your southern birth and breeding gift you with a winning warmth of manners in strong contrast to the colder natures around you; and your love for me lends an almost tender deference to your intercourse with all womankind. Amuse, console this poor girl, and show her husband what he should be; I have no fear of losing your heart nor need you fear for hers; she is one of those spaniel-like creatures who love the hand that strikes them and fawn upon the foot that spurns them.'

'Am I to be the sole actor in the drama of deceit? While I woo Babie, what will you do, Pauline?'

'Let Gilbert woo me – have patience till you understand my meaning; he still loves me and believes I still return that love. I shall not undeceive him yet, but let silence seem to confess what I do not own in words. He fed me with false promises, let me build my life's happiness on baseless hopes, and rudely woke me when he could delude no longer, leaving me to find I had pursued a shadow. I will do the same. He shall follow me undaunted, undeterred by all obstacles, all ties; shall stake his last throw and lose it, for when the crowning moment comes I shall show him that through me he is made bankrupt in love, honor, liberty, and hope, tell him I am yours entirely and forever, then vanish like an *ignis-fatuus*, leaving him to the darkness of despair and defeat. Is not this a better retribution than the bullet that would give him peace at once?'

Boy, lover, husband though he was, Manuel saw and stood aghast at the baleful spirit which had enslaved this woman, crushing all generous impulses, withering all gentle charities, and making her the saddest spectacle this world can show – one human soul rebelling against Providence, to become the nemesis of another. Involuntarily he recoiled from her, exclaiming, 'Pauline! Are you possessed of a devil?'

'Yes! One that will not be cast out till every sin, shame, and sorrow mental ingenuity can conceive and inflict has been heaped on that man's head. I thought I should be satisfied with one accusing look, one bitter word; I am not, for the evil genii once let loose cannot be recaptured. Once

I ruled it, now it rules me, and there is no turning back. I have come under the law of fate, and henceforth the powers I possess will ban, not bless, for I am driven to whet and wield them as weapons which may win me success at the price of my salvation. It is not yet too late for you to shun the spiritual contagion I bear about me. Choose now, and abide by that choice without a shadow of turning, as I abide by mine. Take me as I am; help me willingly and unwillingly; and in the end receive the promised gift – years like the days you have called heaven upon earth. Or retract the vows you plighted, receive again the heart and name you gave me, and live unvexed by the stormy nature time alone can tame. Here is the ring. Shall I restore or keep it, Manuel?'

Never had she looked more beautiful as she stood there, an image of will, daring, defiant, and indomitable, with eyes darkened by intensity of emotion, voice half sad, half stern, and outstretched hand on which the wedding ring no longer shone. She felt her power, yet was wary enough to assure it by one bold appeal to the strongest element of her husband's character: passions, not principles, were the allies she desired, and before the answer came she knew that she had gained them at the cost of innocence and self-respect.

As Manuel listened, an expression like a dark reflection of her own settled on his face; a year of youth seemed to drop away; and with the air of one who puts fear behind him, he took the hand, replaced the ring, resolutely accepted the hard conditions, and gave all to love, only saying as he had said before, 'Soul and body, I belong to you; do with me as you will.'

A fortnight later Pauline sat alone, waiting for her husband. Under the pretext of visiting a friend, she had absented herself a week, that Manuel might give himself entirely to the distasteful task she set him. He submitted to the separation, wrote daily, but sent no tidings of his progress, told her nothing when they met that night, and had left her an hour before asking her to have patience till he could show his finished work. Now, with her eye upon the door, her ear alert to catch the coming step, her mind disturbed by contending hopes and fears, she sat waiting with the vigilant immobility of an Indian on the watch. She had not long to look and listen. Manuel entered hastily, locked the door, closed the windows, dropped the curtains, then paused in the middle of the room and broke into a low, triumphant laugh as he eyed his wife with an expression she had never seen in those dear eyes before. It startled her, and, scarcely knowing what to desire or dread, she asked eagerly, 'You are come to tell me you have prospered.'

'Beyond your hopes, for the powers of darkness seem to help us, and lead the man to his destruction faster than any wiles of ours can do. I am tired, let me lie here and rest. I have earned it, so when I have told all say, "Love, you have done well," and I am satisfied.'

He threw himself along the couch where she still sat and laid his head in her silken lap, her cool hand on his hot forehead, and continued in a muffled voice.

'You know how eagerly Gilbert took advantage of my willingness to play, and soon how recklessly he pursued it, seeming to find the satisfaction you foretold, till, obeying your commands, I ceased losing and won sums which surprised me. Then you went, but I was not idle, and in the effort to extricate himself, Gilbert plunged deeper into debt; for my desire to please you seemed to gift me with redoubled skill. Two days ago I refused to continue the unequal conflict, telling him to give himself no uneasiness, for I could wait. You were right in thinking it would oppress him to be under any obligation to me, but wrong in believing he would endure, and will hardly be prepared for the desperate step he took to free himself. That night he played falsely, was detected, and though his opponent generously promised silence for Babie's sake, the affair stole out – he is shunned and this resource has failed. I thought he had no other, but yesterday he came to me with a strange expression of relief, discharged the debt to the last farthing, then hinted that my friendship with his wife was not approved by him and must cease. This proves that I have obeyed you in all things, though the comforting of Babie was an easy task, for, both loving you, our bond of sympathy and constant theme has been Pauline and her perfections.'

'Hush! No praise – it is a mockery. I am what one man's perfidy has made; I may yet learn to be worthy of another man's devotion. What more, Manuel?'

'I thought I should have only a defeat to show you, but today has given me a strange success. At noon a gentleman arrived and asked for Gilbert. He was absent, but upon offering information relative to the time of his return, which proved my intimacy with him, this Seguin entered into conversation with me. His evident desire to avoid Mrs Redmond and waylay her husband interested me, and when he questioned me somewhat closely concerning Gilbert's habits and movements of late, my suspicions were roused; and on mentioning the debt so promptly discharged, I received a confidence that startled me. In a moment of despair Gilbert had forged the name of his former friend, whom he believed abroad, had drawn the money and freed himself from my power, but not for long. The good fortune which has led him safely through many crooked ways seems to have deserted him in this strait. For the forgery was badly executed, inspection raised doubts, and Seguin, just returned, was at his banker's an hour after Gilbert, to prove the fraud; he came hither at once to accuse him of it and made me his confidant. What would you have had me do, Pauline? Time was short, and I could not wait for you.'

'How can I tell at once? Why pause to ask? What did you do?'

'Took a leaf from your book and kept accusation, punishment, and power in my own hands, to be used in your behalf. I returned the money, secured the forged check, and prevailed on Seguin to leave the matter in my hands, while he departed as quietly as he had come. Babie's presence when we met tonight prevented my taking you into my counsels. I had prepared this surprise for you and felt a secret pride in working it out alone. An hour ago I went to watch for Gilbert. He came, I took him to his rooms, told him what I had done, added that compassion for his wife had actuated me. I left him saying the possession of the check was a full equivalent for the money, which I now declined to receive from such dishonorable hands. Are you satisfied, Pauline?'

With countenance and gestures full of exultation she sprang up to pace the room, exclaiming, as she seized the forged paper, 'Yes, that stroke was superb! How strangely the plot thickens. Surely the powers of darkness are working with us and have put this weapon in our hands when that I forged proved useless. By means of this we have a hold upon him which nothing can destroy unless he escape by death. Will he, Manuel?'

'No; there was more wrath than shame in his demeanor when I accused him. He hates me too much to die yet, and had I been the only possessor of this fatal fact, I fancy it might have gone hard with me; for if ever there was murder in a man's heart it was in his when I showed him that paper and then replaced it next the little poniard you smile at me for wearing. This is over. What next, my queen?'

There was energy in the speaker's tone but none in attitude or aspect, as, still lying where she had left him, he pillowed his head upon his arm and turned toward her a face already worn and haggard with the feverish weariness that had usurped the blithe serenity which had been his chiefest charm a month ago. Pausing in her rapid walk, as if arrested by the change that seemed to strike her suddenly, she recalled her thoughts from the dominant idea of her life and, remembering the youth she was robbing of its innocent delights, answered the wistful look which betrayed the hunger of a heart she had never truly fed, as she knelt beside her husband and, laying her soft cheek to his, whispered in her tenderest accents, 'I am not wholly selfish or ungrateful, Manuel. You shall rest now while I sing to you, and tomorrow we will go away among the hills and leave behind us for a time the dark temptation which harms you through me.'

'No! Finish what you have begun. I will have all or nothing, for if we pause now you will bring me a divided mind, and I shall possess only the shadow of a wife. Take Gilbert and Babie with us, and end this devil's work without delay. Hark! What is that?'

Steps came flying down the long hall, a hand tried the lock, then beat impetuously upon the door, and a low voice whispered with shrill importunity, 'Let me in! Oh, let me in!'

Manuel obeyed the urgent summons, and Mrs Redmond, half dressed, with streaming hair and terror-stricken face, fled into Pauline's arms, crying incoherently, 'Save me! Keep me! I never can go back to him; he said I was a burden and a curse, and wished I never had been born!'

'What has happened, Babie? We are your friends. Tell us, and let us comfort and protect you if we can.'

But for a time speech was impossible, and the poor girl wept with a despairing vehemence sad to see, till their gentle efforts soothed her; and, sitting by Pauline, she told her trouble, looking oftenest at Manuel, who stood before them, as if sure of redress from him.

'When I left here an hour or more ago I found my rooms still empty, and, though I had not seen my husband since morning, I knew he would be displeased to find me waiting, so I cried myself to sleep and dreamed of the happy time when he was kind, till the sound of voices woke me. I heard Gilbert say, "Babie is with your wife, her maid tells me; therefore we are alone here. What is this mysterious affair, Laroche?" That tempted me to listen, and then, Manuel, I learned all the shame and misery you so generously tried to spare me. How can I ever repay you, ever love and honor you enough for such care of one so helpless and forlorn as I?'

'I am repaid already. Let that pass, and tell what brings you here with such an air of fright and fear?'

'When you were gone he came straight to the inner room in search of something, saw me, and knew I must have heard all he had concealed from me so carefully. If you have ever seen him when that fierce temper of his grows ungovernable, you can guess what I endured. He said such cruel things I could not bear it, and cried out that I would come to you, for I was quite wild with terror, grief, and shame, that seemed like oil to fire. He swore I should not, and oh, Pauline, he struck me! See, if I do not tell the living truth!'

Trembling with excitement, Mrs Redmond pushed back the wide sleeve of her wrapper and showed the red outline of a heavy hand. Manuel set his teeth and stamped his foot into the carpet with an indignant exclamation and the brief question, 'Then you left him, Babie?'

'Yes, although he locked me in my room, saying the law gave him the right to teach obedience. I flung on these clothes, crept noiselessly along the balcony till the hall window let me in, and then I ran to you. He will come for me. Can he take me away? Must I go back to suffer any more?'

In the very act of uttering the words, Mrs Redmond clung to Manuel with a cry of fear, for on the threshold stood her husband. A comprehensive glance seemed to stimulate his wrath and lend the hardihood wherewith to confront the three, saying sternly as he beckoned, 'Babie, I am waiting for you.'

She did not speak, but still clung to Manuel as if he were her only hope. A glance from Pauline checked the fiery words trembling on his lips, and he too stood silent while she answered with a calmness that amazed him:

'Your wife has chosen us her guardians, and I think you will scarcely venture to use force again with two such witnesses as these to prove that you have forfeited your right to her obedience and justify the step she has taken.'

With one hand she uncovered the discolored arm, with the other held the forgery before him. For a moment Gilbert stood daunted by these mute accusations, but just then his ire burned hottest against Manuel; and believing that he could deal a double blow by wounding Pauline through her husband, he ignored her presence and, turning to the young man, asked significantly, 'Am I to understand that you refuse me my wife, and prefer to abide by the consequences of such an act?'

Calmed by Pauline's calmness, Manuel only drew the trembling creature closer, and answered with his haughtiest mien, 'I do; spare yourself the labor of insulting me, for having placed yourself beyond the reach of a gentleman's weapon, I shall accept no challenge from a –'

A soft hand at his lips checked the opprobrious word, as Babie, true woman through it all, whispered with a broken sob, 'Spare him, for I loved him once.'

Gilbert Redmond had a heart, and, sinful though it was, this generous forbearance wrung it with a momentary pang of genuine remorse, too swiftly followed by a selfish hope that all was not lost if through his wife he could retain a hold upon the pair which now possessed for him the strong attraction of both love and hate. In that brief pause this thought came, was accepted and obeyed, for, as if yielding to an uncontrollable impulse of penitent despair, he stretched his arms to his wife, saying humbly, imploringly, 'Babie, come back to me, and teach me how I may retrieve the past. I freely confess I bitterly repent my manifold transgressions, and submit to your decree alone; but in executing justice, oh, remember mercy! Remember that I was too early left fatherless, motherless, and went astray for want of some kind heart to guide and cherish me. There is still time. Be compassionate and save me from myself. Am I not punished enough? Must death be my only comforter? Babie, when all others cast me off, will you too forsake me?'

'No, I will not! Only love me, and I can forgive, forget, and still be happy!'

Pauline was right. The spaniel-like nature still loved the hand that struck it, and Mrs Redmond joyfully returned to the arms from which she had so lately fled. The tenderest welcome she had ever received from him welcomed the loving soul whose faith was not yet dead, for Gilbert felt the value this once neglected possession had suddenly acquired, and he held it close; yet as he soothed with gentle touch and tone, could not forbear a glance of triumph at the spectators of the scene.

Pauline met it with that inscrutable smile of hers, and a look of intelligence toward her husband, as she said, 'Did I not prophesy truly, Manuel? Be kind to her, Gilbert, and when next we meet show us a happier wife than the one now sobbing on your shoulder. Babie, good night and farewell, for we are off to the mountains in the morning.'

'Oh, let us go with you as promised! You know our secret, you pity me and will help Gilbert to be what he should. I cannot live at home, and places like this will seem so desolate when you and Manuel are gone. May we, can we be with you a little longer?'

'If Gilbert wishes it and Manuel consents, we will bear and forbear much for your sake, my poor child.'

Pauline's eye said, 'Dare you go?' and Gilbert's answered, 'Yes,' as the two met with a somber fire in each; but his lips replied, 'Anywhere with you, Babie,' and Manuel took Mrs Redmond's hand with a graceful warmth that touched her deeper than his words.

'Your example teaches me the beauty of compassion, and Pauline's friends are mine.'

'Always so kind to me! Dear Manuel, I never can forget it, though I have nothing to return but this,' and, like a grateful child, she lifted up her innocent face so wistfully he could only bend his tall head to receive the kiss she offered.

Gilbert's black brows lowered ominously at the sight, but he never spoke; and, when her good nights were over, bowed silently and carried his little wife away, nestling to him as if all griefs and pains were banished by returning love.

'Poor little heart! She should have a smoother path to tread. Heaven grant she may hereafter; and this sudden penitence prove no sham.' Manuel paused suddenly, for as if obeying an unconquerable impulse, Pauline laid a hand on either shoulder and searched his face with an expression which baffled his comprehension, though he bore it steadily till her eyes fell before his own, when he asked smilingly:

'Is the doubt destroyed, *cariña*?'

'No; it is laid asleep.'

Then as he drew her nearer, as if to make his peace for his unknown offense, she turned her cheek away and left him silently. Did she fear to find Babie's kiss upon his lips?

Chapter 4

The work of weeks is soon recorded, and when another month was gone these were the changes it had wrought. The four so strangely bound together by ties of suffering and sin went on their way, to the world's eye, blessed with every gracious gift, but below the tranquil surface rolled that undercurrent whose mysterious tides ebb and flow in human hearts unfettered by race or rank or time. Gilbert was a good actor, but, though he curbed his fitful temper, smoothed his mien, and sweetened his manner, his wife soon felt the vanity of hoping to recover that which never had been hers. Silently she accepted the fact and, uttering no complaint, turned to others for the fostering warmth without which she could not live. Conscious of a hunger like her own, Manuel could offer her sincerest sympathy, and soon learned to find a troubled pleasure in the knowledge that she loved him and her husband knew it, for his life of the emotions was rapidly maturing the boy into the man, as the fierce ardors of his native skies quicken the growth of wondrous plants that blossom in a night. Mrs Redmond, as young in character as in years, felt the attraction of a nature generous and sweet, and yielded to it as involuntarily as an unsupported vine yields to the wind that blows it to the strong arms of a tree, still unconscious that a warmer sentiment than gratitude made his companionship the sunshine of her life. Pauline saw this, and sometimes owned within herself that she had evoked spirits which she could not rule, but her purpose drove her on, and in it she found a charm more perilously potent than before. Gilbert watched the three with a smile darker than a frown, yet no reproach warned his wife of the danger which she did not see; no jealous demonstration roused Manuel to rebel against the oppression of a presence so distasteful to him; no rash act or word gave Pauline power to banish him, though the one desire of his soul became the discovery of the key to the inscrutable expression of her eyes as they followed the young pair, whose growing friendship left their mates alone. Slowly her manner softened toward him, pity seemed to bridge across the gulf that lay between them, and in rare moments time appeared to have retraced its steps, leaving the tender woman of a year ago. Nourished by such unexpected hope, the early passion throve and strengthened until it became the mastering ambition of his life, and, only pausing to make assurance doubly sure, he waited the advent of the hour when he could 'put his fortune to the touch and win or lose it all.'

'Manuel, are you coming?'

He was lying on the sward at Mrs Redmond's feet, and, waking from the reverie that held him, while his companion sang the love lay he was teaching her, he looked up to see his wife standing on the green slope before him. A black lace scarf lay over her blonde hair as Spanish women wear their veils, below it the violet eyes shone clear, the cheek glowed with the color fresh winds had blown upon their paleness, the lips parted with a wistful smile, and a knot of bright-hued leaves upon her bosom made a mingling of snow and fire in the dress, whose white folds swept the grass. Against a background of hoary cliffs and somber pines, this figure stood out like a picture of blooming womanhood, but Manuel saw three blemishes upon it – Gilbert had sketched her with that shadowy veil upon her head, Gilbert had swung himself across a precipice to reach the scarlet nosegay for her breast, Gilbert stood beside her with her hand upon his arm; and troubled by the fear that often haunted him since Pauline's manner to himself had grown so shy and sad, Manuel leaned and looked forgetful of reply, but Mrs Redmond answered blithely:

'He is coming, but with me. You are too grave for us, so go your ways, talking wisely of heaven and earth, while we come after, enjoying both as we gather lichens, chase the goats, and meet you at the waterfall. Now señor, put away guitar and book, for I have learned my lesson; so help me with this unruly hair of mine and leave the Spanish for today.'

They looked a pair of lovers as Manuel held back the long locks blowing in the wind, while Babie tied her hat, still chanting the burthen of the tender song she had caught so soon. A voiceless sigh stirred the ruddy leaves on Pauline's bosom as she turned away, but Gilbert embodied it in words, 'They are happier without us. Let us go.'

Neither spoke till they reached the appointed tryst. The others were not there, and, waiting for them, Pauline sat on a mossy stone, Gilbert leaned against the granite boulder beside her, and both silently surveyed a scene that made the heart glow, the eye kindle with delight as it swept down from that airy height, across valleys dappled with shadow and dark with untrodden forests, up ranges of majestic mountains, through gap after gap, each hazier than the last, far out into that sea of blue which rolls around all the world. Behind them roared the waterfall swollen with autumn rains and hurrying to pour itself into the rocky basin that lay boiling below, there to leave its legacy of shattered trees, then to dash itself into a deeper chasm, soon to be haunted by a tragic legend and go glittering away through forest, field, and intervale to join the river rolling slowly to the sea. Won by the beauty and the grandeur of the scene, Pauline forgot she was not alone, till turning, she suddenly became aware that while she scanned the face of nature her companion had been scanning hers. What he saw there she could not tell, but all restraint had vanished from his manner, all reticence from his speech, for with the old ardor in his eye, the old impetuosity in his voice, he said, leaning down as if to read her heart, 'This is the moment I have waited for so long. For now you see what I see, that

30

both have made a bitter blunder, and may yet repair it. Those children love each other; let them love, youth mates them, fortune makes them equals, fate brings them together that we may be free. Accept this freedom as I do, and come out into the world with me to lead the life you were born to enjoy.'

With the first words he uttered Pauline felt that the time had come, and in the drawing of a breath was ready for it, with every sense alert, every power under full control, every feature obedient to the art which had become a second nature. Gilbert had seized her hand, and she did not draw it back; the sudden advent of the instant which must end her work sent an unwonted color to her cheek, and she did avert it; the exultation which flashed into her eyes made it unsafe to meet his own, and they drooped before him as if in shame or fear, her whole face woke and brightened with the excitement that stirred her blood. She did not seek to conceal it, but let him cheat himself with the belief that love touched it with such light and warmth, as she softly answered in a voice whose accents seemed to assure his hope.

'You ask me to relinquish much. What do you offer in return, Gilbert, that I may not for a second time find love's labor lost?'

It was a wily speech, though sweetly spoken, for it reminded him how much he had thrown away, how little now remained to give, but her mien inspired him, and nothing daunted, he replied more ardently than ever:

'I can offer you a heart always faithful in truth though not in seeming, for I never loved that child. I would give years of happy life to undo that act and be again the man you trusted. I can offer you a name which shall yet be an honorable one, despite the stain an hour's madness cast upon it. You once taunted me with cowardice because I dared not face the world and conquer it. I dare do that now; I long to escape from this disgraceful servitude, to throw myself into the press, to struggle and achieve for your dear sake. I can offer you strength, energy, devotion – three gifts worthy any woman's acceptance who possesses power to direct, reward, and enjoy them as you do, Pauline. Because with your presence for my inspiration, I feel that I can retrieve my faultful past, and with time become God's noblest work – an honest man. Babie never could exert this influence over me. You can, you will, for now my earthly hope is in your hands, my soul's salvation in your love.'

If that love had not died a sudden death, it would have risen up to answer him as the one sincere desire of an erring life cried out to her for help, and this man, as proud as sinful, knelt down before her with a passionate humility never paid at any other shrine, human or divine. It seemed to melt and win her, for he saw the color ebb and flow, heard the rapid beating of her heart, felt the hand tremble in his own, and received no denial but a lingering doubt, whose removal was a keen satisfaction to himself.

'Tell me, before I answer, are you sure that Manuel loves Babie?'

'I am; for every day convinces me that he has outlived the brief delusion, and longs for liberty, but dares not ask it. Ah! that pricks pride! But it is so. I have watched with jealous vigilance and let no sign escape me; because in his infidelity to you lay my chief hope. Has he not grown melancholy, cold, and silent? Does he not seek Babie and, of late, shun you? Will he not always yield his place to me without a token of displeasure or regret? Has he ever uttered reproach, warning, or command to you, although he knows I was and am your lover? Can you deny these proofs, or pause to ask if he will refuse to break the tie that binds him to a woman, whose superiority in all things keeps him a subject where he would be a king? You do not know the heart of man if you believe he will not bless you for his freedom.'

Like the cloud which just then swept across the valley, blotting out its sunshine with a gloomy shadow, a troubled look flitted over Pauline's face. But if the words woke any sleeping fear she cherished, it was peremptorily banished, for scarcely had the watcher seen it than it was gone. Her eyes still shone upon the ground, and still she prolonged the bittersweet delight at seeing this humiliation of both soul and body by asking the one question whose reply would complete her sad success.

'Gilbert, do you believe I love you still?'

'I know it! Can I not read the signs that proved it to me once? Can I forget that, though you followed me to pity and despise, you have remained to pardon and befriend? Am I not sure that no other power could work the change you have wrought in me? I was learning to be content with slavery, and slowly sinking into that indolence of will which makes submission easy. I was learning to forget you, and be resigned to hold the shadow when the substance was gone, but you came, and with a look undid my work, with a word destroyed my hardwon peace, with a touch roused the passion which was not dead but sleeping, and have made this month of growing certainty to be the sweetest in my life – for I believed all lost, and you showed me that all was won. Surely that smile is propitious, and I may hope to hear the happy confirmation of my faith from lips that were formed to say "I love!"'

She looked up then, and her eyes burned on him, with an expression which made his heart leap with expectant joy, as over cheek and forehead spread a glow of womanly emotion too genuine to be feigned, and her voice thrilled with the fervor of that sentiment which blesses life and outlives death.

'Yes, I love; not as of old, with a girl's blind infatuation, but with the warmth and wisdom of heart, mind, and soul – love made up of honor, penitence and trust, nourished in secret by the better self which lingers in the most tried and tempted of us, and now ready to blossom and bear fruit, if God so wills. I have been once deceived, but faith still endures, and I believe that I may yet earn this crowning gift of a woman's life for the man who shall make my happiness as I make his – who shall find me the prouder for past coldness, the humbler for past pride – whose life shall pass serenely loving. And that beloved is – my husband.'

If she had lifted her white hand and stabbed him, with that smile upon her face, it would not have shocked him with a more pale dismay than did those two words as Pauline shook him off and rose up, beautiful and stern as an avenging angel. Dumb with an amazement too fathomless for words, he knelt there motionless and aghast. She did not speak. And, passing his hand across his eyes as if he felt himself the prey to some delusion, he rose slowly, asking, half incredulously, half imploringly, 'Pauline, this is a jest?'

'To me it is; to you – a bitter earnest.'

A dim foreboding of the truth fell on him then, and with it a strange sense of fear; for in this apparition of human judgment he seemed to receive a premonition of the divine. With a sudden gesture of something like entreaty, he cried out, as if his fate lay in her hands, 'How will it end? how will it end?'

'As it began – in sorrow, shame and loss.'

Then, in words that fell hot and heavy on the sore heart made desolate, she poured out the dark history of the wrong and the atonement wrung from him with such pitiless patience and inexorable will. No hard fact remained unrecorded, no subtle act unveiled, no hint of her bright future unspared to deepen the gloom of his. And when the final word of doom died upon the lips that should have awarded pardon, not punishment, Pauline tore away the last gift he had given, and dropping it to the rocky path, set her foot upon it, as if it were the scarlet badge of her subjection to the evil spirit which had haunted her so long, now cast out and crushed forever.

Gilbert had listened with a slowly gathering despair, which deepened to the blind recklessness that comes to those whose passions are their masters, when some blow smites but cannot subdue. Pale to his very lips, with the still white wrath, so much more terrible to witness than the fiercest ebullition of the ire that flames and feeds like a sudden fire, he waited till she ended, then used the one retaliation she had left him. His hand went to his breast, a tattered glove flashed white against the cliff as he held it up before her, saying, in a voice that rose gradually till the last words sounded clear above the waterfall's wild song:

'It was well and womanly done, Pauline, and I could wish Manuel a happy life with such a tender, frank, and noble wife; but the future which you paint so well never shall be his. For, by the Lord that hears me! I swear

I will end this jest of yours in a more bitter earnest than you prophesied. Look; I have worn this since the night you began the conflict, which has ended in defeat to me, as it shall to you. I do not war with women, but you shall have one man's blood upon your soul, for I will goad that tame boy to rebellion by flinging this in his face and taunting him with a perfidy blacker than my own. Will that rouse him to forget your commands and answer like a man?'

'Yes!'

The word rang through the air sharp and short as a pistol shot, a slender brown hand wrenched the glove away, and Manuel came between them. Wild with fear, Mrs Redmond clung to him. Pauline sprang before him, and for a moment the two faced each other, with a year's smoldering jealousy and hate blazing in fiery eyes, trembling in clenched hands, and surging through set teeth in defiant speech.

'This is the gentleman who gambles his friend to desperation, and skulks behind a woman, like the coward he is,' sneered Gilbert.

'Traitor and swindler, you lie!' shouted Manuel, and, flinging his wife behind him, he sent the glove, with a stinging blow, full in his opponent's face.

Then the wild beast that lurks in every strong man's blood leaped up in Gilbert Redmond's, as, with a single gesture of his sinewy right arm he swept Manuel to the verge of the narrow ledge, saw him hang poised there one awful instant, struggling to save the living weight that weighed him down, heard a heavy plunge into the black pool below, and felt that thrill of horrible delight which comes to murderers alone.

So swift and sure had been the act it left no time for help. A rush, a plunge, a pause, and then two figures stood where four had been – a man and woman staring dumbly at each other, appalled at the dread silence that made high noon more ghostly than the deepest night. And with that moment of impotent horror, remorse, and woe, Pauline's long punishment began.

LISA St AUBIN de TERÁN

The Spider's Web

La Rusa was spending her second year in bed, and her fantasies were running dry. Although she was still, nominally, the madame of the finest brothel in the neighbourhood, her life at 'The Rainbow' was more like that of a spider trapped in her own web. In another month the rainy season would begin. And another month would see the anniversary of the time when she fell down the stairs and broke her back. Every morning, as her girls slept and only the sound of insects relieved the monotony of the silence, La Rusa tried not to feel again the push that had sent her down the carved staircase. Falls were healthier. Pushes had too many other implications. She was a helpless invalid; it didn't do to dwell on how she came to be so.

Beyond the slatted shutters and the grid-iron bars, across the street, lay Maria Elena Rosales who had been shrivelling back to a sackful of bones and skin for the last ten years. She was wasting away without a murmur of complaint. Some of the girls, fascinated by this illness that had taken on aspects of a circus act, monitored her gradual disappearance and declared her a saint. The same could never be said for La Rusa, whose only relief from the fear and humiliation of her condition was to protest in an outraged monologue that continued in whispers, even in her sleep. It could have been guilt or merely boredom that kept the girls away from the icon-filled relic of La Rusa's room, but for whatever reason, she spent most of her hot helpless hours on her own.

Nobody knew for sure how the new girl came to be sitting on the end of La Rusa's bed that day when the morning coffee was brought. The other girls went down and scrutinised the intruder. They themselves all ranged in age between fifteen and forty (although the elder ones would not admit this much), while the new girl, as La Rusa called her, was no bigger than a child of seven. She was also excessively plain, and wide-mouthed, with an unnatural pallor that made her look like a flat-faced toad. Her round freckled eyes were disturbingly knowing in their expression.

'This child has come to sit with me in my solitude,' La Rusa announced. When the girls had left her, she turned to the newcomer, and laughed for the first time since her accident.

'What will they make of that!' she gloated, 'what will they think!'

They thought it was witchcraft, and upstairs, all the old potions and spells were brought out of their drawers and boxes. Ilario Gomez, who took the money and paid the wages and the bills in La Rusa's stead now that she was unable to hold her own purse strings any more, declared that the new girl had crawled through the window bars, drawn in by La Rusa's incessant muttering. While La Rusa herself had no doubt in her mind that this child companion had arrived by means of a miracle. She would have liked to have woven her arrival into the story of the last grand duchess: to make the waif an emissary from the doomed court of Russia. But since the child refused to speak about herself, and had a dazed, almost half-witted air about her, it seemed best just to tell her about the Russian royal family rather than try to turn her into one of them. The mystery of La Rusa's own origins no longer kept the townspeople debating into the night. Nobody seemed to care any more whether she was or was not the glamorous Anastasia. She was merely a cripple whose image had broken with her back.

Every morning La Rusa awoke, fully expecting the child to have disappeared as miraculously as she had come. It sunk her ageing chest and head in a suffusing sweetness each time she heard the gentle swish of the child's broom across the floor. La Rusa was immune to the reptilian qualities of her new companion; she was aware of, and quickly came to love, only her graceful choreography as she swept and re-swept the formerly unkempt room. Also the devotion with which the child (whose skills belied her stunted size) manicured the aching nails, and tended her body and her hair. La Rusa saw too how this strange creature actually believed all her tales and inventions. Here, at last, was a fellow Russophile and a romantic. Here was a draught of sweetness in her cup of gall. In the absence of any other name, she called the new girl Dulce.

Every day the girls eyed La Rusa's protégée with growing distaste. They stared into her eyes, hoping that it would drive her back to whatever sunless underworld she had crawled in from. Had they known how starved the child had always been of adult love, and how in need of protection she then was, they might have seen that she was immune to their subtle threats. They laughed at her uncouth ways and at her astonishment at such things as inside plumbing, hot water, electric lights, ice and machinery. They teased and bullied her, while she ran willingly from room to room, polishing shoes and manicuring nails for these girls who were as strange and fantastic to her as any of La Rusa's stories. She was a refugee from the uplands with its chill and its daily drudgery.

Gradually, Dulce became so much a part of the Rainbow that she was as familiar to everyone there as the pattern on the floor tiles or the stained patchwork quilts that covered all the beds. Before her accident, La Rusa had insisted on training her girls not only to be superlative whores but also to make exemplary wives. So needlework and housekeeping had been a part of each girl's life. And many of the girls had left the Rainbow to get married. Yet, in the two years since her fall not a single girl had left. It was almost as though they were all waiting for her to die so that they could dig up the floor under her bed and claim their share of her much-talked-of fortune.

Since no one left, no new girls came, and the spice of the unknown was noted and missed by the numerous clients. It was the only element of change that was ever referred to. Other things, like the atmosphere of unease, the gradual dilapidation of the house and the lack of interest that the girls themselves showed in their work, were left unmentioned. In a world held together entirely by habit and ritual, no one wanted to be the first to admit to a change. The old feeling of contentment had given way to an aura of suppressed aggression. Only the new girl, Dulce, seemed happy with her lot. It was confusing to call her a girl, she wasn't one of the girls at all, she was just a child, and such a plain strange child at that.

All through the rainy season, when everyone's emotions mildewed with the inescapable dampness, the men petted and spoilt Dulce. They brought her sticks of barley sugar and twists of liquorice, and ribbons for her straggly hair. What she liked best were emery boards and manicure sets, miniature scalpels, varnish and polish, anything, in fact, that could enhance her already beautiful fingernails. Ilario Gomez, who had a sixth sense for money, was the first to realise that it was wizened little Dulce, with her pond-dweller's face, who was bringing in the clients. She had found an old usherette's tray in a cupboard and had taken to giving manicures to the otherwise dissatisfied patrons of the house. Ilario Gomez spent many hours watching her, wondering if her air of innocence were true or false. Was she really as unaware as she seemed of her customers squirming in their chairs as she caressed their debauched fingers? He would never understand that she herself found such exquisite pleasure in the attention to her nails that any orgasmic writhing would seem to be a natural reaction to her expert probing.

La Rusa missed Dulce when she set off with her tray of tools to do the rounds of the clients' hands. She began to day-dream about a different life for her and Dulce, somewhere far away from the Rainbow. She also began to complain less about her plight, and even to enjoy herself again. She realised that her greatest pleasure had really been in the fabricating of her stories. She had created a mystery that could only exist if other people believed in her fantasies. Dulce believed her to such a point that she herself dreamt of the Russian steppes covered, as she knew they were, with the scrapings of a million refrigerators and patrolled by dogs that slunk like armadillos and bit like mapamare snakes. She dreamt too of a room higher than all the rooms of the Rainbow put together and streaked with gold where people as beautiful and elegant as La Rusa herself leapt through the air and never fell or broke their backs. La Rusa need not have worried, Dulce was always anxious to return to her. The pleasure of doing someone else's nails could never compete with the thrill of doing her own.

Ilario Gomez was only interested in counting up the takings, falsifying the accounts, pocketing the difference and banking the rest. He saw the men surreptitiously taking their pleasure with little Dulce, but he failed to see either the measure of love that was growing between the child and La Rusa, or the measure of hate that was gathering steadily towards them from the other girls. Now that no maintenance took place on the building, the persistent rains were rotting away its fabric; just as the general discontent among the girls was rotting away their common sense. From the galleried landing they watched Dulce at work, manicuring their clients into various states of ecstasy. Seeing these faces reminded them of the days when such looks and groans were reserved exclusively for themselves. Even their lovemaking had come to be perfunctory and incomplete. They remembered the times when they used to be happy at the Rainbow. They compared such times to their present loss, and they blamed Dulce, not only for dulling their senses, but also for stealing their youth and even somehow for the mangled state of La Rusa's spinal column.

In the days when La Rusa was vigilant and patrolled the Rainbow maintaining standards and encouraging her girls to excel, they used to hide in their rooms and plot minor rebellions behind her back. Some of that old thrill returned to them as they locked themselves in a conclave to discuss how best to bring down Dulce. No one dared get rid of her altogether. They had tried, on impulse, to do so to La Rusa and it had brought nothing but bad luck. They wanted something subtle and nasty, painful but not dangerous: something that would hurt her inside to such a degree that she would lose all her naive power.

The dry season had taken its place on the calendar, and the heat seemed to be so entrenched that there was talk of a drought. Dulce was unused to the heat. She had grown up in the temperate uplands, and although she loved the profusion of flowers and the incessant croaking of tree frogs and the patterns of sunlight that pushed through the window bars and forced themselves into the rooms like dancers on the tiles, she could not sleep. So she moved her bed from the space beside La Rusa's own, away from the photographs of Valentino and Fred Astaire and the Russian émigrés, and slept on a mat on a balcony under the stars.

This decampment made the other girls' trick all the easier to play. Before it began, they were all agreed to take part in the punishing. But when the time came to hold the ether pad over Dulce's broad gash of a mouth and hold down her thin pale body until it was still, one of the gang refused to continue.

'It's like killing her,' she said.

'Don't be stupid, Sophie, it's just a lesson, and how come you're so squeamish. When it comes to killing I've seen you try your bit; and don't forget it.'

'It's just that she's only a kid.'

'Then she should act like one . . . Didn't you get enough thrashings when you were one?'

Next morning Dulce woke up with a heavy head and a strange taste in her mouth but with a familiar feeling inside her. She felt a sense of injustice and she ached the way she had ached at home in the uplands. Every time she remembered that her mother had run away and left her in a burning hut, she felt it, and every time her cousins beat her with her yard broom until all her bones ached she felt it. When the uncle who had taken her into his house to live with his own children turned her out in the night to fend for herself without so much as an explanation she had felt it. It had trudged with her from the cane fields to the town. La Rusa's voice had been the only balm strong enough to make her forget her early troubles. All of Dulce's person was contained between the web of La Rusa's stories and the reality of her own fingernails. Now her arms ached and her hands were weighted.

No violation could have hurt her more than this. She knew even before she looked that her hands were disfigured. It took a long while for her to focus her frightened eyes on her swollen blood-stained fingertips. Carved across the nails of each hand was the word *zapa*, which means toad. She wanted to cry, but the ache was too great; like the aches of home, it would smother her with its silence. Until Sophie came out to see her and to bathe and bandage her hands, she had no idea that she was a despised usurper. In its way, Sophie's attempt at kindness only hurt her the more. So the girls have done this, she thought, and her mind went a dull black, too dense even to allow the frogs or cicadas to penetrate the void.

Downstairs, La Rusa called for her, but Dulce could not hear. Upstairs, the girls were frightened by her trance-like silence and they hovered round her. When she eventually picked herself up from her mat and went down to La Rusa, she found her patron aged and anxious. Despite the other girls' protests and promises, she believed that Dulce had gone. The child herself, who until she entered that cluttered reliquary of a room had thought all her feelings were dead, ran to the old lady and buried her head in the musk and silk that covered her. Her own bandaged hands seemed suddenly irrelevant beside the greater pain of a life ruined by a snapped spine.

Paradoxically, La Rusa, who had managed to overlook the spite involved in her own accident, determined to repay the damage done to her companion's hands. Under the high-pitched droning of the cicadas and through the buzz of humming birds darting through the papery blossoms of hibiscus and bougainvillaea there could be heard a continual whispering. Ilario Gomez said that it sounded like the house slowly subsiding on its foundations or the crumbling of wood under the onslaughts of silently drilling worms. La Rusa whispered the sweetness back into her injured child.

'Sometimes, ' she murmured, 'the only sweetness in life is to remember your scores: those that are settled and those still to be so. I was wrong, Dulce, to let those girls get away with crippling me. I was a coward and I gave in. But we have debts to pay now, so listen . . .'

As Dulce listened, she realised how little the loss of her one point of pride was when compared to the atrocity carried out on La Rusa. The lethargy that had threatened to swallow her up since the morning when she found her nails ruined could not hold against the surge of rage and injustice that she felt for her friend's injury. The girls must all lose what was dearest to them to atone for the robbery of two such qualities.

'The main thing', La Rusa told her, 'is total secrecy. We don't want a battle, we want a victory.'

From midday to dusk the sun pulsated on the dusty street, pressing its heat against the peeling walls of the Rainbow. Inside, there was a feeling of uneasiness so great that it seemed to get trapped inside the cornbread and even float on top of the sickly cups of coffee. Only one girl, Sophie, left the house, unable to cope with the tension there. No one could say for sure where she went to, but rumour had it that she had hitch-hiked for ten days to the coast and then tried to reach Trinidad. None of the other girls tried to leave, they were all mesmerised by the thought of La Rusa's gold. Although they had never really believed in her stories, they were convinced that the Romanov millions, or at least a large part of them, were interred somewhere in La Rusa's room. They didn't even discuss the subject. They just knew, intuitively, that it was so. They felt the change in the air, and mistook it in their greed for a sign of the old madame's weakening.

'The old cow is shuddering in her sleep, she can't have long,' the scout reported.

The clients were as discontented as they had ever been. The girls themselves seemed obsessed by something so far removed from sex that they even forgot to open their legs when they lay down, let alone fake any pleasure. While their Dulce, their pet, no longer tickled their fingers or held their hands. She had thrown away her manicurist's tray and she responded only dully to presents of any kind. It was clear that she had hurt her hands, but how long would the bandages remain, and how long would they be expected to restrain from their pleasures? What kind of a house was the Rainbow after all?

A week passed by, and then another, and then so many weeks that they got lost in the stifling heat and joined that continuum of time which is divided in the tropics only by rain. But the weather held and Madame, sensing the unrest reach its peak even from the inner sanctum of her web, proposed an outing for the girls and their favourite clients to the waterfall of Trujillito. In the early years, there had been outings, but only to the cinema matinées, the market or the travelling circus. There had never been a real outing with food and barrels of rum and trucks and drivers.

At seven o'clock in the morning the first of the trucks rattled down the narrow cobbled street outside the Rainbow. The girls, dressed up for once in all their finery, piled in. At seven fifteen, from a discreet corner on the edge of town, twenty-five men in their Sunday best clambered over the sides of a second truck. At eight o'clock, a third one stopped outside the demurely shuttered Rainbow, and two men began to load it with the furniture from inside. The street soon filled with curious gossipers, as truck-load after truck-load was carted away. By half past ten the last of the contents had been despatched, and Ilario Gomez had paid the cook and the cross-eyed girl who helped her their paltry wages. Ilario Gomez had not been sorry when La Rusa asked him to organise her flight. He lived on a permanent tightrope between the dread of having his embezzlements discovered and his desire to keep stealing. Since Madame was so graciously leaving without having discovered his years of theft, he lifted her with real tenderness from her bed in the stripped room of the Rainbow to a bed in the back of the last of the trucks. Then he assisted the pale blinking Dulce to her place beside her, patting her thin stiff arm with relief, for he too had begun to have designs on the waif, and he was a family man, and such things weren't right. The lease had, by chance, been due for renewal, so it had been a simple matter to let La Rusa's option drop. The deadline was midday, although the landlord had insisted on flexibility, should it be needed. It took some time for him to grasp that there was a game at stake, and the locks must be changed forthwith.

As the last truck drove away, there were boxes of records in the street curling up in the sun, and there were scattered letters and clothes. During the afternoon, these were all picked over and taken or discarded according to merit. Outside the front door there were twelve patchwork quilts, one for each girl, twelve legacies from the days when they were training to be ladies. Each square had been stitched by their own hands. These last years of neglect had taken their toll, though, even on the quilts, because each one was stained with the vestigial remains of thousands of bought orgasms. Stiff with seed, they crackled in the sun.

Dulce and La Rusa travelled almost as far as the missing Sophie was said to have done, and they took a small house with a verandah covered with climbing plants and humming birds. There were no bars on the windows, and there was no upstairs at all. They lived on La Rusa's savings and on the stories that she spun like fine silk from herself. Sometimes, when the evenings were unduly hot and long, they talked over their flight from the Rainbow and tried to imagine each girl's reaction to finding them gone. They both hoped that the shock would last for a long time. They would have been gratified.

The night of the move and the excursion was one of scandal in the town. There was a crowd gathered and waiting long before the girls got home. As the wailing and anger, the recriminations and cursing increased, the street vendors gathered and began to sell plantain chips and popcorn to the audience. Eventually, the National Guard arrived and hauled the former inmates off the house that they were trying to break into. The next morning they had no choice but to hawk their services around the lesser brothels in the town. Once, any girl from the Rainbow would have been welcomed with open arms, but the gossip had stuck together like a cloud of gnats and there were questions and criticisms everywhere.

'I heard there was a mere child working there. Is it true she was so young she could hardly speak?'

Everyone had a different story to tell about Dulce, but in all of them, although the rumours grew, Dulce herself shrank until she was scarcely more than a babe in arms. The less the other girls said about her, the more the curiosity grew, so that wherever they went, and wherever they worked, her name and her flat toad face followed them, until the very colours of the Rainbow ran into one dull blob of ill-conceived slander that sat like a heaviness in each chest. They would never be able to forget her. Every dusk with its ephemeral pink halo reminded them of the once perfect fingertips they had defiled. Dulce's memory was everywhere and it was as insistent as the voices of the tree frogs croaking and gloating through the tropical nights.

WINIFRED HOLTBY

Why Herbert Killed His Mother

Once upon a time there was a Model Mother who had a Prize Baby. Nobody had ever had such a Baby before. He was a Son, of course. All prize babies are masculine, for should there be a flaw in their gender this might deprive them of at least twenty-five per cent of the marks merited by their prize-worthiness.

The Mother's name was Mrs Wilkins, and she had a husband called Mr Wilkins, but he did not count much. It is true that he was the Baby's father, and on the night after the child was born he stood Drinks All Round at the Club; though he was careful to see that there were only two other members in the bar at the time he suggested it, because although one must be a Good Father and celebrate properly, family responsibilities make a man remember his bank balance. Mr Wilkins remembered his very often, particularly when Mrs Wilkins bought a copy of *Vogue*, or remarked that the Simpsons, who lived next door but one, had changed their Austin Seven for a Bentley. The Wilkinses had not even an old Ford; but then the buses passed the end of their road, and before the Prize Baby arrived, Mrs Wilkins went to the stores and ordered a very fine pram.

Mrs Wilkins had determined to be a Real Old-Fashioned Mother. She had no use for these Modern Women who Drink Cocktails, Smoke Cigarettes, and dash about in cars at all hours with men who are not their husbands. She believed in the true ideal of Real Womanliness, Feminine Charm, and the Maternal Instinct. She won a ten-shilling prize once from a daily paper, with a circulation of nearly two million, for saying so, very prettily, on a postcard.

Before the Baby came she sat with her feet up every afternoon sewing little garments. She made long clothes with twenty tucks round the hem of each robe, and embroidered flannels, fifty inches from hem to shoulder tape, and fluffy bonnets, and teeny-weeny little net veils; she draped a

43

bassinet with white muslin and blue ribbons, and she thought a great deal about violets, forget-me-nots and summer seas in order that her baby might have blue eyes. When Mrs Burton from 'The Acacias' told her that long clothes were unhygienic, and that drapery on the bassinet held the dust, and that heredity had far more to do with blue eyes than thoughts about forget-me-nots, she shook her head charmingly, and said: 'Ah, well. You *clever* women know so much. I can only go by what my darling mother told me.' Mrs Burton said: 'On the contrary. You have a lot of other authority to go by nowadays,' and she produced three pamphlets, a book on infant psychology, and a programme of lectures on 'Health, Happiness and Hygiene in the Nursery'. But Mrs Wilkins sighed, and said: 'My poor little brain won't take in all that stuff. I have only my Mother Love to guide me.' And she dropped a pearly tear on to a flannel binder.

Mrs Burton went home and told Mr Burton that Mrs Wilkins was hopeless, and that her baby would undoubtedly suffer from adenoids, curvature of the spine, flat feet, halitosis, bow legs, indigestion and the Œdipus complex. Mr Burton said 'Quite, quite'. And everyone was pleased.

The only dissentient was the Wilkins baby, who was born without any defect whatsoever. He was a splendid boy, and his more-than-proud parents had him christened Herbert James Rodney Stephen Christopher, which names they both agreed went very well with Wilkins. He wore for the ceremony two binders, four flannels, an embroidered robe with seventeen handmade tucks, a woolly coat, two shawls, and all other necessary and unnecessary garments, and when he stared into the Rector's face, and screamed lustily, his aunts said: 'That means he'll be musical, bless him'. But his mother thought: 'What a strong will he has! And what sympathy there is between us! Perhaps he knows already what I think about the Rector.'

As long as the monthly nurse was there, Mrs Wilkins and Herbert got along very nicely on Mother Love; but directly she left trouble began.

'My baby,' Mrs Wilkins had said, 'shall never be allowed to lie awake and cry like Mrs Burton's poor little wretch. Babies need cuddling.' So whenever Herbert cried at first she cuddled him. She cuddled him in the early morning when he woke up Mr Wilkins and wanted his six o'clock bottle at four. She cuddled him at half-past six and half-past seven and eight. She cuddled him half-hourly for three days and then she smacked him. It was a terrible thing to do, but she did it. She fed him when he seemed hungry, and showed him to all the neighbours who called, and kept him indoors when it rained, which it did every day, and nursed him while she had her own meals, and when she didn't gave him Nestlé's. And he still flourished.

But what with the crying and the washing that hung in the garden, the neighbours began to complain, and Mrs Burton said: 'Of course, you're killing that child.'

Mrs Wilkins knew that the Maternal Instinct was the safest guide in the world; but when her husband showed her an advertisement in the evening paper which began: 'Mother, does your child cry?' she read it. She learned there that babies cry because their food does not agree with them. 'What-not's Natural Digestive Infants' Milk solves the Mother's problem.' Mrs Wilkins thought that no stone should be left unturned and bought a specimen tin of What-not's Natural Digestive Infants' Milk, and gave it to Herbert. Herbert flourished. He grew larger and rounder and pinker, and more dimpled than ever. But he still cried.

So Mrs Wilkins read another advertisement in the evening paper. And there she learned that when babies cry it is because they are not warm enough, and that all good mothers should buy Flopsy's Fleecy Pram Covers. So, being a good mother, she bought a Flopsy's Fleecy Pram Cover and wrapped Herbert in it. And still Herbert flourished. And still he cried.

So she continued to read the evening papers, for by this time both she and Mr Wilkins were nearly distracted, and one of the neighbours threatened to complain to the landlord, and Mrs Simpson kept her loud speaker going all night and day to drown the noise, she said. And now Mrs Wilkins learned that the reason her baby cried was because his Elimination was inadequate so she bought him a bottle of Hebe's Nectar for the Difficult Child, and gave him a teaspoonful every morning. But still he cried.

Then the spring came, and the sun shone, and the bulbs in the garden of Number Seven were finer than they had ever been before, and Mrs Wilkins put Herbert out in the garden in his pram, and he stopped crying.

She was such a nice woman and such a proud mother that she wrote at once to the proprietors of What-not's Natural Digestive Infants' Milk, and Flopsy's Fleecy Pram Covers, and Hebe's Nectar for the Difficult Child, and told them that she had bought their things for Herbert and that he had stopped crying.

Two days later a sweet young woman came to the Wilkins' house, and said that What-not's Limited had sent her to see Herbert, and what a fine baby he was, and how healthy, and could she take a photograph? And Mrs Wilkins was very pleased, and thought: 'Well, Herbert is the most beautiful baby in the world, and won't this be a sell for Mrs Burton,' and was only too delighted. So the young woman photographed Herbert in his best embroidered robe drinking Natural Digestive Infants' Milk from a bottle, and went away.

The next day a kind old man came from Flopsy's Fleecy Pram Covers Limited, and photographed Herbert lying under a Fleecy Pram Cover. It was a hot afternoon and a butterfly came and settled on the pram; but the kind old man said that this was charming.

The next day a scientific-looking young man with horn-rimmed spectacles came from Hebe's Nectar Limited and photographed Herbert lying on a fur rug wearing nothing at all. And when Mr Wilkins read his Sunday paper, there he saw his very own baby, with large black capitals printed above him, saying: 'My Child is now no longer Difficult, declares Mrs Wilkins, of Number 9, The Grove, SW10.'

Mrs Burton saw it too, and said to Mr Burton: 'No wonder, when at last they've taken a few stones of wool off the poor little wretch.'

But Mr and Mrs Wilkins saw it differently. They took Herbert to a Court photographer and had him taken dressed and undressed, with one parent, with both parents, standing up and sitting down; and always he was the most beautiful baby that the Wilkinses had ever seen.

One day they saw an announcement in a great Sunday paper of a £10,000 prize for the loveliest baby in the world. 'Well, dear, this will be nice,' said Mrs Wilkins. 'We shall be able to buy a saloon car now.' Because, of course, she knew that Herbert would win the prize.

And so he did. He was photographed in eighteen different poses for the first heat; then he was taken for a personal inspection in private for the second heat; then he was publicly exhibited at the Crystal Palace for the semi-finals, and for the Final Judgment he was set in a pale blue bassinet and examined by three doctors, two nurses, a Child Psychologist, a film star, and Mr Cecil Beaton. After that he was declared the Most Beautiful Baby in Britain.

That was only the beginning. Baby Britain had still to face Baby France, Baby Spain, Baby Italy, and Baby America. Signor Mussolini sent a special message to Baby Italy, which the other national competitors thought unfair. The Free State insisted upon sending twins, which were disqualified. The French President cabled inviting the entire contest to be removed to Paris, and the Germans declared that the girl known as Baby Poland, having been born in the Polish Corridor, was really an East Prussian and should be registered as such.

But it did not matter. These international complications made no difference to Herbert. Triumphantly he overcame all his competitors, and was crowned as World Baby on the eve of his first birthday.

Then, indeed, began a spectacular period for Mr and Mrs Wilkins. Mrs Wilkins gave interviews to the Press on 'The Power of Mother Love', 'The Sweetest Thing in the World', and 'How I Run My Nursery'. Mr Wilkins wrote some fine manly articles on 'Fatherhood Faces Facts', and 'A Man's Son' – or, rather, they were written for him by a bright young woman until Mrs Wilkins decided that she should be present at the collaborations.

Then a firm of publishers suggested to Mr Wilkins that he should write a Christmas book called *Herbert's Father*, all about what tender feelings fathers had, and what white, pure thoughts ran through their heads when they looked upon the sleeping faces of their sons, and about how strange and wonderful it was to watch little images of themselves growing daily in beauty, and how gloriously unspotted and magical were the fairy-like actions of little children. Mr Wilkins thought that this was a good idea if someone would write the book for him, and if the advance royalties were not less than £3,000 on the date of publication; but he would have to ask Mrs Wilkins. Mrs Wilkins was a trifle hurt. Why *Herbert's Father*? What right had Paternity to override Maternity? The publisher pointed out the success of Mr A. A. Milne's *Christopher Robin*, and Mr Lewis Hind's *Julius Caesar*, and of Mr A. S. M. Hutchinson's *Son Simon*, to say nothing of Sir James Barrie's *Little White Bird*. 'But none of these children was my Herbert,' declared Mrs Wilkins – which, indeed, was undeniable. So the contract was finally signed for *The Book of Herbert*, by His Parents.

It was a success. Success? It was a Triumph, a Wow, a Scream, an Explosion. There was nothing like it. It was The Christmas Gift. It went into the third hundredth thousand before December 3rd. It was serialized simultaneously in the *Evening Standard*, *Home Chat*, and *The Nursery World*. Mr Baldwin referred to it at a Guildhall Banquet. The Prince used a joke from it in a broadcast speech on England and the Empire. The Book Society failed to recommend it, but every bookstall in the United Kingdom organized a display stand in its honour, with photographs of Herbert and copies signed with a blot 'Herbert, His Mark' exquisitely arranged.

The Herbert boom continued. Small soap Herberts (undressed for the bath) were manufactured and sold for use in delighted nurseries. Royalty graciously accepted an ivory Herbert, designed as a paperweight, from the loyal sculptor. A Herbert Day was instituted in order to raise money for the children's hospitals of England, and thirty-seven different types of Herbert calendars, Christmas cards, and penwipers were offered for sale – and sold.

Mrs Wilkins felt herself justified in her faith. This, she said, was what mother love could do. Mr Wilkins demanded 10 per cent royalties on every Herbert article sold. And they all bought a country house near Brighton, a Bentley car, six new frocks for Mrs Wilkins, and an electric refrigerator, and lived happily ever after until Herbert grew up.

But Herbert grew up.

When he was four he wore curls and a Lord Fauntleroy suit and posed for photographers. When he was fourteen he wore jerseys and black fingernails and collected beetles. When he left one of England's Great Public Schools he wore plus-fours and pimples and rode a motorcycle and changed his tie three times in half an hour before he called on the young lady at the tobacconist's round the corner. He knew what a Fella does, by Jove, and he knew what a Fella doesn't. His main interests in life were etiquette, Edgar Wallace, and the desire to live down his past. For on going to a preparatory school he had carefully insisted that his name was James. His father, who knew that boys will be boys, supported him, and as he grew to maturity, few guessed that young James Wilkins, whose beauty was certainly not discernible to the naked eye, was Herbert, the Loveliest Baby in the World. Only Mrs Wilkins, in a locked spare bedroom, cherished a museum of the Herbert photographs, trophies, first editions, soap images, ivory statuettes, silver cups, and Christmas cards. The Herbert vogue had faded, as almost all vogues do, until not even a gag about Herbert on the music hall stage raised a feeble smile.

But Mrs Wilkins found the position hard to bear. It is true that the fortunes of the family were soundly laid, that Mr Wilkins had invested the profits of his son's juvenile triumphs in trustee stock, and that no household in South Kensington was more respected. But Mrs Wilkins had tasted the sweet nectar of publicity and she thirsted for another drink.

It happened that one day, when (Herbert) James was twenty-three, he brought home the exciting news that he had become engaged to Selena Courtney, the daughter of Old Man Courtney, whose office in the city Herbert adorned for about six hours daily.

Nothing could have been more fortunate. Mr Wilkins was delighted, for Courtney, of Courtney, Gilbert and Co., was worth nearly half a million. Herbert was delighted, for he was enjoying the full flavour of Young Love and Satisfied Snobbery combined, which is, as everyone knows, the perfect fulfilment of a True Man's dreams. The Courtneys were delighted, because they thought young Wilkins a very decent young man, with none of this damned nonsense about him. And Mrs Wilkins – well, her feelings were mixed. It was she, after all, who had produced this marvel, and nobody seemed to remember her part in the production, nor to consider the product specially marvellous. Besides, she was a little jealous, as model mothers are allowed to be, of her prospective daughter-in-law.

The engagement was announced in *The Times* – the reporters came, rather bored, to the Kensington home of Mrs Wilkins. She was asked to supply any details about her son's career. 'Any adventures? Any accidents? Has he ever won any prizes?' asked a reporter.

This was too much. 'Come here!' said Mrs Wilkins; and she led the reporters up to the locked spare bedroom.

What happened there was soon known to the public. When (Herbert) James, two evenings later, left the office on his way to his future father-in-law's house in Belgrave Square, hoping to take his fiancée after dinner to a dance given by Lady Soxlet, he was confronted by placards announcing 'The Perfect Baby to Wed'. Taking no notice he went on to the tube station, but there he saw yet further placards. 'The World's Loveliest Baby now a Man', and 'Little Herbert Engaged'.

Still hardly conscious of the doom awaiting him, he bought an evening paper, and there he saw in black letters across the front page: 'Herbert's Identity at last Discovered', and underneath the fatal words: 'The young City man, Mr James Wilkins, whose engagement to Miss Selena Courtney, of 299 Belgrave Square, was announced two days ago, has been revealed by his mother, Mrs Wilkins, to be Herbert, the Wonder Baby.' There followed descriptions of the Perfect Childhood, stories taken from the Herbert Legend; rapid advertisements rushed out by What-not's Natural Digestive Infants' Milk, Flopsy's Fleecy Pram Covers, and Hebe's Nectar for the Difficult Child, illustrated by photographs of the Infant Herbert. The publishers of the *Book of Herbert* announced a new edition, and a famous daily paper, whose circulation was guaranteed to be over 2,000,000, declared its intention of publishing a series of articles called 'My Herbert is a Man, by Herbert's Mother'.

Herbert did not proceed to Belgrave Square. He went to Kensington. With his own latchkey he opened the door and went up to his mother's boudoir. He found her laughing and crying with joy over the evening paper. She looked up and saw her son.

'Oh, darling,' she said. 'I thought you were taking Selena to a dance.'

'There is no Selena,' declared Herbert grimly. 'There is no dance. There is only you and me.'

He should, doubtless, have said: 'You and I,' but among the things a Fella does, correct grammar is not necessarily included.

'Oh, Herbert,' cried Mrs Wilkins, with ecstatic joy. 'My mother instinct was right. Mother always knows, darling. You have come back to me.'

'I have,' said Herbert.

And he strangled her with a rope of twisted newspapers.

The judge declared it justifiable homicide, and Herbert changed his name to William Brown and went to plant tea or rubber or something in the Malay states, where Selena joined him two years later – and Mr Wilkins lived to a ripe old age at the Brighton house and looked after his dividends, and everyone was really very happy after all.

CANDIA McWILLIAM

Being a People Person

'And, above all, you've got to be a people person,' finished the person, addressing a number of people in the personnel room. As though, thought Patrick, one could ever get away from being so. Since the last tangle with a person, I don't care if I become a louse-person, or a concrete-person, anything at all in fact but a people person.

A person laughed in a most unseemly way and Patrick followed the sound in case it was he himself who had made the noise. Since Frances had gone, leaving the teapot warm and the paper folded at the 'How to Spend It' page of *The Financial Times*, he had suffered from bouts of disembodiment. One time he had seen a very drunk man fall down in the distant purple mirror behind a cocktail bar. Red cherries and tall cocktail spoons made a Miró of the mirror. Only in the morning did he realise that it had been himself, Patrick, who could wash in rye and stay dry behind the ears. Corny jokes come easily to admen, he thought. I think in phrases which would fit on a bus-side. Was his id riddled with quick quips and reflex associations too? He admired the notion that he might be a perfectly functioning phenomenon, a faultless free-market capitalist. A credit to any mother, though in fact considered a debit by his own, since taking up this job. She'd sooner he were a teacher or a preacher. Or anything but what he was.

Patrick was twenty-nine and he was going to live for ever. Or he had been until Frances went. In actual fact, maybe he'd live for ever anyway. That would spite her.

Now, where was that laugh coming from? Patrick minded people looking instantly towards the source of some irregularity, a lunatic on the tube, or a raving prophet on the bus, so he dropped something behind himself in order to pick it up in the most natural way in the world and lift his head, at the same moment darting his eyes to the source of the laugh.

His glance struck and stuck. If that was a person, he certainly was a people person. 'Certainly am', the other guys in the office would say if you asked them if they were going out that night. Was Patrick a people person? Certainly was.

Catch a load of *her*. She resembled everyone's sweetest fantasy. Sisterly sexiness shone from her, asking to be licked off like butterscotch sauce. She had that kind of French colouring which looks good with lace and an old bike in some campaign shot in an attic for five hundred grand. Dipped in water, she'd just get shiny, and deepen fractionally in colour, like damp sand. Twenty-four-ish, he supposed, just turning the corner from legwear to food products. None the worse for that, though. Older is bolder, thought Patrick. It was not his own phrase, though he prided himself on learning fast.

But she didn't look bold, he thought, in relief. Demure was the word, which was how you wanted them when it came down to it, to look at at any rate. That folksy old saying about the perfect chick being a maid in the kitchen and a whore in the bedroom was the one Patrick intended sticking to from here on in; he preferred the old ways, the good ways, tried and trusted, passed down from father to son, or was it from hand to mouth?

Her name was Louella and she was a doll. No one didn't like her. Right then in the personnel room of Drive, Torque, MacIsmo, the cream of the firm's team was busy liking her a lot. Patrick couldn't think for the moment why she was there, but they often got visitors at Drive, Torque. It was the coming agency.

Several of the men in the room were plotting. They were people people, after all. How to get rid of the evening's domestic arrangements and insinuate this toasty, sugary young woman into those valued leisure hours? Work hard, play hard, that was the form. And they believed women were people, these men; certainly did. One or two of them had even learnt the lingo necessary to trap the new people women; there were certain key lines to put forth which would almost guarantee a lady'd put out. A bit of jaw about freedom, space, quality time, and the figgy treat was on the table, all but.

The biggest account held by Drive, Torque was a confectionery bar aimed at the homebound housewife; like her, Jeremy Drive was fond of saying, it was soft with little hard bits, sweet but with only natural sweetness, and could be eaten at any time when nothing more leisurely was possible. The bar's shape was that of many of the bottles to be found in any household cupboard, straight-sided with a neatly rounded swelling at the top. The product developers have long known this shape is specially congenial to the female grip. In the case of the bar the swelling was coated with chocolate over a bullet of vanilla cream, which tipped a core of honeycomb. As the marketing director said, 'Show me the bird who didn't learn French kissing on a Crunchie bar and I'll show you a nun in the Rasputin.' The Rasputin was a club where advertising men met up with each other in a leisure situation. It stayed in the swim with a total makeover every couple of years. Last time it was done over had been when the promotion for a kind of dogfood had got out of hand. It was like the dogs hadn't known how to behave at a big do.

The icecream at the Rasputin was said to be made by a deaf mute from the Bombay Taj. ('What other Taj is there?', the club's manager asked.) None of the members had seen the subcontinental icecream man and his legend grew. Jeremy Drive said it stood to reason, 'The deprived are the best at luxury goods, take it from me.'

The confectionery bar was called Goldenrod; its tag was 'the molten gold bar'. The teaser slots on TV, between long stories for washing powder and baby alarms, ran 'The at-home bar – guilt-free gold, in YOUR mouth NOW'. The direct reference to the act of eating had been thought a bit near the edge by one of the girl juniors in media, but the client had explained matters to her. After all, the bar contained not less than 20 per cent full farm yoghurt, the only food known to peel off pounds whether you slap it on or slurp it down. She was a big girl, and that stopped her mouth.

Late at night in the Rasputin (some tyros called it the Raz of course, but this did them no good at all among the real helium warriors who called it the Monk), the Goldenrod bar was referred to as the choc cock and the men felt they had isolated a great truth not merely about the advertising business but about women.

Drive, Torque, MacIsmo had a considerable number of accounts, but the big one at the moment was definitely Goldenrod. There was a Goldenrod guy, a man whose career was not in modelling, so he had the right homey feel. His parents had come from a small part of what was now East Germany; his name was Axel and he needed the money badly. It was good money. He wore specs and didn't look like a woman when wardrobe put him in a cardigan for C2 credibility at personal appearances.

Patrick's brief at the moment was to find a Goldenrod girl. Axel's own girlfriend, who was in fact his wife, would not do. She had to be, excuse the double meaning, kept pretty dark. Patrick liked her fine and she was beautiful, but she was black as your hat and incredibly serious. Like a lot of Senegalese, she was a catwalk model, which left her quite a lot of time for Axel. Most of the girls who lasted, she'd explained to Patrick, just looked extraordinary. Most of them simply lived their lives; it was the minority who changed racing drivers every season. Anyhow, catch Roxanne eating a Goldenrod, all those refined sugars.

Those executives of Drive, Torque who had seen Roxanne talked about her as though she were a bit alarming, like a big cat with good manners. After a few bevvies, they'd discuss her, in depth; last thing she needed was a choc cock. Axel was completing his doctorate in insects' nervous systems; mayflies were his special interest. Did the shortness of their lives make for speeded-up messages between neurones? Axel worried that his own time would run out before he found an answer.

The meeting in the personnel room had been on Goldenrod. For the first time since Frances's departure, Patrick felt sentimental as well as physiological lust, something less itchy than simple appetite. He was determined to win the nut-brown girl. It was the end of a long day and he felt he owed himself a reward, something soft and creamy and delicious.

'Meeting adjourned,' said the person at the head of the long white table, 'I'll be interested to see what you can come up with.' Patrick could not remember how the last hour or so had been spent. The words had been the same as ever, maybe in a different order, that's all. There was a shuffling and dealing of bits of paper; the secretaries left the personnel room, followed by the girl. Who would be the first to reach her without seeming uncool? Patrick hung back, and, once the room had emptied, took the chairman's private lift down, intending to catch her at the door of the mirrored building – it was worth the risk. He looked at his own face in the walls of the lift. He was satisfactorily reflected back to himself on all sides. He wouldn't take her to the Monk, he decided, careful even in his private thoughts to use the most exclusive slang. Strive to belong, behave as though you belong, and you will belong, he told himself regularly throughout each day. Act as though you are one of them and you will become one of them. It was not that hard, mostly just a matter of not speaking first, laughing in the right place, and copying their gestures and phrases. If you wanted something enough, you generally got it, and Patrick wanted to be one of them. They were sleek. They knew what to do. They weren't losers.

Not the Monk, then, but somewhere he could receive her undivided attention. He allowed his thoughts to soften. He might even have begun to feel a stirring in his imagination had he not gained the revolving glass door just as she did. There she miraculously was, in deep brown fur and pale leather boots. No one else seemed to be about.

'How do you do? I noticed you in that meeting. Where do you fit into the campaign? I'm Patrick Hunter, by the way.' He was keeping things light, important with really pretty ones. The better looking they were, the more offhand you'd to be or they thought you were a woman. Peter Torque slipped him that tip one night they'd been working late on a flowchart.

'Hello, I'm Louella Drummond, and I'm in market research.' She had quite a deep voice and white teeth without ridges. Rich girl's teeth. No sugar abuse there. There was a candied scent from her hair and skin. Her gaze had an interesting blankness. Patrick gained confidence.

'I was wondering if you were free for a bite of supper?' he heard himself asking in an almost perfect imitation of the tones he knew got results, because he'd heard them time and again in the Monk. He sounded offhand but full of potential.

'Oh, that would be really nice, Patrick,' said this delicious girl, with her fresh hair and small brown gloves.

'Shall we go then? How do you like to eat? Korean? Thai? Japanese?' First time he'd been asked how he liked to eat, Patrick had said, 'Sitting down.' That had torn them up laughing. 'God, you kill me, Paddy,' Jeremy said, hitting him repeatedly in the chest.

Patrick had not been brought up in the knowledge of foreign food and he found its demands confusing. If pushed, he could do that hairstyling thing with a fork and spaghetti.

'Actually,' she replied, 'I'm not good at fancy food. I'd really like something simple.'

They ate at a restaurant he'd picked up on from his colleagues. The cost legitimised the simplicity of the food.

All about sat refugees from complicated foodstuffs. Patrick ordered tomato soup, mixed grill, and crumble with cream for both of them. She was quite happy to eat what he ate; she drank water. Patrick had a beer. He didn't, frankly, like wines. He'd said as much once at a business lunch and there was a bit of a hush.

'Prefer a milky drink, do you?' Jeremy asked, which was quite nice of him really, to make a joke of something people like him clearly held to be serious.

Patrick was soon absorbed. She was an amazing listener. Not seeming to say, let alone tell, much, she soon had it all out of him about his mum and the house in Weston. Then she had it out of him like a tooth he was happy to lose about Frances and her stuck-up parents with their indoor pool and gins you could do backstroke in. Then it came out about Frances's ideas on women. He did not go so far as to tell this soft creature about Frances's active role in the Anti-Infibulation Association. Frances had been quite unfeminine in that way. Even to talk about those sort of matters would surely offend and confuse Louella, never mind the problem of defining infibulation for her over the mixed grill's selected inner parts and their modest parsley leaf.

He began to feel that his sensation on Frances's departure had been relief, with a dash of self-pity. She had known how to iron and Patrick, with all his shirts, had appreciated that. He missed it still.

'Not that I don't want a girl to be independent,' he was saying. This was a line which had led him more than once through feint and skirmish to surrender. He spoke to girls in this mode as though he were handing them a bag of sweeties.

'Oh, I just don't want independence,' she responded, making wide eyes and drawing her spoon out of her mouth upwards, so that he could see part of her tongue and the silver bowl tipped to reflect, upside down, his own face, made paler by the patina of the silver.

'I really just want to make someone happy.' An emotion more often felt than heard, Patrick thought. It was the sort of thing his mother believed in.

'But how does that fit in with your work commitments, Louella?' He enunciated her name as though it were a new way of twisting her for her own pleasure.

'I don't find it hard,' she confessed, and he had a great rush of simplification such as can accompany the birth of love. Worry and fret were shelved, and he saw with the flat clarity of comprehensive benevolence. He felt the complications of which Frances had forced him to be aware melt and fuse and he was home, safe, a whole man again, feeling one direct emotion towards each thing which presented itself to him. He was freed from the multiple apprehensions he had endured since Frances's first eruption into his life, and even more acutely since her disappearance from it.

At once nothing vibrated with unpleasant implications beyond itself. Everything felt fat, replete with simple happy meaning. Life seemed plotless but pointful. Everything was extra real. Patrick's senses were a child's. It was this girl.

They didn't take coffee. She admitted that she'd never got used to the taste, and he was happy to agree. He helped her into her fur coat. Its biscuit-coloured silk lining shone and the fur itself seemed to promise something about Louella. Frances's mother's fur had been a solid bank reference, Frances's own had been 'hocked' – her word, horsy cow – long ago. Patrick imagined Louella saving for her fur; what could be more natural, more feminine, than to want a soft, warm, outer wrapping? How sweet that she had earned it.

Drunk at heart, sober at head, he drove her home. Though she must at least have guessed something of what might be to come, there was a coating of innocence to her. She kept her eyes down. They chatted lightly of routes through central London. Frances had judged this topic as dull as swapping inflation stories. But things *had* been dull before, Patrick now saw, until he'd found the one, the only, the golden girl.

To his own surprise, he did not worry about his flat and the messages the girl might read in its bottles, its posters, coffee table and rowing machine. He kicked the bullworker under his new leather-jacketed sofa, tooled, the salesman crooned at him, by the very suppliers who fitted out the classic motors, your Jag, your Rolls, your Aston.

He went to the kitchen to make tea and turned to look through the hatch into his walkthrough diner/rec room. One asset the agent hadn't drawn to his attention on the guided tour. You could see your date even when you were coming on domestic.

There she sat, nice as sugar pie, knees together, hands on them, head on one side, hair touching each shoulder, just. She was pale brown all over, dipped in pale brown. He did not allow her nakedness to hurry his teamaking. You had to be cool.

He laid a pretty tray, two white cups, white sugar lumps in a bowl with beige roses and a brown jug of milk. He also laid a small white dish of chocolates, dusty truffles and a few dragees. He had some white chocs too, from when his mother visited. Jeremy had told him white chocolate was women's chocolate – feminine and not too strong. The brown teapot was from his mother. Heat came out of the tiny hole in its lid, an aromatic breath of home.

He took his tray in to the brown waiting girl. They passed chocolates from mouth to mouth for a while. He laid her down and put one dragee beneath each ear. Her ears were not pierced. He journeyed in her hair and neck. He fed her. He lifted her up and gave her tea, very milky and sweet, from a spoon. When the chocolates were done, he licked each of her fingers and dried them. He put his own fingers, one by one, into her sweet mouth. There was no bit of her which was not brown. Her irises were the darkest brown, and shining, shining.

They gorged on each other. When they woke up he wanted more. She was pepperminty, still with that slight warm-sugar smell he now knew to be her most intimate flavour.

'When can I see you again?' he asked.

'Whenever you want,' said Louella, 'but for now I really must be off.'

'Well, pulled her, did you?' asked Doug MacIsmo in the executive carpark. Another of the guys was there too.

'We had dinner,' Patrick replied.

'Stand her a spot of savoury, did you?' roared Doug.

Patrick did not really mind that he was blushing. So, they knew. They'd have to know sometime, and he didn't want any of them going after his baby. Doug and the other bloke exchanged gestures of lewd envy and looks of something else which Patrick couldn't place.

All day enquiries about his night irked and elated him, reminding him of the hoard of beauty now his.

'Pat, a word,' said the person who had been giving – was it yesterday? – the talk on people people, and beckoned him with an arch finger into the personnel room.

'Do sit down, there's a good man, have a cappuccino, the choc dust sprayer's been replaced. It really is something of a winning little gadget . . .'

The person stretched out his legs before him; he appeared to be burdened with a codpiece, which he adjusted. Could *that* be cavalry twill, too? The legs were about the length of the front bit of a Porsche, which was just as well. These legs terminated in strangely orange suede brogues, all the nap smoothed one way.

'About the Goldenrod girl, Pat, we've decided to pull the chain on that, but the creative boys came up with a big one a couple of weeks ago and we've been giving it a good kick around. I really wanted to ask you a few to the point thrusters, your views and so on.'

'A couple of weeks,' thought Patrick, 'that's how knocked back I was about Frances. I never took a new campaign on board.' He said nothing. He'd thought yesterday afternoon's meeting had been about the Goldenrod girl. He knew keeping quiet was the best thing.

'Now, Pat, I'm not sure what your thinking is here, but if we're talking a hard yet soft, get my meaning, product for the ladies, I hazard' (the diffidence was so utter as to be implausible) 'I hazard the guys want something soft all through, but easy to handle. Am I right here would you say or am I right?' The codpiece was shifted.

'Um . . .'

'I mean, while the ladies want something that's never going to get confectioner's droop, if you take me, we want something here that's never going to say no, a really soft, yielding unit, but not one that's going to embarrass us in a public place, something you can eat out of doors without feeling you're out of tune with Mother Nature, yet something you can browse from your briefcase without the other chaps thinking you're a lady. The pack's got to be virile without being so butch it's fetishy, and I think we're looking to a non-design design on this, a kind of street-naturalness, you have me?'

'What's its name to be?' Patrick asked. It was awesome that a chocolate bar could have all this meaning. What had people been doing without it all these years?

'I'm wanting something with overtones of Adam's rib if you know your Good Book at all, Pat, but eventually we decided we'd open the name question pretty well up to you.'

'Me?' The creative side of the biz were pretty aloof as a rule, being creative.

'Yup. Well, Pat, you see, you are pretty much the only guy who's had the ultimate experience of all we feel our target group wants from a choc bar.'

'Me?' asked Patrick again. He was silly with new love. The person before him had very likely gone mad; perhaps he'd fallen in love overnight, too. Stranger things happen, truth stranger than fiction, all that . . .

57

'Pat, old thing, am I right in thinking you gave one to that little pot of honey who by chance cropped up at our yesterday meeting?' The words 'by chance' had a cheesy tone.

Of course he was disgusted, but he couldn't deny it. Nor could he see the harm in admitting to love. He loved her, would marry her, keep her always, cherish her.

'Wake up, Patrick, did you or did you not? Ah, I see you did; one better you'll agree than the boss's daughter type you were porking, all opinions and poncho?'

Patrick made as if to look outraged. He knew that a man's private life was fair game, being as it was closely related to his image. But still . . .

'Never mind, Pat, old thing, I see from your face you did get some joy from Louella.'

How did this person know her name?

'Surprised, Pat? You are an old love, really. Didn't you even whiff a wolverine when none of the other guys went for the little box of tricks?'

'I beat them to it.' He was startled into openness.

'That gag with the chairman's lift is as old as the proverbials, and you must know it. Wilful suspension of disbelief in the grip of hunger, like a man forgetting he'll get fat on cocoa butter and nougat and caramel and Uncle Tom Chocco and all.'

Patrick was just about following.

The person resumed. The codpiece seemed to be giving him a disposition problem. He moved it decisively in one cupped palm, to the left, and settled it as though for a sleep. In vain. It flexed, with assertion.

'Truth is, Louella's by way of being quite a pal of mine, been modelling since she was doing teething rusks. I thought we could put this bit of business her way.'

'Business?' Patrick's stomach moved as though he had seen into the secrets of pouch and knot and gloss inside the horrible twill codpiece. He was going to be sick, unless it wasn't true.

'Nothing nasty, dear old thing, just that I, that is the whole team, thought that she'd be the perfect peg for this new bar. You've got to agree.'

'Me?'

'Well, you know the market for Goldenrod; even though Axel's so very dandy, it's the female C2s, the gross confectionery purchasers, the checkout punters and afternoon timekillers and old bags with Hoover hangovers. And we feel the new bar has got to be for . . .'

'The male equivalent.' Patrick tasted bile as he spoke. This was their punishment of him for trying to be one of them.

'In a nutshell, That's broadly it, old son. The thing of it was, when we were all around the table, we realised (it was the day after you'd tied one on when that girl dumped you) that we were going to have to do a touch of product testing. We wanted the name for the bar to come from the experience we wanted the bar to reflect, soft, sweet, you know the sort of thing. And if possible firing a bloke up to want another about every eight hours. Not just one a day helping work rest and play, but three a day, Pat, assisting slog, sleep and shag. The long and the short of it was that we needed you, you, Patrick, because you may earn like an alpha but you're the only man in the office with the distinction of having known life as a C2. Now, do tell, what would you dub the bar, never forgetting this could carry a hefty slice of the sweet folding stuff when the product hits the shelves? How would you describe last night?'

He leered, but his real expression was one of attentive pecuniary acumen.

'Melted Dreams,' answered Patrick, knowing bitterness for the true opposite of sweetness.

ELIZABETH GASKELL

The Doom of the Griffiths

Chapter 1

I have always been much interested by the traditions which are scattered up and down North Wales relating to Owen Glendower (Owain Glendwr is the national spelling of the name), and I fully enter into the feeling which makes the Welsh peasant still look upon him as the hero of his country. There was great joy among many of the inhabitants of the principality, when the subject of the Welsh prize poem at Oxford, some fifteen or sixteen years ago, was announced to be 'Owain Glendwr.' It was the most proudly national subject that had been given for years.

Perhaps, some may not be aware that this redoubted chieftain is, even in the present days of enlightenment, as famous among his illiterate countrymen for his magical powers as for his patriotism. He says himself – or Shakespeare says it for him, which is much the same thing –

> 'At my nativity
> The front of heaven was full of fiery
> > shapes
> Of burning cressets . . .
> . . . I can call spirits from the vasty deep.'

And few among the lower orders in the principality would think of asking Hotspur's irreverent question in reply.

Among other traditions preserved relative to this part of the Welsh hero's character, is the old family prophecy which gives title to this tale. When Sir David Gam, 'as black a traitor as if he had been born in Builth,' sought to murder Owen at Machynlleth, there was one with him whose name Glendwr little dreamed of having associated with his enemies. Rhys ap Gryfydd, his 'old familiar friend,' his relation, his more than brother, had consented unto his blood. Sir David Gam might be forgiven, but one whom he had loved, and who had betrayed him, could never be forgiven. Glendwr

60

was too deeply read in the human heart to kill him. No, he let him live on, the loathing and scorn of his compatriots, and the victim of bitter remorse. The mark of Cain was upon him.

But before he went forth – while yet he stood a prisoner, cowering beneath his conscience before Owain Glendwr – that chieftain passed a doom upon him and his race:

'I doom thee to live, because I know thou wilt pray for death. Thou shalt live on beyond the natural term of the life of man, the scorn of all good men. The very children shall point to thee with hissing tongue, and say, "There goes one who would have shed a brother's blood!" For I loved thee more than a brother, oh Rhys ap Gryfydd! Thou shalt live on to see all of thy house, except the weakling in arms, perish by the sword. Thy race shall be accursed. Each generation shall see their lands melt away like snow; yea, their wealth shall vanish, though they may labour night and day to heap up gold. And when nine generations have passed from the face of the earth, thy blood shall no longer flow in the veins of any human being. In those days the last male of thy race shall avenge me. The son shall slay the father.'

Such was the traditional account of Owain Glendwr's speech to his once-trusted friend. And it was declared that the doom had been fulfilled in all things; that, live in as miserly a manner as they would, the Griffiths never were wealthy and prosperous – indeed, that their worldly stock diminished without any visible cause.

But the lapse of many years had almost deadened the wonder-inspiring power of the whole curse. It was only brought forth from the hoards of memory when some untoward event happened to the Griffiths family; and in the eighth generation the faith in the prophecy was nearly destroyed, by the marriage of the Griffiths of that day, to a Miss Owen, who, unexpectedly, by the death of a brother, became an heiress – to no considerable amount, to be sure, but enough to make the prophecy appear reversed. The heiress and her husband removed from his small patrimonial estate in Merionethshire, to her heritage in Caenarvonshire, and for a time the prophecy lay dormant.

If you go from Tremadoc to Criccaeth you pass by the parochial church of Ynysynhanarn, situated in a boggy valley running from the mountains, which shoulder up to the Rivals, down to Cardigan Bay. This tract of land has every appearance of having been redeemed at no distant period of time from the sea, and has all the desolate rankness often attendant upon such marshes. But the valley beyond, similar in character, had yet more of gloom at the time of which I write. In the higher part there were large plantations of firs, set too closely to attain any size, and remaining stunted in height and scrubby in appearance. Indeed, many of the smaller and more weakly had died, and the bark had fallen down on the brown soil neglected and unnoticed. These trees had a ghastly appearance, with their white trunks, seen by the dim light which struggled through the thick boughs above. Nearer to the sea, the valley assumed a more open, though hardly a more cheerful character; it looked dark and overhung by sea-fog through the greater part of the year, and even a farm-house, which usually imparts something of cheerfulness to a landscape, failed to do so here. This valley formed the greater part of the estate to which Owen Griffiths became entitled by right of his wife. In the higher part of the valley was situated the family mansion, or rather dwelling-house, for 'mansion,' is too grand a word to apply to the clumsy, but substantially-built Bodowen. It was square and heavy-looking, with just that much pretension to ornament necessary to distinguish it from the mere farm-house.

In this dwelling Mrs Owen Griffiths bore her husband two sons – Llewellyn, the future squire, and Robert, who was early destined for the church. The only difference in their situation, up to the time when Robert was entered at Jesus College, was that the elder was invariably indulged by all around him, while Robert was thwarted and indulged by turns; that Llewellyn never learned anything from the poor Welsh parson who was nominally his private tutor; while occasionally Squire Griffiths made a great point of enforcing Robert's diligence, telling him that, as he had his bread to earn, he must pay attention to his learning. There is no knowing how far the very irregular education he had received would have carried Robert through his college examinations; but, luckily for him in this respect, before such a trial of his learning came round, he heard of the death of his elder brother, after a short illness, brought on by a hard drinking-bout. Of course, Robert was summoned home, and it seemed quite as much of course, now that there was no necessity for him to 'earn his bread by his learning,' that he should not return to Oxford. So the half-educated, but not unintelligent, young man continued at home, during the short remainder of his parents' lifetime.

His was not an uncommon character. In general he was mild, indolent, and easily managed; but once thoroughly roused, his passions were vehement and fearful. He seemed, indeed, almost afraid of himself, and in common hardly dared to give way to justifiable anger – so much did he dread losing his self-control. Had he been judiciously educated, he would, probably, have distinguished himself in those branches of literature which call for taste and imagination, rather than any exertion of reflection or judgement. As it was, his literary taste showed itself in making collections of Cambrian antiquities of every description, till his stock of Welsh MSS would have excited the envy of Dr Pugh himself, had he been alive at the time of which I write.

There is one characteristic of Robert Griffiths which I have omitted to note, and which was peculiar among his class. He was no hard drinker;

whether it was that his head was very easily affected, or that his partially-refined taste led him to dislike intoxication and its attendant circumstances, I cannot say; but at five-and-twenty Robert Griffiths was habitually sober – a thing so rare in Llyn, that he was almost shunned as a churlish, unsociable being, and passed much of his time in solitude.

About this time, he had to appear in some case that was tried at the Caernarvon assizes; and while there, was a guest at the house of his agent, a shrewd, sensible Welsh attorney, with one daughter, who had charms enough to captivate Robert Griffiths. Though he remained only a few days at her father's house, they were sufficient to decide his affections, and short was the period allowed to elapse before he brought home a mistress to Bodowen. The new Mrs Griffiths was a gentle, yielding person, full of love toward her husband, of whom, nevertheless, she stood something in awe, partly arising from the difference in their ages, partly from his devoting much time to studies of which she could understand nothing.

She soon made him the father of a blooming little daughter, called Augharad after her mother. Then there came several uneventful years in the household of Bodowen; and when the old women had one and all declared that the cradle would not rock again, Mrs Griffiths bore the son and heir. His birth was soon followed by his mother's death: she had been ailing and low-spirited during her pregnancy, and she seemed to lack the buoyancy of body and mind requisite to bring her round after her time of trial. Her husband, who loved her all the more from having few other claims on his affections, was deeply grieved by her early death, and his only comforter was the sweet little boy whom she had left behind. That part of the Squire's character, which was so tender, and almost feminine, seemed called forth by the helpless situation of the little infant, who stretched out his arms to his father with the same earnest cooing that happier children make use of to their mother alone. Augharad was almost neglected, while the little Owen was king of the house; still, next to his father, none tended him so lovingly as his sister. She was so accustomed to give way to him that it was no longer a hardship. By night and by day Owen was the constant companion of his father, and increasing years seemed only to confirm the custom. It was an unnatural life for the child, seeing no bright little faces peering into his own (for Augharad was, as I said before, five or six years older, and her face, poor motherless girl, was often anything but bright), hearing no din of clear ringing voices, but day after day sharing the otherwise solitary house of his father, whether in the dim room, surrounded by wizard-like antiquities, or pattering his little feet to keep up with his 'tada' in his mountain rambles or shooting excursions. When the pair came to some little foaming brook, where the stepping-stones were far and wide, the father carried his little boy across with the tenderest care; when the lad was weary, they rested, he cradled in his father's arms, or the Squire would lift him up and carry him to his home again. The boy was indulged (for his father felt flattered by the desire) in his wish of sharing his meals and keeping the same hours. All this indulgence did not render Owen unamiable, but it made him wilful, and not a happy child. He had a thoughtful look, not common to the face of a young boy. He knew no games, no merry sports; his information was of an imaginative and speculative character. His father delighted to interest him in his own studies, without considering how far they were healthy for so young a mind.

Of course Squire Griffiths was not unaware of the prophecy which was to be fulfilled in his generation. He would occasionally refer to it when among his friends, with sceptical levity; but in truth it lay nearer to his heart than he chose to acknowledge. His strong imagination rendered him peculiarly impressible on such subjects; while his judgement, seldom exercised or fortified by severe thought, could not prevent his continually recurring to it. He used to gaze on the half-sad countenance of the child, who sat looking up into his face with his large dark eyes, so fondly yet so inquiringly, till the old legend swelled around his heart, and became too painful for him not to require sympathy. Besides, the overpowering love he bore to the child seemed to demand fuller vent than tender words; it made him like, yet dread, to upbraid its object for the fearful contrast foretold. Still Squire Griffiths told the legend, in a half-jesting manner, to his little son, when they were roaming over the wild heaths in the autumn days, 'the saddest of the year,' or while they sat in the oak-wainscoted room, surrounded by mysterious relics that gleamed strangely forth by the flickering fire-light. The legend was wrought into the boy's mind, and he would crave, yet tremble, to hear it told over and over again, while the words were intermingled with caresses and questions as to his love. Occasionally his living words and actions were cut short by his father's light yet bitter speech – 'Get thee away, my lad; thou knowest not what is to come of all this love.'

When Augharad was seventeen, and Owen eleven or twelve, the rector of the parish in which Bodowen was situated, endeavoured to prevail on Squire Griffiths to send the boy to school. Now, this rector had many congenial tastes with his parishioner, and was his only intimate; and, by repeated arguments, he succeeded in convincing the Squire that the unnatural life Owen was leading was in every way injurious. Unwillingly was the father wrought to part from his son; but he did at length send him to the Grammar School at Bangor, then under the management of an excellent classic. Here Owen showed that he had more talents than the rector had given him credit for, when he affirmed that the lad had been completely stupefied by the life he led at Bodowen. He bade fair to do credit to the school in the peculiar branch of learning for which it was famous. But he was not popular among his schoolfellows. He was wayward, though, to a certain degree, generous and unselfish; he was reserved but gentle, except when the tremendous bursts of passion (similar in character to those of his father) forced their way.

On his return from school one Christmas-time, when he had been a year or so at Bangor, he was stunned by hearing that the undervalued Augharad was about to be married to a gentleman of South Wales, residing near Aberystwyth. Boys seldom appreciate their sisters; but Owen thought of the many slights with which he had requited the patient Augharad, and he gave way to bitter regrets, which, with a selfish want of control over his words, he kept expressing to his father, until the Squire was thoroughly hurt and chagrined at the repeated exclamations of 'What shall we do when Augharad is gone?' 'How dull we shall be when Augharad is married!' Owen's holidays were prolonged a few weeks, in order that he might be present at the wedding; and when all the festivities were over, and the bride and bridegroom had left Bodowen, the boy and his father really felt how much they missed the quiet, loving Augharad. She had performed so many thoughtful, noiseless little offices, on which their daily comfort depended; and now she was gone, the household seemed to miss the spirit that peacefully kept it in order; the servants roamed about in search of commands and directions, the rooms had no longer the unobtrusive ordering of taste to make them cheerful, the very fires burned dim, and were always sinking down into dull heaps of grey ashes. Altogether Owen did not regret his return to Bangor, and this also the mortified parent perceived. Squire Griffiths was a selfish parent.

Letters in those days were a rare occurrence. Owen usually received one during his half-yearly absences from home, and occasionally his father paid him a visit. This half-year the boy had no visit, nor even a letter, till very near the time of his leaving school, and then he was astounded by the intelligence that his father was married again.

Then came one of his paroxysms of rage; the more disastrous in its effects upon his character because it could find no vent in action. Independently of slight to the memory of the first wife, which children are so apt to fancy such an action implies, Owen had hitherto considered himself (and with justice) the first object of his father's life. They had been so much to each other; and now a shapeless, but too real something had come between him and his father there for ever. He felt as if his permission should have been asked, as if he should have been consulted. Certainly he ought to have been told of the intended event. So the Squire felt, and hence his constrained letter, which had so much increased the bitterness of Owen's feelings.

With all this anger, when Owen saw his stepmother, he thought he had never seen so beautiful a woman for her age; for she was no longer in the bloom of youth, being a widow when his father married her. Her manners, to the Welsh lad, who had seen little of female grace among the families of the few antiquarians with whom his father visited, were so fascinating that he watched her with a sort of breathless admiration. Her measured grace, her faultless movements, her tones of voice, sweet, till the ear was sated with their sweetness, made Owen less angry at his father's marriage. Yet he felt, more than ever, that the cloud was between him and his father; that the hasty letter he had sent in answer to the announcement of his wedding was not forgotten, although no allusion was ever made to it. He was no longer his father's confidant – hardly ever his father's companion, for the newly-married wife was all in all to the Squire, and his son felt himself almost a cipher, where he had so long been everything. The lady herself had ever the softest consideration for her stepson; almost too obtrusive was the attention paid to his wishes, but still he fancied that the heart had no part in the winning advances. There was a watchful glance of the eye that Owen once or twice caught when she had imagined herself unobserved, and many other nameless little circumstances, that gave him a strong feeling of want of sincerity in his stepmother. Mrs Owen brought with her into the family her little child by her first husband, a boy nearly three years old. He was one of those elfish, observant, mocking children, over whose feelings you seem to have no control: agile and mischievous, his little practical jokes, at first performed in ignorance of the pain he gave, but afterward proceeding to a malicious pleasure in suffering, really seemed to afford some ground to the superstitious notion of some of the common people that he was a fairy changeling.

Years passed on; and as Owen grew older he became more observant. He saw, even in his occasional visits at home (for from school he had passed on to college), that a great change had taken place in the outward manifestations of his father's character; and, by degrees, Owen traced this change to the influence of his stepmother; so slight, so imperceptible to the common observer, yet so resistless in its effects. Squire Griffiths caught up his wife's humbly advanced opinions, and, unawares to himself, adopted them as his own, defying all argument and opposition. It was the same with her wishes; they met with their fulfilment, from the extreme and delicate art with which she insinuated them into her husband's mind, as his own. She sacrificed the show of authority for the power. At last, when Owen perceived some oppressive act in his father's conduct toward his dependants, or some unaccountable thwarting of his own wishes, he fancied he saw his stepmother's secret influence thus displayed, however much she might regret the injustice of his father's actions in her conversations with him when they were alone. His father was fast losing his temperate habits, and frequent intoxication soon took its usual effect upon the temper. Yet even here was the spell of his wife upon him. Before her he placed a restraint upon his passion, yet she was perfectly aware of his irritable disposition, and directed it hither and thither with the same apparent ignorance of the tendency of her words.

Meanwhile Owen's situation became peculiarly mortifying to a youth whose early remembrances afforded such a contrast to his present state. As a child, he had been elevated to the consequence of a man before his years gave any mental check to the selfishness which such conduct was likely to engender; he could remember when his will was law to the servants and dependants, and his sympathy necessary to his father: now he was as a cipher in his father's house; and the Squire, estranged in the first instance by a feeling of the injury he had done his son in not sooner acquainting him with his purposed marriage, seemed rather to avoid than to seek him as a companion, and too frequently showed the most utter indifference to the feelings and wishes which a young man of a high and independent spirit might be supposed to indulge.

Perhaps Owen was not fully aware of the force of all these circumstances; for an actor in a family drama is seldom unimpassioned enough to be perfectly observant. But he became moody and soured; brooding over his unloved existence, and craving with a human heart after sympathy.

This feeling took more full possession of his mind when he had left college, and returned home to lead an idle and purposeless life. As the heir, there was no worldly necessity for exertion: his father was too much of a Welsh squire to dream of the moral necessity, and he himself had not sufficient strength of mind to decide at once upon abandoning a place and mode of life which abounded in daily mortifications; yet to this course his judgement was slowly tending, when some circumstances occurred to detain him at Bodowen.

It was not to be expected that harmony would long be preserved, even in appearance, between an unguarded and soured young man, such as Owen, and his wary stepmother, when he had once left college, and come, not as a visitor, but as the heir to his father's house. Some cause of difference occurred, where the woman subdued her hidden anger sufficiently to become convinced that Owen was not entirely the dupe she had believed him to be. Henceforward there was no peace between them. Not in vulgar altercations did this show itself; but in moody reserve on Owen's part, and in undisguised and contemptuous pursuance of her own plans by his stepmother. Bodowen was no longer a place where, if Owen was not loved or attended to, he could at least find peace, and care for himself: he was thwarted at every step, and in every wish, by his father's desire apparently, while the wife sat by with a smile of triumph on her beautiful lips.

So Owen went forth at the early day dawn, sometimes roaming about on the shore or the upland, shooting or fishing, as the season might be, but oftener 'stretched in indolent repose' on the short, sweet grass, indulging in gloomy and morbid reveries. He would fancy that this mortified state of existence was a dream, a horrible dream, from which he should awake and find himself again the sole object and darling of his father. And then he would start up and strive to shake off the incubus. There was the molten sunset of his childish memory; the gorgeous crimson piles of glory in the west, fading away into the cold, calm light of the rising moon, while here and there a cloud floated across the western heaven, like a seraph's wing, in its flaming beauty; the earth was the same as in his childhood's days, full of gentle evening sounds, and the harmonies of twilight – the breeze came sweeping low over the heather and blue-bells by his side, and the turf was sending up its evening incense of perfume. But life, and heart, and hope were changed for ever since those bygone days!

Or he would seat himself in a favourite niche of the rocks on Meol Gêst, hidden by a stunted growth of the whitty, or mountain-ash, from general observation with a rich-tinted cushion of stone-crop for his feet, and a straight precipice of rock rising just above. Here would he sit for hours, gazing idly at the bay below with its background of purple hills, and the little fishing-sail on its bosom, showing white in the sunbeam, and gliding on in such harmony with the quiet beauty of the glassy sea; or he would pull out an old school volume, his companion for years, and in morbid accordance with the dark legend that still lurked in the recesses of his mind – a shape of gloom in those innermost haunts awaiting its time to come forth in distinct outline – would he turn to the old Greek dramas which treat of a family foredoomed by an avenging Fate. The worn page opened of itself at the play of the Œdipus Tyrannus, and Owen dwelt with the craving of disease upon the prophecy so nearly resembling that which concerned himself. With his consciousness of neglect, there was a sort of self-flattery in the consequence which the legend gave him. He almost wondered how they durst, with slights and insults, thus provoke the Avenger.

The days drifted onward. Often he would vehemently pursue some sylvan sport, till thought and feeling were lost in the violence of bodily exertion. Occasionally his evenings were spent at a small public house, such as stood by the unfrequented wayside, where the welcome, hearty though bought, seemed so strongly to contrast with the gloomy negligence of home – unsympathizing home.

One evening (Owen might be four or five-and-twenty), wearied with a day's shooting on the Clenneny Moors, he passed by the open door of 'The Goat' at Penmorfa. The light and the cheeriness within tempted him, poor self-exhausted man! as it has done many a one more wretched in worldly circumstances, to step in, and take his evening meal where at least his presence was of some consequence. It was a busy day in that little hostel. A flock of sheep, amounting to some hundreds, had arrived at Penmorfa, on their road to England, and thronged the space before the house. Inside was the shrewd, kind-hearted hostess, bustling to and fro, with merry greetings for every tired drover who was to pass the night in her house, while the sheep were penned in a field close by. Ever and anon, she kept attending to the second crowd of guests, who were celebrating a rural wedding in her house. It was busy work to Martha Thomas, yet her smile never flagged; and when Owen Griffiths had finished his evening meal she was there, ready with a hope that it had done him good, and was to his mind, and a word of intelligence that the wedding-folk were about to dance in the kitchen, and the harper was the famous Edward of Corwen.

Owen, partly from good-natured compliance with his hostess's implied wish, and partly from curiosity, lounged to the passage which led to the kitchen − not the every-day, working, cooking kitchen which was beyond, but a good-sized room where the mistress sat when her work was done, and where the country people were commonly entertained at such merry-makings as the present. The lintels of the door formed a frame for the animated picture which Owen saw within, as he leaned against the wall in the dark passage. The red light of the fire, with every now and then a falling piece of turf sending forth a fresh blaze, shone full upon four young men who were dancing a measure something like a Scotch reel, keeping admirable time in their rapid movements to the capital tune the harper was playing. They had their hats on when Owen first took his stand, but as they grew more and more animated they flung them away, and presently their shoes were kicked off with like disregard to the spot where they might happen to alight. Shouts of applause followed any remarkable exertion of agility, in which each seemed to try to excel his companions. At length, wearied and exhausted, they sat down, and the harper gradually changed to one of those wild, inspiring national airs for which he was so famous. The thronged audience sat earnest and breathless, and you might have heard a pin drop, except when some maiden passed hurriedly, with flaring candle and busy look, through to the real kitchen beyond. When he had finished playing his beautiful theme on 'The march of the men of Harlech,' he changed the measure again to 'Tri chant o' bunnan' (Three hundred pounds), and immediately a most unmusical-looking man began chanting 'Pennillion,' or a sort of recitative stanzas, which were soon taken up by another, and this amusement lasted so long that Owen grew weary, and was thinking of retreating from his post by the door, when some little bustle was occasioned, on the opposite side of the room, by the entrance of a middle-aged man, and a young girl, apparently his daughter. The man advanced to the bench occupied by the seniors of the party, who welcomed him with the usual pretty Welsh greeting, 'Pa sut mae dy galon?' ('How is thy heart?') and drinking his health, passed on to him the cup of excellent *cwrw*. The girl, evidently a village belle, was as warmly greeted by the young men, while the girls eyed her rather askance with a half-jealous look, which Owen set down to the score of her extreme prettiness. Like most Welsh women, she was of middle size as to height, but beautifully made, with the most perfect yet delicate roundness in every limb. Her little mobcap was carefully adjusted to a face which was excessively pretty, though it never could be called handsome. It also was round, with the slightest tendency to the oval shape, richly coloured, though somewhat olive in complexion, with dimples in cheek and chin, and the most scarlet lips Owen had ever seen, that were too short to meet over the small pearly teeth. The nose was the most defective feature; but the eyes were splendid. They were so long, so lustrous, yet at times so very soft under their thick fringe of eyelash! The nut-brown hair was carefully braided beneath the border of delicate lace: it was evident the little village beauty knew how to make the most of all her attractions, for the gay colours which were displayed in her neckerchief were in complete harmony with the complexion.

Owen was much attracted, while yet he was amused, by the evident coquetry the girl displayed, collecting around her a whole bevy of young fellows, for each of whom she seemed to have some gay speech, some attractive look or action. In a few minutes, young Griffiths of Bodowen was at her side, brought thither by a variety of idle motives, and as her undivided attention was given to the Welsh heir, her admirers, one by one, dropped off, to seat themselves by some less fascinating but more attentive fair one. The more Owen conversed with the girl, the more he was taken; she had more wit and talent than he had fancied possible; a self-abandon and thoughtfulness, to boot, that seemed full of charms; and then her voice was so clear and sweet, and her actions so full of grace, that Owen was fascinated before he was well aware, and kept looking into her bright, blushing face, till her uplifted flashing eye fell beneath his earnest gaze.

While it thus happened that they were silent – she from confusion at the unexpected warmth of his admiration, he from an unconsciousness of anything but the beautiful changes in her flexile countenance – the man whom Owen took for her father came up and addressed some observation to his daughter, from whence he glided into some commonplace though respectful remark to Owen, and at length engaging him in some slight local conversation, he led the way to the account of a spot on the peninsula of Penthryn, where teal abounded, and concluded with begging Owen to allow him to show him the exact place, saying that whenever the young Squire felt so inclined, if he would honour him by a call at his house, he would take him across in his boat. While Owen listened, his attention was not so much absorbed as to be unaware that the little beauty at his side was refusing one or two who endeavoured to draw her from her place by invitations to dance. Flattered by his own construction of her refusals, he again directed all his attention to her, till she was called away by her father, who was leaving the scene of festivity. Before he left he reminded Owen of his promise, and added,

'Perhaps, Sir, you do not know me. My name is Ellis Pritchard, and I live at Ty Glas, on this side of Moel Gêst; any one can point it out to you.'

When the father and daughter had left, Owen slowly prepared for his ride home; but, encountering the hostess, he could not resist asking a few questions relative to Ellis Pritchard and his pretty daughter. She answered shortly but respectfully, and then said rather hesitatingly —

'Master Griffiths, you know the triad, "Tri pheth tebyg y naill i'r llall, ysgnbwr heb yd, mail deg heb ddiawd, a merch deg heb ei geirda" (Three things are alike: a fine barn without corn, a fine cup without drink, a fine woman without her reputation).' She hastily quitted him, and Owen rode slowly to his unhappy home.

Ellis Pritchard, half farmer and half fisherman, was shrewd, and keen, and worldly; yet he was good-natured, and sufficiently generous to have become rather a popular man among his equals. He had been struck with the young Squire's attention to his pretty daughter, and was not insensible to the advantages to be derived from it. Nest would not be the first peasant girl, by any means, who had been transplanted to a Welsh manor-house as its mistress; and, accordingly, her father had shrewdly given the admiring young man some pretext for further opportunities of seeing her.

As for Nest herself, she had somewhat of her father's worldliness, and was fully alive to the superior station of her new admirer, and quite prepared to slight all her old sweethearts on his account. But then she had something more of feeling in her reckoning; she had not been insensible to the earnest yet comparatively refined homage which Owen paid her; she had noticed his expressive and occasionally handsome countenance with admiration, and was flattered by his so immediately singling her out from her companions. As to the hint which Martha Thomas had thrown out, it is enough to say that Nest was very giddy, and that she was motherless. She had high spirits and a great love of admiration, or, to use a softer term, she loved to please; men, women, and children, all, she delighted to gladden with her smile and voice. She coquetted, and flirted, and went to the extreme lengths of Welsh courtship, till the seniors of the village shook their heads, and cautioned their daughters against her acquaintance. If not absolutely guilty, she had too frequently been on the verge of guilt.

Even at the time, Martha Thomas's hint made but little impression on Owen, for his senses were otherwise occupied; but in a few days the recollection thereof had wholly died away, and one warm glorious summer's day, he bent his steps toward Ellis Pritchard's with a beating heart; for, except some very slight flirtations at Oxford, Owen had never been touched; his thoughts, his fancy, had been otherwise engaged.

Ty Glas was built against one of the lower rocks of Moel Gêst, which, indeed, formed a side to the low lengthy house. The materials of the cottage were the shingly stones which had fallen from above, plastered rudely together, with deep recesses for the small oblong windows. Altogether, the exterior was much ruder than Owen had expected; but inside there seemed no lack of comforts. The house was divided into two apartments, one large, roomy, and dark, into which Owen entered immediately; and before the blushing Nest came from the inner chamber (for she had seen the young Squire coming, and hastily gone to make some alteration in her dress), he had had time to look around him, and note the various little particulars of the room. Beneath the window (which commanded a magnificent view) was an oaken dresser, replete with drawers and cupboards, and brightly polished to a rich dark colour. In the farther part of the room, Owen could at first distinguish little, entering as he did from the glaring sunlight, but he soon saw that there were two oaken beds, closed up after the manner of the Welsh: in fact, the dormitories of Ellis Pritchard and the man who served under him, both on sea and on land. There was the large wheel used for spinning wool, left standing on the middle of the floor, as if in use only a few minutes before; and around the ample chimney hung flitches of bacon, dried kids'-flesh, and fish, that was in process of smoking for winter's store.

Before Nest had shyly dared to enter, her father, who had been mending his nets down below, and seen Owen winding up to the house, came in and gave him a hearty yet respectful welcome; and then Nest, downcast and blushing, full of the consciousness which her father's advice and conversation had not failed to inspire, ventured to join them. To Owen's mind this reserve and shyness gave her new charms.

It was too bright, too hot, too anything, to think of going to shoot teal till later in the day, and Owen was delighted to accept a hesitating invitation to share the noonday meal. Some ewe-milk cheese, very hard and dry, oatcake, slips of the dried kids'-flesh broiled, after having been previously soaked in water for a few minutes, delicious butter and fresh buttermilk, with a liquor called 'diod griafol' (made from the berries of the Sorbus aucuparia, infused in water and then fermented), composed the frugal repast; but there was something so clean and neat, and withal such a true welcome, that Owen had seldom enjoyed a meal so much. Indeed, at that time of day the Welsh squires differed from the farmers more in the plenty and rough abundance of their manner of living than in the refinement of style of their table.

At the present day, down in Llyn, the Welsh gentry are not a whit behind their Saxon equals in the expensive elegances of life; but then (when there was but one pewter-service in all Northumberland) there was nothing in Ellis Pritchard's mode of living that grated on the young Squire's sense of refinement.

Little was said by that young pair of wooers during the meal: the father had all the conversation to himself, apparently heedless of the ardent looks and inattentive mien of his guest. As Owen became more serious in his feelings, he grew more timid in their expression, and at night, when they returned from their shooting-excursion, the caress he gave Nest was almost as bashfully offered as received.

This was but the first of a series of days devoted to Nest in reality, though at first he thought some little disguise of his object was necessary. The past, the future, was all forgotten in those happy days of love.

And every worldly plan, every womanly wile was put in practice by Ellis Pritchard and his daughter, to render his visits agreeable and alluring. Indeed, the very circumstance of his being welcome was enough to attract the poor young man, to whom the feeling so produced was new and full of charms. He left a home where the certainty of being thwarted made him chary in expressing his wishes; where no tones of love ever fell on his ear, save those addressed to others; where his presence or absence was a matter of utter indifference; and when he entered Ty Glas, all, down to the little cur which, with clamorous barkings, claimed a part of his attention, seemed to rejoice. His account of his day's employment found a willing listener in Ellis; and when he passed on to Nest, busy at her wheel or at her churn, the deepened colour, the conscious eye, and the gradual yielding of herself up to his lover-like caress, had worlds of charms. Ellis Pritchard was a tenant on the Bodowen estate, and therefore had reasons in plenty for wishing to keep the young Squire's visits secret; and Owen, unwilling to disturb the sunny calm of these halcyon days by any storm at home, was ready to use all the artifice which Ellis suggested as to the mode of his calls at Ty Glas. Nor was he unaware of the probable, nay, the hoped-for termination of these repeated days of happiness. He was quite conscious that the father wished for nothing better than the marriage of his daughter to the heir of Bodowen; and when Nest had hidden her face in his neck, which was encircled by her clasping arms, and murmured into his ear her acknowledgement of love, he felt only too desirous of finding some one to love him for ever. Though not highly principled, he would not have tried to obtain Nest on other terms save those of marriage: he did so pine after enduring love, and fancied he should have bound her heart for evermore to his, when they had taken the solemn oaths of matrimony.

There was no great difficulty attending a secret marriage at such a place and at such a time. One gusty autumn day, Ellis ferried them round Penthryn to Llandutrwyn, and there saw his little Nest become future Lady of Bodowen.

How often do we see giddy, coquetting, restless girls become sobered by marriage? A great object in life is decided; one on which their thoughts have been running in all their vagaries, and they seem to verify the beautiful fable of Undine. A new soul beams out in the gentleness and repose of their future lives. An indescribable softness and tenderness takes place of the wearying vanity of their former endeavours to attract admiration. Something of this sort took place in Nest Pritchard. If at first she had been anxious to attract the young Squire of Bodowen, long before her marriage this feeling had merged into a truer love than she had ever felt before; and now that he was her own, her husband, her whole soul was bent toward making him amends, as far as in her lay, for the misery which, with a woman's tact, she saw that he had to endure at his home. Her greetings were abounding in delicately-expressed love; her study of his tastes unwearying, in the arrangement of her dress, her time, her very thoughts.

No wonder that he looked back on his wedding-day with a thankfulness which is seldom the result of unequal marriages. No wonder that his heart beat aloud as formerly when he wound up the little path to Ty Glas, and saw – keen though the winter's wind might be – that Nest was standing out at the door to watch for his dimly-seen approach, while the candle flared in the little window as a beacon to guide him aright.

The angry words and unkind actions of home fell deadened on his heart; he thought of the love that was surely his, and of the new promise of love that a short time would bring forth, and he could almost have smiled at the impotent efforts to disturb his peace.

A few more months, and the young father was greeted by a feeble little cry, when he hastily entered Ty Glas, one morning early, in consequence of a summons conveyed mysteriously to Bodowen; and the pale mother, smiling, and feebly holding up her babe to its father's kiss, seemed to him even more lovely than the bright gay Nest who had won his heart at the little inn of Penmorfa.

But the curse was at work! The fulfilment of the prophecy was nigh at hand!

Chapter 2

It was the autumn after the birth of their boy: it had been a glorious summer, with bright, hot, sunny weather; and now the year was fading away as seasonably into mellow days, with mornings of silver mists and clear frosty nights. The blooming look of the time of flowers was past and gone; but instead there were even richer tints abroad in the sun-coloured leaves, the lichens, the golden-blossomed furze: if it was the time of fading, there was a glory in the decay.

Nest, in her loving anxiety to surround her dwelling with every charm for her husband's sake, had turned gardener, and the little corners of the rude court before the house were filled with many a delicate mountain flower, transplanted more for its beauty than its rarity. The sweetbriar bush may even yet be seen, old and grey, which she and Owen planted a green slipling beneath the window of her little chamber. In those moments Owen forgot all besides the present; all the cares and griefs he had known in the past, and all that might await him of woe and death in the future. The boy, too, was as lovely a child as the fondest parent was ever blessed with; and crowed with delight, and clapped his little hands, as his mother held him in her arms at the cottage door to watch his father's ascent up the rough path that led to Ty Glas, one bright autumnal morning; and when the three entered the house together, it was difficult to say which was the happiest. Owen carried his boy, and tossed and played with him, while Nest sought out some little article of work, and seated herself on the dresser beneath the window, where, now busily plying the needle, and then again looking at her husband, she eagerly told him the little pieces of domestic intelligence, the winning ways of the child, the result of yesterday's fishing, and such of the gossip of Penmorfa as came to the ears of the now retired Nest. She noticed that, when she mentioned any little circumstance which bore the slightest reference to Bodowen, her husband appeared chafed and uneasy, and at last avoided anything that might in the least remind him of home. In truth, he had been suffering much of late from the irritability of his father, shown in trifles to be sure, but not the less galling on that account.

While they were thus talking, and caressing each other and the child, a shadow darkened the room, and before they could catch a glimpse of the object that had occasioned it, it vanished, and Squire Griffiths lifted the door-latch and stood before them. He stood and looked – first at his son, so different (in his buoyant expression of content and enjoyment, with his noble child in his arms, like a proud and happy father, as he was) from the depressed, moody young man he too often appeared at Bodowen; then on Nest – poor, trembling, sickened Nest! – who dropped her work, but yet durst not stir from her seat on the dresser, while she looked to her husband as if for protection from his father.

The Squire was silent, as he glared from one to the other, his features white with restrained passion. When he spoke, his words came most distinct in their forced composure. It was to his son he addressed himself:

'That woman! who is she?'

Owen hesitated one moment, and then replied, in a steady, yet quiet voice:

'Father, that woman is my wife.'

He would have added some apology for the long concealment of his marriage; have appealed to his father's forgiveness; but the foam flew from Squire Owen's lips as he burst forth with invective against Nest:

'You have married her! It is as they told me! Married Nest Pritchard yr buten! And you stand there as if you had not disgraced yourself for ever and ever with your accursed wiving! And the fair harlot sits there, in her mocking modesty, practising the mimming airs that will become her state as future Lady of Bodowen. But I will move heaven and earth before that false woman darken the doors of my father's house as mistress!'

All this was said with such rapidity that Owen had no time for the words that thronged to his lips. 'Father!' (he burst forth at length) 'Father, whosoever told you that Nest Pritchard was a harlot told you a lie as false as hell! Ay! a lie as false as hell!' he added, in a voice of thunder, while he advanced a step or two nearer to the Squire. And then, in a lower tone, he said:

'She is as pure as your own wife; nay, God help me! as the dear, precious mother who brought me forth, and then left me – with no refuge in a mother's heart – to struggle on through life alone. I tell you Nest is as pure as that dear, dead mother!'

'Fool – poor fool!'

At this moment the child – the little Owen – who had kept gazing from one angry countenance to the other, and with earnest look, trying to understand what had brought the fierce glare in the face when till now he had read nothing but love, in some way attracted the Squire's attention, and increased his wrath.

'Yes!' he continued, 'poor, weak fool that you are, hugging the child of another as if it were your own offspring!' Owen involuntarily caressed the affrighted child, and half smiled at the implication of his father's words. This the Squire perceived, and raising his voice to a scream of rage, he went on:

'I bid you, if you call yourself my son, to cast away that miserable, shameless woman's offspring; cast it away this instant – this instant!'

In his ungovernable rage, seeing that Owen was far from complying with his command, he snatched the poor infant from the loving arms that held it, and throwing it at its mother, left the house inarticulate with fury.

Nest – who had been pale and still as marble during this terrible dialogue, looking on and listening as if fascinated by the words that smote her heart – opened her arms to receive and cherish her precious babe; but the boy was not destined to reach the white refuge of her breast. The furious action of the Squire had been almost without aim, and the infant fell against the sharp edge of the dresser down on to the stone floor.

Owen sprang up to take the child, but he lay so still, so motionless, that the awe of death came over the father, and he stooped down to gaze more closely. At that moment, the upturned, filmy eyes rolled convulsively – a spasm passed along the body – and the lips, yet warm with kissing, quivered into everlasting rest.

A word from her husband told Nest all. She slid down from her seat, and lay by her little son as corpse-like as he, unheeding all the agonizing endearments and passionate adjurations of her husband. And that poor, desolate husband and father! Scarce one little quarter of an hour, and he had been so blessed in his consciousness of love! the bright promise of many years on his infant's face, and the new, fresh soul beaming forth in its awakened intelligence. And there it was; the little clay image, that would never more gladden up at the sight of him, nor stretch forth to meet his embrace; whose inarticulate, yet most eloquent cooings might haunt him in his dreams, but would never more be heard in waking life again! And by the dead babe, almost as utterly insensate, the poor mother had fallen in a merciful faint – the slandered, heart-pierced Nest! Owen struggled against the sickness that came over him, and busied himself in vain attempts at her restoration.

It was now near noonday, and Ellis Pritchard came home, little dreaming of the sight that awaited him; but, though stunned, he was able to take more effectual measures for his poor daughter's recovery than Owen had done.

By-and-by she showed symptoms of returning sense, and was placed in her own little bed in a darkened room, where, without ever waking to complete consciousness, she fell asleep. Then it was that her husband, suffocated by pressure of miserable thought, gently drew his hand from her tightened clasp, and printing one long soft kiss on her waxen forehead, hastily stole out of the room, and out of the house.

Near the base of Moel Gêst – it might be a quarter of a mile from Ty Glas – was a little neglected solitary copse, wild and tangled with the trailing branches of the dog-rose and the tendrils of the white bryony. Toward the middle of this thicket lay a deep crystal pool – a clear mirror for the blue heavens above – and round the margin floated the broad green leaves of the water-lily, and when the regal sun shone down in his noonday glory the flowers arose from their cool depths to welcome and greet him. The copse was musical with many sounds; the warbling of birds rejoicing in its shades, the ceaseless hum of the insects that hovered over the pool, the chime of the distant waterfall, the occasional bleating of the sheep from the mountain-top, were all blended into the delicious harmony of nature.

It had been one of Owen's favourite resorts when he had been a lonely wanderer – a pilgrim in search of love in the years gone by. And thither he went, as if by instinct, when he left Ty Glas; quelling the uprising agony till he should reach that little solitary spot.

It was the time of day when a change in the aspect of the weather so frequently takes place; and the little pool was no longer the reflection of a blue and sunny sky: it sent back the dark and slaty clouds above, and, every now and then, a rough gust shook the painted autumn leaves from their branches, and all other music was lost in the sound of the wild winds piping down from the moorlands, which lay up and beyond the clefts in the mountain-side. Presently the rain came on and beat down in torrents.

But Owen heeded it not. He sat on the dank ground, his face buried in his hands, and his whole strength, physical and mental, employed in quelling the rush of blood, which rose and boiled and gurgled in his brain as if it would madden him.

The phantom of his dead child rose ever before him, and seemed to cry aloud for vengeance. And when the poor young man thought upon the victim whom he required in his wild longing for revenge, he shuddered, for it was his father!

Again and again he tried not to think; but still the circle of thought came round, eddying through his brain. At length he mastered his passions, and they were calm; then he forced himself to arrange some plan for the future.

He had not, in the passionate hurry of the moment, seen that his father had left the cottage before he was aware of the fatal accident that befell the child. Owen thought he had seen all; and once he planned to go to the Squire and tell him of the anguish of heart he had wrought, and awe him, as it were, by the dignity of grief. But then again he durst not – he distrusted his self-control – the old prophecy rose up in its horror – he dreaded his doom.

At last he determined to leave his father for ever; to take Nest to some distant country where she might forget her first-born, and where he himself might gain a livelihood by his own exertions.

But when he tried to descend to the various little arrangements which were involved in the execution of this plan, he remembered that all his money (and in this respect Squire Griffiths was no niggard) was locked up in his escritoire at Bodowen. In vain he tried to do away with this matter-of-fact difficulty; go to Bodowen he must: and his only hope – nay his determination – was to avoid his father.

He rose and took a by-path to Bodowen. The house looked even more gloomy and desolate than usual in the heavy down-pouring rain, yet Owen gazed on it with something of regret – for sorrowful as his days in it had been, he was about to leave it for many, many years, if not for ever. He entered by a side-door, opening into a passage that led to his own room, where he kept his books, his guns, his fishing-tackle, his writing materials, etcetera.

Here he hurriedly began to select the few articles he intended to take; for, besides the dread of interruption, he was feverishly anxious to travel far that very night, if only Nest was capable of performing the journey. As he was thus employed, he tried to conjecture what his father's feelings would be on finding that his once-loved son was gone away for ever. Would he then awaken to regret for the conduct which had driven him from home, and bitterly think on the loving and caressing boy who haunted his footsteps in former days? Or, alas! would he only feel that an obstacle to his daily happiness – to his contentment with his wife, and his strange, doting affection for the child – was taken away? Would they make merry over the heir's departure? Then he thought of Nest – the young childless mother, whose heart had not yet realized her fullness of desolation. Poor Nest! so loving as she was, so devoted to her child – how should he console her? He pictured her away in a strange land, pining for her native mountains, and refusing to be comforted because her child was not.

Even this thought of the homesickness that might possibly beset Nest hardly made him hesitate in his determination; so strongly had the idea taken possession of him that only by putting miles and leagues between him and his father could he avert the doom which seemed blending itself with the very purposes of his life as long as he stayed in proximity with the slayer of his child.

He had now nearly completed his hasty work of preparation, and was full of tender thoughts of his wife, when the door opened, and the elfish Robert peered in, in search of some of his brother's possessions. On seeing Owen he hesitated, but then came boldly forward, and laid his hand on Owen's arm, saying,

'Nesta yr buten! How is Nest yr buten?'

He looked maliciously into Owen's face to mark the effect of his words, but was terrified at the expression he read there. He started off and ran to the door, while Owen tried to check himself, saying continually, 'He is but a child. He does not understand the meaning of what he says. He is but a child!' Still Robert, now in fancied security, kept calling out his insulting words, and Owen's hand was on his gun, grasping it as if to restrain his rising fury.

But when Robert passed on daringly to mocking words relating to the poor dead child, Owen could bear it no longer; and before the boy was well aware, Owen was fiercely holding him in an iron clasp with one hand, while he struck him hard with the other.

In a minute he checked himself. He paused, relaxed his grasp, and, to his horror, he saw Robert sink to the ground; in fact, the lad was half-stunned, half-frightened, and thought it best to assume insensibility.

Owen – miserable Owen – seeing him lie there prostrate, was bitterly repentant, and would have dragged him to the carved settle, and done all he could to restore him to his senses, but at this instant the Squire came in.

Probably, when the household at Bodowen rose that morning, there was but one among them ignorant of the heir's relation to Nest Pritchard and her child; for secret as he had tried to make his visits to Ty Glas, they had been too frequent not to be noticed, and Nest's altered conduct – no longer frequenting dances and merry-making – was a strongly corroborative

circumstance. But Mrs Griffiths' influence reigned paramount, if unac-
knowledged, at Bodowen, and till she sanctioned the disclosure, none
would dare to tell the Squire.

Now, however, the time drew near when it suited her to make her
husband aware of the connexion his son had formed; so, with many tears,
and much seeming reluctance, she broke the intelligence to him – taking
good care, at the same time, to inform him of the light character Nest had
borne. Nor did she confine this evil reputation to her conduct before her
marriage, but insinuated that even to this day she was a 'woman of the
grove and brake' – for centuries the Welsh term of opprobrium for the
loosest female characters.

Squire Griffiths easily tracked Owen to Ty Glas; and without any aim
but the gratification of his furious anger, followed him to upbraid as we
have seen. But he left the cottage even more enraged against his son than
he had entered it, and returned home to hear the evil suggestions of the
stepmother. He had heard a slight scuffle in which he caught the tones of
Robert's voice, as he passed along the hall, and an instant afterwards he
saw the apparently lifeless body of his little favourite dragged along by the
culprit Owen – the marks of strong passion yet visible on his face. Not
loud, but bitter and deep were the evil words which the father bestowed on
the son; and as Owen stood proudly and sullenly silent, disdaining all
exculpation of himself in the presence of one who had wrought him so
much graver – so fatal an injury – Robert's mother entered the room. At
sight of her natural emotion the wrath of the Squire was redoubled, and his
wild suspicions that this violence of Owen's to Robert was a premeditated
act appeared like the proven truth through the mists of rage. He summoned
domestics as if to guard his own and his wife's life from the attempts of his
son; and the servants stood wondering around – now gazing at Mrs
Griffiths, alternately scolding and sobbing, while she tried to restore the lad
from his really bruised and half-unconscious state; now at the fierce and
angry Squire; and now at the sad and silent Owen. And he – he was hardly
aware of their looks of wonder and terror; his father's words fell on a
deadened ear; for before his eyes there rose a pale dead babe, and in that
lady's violent sounds of grief he heard the wailing of a more sad, more
hopeless mother. For by this time the lad Robert had opened his eyes, and
though evidently suffering a good deal from the effects of Owen's blows,
was fully conscious of all that was passing around him.

Had Owen been left to his own nature, his heart would have worked
itself to doubly love the boy whom he had injured; but he was stubborn
from injustice, and hardened by suffering. He refused to vindicate himself;
he made no effort to resist the imprisonment the Squire had decreed, until
a surgeon's opinion of the real extent of Robert's injuries was made known.
It was not until the door was locked and barred, as if upon some wild and

furious beast, that the recollection of poor Nest, without his comforting presence, came into his mind. Oh! thought he, how she would be wearying, pining for his tender sympathy; if, indeed, she had recovered the shock of mind sufficiently to be sensible of consolation! What would she think of his absence? Could she imagine he believed his father's words, and had left her, in this her sore trouble and bereavement? The thought maddened him, and he looked around for some mode of escape.

He had been confined in a small unfurnished room on the first floor, wainscoted, and carved all round, with a massy door, calculated to resist the attempts of a dozen strong men, even had he afterward been able to escape from the house unseen, unheard. The window was placed (as is common in old Welsh houses) over the fireplace; with branching chimneys on either hand, forming a sort of projection on the outside. By this outlet his escape was easy, even had he been less determined and desperate than he was. And when he had descended, with a little care, a little winding, he might elude all observation and pursue his original intention of going to Ty Glas.

The storm had abated, and watery sunbeams were gilding the bay, as Owen descended from the window, and, stealing along in the broad afternoon shadows, made his way to the little plateau of green turf in the garden at the top of a steep precipitous rock, down the abrupt face of which he had often dropped, by means of a well-secured rope, into the small sailing-boat (his father's present, alas! in days gone by) which lay moored in the deep seawater below. He had always kept his boat there, because it was the nearest available spot to the house; but before he could reach the place – unless, indeed, he crossed a broad sun-lighted piece of ground in full view of the windows on that side of the house, and without the shadow of a single sheltering tree or shrub – he had to skirt round a rude semicircle of underwood, which would have been considered as a shrubbery had any one taken pains with it. Step by step he stealthily moved along – hearing voices now, again seeing his father and stepmother in no distant walk, the Squire evidently caressing and consoling his wife, who seemed to be urging some point with great vehemence, again forced to crouch down to avoid being seen by the cook, returning from the rude kitchen garden with a handful of herbs. This was the way the doomed heir of Bodowen left his ancestral house for ever, and hoped to leave behind him his doom. At length he reached the plateau – he breathed more freely. He stooped to discover the hidden coil of rope, kept safe and dry in a hole under a great round flat piece of rock: his head was bent down and he did not see his father approach, nor did he hear his footstep for the rush of blood to his head in the stooping effort of lifting the stone; the Squire had grappled with him before he rose up again, before he fully knew whose hands detained him, now, when his liberty of person and action seemed secure. He made a vigorous struggle to free himself; he wrestled with his father for a moment – he pushed him hard, and drove him on to the great displaced stone, all unsteady in its balance.

Down went the Squire, down into the deep waters below – down after him went Owen, half consciously, half unconsciously, partly compelled by the sudden cessation of any opposing body, partly from a vehement irrepressible impulse to rescue his father. But he had instinctively chosen a safer place in the deep seawater pool than that into which his push had sent his father. The Squire had hit his head with much violence against the side of the boat, in his fall; it is, indeed, doubtful whether he was not killed before ever he sank into the sea. But Owen knew nothing save that the awful doom seemed even now present. He plunged down, he dived below the water in search of the body, which had none of the elasticity of life to buoy it up; he saw his father in those depths, he clutched at him, he brought him up and cast him, a dead weight, into the boat, and, exhausted by the effort, he had begun himself to sink again before he instinctively strove to rise and climb into the rocking boat. There lay his father, with a deep dent in the side of his head where the skull had been fractured by his fall; his face blackened by the arrested course of the blood. Owen felt his pulse, his heart – all was still. He called him by his name.

'Father, father!' he cried, 'come back! come back! You never knew how I loved you! how I could love you still – if – Oh God!'

And the thought of his little child rose before him.

'Yes, father,' he cried afresh, 'you never knew how he fell – how he died! Oh, if I had but had patience to tell you! If you would but have borne with me and listened! And now it is over! Oh father ! father!'

Whether she had heard this wild wailing voice, or whether it was only that she missed her husband and wanted him for some little everyday question, or, as was perhaps more likely, she had discovered Owen's escape, and come to inform her husband of it, I do not know, but on the rock, right above his head, as it seemed, Owen heard his stepmother calling her husband.

He was silent, and softly pushed the boat right under the rock till the sides grated against the stones, and the overhanging branches concealed him and it all not on a level with the water. Wet as he was, he lay down by his dead father the better to conceal himself; and, somehow, the action recalled those early days of childhood – the first in the Squire's widowhood – when Owen had shared his father's bed, and used to waken him in the morning to hear one of the old Welsh legends. How long he lay thus – body chilled, and brain hard-working through the heavy pressure of a reality as terrible as a nightmare – he never knew; but at length he roused himself up to think of Nest.

Drawing out a great sail, he covered up the body of his father with it where he lay in the bottom of the boat. Then with his numbed hands he took the oars, and pulled out into the more open sea toward Criccaeth. He skirted along the coast till he found a shadowed cleft in the dark rocks; to that point he rowed, and anchored his boat close in land. Then he mounted, staggering, half longing to fall into the dark waters and be at rest – half instinctively finding out the surest foot-rests on that precipitous face of rock, till he was high up, safe landed on the turfy summit. He ran off, as if pursued, toward Penmorfa; he ran with maddened energy. Suddenly he paused, turned, ran again with the same speed, and threw himself prone on the summit, looking down into his boat with straining eyes to see if there had been any movement of life – any displacement of a fold of sail-cloth. It was all quiet deep down below, but as he gazed the shifting light gave the appearance of a slight movement. Owen ran to a lower part of the rock, stripped, plunged into the water, and swam to the boat. When there, all was still – awfully still! For a minute or two, he dared not lift up the cloth. Then reflecting that the same terror might beset him again – of leaving his father unaided while yet a spark of life lingered – he removed the shrouding cover. The eyes looked into his with a dead stare! He closed the lids and bound up the jaw. Again he looked. This time he raised himself out of the water and kissed the brow.

'It was my doom, father! It would have been better if I had died at my birth!'

Daylight was fading away. Precious daylight! He swam back, dressed, and set off afresh for Penmorfa. When he opened the door of Ty Glas, Ellis Pritchard looked at him reproachfully, from his seat in the darkly-shadowed chimney corner.

'You're come at last,' said he. 'One of our kind (i.e. station) would not have left his wife to mourn by herself over her dead child; nor would one of our kind have let his father kill his own true son. I've a good mind to take her from you for ever.'

'I did not tell him,' cried Nest, looking piteously at her husband; 'he made me tell him part, and guessed the rest.'

She was nursing her babe on her knee as if it was alive. Owen stood before Ellis Pritchard.

'Be silent,' said he, quietly. 'Neither words nor deeds but what are decreed can come to pass. I was set to do my work, this hundred years and more. The time waited for me, and the man waited for me. I have done what was foretold of me for generations!'

Ellis Pritchard knew the old tale of the prophecy, and believed in it in a dull, dead kind of way, but somehow never thought it would come to pass in his time. Now, however, he understood it all in a moment, though he mistook Owen's nature so much as to believe that the deed was intentionally done, out of revenge for the death of his boy; and viewing it in this light, Ellis thought it little more than a just punishment for the cause of all the wild despairing sorrow he had seen his only child suffer during the hours of this long afternoon. But he knew the law would not so regard it. Even the lax Welsh law of those days could not fail to examine into the death of a man of Squire Griffiths' standing. So the acute Ellis thought how he could conceal the culprit for a time.

'Come,' said he; 'don't look so scared! It was your doom, not your fault;' and he laid a hand on Owen's shoulder.

'You're wet,' said he, suddenly. 'Where have you been? Nest, your husband is dripping, drookit wet. That's what makes him look so blue and wan.'

Nest softly laid her baby in its cradle; she was half stupefied with crying, and had not understood to what Owen alluded, when he spoke of his doom being fulfilled, if indeed she had heard the words.

Her touch thawed Owen's miserable heart.

'Oh, Nest!' said he, clasping her in his arms; 'do you love me still – can you love me, my own darling?'

'Why not?' asked she, her eyes filling with tears. 'I only love you more than ever, for you were my poor baby's father!'

'But, Nest – Oh, tell her, Ellis! *you* know.'

'No need, no need!' said Ellis. 'She's had enough to think on. Bustle, my girl, and get out my Sunday clothes.'

'I don't understand,' said Nest, putting her hand up to her head. 'What is to tell? and why are you so wet? God help me for a poor crazed thing, for I cannot guess at the meaning of your words and your strange looks! I only know my baby is dead!' and she burst into tears.

'Come, Nest! go and fetch him a change, quick!' and as she meekly obeyed, too languid to strive further to understand, Ellis said rapidly to Owen, in a low hurried voice,

'Are you meaning that the Squire is dead? Speak low, lest she hear! Well, well, no need to talk about how he died. It was sudden, I see; and we must all of us die; and he'll have to be buried. It's well the night is near. And I should not wonder now if you'd like to travel for a bit; it would do Nest a power of good; and then – there's many a one goes out of his own house and never comes back again; and – I trust he's not lying in his own house – and there's a stir for a bit, and a search, and a wonder – and, by-and-by, the heir just steps in, as quiet as can be. And that's what you'll do, and bring Nest to Bodowen after all. Nay, child, better stockings nor those; find the blue woollens I bought at Llanrwst fair. Only don't lose heart. It's done now and can't be helped. It was the piece of work set you to do from the days of the Tudors, they say. And he deserved it. Look in yon cradle. So tell us where he is, and I'll take heart of grace and see what can be done for him.'

84

But Owen sat wet and haggard, looking into the peat fire as if for visions of the past, and never heeding a word Ellis said. Nor did he move when Nest brought the armful of dry clothes.

'Come, rouse up, man!' said Ellis, growing impatient.

But he neither spoke nor moved.

'What is the matter, father?' asked Nest, bewildered.

Ellis kept on watching Owen for a minute or two, till, on his daughter's repetition of the question, he said,

'Ask him yourself, Nest.'

'Oh, husband, what is it?' said she, kneeling down and bringing her face to a level with his.

'Don't you know?' said he, heavily. 'You won't love me when you do know. And yet it was not my doing. It was my doom.'

'What does he mean, father?' asked Nest, looking up; but she caught a gesture from Ellis urging her to go on questioning her husband.

'I will love you, husband, whatever has happened. Only let me know the worst.'

A pause, during which Nest and Ellis hung breathless.

'My father is dead, Nest.'

Nest caught her breath with a sharp gasp.

'God forgive him!' said she, thinking on her babe.

'God forgive *me*!' said Owen.

'You did not – ' Nest stopped.

'Yes, I did. Now you know it. It was my doom. How could I help it? The devil helped me – he placed the stone so that my father fell. I jumped into the water to save him. I did, indeed, Nest. I was nearly drowned myself. But he was dead – dead – killed by the fall!'

'Then he is safe at the bottom of the sea?' said Ellis, with hungry eagerness.

'No, he is not; he lies in my boat,' said Owen, shivering a little, more at the thought of his last glimpse at his father's face than from cold.

'Oh, husband, change your wet clothes!' pleaded Nest, to whom the death of the old man was simply a horror with which she had nothing to do, while her husband's discomfort was a present trouble.

While she helped him to take off the wet garments which he would never have had energy enough to remove of himself, Ellis was busy preparing food, and mixing a great tumbler of spirits and hot water. He stood over the unfortunate young man and compelled him to eat and drink, and made Nest, too, taste some mouthfuls – all the while planning in his own mind how best to conceal what had been done, and who had done it; not altogether without a certain feeling of vulgar triumph in the reflection that Nest, as she stood there, carelessly dressed, dishevelled in her grief, was in reality the mistress of Bodowen, than which Ellis Pritchard had never seen a grander house, though he believed such might exist.

By dint of a few dexterous questions he found out all he wanted to know from Owen, as he ate and drank. In fact, it was almost a relief to Owen to dilute the horror by talking about it. Before the meal was done, if meal it could be called, Ellis knew all he cared to know.

'Now, Nest, on with your cloak and haps. Pack up what needs to go with you, for both you and your husband must be half way to Liverpool by tomorrow's morn. I'll take you past Rhyl Sands in my fishing boat, with yours in tow; and, once over the dangerous part, I'll return with my cargo of fish, and learn how much stir there is at Bodowen. Once safe hidden in Liverpool, no one will know where you are, and you may stay quiet till your time comes for returning.'

'I will never come home again,' said Owen, doggedly. 'The place is accursed!'

'Hoot! be guided by me, man. Why, it was but an accident, after all! And we'll land at the Holy Island, at the Point of Llyn; there is an old cousin of mine, the parson, there – for the Pritchards have known better days, Squire – and we'll bury him there. It was but an accident, man. Hold up your head! You and Nest will come home yet and fill Bodowen with children, and I'll live to see it.'

'Never!' said Owen. 'I am the last male of my race, and the son has murdered his father!'

Nest came in laden and cloaked. Ellis was for hurrying them off. The fire was extinguished, the door was locked.

'Here, Nest, my darling, let me take your bundle while I guide you down the steps.' But her husband bent his head, and spoke never a word. Nest gave her father the bundle (already loaded with such things as he himself had seen fit to take), but clasped another softly and tightly.

'No one shall help me with this,' said she, in a low voice.

Her father did not understand her; her husband did, and placed his strong helping arm round her waist, and blessed her.

'We will all go together, Nest,' said he. 'But where?' and he looked up at the storm-tossed clouds coming up from windward.

'It is a dirty night,' said Ellis, turning his head round to speak to his companions at last. 'But never fear, we'll weather it!' And he made for the place where his vessel was moored. Then he stopped and thought a moment.

'Stay here!' said he, addressing his companions. 'I may meet folk, and I shall, maybe, have to hear and to speak. You wait here till I come back for you.' So they sat down close together in a corner of the path.

'Let me look at him, Nest!' said Owen.

She took her little dead son out from under her shawl; they looked at his waxen face long and tenderly; kissed it, and covered it up reverently and softly.

'Nest,' said Owen, at last, 'I feel as though my father's spirit had been near us, and as if it had bent over our poor little one. A strange chilly air met me as I stooped over him. I could fancy the spirit of our pure, blameless child guiding my father's safe over the paths of the sky to the gates of heaven, and escaping those accursed dogs of hell that were darting up from the north in pursuit of souls not five minutes since.'

'Don't talk so, Owen,' said Nest, curling up to him in the darkness of the copse. 'Who knows what may be listening?'

The pair were silent, in a kind of nameless terror, till they heard Ellis Pritchard's loud whisper. 'Where are ye? Come along, soft and steady. There were folk about even now, and the Squire is missed, and madam in a fright.'

They went swiftly down to the little harbour, and embarked on board Ellis's boat. The sea heaved and rocked even there; the torn clouds went hurrying overhead in a wild tumultuous manner.

They put out into the bay; still in silence, except when some word of command was spoken by Ellis, who took the management of the vessel. They made for the rocky shore, where Owen's boat had been moored. It was not there. It had broken loose and disappeared.

Owen sat down and covered his face. This last event, so simple and natural in itself, struck on his excited and superstitious mind in an extraordinary manner. He had hoped for a certain reconciliation, so to say, by laying his father and his child both in one grave. But now it appeared to him as if there was to be no forgiveness; as if his father revolted even in death against any such peaceful union. Ellis took a practical view of the case. If the Squire's body was found drifting about in a boat known to belong to his son, it would create terrible suspicion as to the manner of his death. At one time in the evening, Ellis had thought of persuading Owen to let him bury the Squire in a sailor's grave; or, in other words, to sew him up in a spare sail, and, weighting it well, sink it for ever. He had not broached the subject, from a certain fear of Owen's passionate repugnance to the plan; otherwise, if he had consented, they might have returned to Penmorfa, and passively awaited the course of events, secure of Owen's succession to Bodowen, sooner or later; or if Owen was too much overwhelmed by what had happened, Ellis would have advised him to go away for a short time, and return when the buzz and the talk was over.

Now it was different. It was absolutely necessary that they should leave the country for a time. Through those stormy waters they must plough their way that very night. Ellis had no fear – would have had no fear, at any rate, with Owen as he had been a week, a day ago; but with Owen wild, despairing, helpless, fate-pursued, what could he do?

They sailed into the tossing darkness, and were never more seen of men.

The house of Bodowen has sunk into damp, dark ruins; and a Saxon stranger holds the lands of the Griffiths.

SHENA MACKAY

Curry at the Laburnums

Rain set in. The hills were hidden and the village enclosed in dull grey curtains of mist. The river threatened the supports of the bridge. Children gauged the water level, hoping, as sometimes happened, that they would be cut off from school. The playground was roofed over by umbrellas, floral patterned, transparent pagodas, under which waiting mothers complained. Little, inadequate sandbags appeared outside some houses. Fields lay under a glaze of water. Some cows were temporarily marooned and a rotten tree trunk, caught under the bridge, bobbed uncannily like the head of a drowned cow. The river continued to rise, grass and nettles disappeared and alders stood in water which poured over the sides of the bridge and reduced the road to a narrow sluice.

Commuters returning to houses draped with wet washing were bored and alienated by tales of muddy dramas, trees swept downstream, rescued water rats, coaches forcing their way through the water and taking children miles round the back roads to school. They were more interested to hear that water had got into the cellars of the pub. They became a different species from the gumbooted inhabitants of the heart of the flood, irritated by wives shut up all day with small children, and felt that the trials of water in the brakes, an abandoned car rota, and a go-slow on the trains were far greater than those of the home front.

The platform was jammed. What many found hardest to bear was the unfailing cheerfulness of Lal, the ticket collector, with whom Ivor, from vague liberal principles, often made a point of speaking, exchanging comment on the weather, and last Christmas he had thrust, almost aggressively, a pound note into his hand. Since the go-slow, he somehow hadn't liked to be seen chatting at the ticket collector's box and had restricted himself to a curt nod.

Lal laughed and joked and even made mock announcements over his microphone. Many were quite indecipherable, and the packed, soaked travellers eagerly turning to gaze at the signal which still showed red, and hearing his high-pitched cackle crackling over their heads, stared angrily up the receding tracks and understood only that they had been duped. In his efforts to entertain them, Lal had brought along his own transistor radio from home and played it loud enough to cheer up those at the farthest ends of the platforms. Many of them seemed not to appreciate Radio One.

'I wonder if you know that it's illegal to play transistor radios in public places?' a lady asked, shaking a rain-drop from her nose.

'Must keep my customers happy,' he replied. She reported him to the Station Manager who told him to turn it off.

'Bolshie so-and-so, playing the radio while his fellow Reds hold us to ransom.' A voice was heard in the aftermath.

'Blacks, more like,' replied another.

Camaraderie flowered among the wet heads and shoulders as stranger muttered to stranger imprecations on Blacks and Reds. Ivor and Roger Henry, his neighbour and old school-friend, were edging along the platform to try to get some sense out of Lal. He seized his microphone and shouted:

'All passengers Wictoria and Vaterloo, you might as well go home,' and cackled. Then, as the two men reached his box, he received a telephone announcement, the signal went green and he called: 'All Stations Wictoria. Stopping train Wictoria!'

Twenty minutes later, the grateful commuters saw the train's round caterpillar face crawling towards them and those who could, fought their way aboard and stood steamily, agonisingly pinioned together, fainters held upright, pregnant women loathed for their bulk, dead limbs slowly filling with pins and needles, trapped ever tighter by a seemingly impossible influx at subsequent stations.

So it went on. Drivers reported late and were sent home. Rule books ruled. Trains ran spasmodically. At least the rain began to peter out and there were occasional flashes of watery sunshine.

Ivor and Roger were on the platform, at the edge of a group of older men, doyens of commuting, whose trousers were of necessity hoisted high over round bellies by braces and fell in soft cuffs onto polished shoes, whose muscles were adapted only to the hoovering of lawns with electric mowers, or hitting golf balls; electors who kept Cubleigh a safe Tory seat. At election times its windows broke out in a blue rash of posters depicting Sir John Upton, who seemed to be conjured up only then, opposed only by an occasional doomed orange placard.

'. . . Harold Wilson,' Ivor caught.

'Heh heh heh,' laughed the old boys; products of small schools set back under the dripping beeches of Surrey. A Pekinese-faced lady, with steel-blue fur brushed up from a pink powdered forehead, bared her little teeth and laughed.

'Just let them try to treat cattle like this,' said one, 'and they'd soon have all the do-gooders up in arms.'

Their two weeks of inconvenience led these men, holding briefcases packed with the data of unnecessary companies, to compare themselves with Jews transported across Poland in freezing cattle trucks. One licked his livery lips, spotted like sloughed snake skins, and said:

'Did you hear about the Epsom incident? Some chaps got hold of one of those blighters and locked him in the, er, Ladies.'

'Heh heh heh,' laughed the old boys.

'Ha ha,' laughed Ivor.

'Next train to Vaterloo approaching Platform One in about twenty minutes,' broadcast Lal.

No train materialised. Some people went home. The coffee machine was jammed; a squirt of dirty water rattled into the plastic cup. Ivor and Roger trailed after the group to a little shack in the forecourt which sold such fare as sausage sandwiches, sulphurous rock cakes and tea. They blocked the doorway and jostled the taxi-drivers seated on benches round the walls, shooting spray over them as they closed their umbrellas, and brayed at the woman in broken slippers frying bacon at the stove. The kettle was shrieking; all was steam, noise and succulent wisps of smoke.

'What's yours, Tony?'

'Name your poison.'

'Your shout, I believe, you old rascal.'

'Heh heh heh.'

The woman removed the whistle from the kettle and unfortunately the words, '. . . Bloody unhygienic, ought to be prosecuted' hung in the air.

A huge man in shirtsleeves hoisted himself up from the bench.

'Right,' he said. 'Everybody out. We don't want your sort here. You're all barred!'

'Now look here . . .'

'Out.'

The taxi-drivers rose, a menacing semi-circle confronting former customers.

'Well really, I must say . . .'

'Out.'

'Now look here, my dear chap, it says "ALL WELCOME" outside. Do you realise you're contravening the Trades Descriptions Act?'

'We demand to be served,' said Ivor from the back.

'Berks.'

The drivers stepped forward. The commuters retreated.

'If that's their attitude . . .'

Step by step, the commuters were forced backwards into the forecourt, out of the delicious smell of bacon and hot tea into the cold drizzle.

'Good mind to call the police.'

'Well, I for one shall be contacting the Inspector of Health and I suggest you all do the same.'

A stomach brayed expressing everyone's disappointment.

'My wife was sold a mouldy pie the other day,' volunteered Roger and was ignored.

Ivor felt specially outraged, like a little boy who arrives late for school dinner and finds the hatches closed and his comrades wiping gravy and custard from their lips. Marian had neglected to make muesli and he had left with only a small, bitter cup of coffee. He and Roger went back through the booking hall and found themselves at Lal's box. Ivor was lightheaded and on the point of telling Roger he was giving up and going home. His mouth opened and hung open. Surely not? It couldn't be – a hot pungent drift of curry caught his nose. He stood swooning as it washed over his empty stomach. Roger caught his arm.

'The last bloody straw.'

He looked. The youngest porter, a lowly boy in a too-big jacket, who swept the platforms, was crossing the line bearing foil dishes of take-away curry.

'As you say, the last straw.'

Lal started across the platform through the passengers, smiling and rubbing a knife and fork in his hands, to receive the food. As he reached the edge of the platform and bent forward, Ivor and Roger exchanged a glance, each took an imperceptible step forward and thrust a foot under Lal's ankles. He swayed, the dishes in his hands, and crashed over, hitting his head on the rail; curry erupted and engulfed him. He sat up and half turned, scalding juice running down his hair, tomatoes, ladyfingers, yellow rice slipping down his face, and fell back, a knife sticking out of his striped waistcoat. Ivor and Roger were among the first to jump down. The tearful boy was sent to phone for an ambulance.

'Heh heh heh.'

The old boys couldn't see the knife, and laughed away their humiliations in the café.

Lal now lay on the pile of empty mail sacks on the platform. It occurred to nobody that it wasn't an accident. The ambulance klaxon overtook the sound of the approaching train.

The incident made the evening paper; a small paragraph on the front page under the banner headline proclaiming a return to work by the railmen after the personal intervention of the Prime Minister. It seemed that Lal was comfortable in hospital with burns and a punctured lung.

*

Ivor rolled uneasily all night in bed, behind the window which still bore an orange shred from the last election; the quisling of the station snack bar; all his principles slithering with scalding curry down Lal's surprised face. If he could become completely evil he could forget all this, or laugh at it, continue his affair with Heather from the office, or a succession of women, refuse to attend Family Service, neglect the garden, drink himself to death, then everybody would be sorry. Would he have to use another station?

He practised a sneer on his changed face as he shaved, but the eyes in the mirror had a puffy frightened look.

'Bye dear, have a good day,' he said as he left.

An incomprehensible curse seemed to batter against the front door as he banged it. He sensed something in the atmosphere as soon as he and Roger arrived at Chubleigh Station.

'Deny everything,' he muttered as they squared their shoulders, the wooden floor of the booking hall resounding hollowly like the hearts in their chests. The young porter, promoted, inspected their seasons. A knot of people was down the platform, by the far seat, obviously holding some sort of conference. Roger's elbow caught Ivor painfully on the muscle of his arm. They stopped and glanced frantically back at the booking hall, but people blocked the entrance.

'Wait for the 9.12?' said Roger, stepping back a pace. A patch of bristle under his nose denoted a shaky hand. Ivor shook his head. The cluster broke. A woman pointed at Ivor and Roger.

'A necktie party,' said Roger.

'I am completely evil,' said Ivor to himself.

His umbrella was slippery in his hand. Two students were coming down the platform towards them, his long blue jeans bent and straightened, eating up the asphalt, her skirt trailed tiny chips of grit; they heard the flap of her bare feet. The two avengers garbed in their tatty integrity moved down the platform towards them. Ivor stared at the yellow tin newspaper stand and became absorbed in a blotch of rust, dog-shaped. He scratched at it with a forefinger, to elongate its stumpy tail, and a flake of rust pierced the soft skin under his nail. He stared at it. 'Your nails are so neat,' Heather had said, 'just like haricot beans.'

He felt detached pity for those polished beans, as if they were to be violated in some inquisition or boiled for soup. Meanwhile Roger was finding it necessary to search his briefcase, and not unexpectedly found only *The Guardian* within, and squinted at its sideways folded print.

'About the accident yesterday – '

'Look here,' Roger started to say, but Ivor caught his sleeve.

'We're getting up a collection for Lal's family from the regulars.'

A balloon burst in Ivor's chest, suffusing his veins and face with warm liquid. His leather wallet leapt to his hand and he was stuffing a fiver into the jagged slit of the improvised collection tin, round which was pasted a piece of white paper with the simple message FOR LAL, which the girl held out.

'Turrific,' she uttered.

The male student scowled in silent accusation of ostentation. Roger managed fifty pence, which landed dully on Ivor's note.

'Right,' said the student, taking the tin and giving it a shake, and they moved on to the next passengers.

Roger and Ivor sat at opposite ends of the compartment, as if each thought the other had behaved rather badly.

The following morning the students were waiting. The boy hovered over them, his jeans seemed to sway with self-effacement.

'Personally I think the little old lady who gave 20p out of her pension should take it, but Maggie,' who had her hair in stubby pigtails today, 'seems to think you genuinely love the guy, so here you are. From us all.'

He thrust the heavy tin at Ivor, who stared up at him hopelessly.

'Give him the address, Maggie.'

She gave him a piece of paper. As if divesting themselves of a necessary but distasteful contact with the spoils of capitalism, they loped off.

'Pompous, sentimental young twit,' said Roger.

Ivor, who had the tin, said nothing.

'You'd better go tonight,' suggested Roger. 'Get it over with.'

'Yes, we will,' said Ivor, rolling the weighty embarrassing tin into his briefcase.

They met in a bar at Waterloo and fortified themselves for their task; from his seat under the red and yellow lights, above the platform, Ivor watched all the lucky commuters going home; all the fortunates who didn't have to take a tin of money to the wife and children of a man they had pushed onto the railway line for no reason.

'The more one thinks about it, the more impossible the whole thing becomes,' said Roger.

Ivor grunted. Roger went to telephone Martha.

'That's settled then,' he said as he came back.

'Same again?'

It struck Ivor that Roger was looking forward to the evening with cheerful or morbid curiosity. He almost told him to go home, but the thought of facing Lal's wife alone was worse.

'No thanks,' he said, standing up. 'The woman will be busy putting the kids to bed, maybe after visiting the hospital, we don't want to turn up stinking of booze.'

Roger sighed and followed him out. It transpired, however, that they had twenty minutes to wait for a train, and they returned to the bar. Marian had hung up on him when he telephoned; too late he remembered that it was madrigal night.

Croydon was golden when they left its station. They hired one of the taxis blazing in the forecourt and gave the driver Lal's address. The street turned out to be a long hill of terraced houses, which the taxi climbed slowly looking at the numbers.

'Bet it's that one.' Roger leaned forward and pointed at a blue-painted house with its brickwork picked out in pink, and windows and door, with hanging baskets of plastic flowers, pale green.

'They go in for that sort of thing. Really lowers the tone.'

It was at none of the picked-out houses that the taxi finally drew up. Lal's house was a discreet cream, with only a wreath of stucco leaves above the door painted dark green and a laburnum tree trailing leaves and pods over the gate, with the name 'The Laburnums'.

Ivor was fumbling with the lock of his briefcase as Roger knocked. A plump dark boy in school trousers opened the door.

'Does Mr Kharma live here?'

'My dad isn't here.'

A voice called something foreign from within. The boy answered in the same language, keeping his lustrous eyes on the two strangers, standing on a hectic yellow-orange carpet which swirled up the staircase behind him like a colony of snakes. The hall glittered with dark eyes from behind doors and the spaces of the bannisters.

'Are you from the newspaper?' asked the boy.

'No, we – '

A woman came from somewhere at the back of the house and stood behind the boy. Ivor thrust the tin at her over his head.

'On behalf of the regulars at Chubleigh Station, we'd like you to accept this small token. We were all very sorry about your husband's accident. He was very popular.'

He spoke slowly and loudly, feeling a flush seep up his neck from his collar. She stared at him almost with hostility. A smell of cooking came from the kitchen. The boy seemed to translate.

'Her eyes are like pansies, those dark velvety pansies,' thought Ivor.

'My mother says please come inside.'

'Well, that's awfully kind of you, but we really mustn't impose,' began Ivor.

'Please.'

The woman and children moved back, the boy held the door wide.

'Well, just for a minute.'

Ivor and Roger stepped in. They were led into the front room and told to sit on a black leatherette sofa backed with red, encrusted with gold thread, embossed by a bright picture of a Bengal tiger. Bamboo pictures hung on the walls and coloured brass ornaments stood on the mantelpiece and windowsill. Roger shifted his feet on the blue carpet.

'Have you seen your dad? How is he getting on? That was a rotten thing to happen.'

'He can talk now. His burns pain him. Did you see the accident?' answered the boy.

'Yes, we were right there. We did what we could.'

The woman interposed a question to her son.

'Is one of you Mr Ivor and Mr Roger?' asked the boy.

'No,' said Ivor at once, but Roger was saying heartily, 'That's us. Great pals of your dad, we are.'

This was translated with some vehemence.

'All is lost,' thought Ivor. He wanted to run.

Three little girls came and sat opposite them, two on chairs and one on the arm, swinging an impossibly thin brown leg and foot in a rubber flip-flop. Lal's wife said something to the boy and went out of the room. Ivor tried to remember if there was a telephone in the hall. He placed the tin, FOR LAL, on the little carved table covered with a silk cloth, beside a Monopoly game.

'My mother says please wait. She is getting you some food. She is very grateful to you.'

The men exchanged a helpless glance. Ivor wondered if the plump boy was teased at school, and if his own children could cope so well with a second language. He was not really like a child, rather a small self-contained man in his white shirt, with sleeves turned back to show a heavy gold watch on his wrist. He seemed not to have inherited his father's jocularity; rather his mother's gloom. But of course they had something to be gloomy about, Ivor reminded himself.

The mother called from the kitchen and one of the girls left the room.

'Lovely kids,' muttered Roger. 'Beautiful eyes.'

'I don't like the way they're staring at us. I think they know. Let's get out.'

'Can't. Look worse.'

He raised his voice to the little girls. 'Do you speak English?'

'Yes.'

'Jolly good.'

The tallest girl returned with two thin conical glasses on a brass tray. Her hair was tied back in a long plait like her mother's and she had tiny gold stars in her ears.

'Would you like a drink?'

'I say, thank you very much.'

The two assassins each lifted a glass and put their lips to the thick sweet liquor.

'Cheers.'

'Cheers,' said the girl, unsmiling. She held the tray behind her back; there was nowhere to put the glasses, so they drained them. She held out the tray and went out again. The younger girls were whispering and stopped when they caught Ivor's eye. He wished someone would turn on the television or the transistor with which Lal had cheered up his customers.

'Please tell your mother she mustn't go to any trouble on our account,' he told the boy.

'She wants to repay your kindness.'

'Mustn't offend Eastern hospitality,' mumbled Roger, 'besides, I could do with some nosh. Wonder what it'll be? Smells good.'

The girl returned with the filigree glasses refilled. This time Ivor took a sip and set his glass on the floor.

'Good stuff,' said Roger, a little thickly.

'Don't know how it mixes with Scotch though.'

The mother called again from the kitchen. The little girls opened a drawer in the sideboard and took cones of incense and stood them in little brass hands and lit them. Ivor thought he heard the front door click. He reached down for his glass, the fragile stem swayed in his hand and slopped the liquor onto the floor. A child ran for a cloth and the oldest girl took his glass and brought it back brimming.

'Very clean,' remarked Roger, jerking his head at the floor.

'Is your house dirty then?' retorted the child.

'Touché,' he laughed.

'Would you like to come through,' said the boy politely. 'I'll show you the bathroom first, if you'd like to wash.'

The strange drink and heavy incense swirled round in Ivor's head, he had to put his hand to the wall as he followed the children. Fresh soap and towels seemed to have been put out in the bathroom; he glanced back as he left to make sure he had left it tidy.

'Did you put the towels back?' he whispered to Roger.

'What?' He pushed past him into the kitchen. There, Ivor felt suddenly gross among these small people as he hovered at the table and sat down clumsily on the indicated chair.

'Aren't you having any?'

'We have eaten earlier, before the hospital,' explained their little host.

Bowls of steaming rice and dishes of food smelling, to Ivor, of every spice of the orient were placed before them. The family grouped round the kitchen to watch the Englishmen eat. Incense was burning here too, the air was thick with it, sweet and acrid scents mingling.

'Please eat,' said the girl. Lal's wife drew out a chair and sat down at the opposite end of the table from Ivor. He heaped his plate until it was swimming with beautiful coloured vegetables and marbled with red and yellow juices. A full glass stood by his plate.

'It's great, it's delicious. I don't know what it is but it's great!' Roger said.

There was no need to translate this; his spoon was already digging again into a dish.

'Have some more ladyfingers, Ive.'

He scooped a heap of the little pods onto Ivor's plate and took another drink.

'Everything's all right,' thought Ivor, as he bit into the delicious lady-fingers, he straightened his shoulders which were stiff with tension, and relaxed in his chair.

'I am totally evil,' he thought, and sniggered a little at himself.

Roger put down his spoon and fork.

'D'you know,' he said, spitting rice, 'd'you know, if every immigrant family in this country was to ask one English family into their homes, just one each, for a meal like this, it would put an end to racial prejudice at one stroke. Eh, Mrs Lal? What do you say to that? I call you Mrs Lal,' he explained, 'because you people put your surnames first.'

Ivor was terrified again. If Roger was drunk would they ever escape those velvet eyes and glittering earrings, fusing, shifting, miniature watchful Lal faces, dark and golden?

'We Anglo-Saxons are a funny lot.' Roger was leaning over the table. 'We're very reserved, but if you people would just take the initiative, not be so stand-offish, you know? We can be very nice when you get to know us, can't we, Ivor?'

'For God's sake, Roger!' Surely Indians were teetotal?

'Now some people think, and I know they're wrong, that your lot are a bit stuck-up, you know, toffee-nosed, unwilling to adopt our customs, living in the past. You spread the word, Mrs Lal, you give us an inch and we'll take a yard.'

He stopped suddenly and resumed shovelling. No one spoke. Ivor kept his eyes on his plate; if he stopped eating his head might crash forward into the curry; like Lal's. He blew his nose.

Roger was waving a fork at the boy; his mouth opening and shutting, trying to get the right words out. He lurched up and put his arms round two of the girls, pulling them together so that they almost kissed. The boy stepped forward to protect his sisters. Roger released them.

'These kids. Our kids. It's up to them. They're the generation that counts. You and me, Ivor, we've had our chance. They're the last chance this rotten old world's got.'

He began to cry and sat down, spooning food now into his wet mouth, now down his tie. Ivor's whole head broke into bubbles of sweat; he blotted it with his handkerchief, and saw runnels under Roger's nose. He loosened his tie. He made an effort to salvage the evening and their honour.

'How did your husband seem, Mrs Lal? In himself, I mean.' He said it very slowly and courteously.

'He is as well as can be expected,' said the boy.

'Good. Good.' Ivor nodded solemnly. His eyes were caught by Mrs Kharma's; the pansies seemed drenched with dew; he had to shake his head to shift the image of himself unwrapping the gauzy sari, like the cellophane round a flower, to reveal the dark orchid within. He thought one of the little brass incense burners clenched and unclenched and almost felt the metal fingers on his throat. He kicked Roger and stood up.

'Mrs Lal, my friend and I would like to thank you for a most excellent meal. We mustn't take up any more of your precious time.'

He hauled Roger to his feet.

'It has been a privilege to meet Dad's friends. Please convey our thanks to all the kind people who contributed. But there is more to come.'

One of the girls was taking from the fridge aluminium shells of ice cream pitted with green chips of pistachio. Roger made a clumsy move towards the table. Now or never. Ivor got him into the hall.

'Mrs Lal, I want you to know,' he heard himself saying, 'I want you to know you can count on me, as a friend of your husband. He's a good man, and I'm proud to be his friend – '

'So long Gunga Din.' Roger was ruffling the boy's hair as the front door nearly clipped his fingers.

'Gloomy lot, never smiled once,' he said. 'Did you notice? No sense of humour.'

He tangled with the laburnum.

'More like some weird ritual than a meal.'

'At least one of us kept his dignity,' replied Ivor.

Ivor woke, clawing his chest as if wrenching out a knife; his pyjamas were sodden. He had a terrible pain; he was about to be sick. He bumped through in the dark, gagging himself with his hand, biting his palm, whooshing and whooping into the bowl, a burning poisonous volcano. At last he lay back on the floor, pressing his forehead on the cold tiles, then doubled up and vomited again where he lay.

'Are you all right?' came Marian's annoyed voice from the bedroom.

Spasm after spasm racked him; it was pouring from his mouth, down his nose, and when there was nothing left his stomach still heaved towards his raw throat. His insides felt sore and pink and mangled.

'Ivor?' She had forced herself out of bed.

'Go away,' he groaned. 'Just go away,' trying to pull the door shut with his foot. She took one look, and fled to be sick in the sink.

'O God, O God, I'm dying, let me die, I can't bear it. Let me die,' a voice was groaning over and over. He lay sweating and shivering for a long time. Then he pulled a towel over himself like a blanket and half dozed in the appalling smell. An iron band was screwed round his head.

Some time later he pulled himself, frozen, to his feet and set about cleaning up the fouled bathroom with newspaper and disinfectant and Ajax, washing its walls and floors and the interstices of the hot water pipes, specked and freckled with his guilt. Every time he bent, the burning vice tightened on his skull and his teeth clattered uncontrollably. He put his pyjamas in the dirty linen basket for Marian to wash. He stood in a towel at the open window, watching the strange sky lighten over the heavy oaks. The telephone drilled.

Martha Henry's frantic voice battered against his caved-in chest. He couldn't bear to put the receiver to his ear.

'He won't die,' he said, and put the phone down.

Sitting on the bath's edge, watching it fill, steam flowering up the turquoise sides, in the sour aftermath, and the draught from the open window, he thought: 'You've got to hand it to them. Not a word of the pain we caused them. Not a flicker of emotion. Just a silent revenge. You've got to respect them for that.'

MARY FLANAGAN

The Wedding Dress

They meet at a dance. It is the Saturday night after Thanksgiving and the York Beach Casino is filled to capacity. Nora wears a white angora sweater which Frank notices right away, because of its contrast with her dark blue eyes and what he likes to call her apple cheeks, a feature which in 1935 is greatly admired.

They spend the rest of the evening in each other's arms. Couples step aside, making way for them as if the whole floor were theirs by right. During the last dance he dares to hold her a little closer.

Nora's brother Jimmy is driving her home. Frank expresses concern about possible snow, the condition of the roads and the number of whiskies Jimmy has consumed. 'Oh it will be all right,' she says, and he suspects that she is not unhappy about going home with this brother of hers. As they separate, Nora sees that Frank's blue serge suit is covered with angora fluff. He looks as if a dozen Easter bunnies have capered on his chest. Nora feels badly but can't help laughing. Frank laughs too, for he is a good-natured man. He is also, like Nora, a sharp dresser. She tells him he can call on her. They part.

Frank presents his sisters with the fuzzy suit. They manage all his domestic difficulties. Always have.

Lizzie and Sadie exchange looks.

'Jimmy! Jimmy stop it!' Nora, in her bathrobe, leans from the bedroom window, trying to shout and whisper at the same time. 'Please Jimmy.'

In the street below, her brother is attempting, as he does every morning at seven thirty, to start the motorcycle which he bought second-hand from the White Mountains Garage.

'Son of a bitch! God damn!' He kicks it. 'God *damn!*' He kicks it again.

100

The Wedding Dress MARY FLANAGAN

'Please Jimmy!'

'You go to hell, Nora.' His breath and the cycle's steam and billow like an enraged dragon's.

'Jimmy, the Floods . . .' Neighbors have complained. Harrison Avenue is a Methodist stronghold.

'Fuck the Floods,' he shouts and tries, again without success, to jump-start his ornery machine. 'And fuck you too, Nora, you dumb bitch.'

Nora slams the window shut, her hands trembling. She throws herself on the bed which she shares with her sister Frannie and sobs. The continuing racket of the machine serves as a background to Jimmy's curses.

Frank does some investigating. As a reporter for the *Daily Democrat*, he knows how. He is good at it, he enjoys it. And he is acquainted with nearly everyone in the Tri-City area.

What Frank discovers: Nora Winkle is a Methodist (may present problems), born in Belfast. Emigrated to the US in 1913. Mother cleans houses. Father, estranged, works in a box factory in East Rochester. Nora Winkle is the eldest of ten children. She is secretary to Huntley Bates, boss of the paper mill, a good job for a girl of her background. She is known for her contralto voice and her ladylike behavior. Nora Winkle has also been engaged three times and she has broken each engagement. There was even a medical student from Montreal, but she changed her mind and wouldn't have him. They say he had a nervous breakdown.

Nevertheless, Frank feels encouraged. Frank is an optimist.

Poor Nora: a mother to her brothers and sisters, a husband to her mother.

She stops crying. Oh, she thinks, to be alone. Alone in a room with a few nice things, where it's all new and clean and mine. Where ten people and their friends are not continually fighting and needing you to settle the arguments, losing things and asking you to find them.

But there was that one time, that only terrible time when she *was* alone. One afternoon during her last year in High School she came home to find the house empty. She called for them all, called every name, but heard no reply, no complaining, no music or arguments. And she felt her heart tighten then abruptly stop. Alone. A black helmet was descending over her eyes. Her head was cold and her body hot. Alone. She was sweating – or rather perspiring. She caught hold of the bannister as her knees gave way. 'Mama,' she murmured, 'I'm dying.' Slowly she backed out the front door, clutching her books. 'Mama.' She staggered across the front porch and sat on the hammock, unable to move, her eyes searching the street for one of them. Any one. 'Please,' she whispered, 'come home.' Then Frannie and Ellie turned the corner into Harrison Avenue. Just at that moment her grandmother emerged from the house across the street. She was taking her three pugs for their afternoon constitutional. Immediately Frannie and Ellie crossed the road and made for the trunk of a large elm tree where they huddled together.

'Ha!' cried Grammy Glick. 'I see ye. Ye can't hide from me, ye dirty wee things.'

Nora pressed her head against her books. Oh, to be just alone.

Nora goes to the mirror, takes out her curling tongs and crimps her short blonde hair. Even with red eyes, she is, as they say, a stunner. Yes, high color is the thing. And white, very white skin. She is healthy and exercises with Indian clubs. If only she could get rid of the giveaway Irish freckles. The bleaching cream doesn't really work, despite the promises on the package. Might as well admit it and stop spending precious money on it. Be careful, Nora. You are becoming vain. It is such an easy thing to slide into. The Bible says so.

She has a passion for clothes and spends whatever is left after she hands her paycheck over to her mother on fabric and accessories. She haunts the sales. Her sister Lillian is an expert seamstress and at thirteen was already earning cash by mending silk stockings – so cleverly that her work was almost invisible. Together they 'cook up frocks' from the latest fashion magazines.

Do not be vain, Nora, she tells herself again, studying the back of her head with a hand mirror, be grateful. And she is grateful, because she is an American now, the citizen of a great and good country that has agreed to accept her and her boisterous family and be responsible for them; to offer them jobs in box factories, in linen and paper mills, in bleacheries and shoe factories, to teach them to read and write so that they may buy galoshes and orange pekoe tea and second-hand motorcycles. She offers thanks every night when she says her prayers and every Sunday at church.

At eight precisely Nora leaves for the mill. On the street she passes Millie Flood who smiles, as usual, as though she had not been awakened yet again by foul language. 'The Irish cannot control themselves,' thinks Millie Flood. 'God help them.'

Fresh from his bath, Frank dons the shirt so carefully laundered by his sister Lizzie. Frank is not handsome, but Frank has 'got something.' He checks the auburn curls which he fears are beginning to thin. Never mind, he reckons he'll have them for just about as long as he'll need them.

On the cedar chest is a three pound box of Whitman's Sampler. He has discovered that the only woman he has ever loved, and to whom he will be faithful until he dies at the age of seventy-six, is a chocolate addict. He will attend the Democratic City Committee meeting then drive the twenty miles to Rochester to deliver his gift. Deftly he loops his striped tie and adjusts the knot.

*

The Wedding Dress MARY FLANAGAN

It has been a terrible week. The week before Christmas always is. The dress she and Lil have been working on has had to be completely unstitched. Timmy has brought home three friends for an indefinite stay. She trips every morning over the bodies on the landing. Her mother cannot say no to Timmy. His friends love Mrs Winkle and they love her cooking. She is an even more cheerful slave than their own mothers.

Frannie has been sleepwalking again. Clayton Flood, who once found her wandering by moonlight in his vegetable patch, thinks it has to do with changes in the weather. Whatever it is, something must be done about it. She's becoming dangerous.

At 3 a.m. on Wednesday, Nora woke to find her sister standing over her with an old tennis racket. Nora screamed and Frannie fainted. Timmy complained that he'd been looking for that racket for months.

Normally her somnambulistic behavior was merely strange, even funny. Someone would hear her on the stairs and wake everyone else. Whispering, on tiptoe, they would follow her to the cellar and watch by flashlight as she lifted the wooden cover and looked down into the well.

'Gives me the goddam willies,' Jimmy would say.

'Shhhhhhhhh!'

Then on Saturday there was the incident with Uncle Brendan. At fifty, Brendan Beckett still lived with his mother, the monstrous Grammy Glick. Everyone said she'd had eight husbands, only two of which had been legitimate, and that she'd only married Solomon Glick, the Jewish tailor from Boston, in order to sneak her disorderly family into the Land of Opportunity by the back door. No one knew what had happened to Mr Glick, though Frannie was convinced her grandmother murdered him with a chamber pot and fed him to the pugs. At four feet eleven inches, she was the bane of Harrison Avenue and its environs, and her memory still struck fear into the hearts of men, schoolchildren and cats throughout County Down.

Nora knew something really bad was going to happen. The sign had come just after breakfast. From their sitting room, the Winkles could look straight into the Glick kitchen opposite. Harry, Timmy and little Vinnie saw Grammy Glick descend her permanently snow-covered front steps (the Floods complained they were a health hazard). She cast a malevolent glance at number twenty-seven, but she wasn't quick enough. Anyone who happened to be in the sitting room knew exactly when to hit the floor. Off she went with the pugs, knowing she'd been outsmarted and swearing vengeance.

'Close call.' Harry breathed a sigh of relief as he got to his knees and peeked over the window sill to make sure the coast was clear.

'Oh-oh,' he cried. 'Fire! Fire!'

Nora, Mama and Ellie ran to the sitting room where they could watch Uncle Brendan shoving log after log into the big black stove. 'O God help us!' wailed Mrs Winkle, flapping her apron. 'Not again!'

Four columns of flame from the open burners shot as high as the ceiling. Uncle Brendan liked it warm.

They all ran across the street in pajamas and bathrobes, just in time to save number twenty-eight from conflagration. Mrs Winkle tried to make her half-brother understand how upsetting this sort of behavior was. She said that she would have to tell his mother if he went on this way. This made Uncle Brendan very sad. He said he was truly sorry. He would never do such a terrible thing again. But he had promised before, and his promises only brought more disaster in their wake.

Sure enough, Sunday morning as Nora was grinding cranberries for the relish, she heard the front door open. She knew with an awful certainty who it was. She called for Jimmy who was in the garage, tinkering with the motorcycle, but Uncle Brendan already stood in the kitchen, wild-eyed and wielding an ax. Jimmy burst in. Too late. Uncle Brendan dashed to the sitting room and proceeded to chop down the Christmas tree before they could lay a hand on him.

'Why?' Mrs Winkle wept into her apron. 'Why?' Hearing her, the younger Winkles began to cry, then Harry and finally Nora. All of them crying together and Uncle Brendan too, not understanding.

'What saps,' Frannie observed.

'I must live somewhere else,' thought Nora.

Jimmy said, as he always did, that Uncle Brendan ought to be locked up. And one day he was. He has been in the Concord Hospital for more than twenty years now. Only Harry, Nora's favorite, still visits him. Of course Uncle Brendan has no idea who Harry is.

For once Frank's instincts are not aligned with his famous brain. He jumps the gun and proposes too soon. She isn't ready for this.

'No,' Nora says. Then more kindly, 'It's been an awful week. Just awful.' And then, 'I can't leave Mama.'

'Ah,' Frank thinks and kisses her and cheerfully departs. Now he understands why the three engagements were broken off.

Nora feels badly. She respects Frank, knows he's kind and smart. But she has told him the truth. She cannot leave her mother. A life of hard work and anxiety has left her looking fifteen years older than she is. Already Mrs Winkle wears old ladies' shoes and thick stockings that bag at the ankle. Her hands are twisted and raw with veins a quarter inch high. (All that yellow washing soap, all that bleach and polish and disinfectant and starch.) It isn't possible to abandon her for something as selfish as one's own home, one's own children, one's own husband, one's own wedding dress. Not when she is Little Nora and her mother is Big Nora, and that is how it's been all her life.

She spies the Whitman's Sampler, lies down on the sofa and devours the entire top layer while listening to Rudy Vallee.

'I'm just a vagabond lover . . .'

Nora hums along. As she bites into a butter cream center she remembers the words of her best friend Vinette. 'It's getting late, Norrie. You're twenty-six.'

She cannot stop eating the chocolate. Chocolate stills her mind and heart.

The next morning she wakes up covered in hives. Mortified, she refuses to come downstairs for a Christmas dinner laid for twenty. Of course there is no tree. Mrs Winkle could not afford another now. Every year the Winkles spend their last penny on Christmas then go into debt for the next eight months.

Harry brings Nora her turkey and cranberry relish in bed. Nora loves Harry best of her six brothers. He was the easiest to rear and is also the one most like her. She'd held him in her arms all the way across the Atlantic while her parents spent the journey in the lavatory. She cannot leave Harry either.

Frank is a smart person. He has 'got something.' This something is not lost on Mrs Winkle and Frank knows it. It has been many years since Mrs Winkle met a man she could trust, and this too is not lost on Frank. He calls her 'Sweetheart' and gives her presents. He always remembers to bring her *The Boston Herald Traveler* which she calls her 'wee book.'

He takes the three youngest Winkles for rides in his Ford and lets them scream and bicker and jump up and down on the back seat. He buys them candy and takes them to Saturday afternoon matinees to watch Tom Mix and Hopalong Cassidy. He, too, is partial to Westerns.

Nora teases him about being in love with Mama. He answers that he only misses his own Mama who died when he was fourteen.

'Poor Frank,' Nora says and strokes his cheek.

'But I have the girls.'

Oh yes, the sisters.

Frank drives twenty miles four nights a week to see Nora. Much of his visit is spent in the kitchen with Mrs Winkle. He has added 'Honey' and 'Sweetie Pie' and 'Old Darling' to his repertoire of endearments. Nora he calls Nora.

Politics are his obsession, and he talks to Mrs Winkle about them with great animation and in a way she can understand. She likes this. No one has ever talked to her about serious things, aside from dog bites, broken arms and unpaid bills. She listens. She asks questions as she makes the tea and rolls out the pie crust. She does not mind that Frank Murnane is a Catholic and a Democrat. Once such a thing would have been unthinkable, but this is America, the greatest country in the world. None of those bad old feelings here. And good riddance too.

He says there will be a presidential election soon and will she vote? Oh yes, Clayton and Millie Flood (staunch Republicans) always arrange for her to be driven to the polling booths. The Floods are good friends and neighbors. Fine people. Very kind to her and her family. They even introduced her to the Methodist minister, though of course she never has much time for church. Nora and Harry go. They seem to like it. Nora was even in the Salvation Army, did he know? And Harry will soon be a fully-fledged Mason. The minister likes Nora because she has a beautiful voice. At home Vinette plays the piano while she sings. She sings in the choir too. Gets lots of solos. She'd heard her daughter once in church and cried. Where did it come from she wondered, this beautiful voice? Of course Mr Winkle is musical in a way. Played the bagpipes in a Black Watch band. Kilts and all. My she'd been proud of him. But not like Nora. Bagpipes never made her want to cry.

Frank tells her stories of the great FDR, how he saved the country of America that she loves so much and of which she is so happy to be a citizen. Roosevelt is a hero, he says, omitting the fact that it was the great FDR who repealed Prohibition. The youngest Winkles come and listen too. Then Nora then Harry when he returns from a Masons' meeting. They all move to the big dining room table in order to accommodate Jimmy, who has been sulking in his den over a letter from his estranged wife, and Timmy with his three friends. Their supper has been kept warm for them by Big Nora.

The talk moves from politics to poker. Frank tells funny stories of late night sessions and tricks played on slower witted cronies, forgetting the Methodist line on games of chance. But no one minds. The Winkles begin to tell their own stories, all of which involve disasters. They giggle and guffaw and let the children stay up until one. Harry is pleading 'Shhh, shhh, she'll hear us,' then laughing louder than anyone else. But they are not so hysterical as to neglect to turn off the porch and sitting room lights. They want no visits from vindictive grandmothers. One of Timmy's friends falls off his chair and cuts his lower lip which Little Nora treats with mercurichrome. Big Nora brews more tea and produces a banana cream pie.

The Winkles adore Frank. All but Jimmy, who says he's a phoney. He hates the way Frank always calls him Seamus. Who the hell does that Harp think he is? Nora tells him he's just jealous.

*

New Year's Eve. There is a dance at the York Beach Casino. Frank takes Nora. Alone this time. No siblings. No little Winkles. She looks like a million dollars, a real lady. He's so proud of her. He will still be proud of her when she shrinks and sags and the color has drained forever from her cheeks – especially then.

'Marry me, Nora,' he says as, the objects of every admiring eye, they sway to the music of Glen Glenn and his orchestra.

'I can't leave Mama,' Nora replies.

When they arrive home at four in the morning, Nora makes them cold baked bean sandwiches, her favorite after-dance snack which Frank is slowly learning to love.

By spring they are close enough to exchange confidences and make confessions.

'I've raised nine children,' Nora says. 'Each one as it came along. When she was forty-six and told us she was pregnant with Sonny I said, "Oh Mama, not again!" Wasn't that awful of me? I was angry because she wouldn't stop seeing Papa. We were all angry. Except Frannie. She loves her father best. I still feel guilty about saying that.'

Frank likes her trace of brogue. He asks her about Belfast. He wants to know everything. She tells him her first memory. She was Queen of May, the prettiest little girl on Shankill Road – at least that's what they all said. She wore a white dress and a wreath of flowers and sang a song, she can't remember the words, and held the maypole while everyone danced round her, entwining their colored streamers. It was so pretty. But the festivities were brought to a sudden end by a raid of Catholic boys. They threw stones. Then there was a big fight and the police came. All the children ran away scared and crying. Someone, she never knew who, picked her up under his arm and ran with her, her bare legs and feet dangling, all the way to the Winkles' door where he handed her over to Big Nora.

More confessions. About her clothes. She knows it is a vice. The minister said so in church two Sundays ago, and she is sure he was looking straight at her.

'But I don't spend a lot of money on it,' she hurriedly tells Frank, almost as if she were assuring him that she would make a thrifty wife despite appearances. 'Just the little I have left over when I've given my paycheck to Mama.' He says he realizes that. 'Lil and I go to the sales. We look in the magazines and get ideas. We don't even buy the magazines. We read them in the news shop and memorize the photographs of the models.' She does not say that clothes are the only things that are hers alone. Her clothes and her voice. Vanity.

She does not tell him that her birth forced a marriage between two unsuited people; that no one was sure of her mother's maiden name; that her father was an Orangeman and had jumped many times over the imaginary bodies of dead Catholics; that when she came to America her mother could not read or write. Nora is ashamed of these things. 'I must tell him,' she thinks. And then, 'I must tell him later.'

'Now you confess,' she says, 'Isn't that what good Catholics are supposed to do?'

He pretends to consider the matter.

'I hate my sisters' cooking.' They laugh.

'Well,' she urges after a moment, 'go ahead. There must be more.'

'They'll be leaving soon and know what? I'll be glad.'

'Leaving? Why then you'll be – '

'All alone.'

Alone. In that big wooden house on the corner with its four bedrooms, its three apple trees, its big back yard with the bridlewreath hedge, its large sunny kitchen . . .

'Sadie's been transferred to the mill in Manchester and Lizzie's finally getting married.'

'Really?'

'There's one more thing.' He hesitates. 'Don't you want to know it?'

'If you want to tell me.' She presses his hand. She looks so appealing, innocent almost. Frank resists the impulse to kiss her. He's never sure how she'll react.

'I've seen you before.'

She looks at him, nervous suddenly, quizzical.

He saw her at a bean supper in South Berwick. Her color was especially high. Vinette accompanied as she sang numbers from their favorite collection, *A Treasure Chest of Songs We Love* – 'Ben Bolt' and 'Just Before the Battle Mother', 'The Letter Edged in Black' and 'Whispering Hope'. It was the loveliest thing Frank had ever heard.

'Well my goodness. But you shouldn't flatter me.'

He does not tell her that on that night he resolved to capture her voice.

Summer. Excursions to Rye and Wallis Sands and Old Orchard Beach in Frank's black Ford. The youngest Winkles run wild at the Amusement Park. They are completely unmanageable. Frank buys them candy apples and cotton candy and popcorn. On the way home they are sick. They fight and cry and finally fall asleep, their faces sticky and dirty, their noses running, their soiled socks runched down into the backs of their shoes. Nora tries not to be embarrassed. She begs them to blow their noses. She always carries a small packet of Kleenex.

During the drive she holds Frank's hand. She feels better when she holds his hand. She thinks of a large kitchen, three empty bedrooms, a white dress . . .

Nora cooks Frank a special Sunday lunch. Mama is to rest (she doesn't, and Frannie is to help.

'Please,' Nora begs her brothers, 'no wells.'

They laugh until they remember that Nora takes wells very seriously. They argue that potatoes taste better with wells. But they promise: just for today. Of course they forget. They heap up their mashed potatoes, make large craters in the centre with the backs of their dessert spoons then fill them to overflowing with gravy. They spend a moment enjoying the effect of their accomplishments then mush the potatoes and gravy into a beige soup. Wells.

Frannie sets the table in a leisurely way, practicing a dance step as she does so. Nora inspects her work. She adjusts the salt and pepper shakers by a quarter inch.

'There.' She smiles at Frannie. 'Isn't that better?'

Frannie smashes a saucer on the floor. 'You wanna see a mess?' she cries. 'I'll show you a mess! Clean it up yourself, Miss Just So!'

November, 1936. The presidential election. The Floods arrive promptly at nine in their recently polished car to drive Mrs Winkle to the polling station, then to the house she is cleaning that day. They have done so ever since Mrs Winkle moved to number twenty-seven nineteen years ago. Mrs Winkle sits in the back seat thanking them repeatedly for their kindness. They nod and smile and are pleased with her and with themselves. They are killing the two birds of civic and Christian duty with one stone. It's not every day a person has a chance to do that.

Mrs Winkle votes. The Floods vote. They wait for her, the motor running, as she chats to the mother of one of Timmy's friends. Mrs Mallon hasn't seen her Michael for two weeks and she's getting a welfare report from Mrs Winkle.

'Well,' says Clayton Flood when Mrs Winkle has climbed into the back seat, 'feel better now that you've helped put Landon in the White House?'

'Oh,' says Mrs Winkle, always cheerful, 'I didn't vote for Landon, Mr Flood.'

'You didn't?'

'I voted for Roosevelt.' She smiles, hands folded in her lap, pleased with her wonderful country.

A silence descends which has no effect whatever on Mrs Winkle.

'Bye bye sir, and all the best.' She waves as she steps from the car.

The Floods do not speak to the Winkles for nearly a year.

*

'When were you happiest, Nora?'

'In the Salvation Army,' she answers promptly.

Frank laughs, but when he sees the expression in her eyes he stops. He tries to be serious.

The Floods introduced her to Captain Daggett. It was one of many efforts to civilize the Winkles. No one but Nora was interested, but her enthusiasm more than compensated for their disappointment. Captain Daggett was taken with her voice. She'd got to sing lots of solos and play the cymbals. She even loved her uniform.

The others were kind and decent people who never spoke ill of anyone and eschewed the drink. Nora admired them. With them she felt protected. It was a world safe from the likes of Jimmy.

'And when have you been happiest?'

'Right now.'

She understands she might not have given the correct answer.

It's official. After dances, drives and amusement parks; after innumerable evenings in the Winkle kitchen and twenty boxes of Whitman's Sampler and Candy Cupboard; after Vinette has warned 'Don't wait too long, Nora. You're twenty-eight'; after Frannie and Lil vow that if she won't have him they'll make a play for him themselves; after the three children beg and plead and Mrs Winkle cries into her apron; after Harry proclaims Frank a wonderful man (he has got Harry an assistant managership at the Ben Franklin five and dime) and promises to drive Mama over to visit Nora twice a week; after thinking for months about the four-bedroom house – empty of sisters – of her own furniture and china cupboard and most of all the wedding dress – the white dress in which she once again will be Queen of May but with no street fighting this time and satin slippers instead of bare feet, and no stranger carrying her home but her own dear Frank – after all this she says yes at last.

Now Frank's Ford is parked outside 27 Harrison Avenue every evening. And now the moment has come which everyone has been dreading. Grammy Glick cannot be put off any longer. At seven forty-five on a Wednesday morning she storms in, the pugs yapping about her long skirts and lunging at Skippy the Winkle's yellow mongrel, and announces that they will not succeed in 'Sweeping her under the carpet', that they are a bunch of damned ingrates and that she insists on meeting this bloody Papist. She announces that she will not be made to wait another day and bangs her cane on the floor, at which the pugs whine and cringe and roll on their backs and Skippy flees, the screen door banging behind him.

Nora has warned Frank and Frank believes he is prepared. He has faith in his charm.

She is waiting for them. She sits in her kitchen by the big black stove, the pugs at her feet, quiet for once, her skirts spread round her like the Queen of the Gnomes. Uncle Brendan is safely locked in his room, for she wants no ructions but those she creates herself. She wants to look long and hard at this Papist. She wants to see an example of this religion which practices idolatry and makes hamburger meat out of Protestant babies.

'Grammy, this is Francis Martin Murnane.'

Grammy Glick does not answer. She leans forward and peers at him as though giving him the evil eye. Frank lets her look.

'Be nice, Grammy. Say hello. Frank's my fiancé.'

'I know that,' she roars. Nora is silent for the rest of the interview.

'You've tricked Little Nora,' (by which she means Mrs Winkle). 'She was always feeble-minded. They'd all a perished without me. Not a brain among em.' She points to the house across the street. 'Twas I got em all in, you know.'

'You're a very smart old woman, Mrs Glick.'

'And don't you just wish I wunt, Mr Murnane. I've got your measure and you know it. You cast a spell on that poor imbecile Little Nora.'

'You've got me there,' he smiles and winks.

'Shameless,' she sniffs. Then she sniffs again. Oh no, thinks Nora, here it comes. She closes her eyes.

Grammy Glick lifts the hem of her black skirt and folds it carefully back over her lap. Underneath is a grey petticoat which once had been white. This too she raises and folds back over her lap. Then she lifts a yellowed petticoat which might once have been pink and repeats the process. Finally she arrives at the red flannel petticoat, the ragged ruffle of which she lifts to her face. With a noise like Captain Daggett's French horn, she blows her nose into the ruffle, examines her achievement and blows again. Then she unfolds the red petticoat and smooths it over her knees. The might-have-been-pink one follows then the grey and lastly the black skirt. Nora can open her eyes now. Grammy Glick turns to her.

'Ye daft thing,' she says. 'You'd give up your religion, surrender your children to the priests, eh? For this *spiv*!'

'Oh Frank,' Nora speaks at last. 'Let's go.'

'Catholics!' she shouts after them. 'Never trust em. They're not Christian.'

'It's true, Frank, isn't it, I'll have to promise to – '

'Plenty of time.' He pats the hand that rests on his arm. 'Plenty of time.'

'It's true, isn't it?' Nora asks Vinette. 'I can't be a Methodist any more. I can't go to my own church or sing in the choir.'

'Nora,' Vinette looks at her hard. 'It's worth it.'

Lizzie and Sadie are calm. They are concerned but they are calm. They would never express disapproval of their brother Frank. But as he leaves to pick up Nora and take her to her first interview with Father Happny, Sadie remarks quietly, 'You know they say the Scotch-Irish have the worst tempers in the world.'

Frank waves and blows a kiss and genially orders them not to wait up. When he's left they discuss the rumor of insanity in the Winkle family.

Sadie and Lizzie have never seen a Protestant church. They treat Protestants with respect, though it is hard for them not to giggle when Toddy McVeigh makes fun of their Bible reading, the fact that their congregations all sing together, and in English, and that they are too cheap to smarten up their churches with a couple of statues.

Father Happny is a kind man. Still, Nora is nervous of him. She has never spoken to a priest before. She says she understands about the children's baptism and education. They will go to the school next door where for eight years they will be taught by those saintly women, the Sisters of Mercy. She understands that they will make their First Holy Communion and their Confirmation here in St Patrick's. Won't it be a wonderful thing, says Father Happny, when she can receive the sacraments with them?

'Wonderful,' says Nora.

He stresses that she need not take instruction immediately, though of course it would be preferable to be married as a Roman Catholic. She agrees, trying not to show her panic.

Frank, she wants to say when they leave, I'm not ready. But he speaks first. 'See? What did I tell you? Plenty of time, plenty of time.'

Frannie is awakened by Nora's sobbing.

'For Christ's sake,' Frannie moans. She puts her arm around her sister's heaving shoulders. 'Come on, Norrie. It doesn't matter that much. I'd get married in a Men's Room if I could marry Frank Murnane.'

'Oh you're disgusting!' Nora cries even harder.

'Well why not?' Frannie squeals.

'Shut up,' hisses Lil at the door. 'Will you just please shut up. Oh-oh. What's the matter, Norrie? Oh no, is it because – '

'It's *because*,' Frannie sighs.

'Look,' Lil embraces Nora. The other two make room for her on the bed. They can see the silhouettes of moving leaves and branches on the green window shade. 'It's not really so important.'

'Naw,' reasons pragmatic Frannie, 'so you can't do it in the big church. What's so bad? The sacristy's still part of the church. I mean God's there too, I suppose, if that's important to you.'

'I don't want to be married in an old sacristy!'

'Shut up,' yells Timmy and bangs on the wall.

'Oh go stick your head in a bucket,' says Frannie.

They can hear Mama in her heavy black shoes going down the stairs. It is 5.30 a.m.

'It's not just the sacristy.' Nora collects herself. 'It's – the dress!'

'Yeah, that stinks,' Frannie agrees.

'His sisters said an off-white suit would be "appropriate".'

'Well, beige is almost white.'

'Beige! With my high color?'

'Your high horse, more like it.'

'Shut up, Frannie.'

'It's as if I'm not good enough,' Nora goes on, 'to wear a proper wedding dress and be married properly in church. It has to be all hidden and quiet somewhere way out back where no one will see. They're ashamed of me. Even Frank – ashamed.'

With her sisters on either side of her, Nora sleeps at last. The alarm goes off at seven. Bravely she rises, crimps her hair, skips breakfast, leaves for work with Mrs Winkle chasing her down the front steps with a cup of tea.

'At least drink this, Nora darlin. Drink it for Mama.'

'She wants beatin not babyin,' shouts Grammy Glick from her porch as she gathers up the pugs' leashes.

All day Nora thinks about the white dress which will exist forever only as an idea. She thinks how terrible a beige suit will be, even with one of those showy orchids pinned to the lapel. She looks awful in beige. Everyone looks awful in beige.

Huntley Bates admires Nora Winkle. She is hard-working, conscientious, honest. Best secretary he's ever had. He decides to give her a wedding present of $200. It is more money than Nora has ever had at one time.

'Well, Honey, you've earned it,' Frank says. He tells her they'll be lucky together. Look, their luck has already begun. Yes, she says, she is holding their luck in her hand, right this minute.

'Wish my sister Lizzie would get lucky.'

'Why?'

'Marriage postponed again.' Lizzie has been engaged for four years to Eddie MacMahon, the local policeman. A nice man with a sick mother.

'Does that mean . . . ?'

'Fraid so, Norrie. It's won't be for long I promise.'

So the house with the four bedrooms will not be empty and hers after all.

113

She will have to share meals, conversation, a kitchen, with a reticent and unsympathetic woman who will be sure to have fixed ideas about how everything should be done.

'Then I think I'll keep on working for a while,' she says, not showing her disappointment but chastening him all the same.

'Sure, Honey. Plenty of time.'

Plenty of time to turn Papist. Plenty of time to share a kitchen with a stranger. And Sadie, it seems, intends to come home every other weekend. And Mrs MacMahon might live forever. Old women went on and on, especially bad-tempered ones. Look at Grammy Glick. No one knew how old she really was, but she had been sixty-nine for an awfully long time.

The luster, Nora thinks, is draining from this beautiful marriage, this Maypole day of her life. What is she doing anyway? She is marrying a man her mother trusts. Nora suddenly feels bound and gagged. Somehow she must restore this seeping luster. She will not allow them to rob her of her May dance. She will not be a demure little beige convert asking to be accepted despite her shortcomings, asking for verification of her existence, married in a sacristy, married in November.

Nora and Lil visit the news shop where they inspect the latest fashion magazines. This time they buy one. They go Mrs Pappas' Dress Salon, and Nora tries on several items, the seams of which Lil inspects in the dressing room. They tell Mrs Pappas' assistant the dresses are too large. Expressions of regret all round. Back on the street they head for J. C. Penney's and the patterns department. Lil finds two which she is sure she can chop and change to suit her sister's odd requirements.

'Remember, this is our secret, Lil.' Not even Harry is aware of what's going on in Lil's room and Mama is far too busy to notice. She's cleaning houses and planning the wedding breakfast.

The next day Nora goes to the bank and withdraws half of Huntley Bates' wedding present. She doesn't take it all. She leaves them half their luck.

She boards a bus for Portsmouth, where she visits the most exclusive department store in southern New Hampshire. There she buys seven yards of the finest silk chiffon which the salesgirl wraps carefully in tissue paper. Her next stop is Carbury's, where she purchases a pair of satin pumps with not too high a heel (at five foot seven, Nora is considered tall for a woman). At Suzette's millinery shop she finds a saucy hat of indeterminate fur. She buys two of them. Lastly she purchases a pair of silk stockings and some underwear. She is home in time to mash the potatoes, set the table and do a pile of ironing before she falls into bed beside Frannie, who knows something's cooking and is burning to find out what.

*

Lil and Nora spend their evenings locked in Lil's room, from which the sound of the sewing machine can be heard for hours at a stretch.

'I suppose you think this is bad of me, Lil.'

But Lil is not the person to ask. She cares only for the dress as dress. Its moral implications are not her concern. Nora finds this comforting. How hard it will be to leave her sisters. She cannot imagine life without them and is suddenly afraid. She sits staring, the chiffon beautifully bunched in her lap.

'Get a move on, Norrie,' prompts Lil. Nora threads her needle.

The wedding day. Nora wakes at 5 a.m. She lies in bed, something she never does, as if she were waiting for the sounds of the motorcycle and her brother's curses. She feels as though she were flying apart, pieces of her hurtling off in all directions like iron filings, never again to be drawn together by the magnet of her self. She can just make out the dress, completed the night before, hanging on the back of the closet door.

At five forty-five she makes a pot of tea. She would like to sit in the hammock on the front porch and drink it and eat a cold baked bean sandwich, all alone. But Grammy Glick would be sure to see her and scurry round for a confrontation. She goes to the back steps instead, her coat over her bathrobe. She likes the morning and the bright cold. She sits and drinks her tea and looks at the littered driveway. Timmy and his friends have been drinking beer (not allowed in the house), and the bottles still lie scattered where they left them. The cats have been at the trash can. No one remembered to take Skippy for a walk, and he is straining at his tether, having messed copiously by the garage door. Nora gets a paper bag and begins to tidy up. It is instinct, something she doesn't think about, a habitual reaction.

Jimmy emerges, monkey wrench in hand, eager to attack his motorcycle. He sees Nora at work and starts to cry.

'Norrie,' he sobs, putting his arms round her and burying his face in her neck. 'How can you be getting married? You're just a kid.'

Nora laughs and hugs him. 'I'm two years older than you are.' She will not cry, she will not, because if she starts she will never stop.

'You haven't even lived yet. You've just raised brats and gone to church and sung in that goddam choir.'

'Jimmy!'

'What'll we do without you Norrie? Won't be the same here any more. What the hell will we do?'

Four automobiles are lined up outside 27 Harrison Avenue. Timmy's friends have come through and have begged, borrowed and possibly stolen sufficient transport to carry the entire family, minus Grammy Glick, to Great Falls.

The Winkles come out into the November sunshine. Here and there a few leaves the color of dried blood still cling to the black trees. One of the Winkle boys wears his army uniform. Mama is very proud.

Uncle Brendan has been subdued lately, so they are risking it and he is allowed to come. He is not quite sure which of his nieces is getting married, but he is very happy. He beams, a carnation in the buttonhole of his ancient overcoat and black rubbers over his shoes. His mother, whose face is pressed to the kitchen window, has insisted. She scowls at her ungrateful, disorganized family. She has been asked to the wedding but has refused, to the relief of all concerned. She would rather, she says, endure the fires of hell.

She is cursing them all, Harry is certain. He averts his eyes as he gets into the car. He will be driving Nora and Mama and Frannie, whom Nora has asked to be bridesmaid. She hopes this act of kindness and inclusion will somehow touch her sister and encourage her to reform. It doesn't. But she does like the dressing up. Harry will also give Nora away. Everyone is secretly sad that Papa is not here to do it. They know that he too is sad, but no one says anything about it.

The Winkles climb into the cars, arguing about who will sit where. They all get car sick on long journeys and want to be in the front seat. Even if they leave immediately, they will be half an hour late, but then no one really expects them to be on time.

They are now seated. They all lean forward, craning their necks for a glimpse of Nora, who is coming down the front step. No one speaks. She walks slowly toward the first car, giving the neighbors who are lined up across the street the opportunity for a good long look. She allows herself a quick glance in order to check their expressions. A few mouths, including Millie Flood's, hang open.

Finally Jimmy breaks the silence with a whistle.

'You look like a goddam million, Norrie. But why the color?'

'I like it,' she says.

Mrs Winkle cries all the way to St Patrick's. She is remembering all the times she slapped and spanked and shouted at Little Nora. (None but Sonny were spared her lightning corporal punishment.) Then she would hold them and cry, just as she is doing now. Frannie passes her Kleenex and keeps repeating 'Oh come on, Ma.'

'I'm a damn fool, amn't I,' blubbers Mrs Winkle, who has barely noticed Nora's dress.

Harry holds Nora's hand and does not let go until they reach St Patrick's.

*

The Wedding Dress MARY FLANAGAN

Yes, there they are: Lizzie and Sadie in dark brown coats and identical felt cloches. Lizzie wears short, wool-trimmed boots on which she shifts her weight. They could have waited inside, Nora thinks. But they'd rather freeze and make her feel guilty for being late. Immediately she's sorry for being uncharitable. Why is it, she wonders, looking at the sisters, that in the family lottery of looks, brains and charm, one member should emerge such a clear winner? But Frank, she knows, has goodness as well. When she stands beside him in this outrage of a dress, she will look in his eyes and still see goodness. But she will see something else too, and that will be knowledge, a knowledge of her that has been hidden from him until today. And the knowledge will hurt him a little. And she will sense that and feel satisfied.

Everyone enters the church, the Catholics stopping at the holy water fonts to bless themselves. The youngest Winkles gape at the decor. Frannie gives a little snort and gets a quick kick from Harry. The brother and two sisters wait in the vestibule watching the others walk the long dim side aisle to the sacristy where there is barely enough room for them all and where they begin to get warm from the closeness of other bodies.

Nora refuses a coat. She wants to be exposed for as long as possible in her wedding dress, because she will never wear it again.

She stands at the sacristy door, head up, straight back very straight. There is no music. She sees Frank, dapper but uneasy in a new three-piece suit. He is wearing his father's watch. Beside him is his best man, Toddy McVeigh, whom he has known since childhood and who is a fellow member of the Great Falls chapter of the Knights of Columbus.

Everyone turns, expectant smiles on their faces, hankies at the ready. Then they see it: seven yards of deep purple crepe fall in five tiers over Nora's slender body. The tiers are cut on the bias, so that the bottom tier hangs longer on the right side, ending in a graceful point, while the left exposes Nora's black silk leg as far as her knee. The sleeves are trimmed at the wrist in black fur, the same fur as the hat which adorns her head, tilted at a rakish angle and covering the top of her face with a black net veil. The neckline is low and rounded, exposing her collar bones and the white, white skin of her chest. For the first time in her life she has made up her face. (She has always been what they call a clean-cut kid.)

She is a stunner, a million bucks, the classiest dame in the Tri-City area. She should be going to a nightclub – Twenty-One, the Stork Club, El Morocco – those famous places they have read about but will never visit. She could be going to lunch on the arm of a congressman or modeling for a fashion magazine. She could be going to a funeral – the glamorous widow, the bereaved heiress. The one place she could not be going is to her own wedding.

117

She takes her best-loved brother's arm. They walk toward the small altar adorned with only two candles and two vases of red roses.

Father Happny's bushy eyebrows shoot up nearly to his white hair. He subdues them with difficulty and tries to smile and look benevolent, which he is.

Lil cannot stop studying her masterpiece.

Frannie thinks this the funniest thing she has ever seen.

Jimmy is embarrassed and can't think why.

Mrs Winkle is crying again.

Toddy McVeigh gives the bride a wink.

Lizzie and Sadie exchange looks.

Nora reaches Frank's side. She searches his eyes and finds there what she expects to find.

Uncle Brendan begins to sing 'The Sash My Father Wore'.

The wedding breakfast is over. Nora steps out of the purple dress and hangs it in the closet that is hers no longer. She removes the black pumps and unrolls the black silk stockings. She takes from a hanger the simple, well-cut, inexpensive dusty-rose going-away suit.

'You're not taking the wow-wee-wow dress?' asks Frannie, who has been smoking a cigarette in the bathroom and Nora knows it. She sniffs but makes no comment.

'Should I?'

'Won't you and Frank be stepping out in DC? Lots of nightclubs there I bet.'

'It's not really what we had in mind.'

'You're a snit, Norrie. Marriage hasn't changed you. I feel sorry for Frank.'

Nora doesn't tell her that their big Washington treat will be a visit to the Senate hearings.

'I'm not ever going to wear it again.'

Frannie calculates that this is not the right moment to ask if she can have it. She'll just borrow it while Nora is away.

'That's stupid to let it rot in a trunk. It was expensive.'

'I'm going to give it to my daughter.'

'For her *wedding*?'

Nora closes the closet door firmly and slips into her coat.

'Don't be silly. To play with when she's little.'

'Play? That beautiful – ?'

'Yes. To dress up in. What's a dress for?'

Nora leaves. Frannie locks the door to the room which will be hers alone until Jimmy brings his wife home to live. She kicks off her shoes, lies back on the bed and smokes another cigarette.

MARY E. BRADDON

Samuel Lowgood's Revenge

From the first to the last we were rivals and enemies. Perhaps it was on my part that the hatred, which eventually became so terrible a passion between us, first arose. Perhaps it was, perhaps it was! At any rate, he always said that it was so. I am an old man, and many memories of the past have lost their vivid colouring; but that portion of my life which relates to him is as fresh in my mind to-night as ever it was fifty years ago, when his gracious Majesty George the Second was king, and Christopher Weldon and I were junior clerks together in the great house of Tyndale and Tyndale, ship-owners, Dockside, Willborough.

He was very handsome. It was hard for a pale-faced, sallow-complexioned, hollow-eyed, insignificant lad as I was to sit at the same desk with Christopher Weldon, and guess the comparisons that every stranger entering the counting-house must involuntarily make as he looked at us – if he looked at us, that is to say; and it was difficult not to look at Christopher. Good heavens! I can see him now, seated at the worn, old, battered, ink-stained desk, with the July sunlight streaming down through the dingy office windows upon his pale golden curls; his bright blue eyes looking out through the smoky panes at the forests of masts, dangling ropes, and grimy sails in the dock outside; one girlish white hand carelessly thrown upon the desk before him, and the delicate fingers of the other twisted in his flowing curls. He was scarcely one-and-twenty, the spoiled pet of a widowed mother, the orphan son of a naval officer, and the idol of half the women in the seaport of Willborough. It was not so much to be wondered at, then, that he was a fop and a maccaroni, and that the pale golden curls which he brushed off his white forehead were tied on his coat-collar with a fine purple ribbon on Sundays and holidays. His cravat and ruffles were always of delicate lace, worked by his loving mother's hands; his coats were made by a London tailor, who had once worked for Mr George Selwyn and Lord

March, and he wore small diamond shoe-buckles and a slender court-sword sometimes out of office hours.

I, too, was an orphan; but I was doubly an orphan. My father and mother had both died in my infancy. I had been reared in a workhouse, had picked up chance waifs and strays of education from the hardest masters, and had been drafted, at the age of ten, into the offices of Tyndale and Tyndale. Errand boy, light porter, office drudge, junior clerk – one by one I had mounted the rounds in this troublesome ladder, which for me could only be begun from the very bottom; and at the age of twenty-one I found myself – where? In a business character, I was on a level with Christopher Weldon, the son of a gentleman. How often I, the pauper orphan of a bankrupt corn-chandler, had to hear this phrase – the son of a gentleman! In a business character, I say, I, Samuel Lowgood, who had worked and slaved and drudged, and been snubbed, throughout eleven long weary years – and in spite of all had become a clever accountant and a thorough arithmetician – was in the same rank as Christopher Weldon, who had been in the office exactly four weeks, just to see, as his mother said, whether it would suit him.

He was about as much good in the counting-house as a wax doll would have been, and, like a wax doll, he looked very pretty; but Messrs Tyndale and Tyndale had known his father; and Tyndale senior knew his uncle, and Tyndale junior was acquainted with his first cousin, who lived at the court-end of London; so he was taken at once into the office as junior clerk, with every chance, as one of the seniors told me confidentially, of rising much higher, if he took care of himself.

He knew about as much arithmetic as a baby; but he was very clever with his pen in sketching pretty girls with powdered heads, flowing sacques, and pannier-hoops; so he found plenty of amusement in doing this and reading Mr Henry Fielding's novels behind the ledger; and the head clerks left him to himself, and snubbed me for not doing his work as well as my own.

I hated him. I hated his foppish ways and his haughty manners; I hated his handsome boyish face, with its frame of golden hair, and its blue, beaming, hopeful eyes; I hated him for the sword which swung across the stiff skirts of his brocaded coat, for the money which he jingled in his waistcoat pockets, for the two watches which he wore on high days and holidays, for his merry laugh, for his melodious voice, for his graceful walk, for his tall, slender figure, for his jovial, winning ways, which won everybody else's friendship. I hated him for all these; but, most of all, I hated him for his influence over Lucy Malden.

Lucy was a humble dependent upon the bounty of the house of Tyndale and Tyndale, and she had the care of the town residence belonging to the firm, a roomy old house which communicated with the offices.

People knew very little about her, except that she was the daughter of a superannuated old clerk, who had gone stone blind over the ledgers of Tyndale and Tyndale, and that she lived with her father in this dreary, old, deserted town house. Once or twice in the year the brothers would take it into their heads to give a dinner party in this disused dwelling; and then the great oak furniture was polished, and clusters of wax candles were lighted in the twisted silver sconces, and the dim pictures of the Tyndales dead and gone, shipowners and merchants in the days of William and Mary, were uncovered: but at other times Lucy Malden and her blind old father had the great place, with its long dark corridors and its lofty chambers, into which the light rarely penetrated, all to themselves. The house joined the offices, and the offices and the house formed three sides of a square, the dock-side forming the fourth. The counting-house in which Christopher Weldon and I sat was exactly opposite the house.

I watched him upon the morning when he first saw her – watched him without his being aware of it. It was a blazing July day; and when she had arranged her father's room and her own, and the little sitting-room which they shared together, which formed part of a range of apartments on the second story, she came to her window, and, opening it to its widest extent, sat down to her needlework. She eked out the slender income which the firm allowed her father by the sale of her needlework, which was very beautiful. A screen of flowers in great stone jars shaded the window, and behind these she placed herself.

He saw her in a moment, and his pen fell from his listless hand.

She was not beautiful; I know that she was not beautiful. I think that many would have scarcely called her even a pretty girl; but to me, from the first to the last, she was the fairest, the dearest, and the loveliest of women, and it is so difficult to me to dispossess myself of her image, as that image shone upon me, that I doubt if I can describe her as she really was.

She was very pale. The dreary, joyless life she led in that dark old house, in the heart of a dingy seaport town, had perhaps blanched the roses in her cheeks, and dimmed the sunlight in her thoughtful brown eyes. She had very light hair – hair of the palest flaxen, perfectly straight and smooth, which she wore turned back over a roll, and fastened in one thick mass at the back of her head. Her eyes, in utter contrast to this light hair, were of the darkest brown, so dark and deep, that the stranger always thought them black. Her features were small and delicate, her lips thin, her figure slender, and below the average height. Her dress, a dimity petticoat, with a gray stuff gown, and a white apron.

Christopher's pen fell out of his hand, and he looked up at her window, and began to hum the air of a favourite song in the new opera about thieves and ragamuffins, which had got Mr Gay, the poet, and a beautiful duchess, into such disgrace up in London.

He was such a conceited beau and lady-killer, that he could not rest till she had looked at the office window by which he sat.

The song attracted her, and she lifted her eyes from her work, and looked down at him.

She started, and blushed – blushed a beautiful, rosy red, that lighted up her pale face like the reflection of a fire; and then, seeing me at my desk, nodded and smiled to me. She and I had been friends for years, and I only waited till I should rise one step higher in the office to tell her how much I loved her.

From that day, on some excuse or other, Christopher Weldon was always dangling about the house. He scraped acquaintance with her blind old father. He was a pretty musician, and he would put his flute in his pocket, after office hours, and stroll over to the house, and sit there in the twilight playing to the father and daughter for the hour together, while I hid myself in the shadow of the counting-house doorway, and stood watching them. O, how I hated him, as I saw across the screen of plants the two fair heads side by side, and the blind old father nodding and smiling, and applauding the music! How I hated that melodious opera of Mr Gay's! How I hated Christopher Weldon, as he and Lucy stood on the step of the hall door, between the tall iron extinguishers under the disused oil-lamp, wishing each other goodnight! I thought that I could see the little white hand tremble when it fluttered a gentle farewell to him, as he strode away through the dusky evening.

Should I dog his steps, and when he got to a lonely place along the narrow quay, dart suddenly upon him, and push him into the water? – push him in where the barges lay thickly clustered together, and where he must sink under their keels down into the black stream? The God of sinners knows I have asked myself this question!

For months I watched them. O, what bitter pain, what cruel torture, what a long fever of anguish and despair!

How could I do him some dire injury, which should redress one atom of this mighty sum of wrong that he had done me? – fancied wrong, perhaps; for if he had not won her love, I might never have won it. But I prayed – I believe I was wicked and mad enough even to pray – for some means of doing him as deadly an injury as I thought he had done me.

He looked up at me one day, in his gay, reckless fashion, and said, suddenly pushing the ledger away from him, with a weary sigh,

'Samuel Lowgood, do you know what a tailor's bill is?'

I cursed him in my heart for his insolence in asking me the question; but I looked down at my greasy white coat-sleeve, and said,

'I have worn this for five years, and I bought it second-hand of a dealer on the quay.'

'Happy devil!' he said, with a laugh, 'if you want to see a tailor's bill, then look at that.'

He tossed me over a long slip of paper, and I looked at the sum total.

It seemed to me something so prodigious, that I had to look at it ever so many times before I could believe my eyes.

'Thirty-seven pounds thirteen and fourpence-halfpenny. I like the four-pence-halfpenny,' he said; 'it looks honest. Samuel Lowgood, my mother's heart would break if she saw that bill. I must pay it in a fortnight from today, or it will come to her ears.'

'How much have you got towards paying it?' I asked.

My heart beat faster at the thought of his trouble, and my face flushed crimson; but he sat with his forehead leaning on his clasped hands, and he never looked at me.

'How much have I got towards it?' he said, bitterly. 'This.' He turned his waistcoat pockets inside out, one after the other. 'Never mind,' he added, in his old reckless tone, 'I may be a rich man before the fortnight's out.'

That evening he was dangling over at the house as usual, and I heard 'Cease your funning' on the flute, and saw the two fair heads across the dark foliage of Lucy Malden's little flower garden.

I was glad of his trouble – I was glad of his trouble! It was small, indeed, compared to the sorrow and despair which I wished him; but it *was* trouble, and the bright, fair-haired, blue-eyed boy knew what it was to suffer.

The days passed, and the fortnight was nearly gone, but my fellow clerk said no more about the tailor's bill. So one day, as we sat as usual at the desk – I working hard at a difficult row of figures, he chewing the end of his pen, and looking rather moodily across the courtyard, I asked him,

'Well, have you got rid of your difficulty?'

'What difficulty?' he asked sharply.

'Your tailor's bill; the thirty-seven thirteen and fourpence-halfpenny.'

He looked at me very much as if he would have liked to have knocked me off my high stool; but he said presently, 'O yes; that's been settled ever so long!' and he began to whistle one of his favourite songs.

'Ever so long!' His trouble lasted a very short time, I thought.

But in spite of this he was by no means himself. He sat at his desk with his head buried in his hands; he was sharp and short in his answers when anybody spoke to him, and we heard a great deal less of the *Beggar's Opera* and 'Polly.'

All of a sudden, too, he grew very industrious, and took to writing a great deal; but he contrived to sit in such a manner that I could never find out what he was writing.

It was some private matter of his own, I felt sure. What could it be?

Love letters, perhaps; letters to her!

A fiendish curiosity took possession of me, and I determined to fathom his secret.

I left the counting-house on some pretence; and after a short absence returned so softly that he could not hear me; and stealing behind him, lifted myself upon tiptoe, and looked over his shoulder.

He was writing over and over again, across and across, upon half a sheet of letter paper, the signature of the firm 'Tyndale and Tyndale.'

What could it mean? Was it preoccupation? Mere absence of mind? Idle trifling with his pen? The fop had a little pocket mirror hanging over his desk. I looked into it, and saw his face.

I knew then what it meant. My hatred of him gave me such a hideous joy in the thought of what I had discovered that I laughed aloud. He turned round, and asked me savagely what I was doing; and as he turned he crumpled the paper in his hand, inking his pretty white fingers with the wet page.

'Spy, sneak, sycophant!' he said; 'what are you crawling about here for?'

'I was only trying to startle you, Mister Weldon,' I answered. 'What are you writing, that you're so frightened of my seeing? Love letters?'

'Mind your own business and look to your own work, you pitiful spy,' he roared out, 'and leave me to do mine my own way.'

'I would, if I were you. It seems such a nice way,' I answered meekly.

Two days after this, at half-past three o'clock in the afternoon, Christopher Weldon asked one of the senior clerks for a quarter of an hour's leave of absence. He wanted to see a fellow round in the High Street, he said, and he couldn't see him after four o'clock.

I felt my sallow face flame up into a scarlet flush as my fellow clerk made this request. Could it be as I thought?

He had been four months in the office, and it was the end of November. The end of November, and almost dark at half-past three o'clock.

They granted his request without the slightest hesitation. He left his desk, took his hat up, and walked slowly to the door; at the door he stopped, turned back to his desk, and throwing his hat down, leaned moodily upon his folded arms.

'I don't know that I care much about seeing the fellow now,' he said.

'Why, Chris,' cried one of the clerks, 'what's the matter with you, man? Are you in love or in debt, that you're so unlike yourself?'

'Neither,' he said, with a short laugh.

'What, not in love, Chris? How about the pretty little fair-haired girl over the way?'

'How about her?' he said savagely. 'She's a cold-hearted little coquette, and she may go to – '

I slapped the ledger on which I was at work violently on to the desk, and looked up at him.

'Christopher Weldon!'

'Your humble servant,' he said mockingly. 'There's a face! Have I been poaching upon your manor, Samuel?'

'If you want to see your friend before four o'clock you'd better be off, Chris!' said the clerk.

He took his hat up once more, twirled it slowly round for a few minutes, then put it on his head, and without saying a word to any one, hurried out of the office and across the courtyard.

Lucy was standing at her window opposite, with her forehead leaning against the dingy framework of the panes, and I watched her start and tremble as she saw him.

'If I'm to take these accounts into the market place I'd better take them now, hadn't I, sir?' I asked of the senior clerk.

'You may as well.'

There was a back way through some narrow courts and squares which led from the dock-side to the High Street, in which the house Tyndale and Tyndale banked with was situated. I was hurrying off this way when I stopped, and changed my mind.

'He'll go the back way,' I thought; 'I'll cut across the market place by the most public road.'

In five minutes I was in the High Street. Opposite the bank there was a tobacconist's shop, at which our clerks were accustomed to buy their pennyworths of snuff. I strolled in, and asked the girl to fill my box. I was quite an old man in most of my ways, and snuff-taking was a confirmed habit with me.

As she weighed the snuff, I stood looking through the low window at the great doors of the bank opposite.

One of the doors swung back upon its hinges. An old man, a stranger to me, came out.

Three minutes more.

'I am waiting for a friend,' I said to the girl at the counter.

Two minutes more. The doors opened again. I was right, and I was not surprised. Christopher Weldon came out of the bank, and walked quickly down the street.

It was too dark for me to see his face; but I knew the tall slim figure and the dashing walk.

'I am not surprised, I am only glad,' I said.

During my long service in the house of Tyndale and Tyndale, I had lived so hard as to have been able to save money from my scanty earnings. I had scraped together, from year to year, the sum of forty-eight pounds fifteen shillings.

'I will save a hundred,' I had said, 'and then I will ask her to marry me.'

But the only dream of my life was broken, and my little hoard was useless to me now.

Useless to purchase love, perhaps; but it might yet bring me revenge.

I put every farthing I possessed into my pocket the next morning, and the first time I could find an excuse for going out hurried down to the bank.

'One of our clerks presented a cheque here yesterday,' I said.

The man looked up with an expression of surprise.

'Yes, certainly; there was a cheque cashed yesterday. Your handsome, fair-haired junior brought it.'

'Will you let me look at it?'

'Well, upon my word, it's rather a strange – '

'Request. Perhaps. On the part of Messrs Tyndale and Tyndale I – '

'O,' he said, 'if you are commissioned by the firm to – '

'Never mind,' I said, 'whether I am or not. As you think my request a strange one, I'll put it in another way. Will you be so good as to look at the cheque yourself?'

'Yes, certainly. Here it is,' he added, selecting a paper from a drawer; 'a cheque for forty. Payable to bearer.'

'Look at the signature of the firm.'

'Well, it's right enough, I think. I ought to know the signature pretty well.'

'Look at the "y" in "Tyndale."'

He scrutinised the signature more closely, and lifted his eyebrows with a strange, perplexed expression.

'It's rather stiff, isn't it?' I said. 'Not quite old Tyndale's flowing calligraphy. Very near it, you know, and a very creditable imitation; but not quite the real thing.'

'It's a forgery!' he said.

'It is.'

'How did you come to know of it?'

'Never mind that,' I answered. 'Mr Simmonds, have you any sons?'

'Three.'

'One about the age of Christopher Weldon, perhaps?'

'One pretty nearly his age.'

'Then you'll help me to save this young man, won't you?'

'How is it to be done?'

'Cancel the cheque, and replace the money.'

'My good young man, who's to find the money?'

I drew a little canvas-bag out of my pocket, and turned out a heap of one-pound notes and spade-guineas upon the clerk's desk.

'Here's the exact sum,' I said; 'forty pounds, ready money, for the slip of paper Christopher Weldon presented here at ten minutes to four yesterday evening.'

'But who finds this money?'

'I do. Christopher Weldon and I have been fellow clerks for four months and upwards. I have seen his mother. I know how much she loves her only son. I know a girl who loves him. I don't mind forty pounds out of my savings to keep this matter a secret. Mr Simmonds, for the sake of your own sons, let me have that slip of paper, and cancel the cheque.'

The old man caught my hand in his, and shook it heartily.

'Young Lowgood,' he said, 'there's not another lad in Willborough capable of such a generous action. If I were not a poor old fellow, with a hard fight of it to get a living, I'd be twenty pounds in this transaction; but I respect and honour you. I dare not give you back the cheque upon my own responsibility; but the senior partner is in his office; I'll go and talk to him. Perhaps, when he hears the real state of the case, he'll consent to hush the matter up and do what you want.'

The old man left me and remained away about a quarter of an hour, during which I sat in the quiet counting-house, with my heart beating loud and fast. I daresay the junior clerk wondered what my business could be as I sat waiting for their senior's return. He came back at last.

'I've had a good deal of trouble,' he said, 'but I have succeeded.'

I burst out laughing as he gave me the forged cheque in exchange for the forty pounds I counted out to him.

'Laugh away, laugh away,' said the old man; 'you've need to have a light heart, Samuel Lowgood, for you're a noble fellow.'

In our back office there was a great chest which had been disused for some years. The clerks let me have it for my own use, and inside it I had a smaller iron-clamped strongbox of my own, which I had bought of a broker on the quay. Into this strongbox I put the forged cheque.

Christopher Weldon's high spirits entirely deserted him. It was such pleasure to me to watch him slyly as I sat beside him, apparently occupied only by my work, that I was almost tempted to neglect my business.

No more *Beggar's Opera*, no more 'Polly,' no more flute-playing in the dusk of the evening over at the gloomy old house.

'That lad Weldon is leaving off his giddy ways and growing industrious,' said the clerks; 'he'll get on in the world, depend upon it.'

'Let him – let him – let him,' I thought; 'let him mount the ladder; and when he reaches the highest round – then – then – '

In the following March there were some changes made in the office. Tyndale and Tyndale had a branch house of business in Thames Street, London; and into this house Christopher Weldon was drafted, with a salary nearly double that which he had received in Willborough.

The change came about very suddenly. They wanted some one of

127

gentlemanly appearance and polished manners in the London office, and Weldon, they said, was the very man.

I had not spoken to Lucy Malden for upwards of two months; but I thought I would go and tell her this piece of news.

'I shall find out whether she really loves him,' I thought.

She sat at her old place at the window, in the cold spring twilight, when I followed her father into the house and bade her good evening.

She was not paler than usual, for she had always been pale; nor graver, for she was always grave; but in spite of this, I saw that she had suffered.

My presence had no more effect upon her than if I had been nothing more sentient than the clumsy high-backed oak chair upon which I leaned as I stood talking to her.

She looked at me when I spoke, answered me sweetly and gently, and then looked down again at her tedious work.

I knew that I had come, coward as I was, to stab this tender innocent heart; but I could not resist the fiendish temptation.

'So our pretty fair-haired boy is going to leave us,' I said, by and by.

She knew whom I meant, and I saw the stiff embroidery shiver in her hand.

'Christopher?' she faltered.

'Young Mr Weldon,' I said. 'Yes, the gentleman clerk. He's going away, never to come back here, I daresay. He's going into the London house to make his fortune.'

She made me no answer, nor did she ask me a single question. She sat very quietly, going on with her work, sorting the gay-coloured silks, straining her eyes in the dusky light over the difficult pattern; but I saw – I saw how sharply I had struck this poor, pitiful, broken heart, and I knew now how much she had loved him.

Ten years from that day, I stood in the same room – she working at the same window – and asked her to be my wife.

'I do not ask,' I said, 'for the love which you gave to another ten years ago. I do not ask for the beauty which those who speak to me of you say is faded out of your mournful face. You will always be to me the most beautiful of women, and your gentle tolerance will be dearer to me than the most passionate love of another. Lucy Malden, will you marry me?'

She started up, letting her work fall out of her lap, and turning her face towards the window, burst into a passion of tears.

I had never seen her cry before.

At last she turned to me, with her face drowned in tears, and said,

'Samuel Lowgood, ten years ago, day after day, and night after night, I waited for another to say the words which have just been said by you. I had every right to expect he should say them. He never did – he never did.

Forgive me, forgive me, if it seems to break my heart afresh to hear them spoken by another!'

'He is a prosperous man in London,' I said. 'Lucy Malden, will you be my wife?'

She dried her tears, and, coming slowly to me, put her little cold hand into mine.

'Does that mean yes?' I asked.

She only bent her head in answer.

'God bless you! and goodnight.'

A year and a half after our marriage, we heard great news in the old Willborough house. Christopher Weldon had married a nobleman's daughter, and was about to become a partner in the house of Tyndale and Tyndale.

A night or two after we heard this news, there came a great rattling knock at the grim dragon's-head knocker of the house door. My wife and I lived in her old apartments, by permission of the firm, and I had advanced to be head clerk in the Willborough office.

I was sitting, going over some accounts that I had not been able to finish in the day; so she looked up at the sound of the knocking, and said,

'I'll answer the door, Samuel! – you're tired.'

She was a good and gentle wife to me, from the first to the last.

Presently I started from my desk, and rushed down the stairs. I had heard a voice that I knew in the hall below.

My wife was lying on the cold stone flags, and Christopher Weldon bending over her.

'Poor little thing!' he said; 'she has fainted.'

'This decides me, this decides me!' I thought; 'I'll have my forty pounds' worth before long.'

Christopher Weldon had come down to the house to announce to us, its custodians, that he was about to occupy it, with his wife, the Lady Belinda Weldon.

He brought a regiment of London upholsterers the next day, and set them to work tearing the gloomy old rooms to pieces. My lady came too, in her gilded chair, and gave orders for a chintz here and damask there, and could not find words to express her contempt for the place and her despair of ever making it habitable; but declared that whatever taste and upholstery could do for such a gloomy dungeon of a place, was to be done. After her ladyship's departure, a prim housekeeper came to inform my wife that we must be prepared to leave the house in a month. In a month the place was transformed, and at the end of the month Christopher Weldon was to give a great dinner party, at which Messrs Tyndale and Tyndale were to be present, to inaugurate his partnership. As senior clerk, I was honoured by an invitation.

My enemy had mounted to the highest round of the ladder. Rich, beloved, honoured, the husband of a lovely and haughty lady, partner in the great and wealthy house which he had entered as junior clerk – what more could fortune bestow upon him?

My time had come – the time at which it was worth my while to crush him.

'I will wait till the dinner is over, and the toasts have been drunk, and all the fine speeches have been made; and when Tyndale senior has proposed the health of the new partner, in a speech full of eulogy, I will hand him the forged cheque across the dinner table.'

The night before the dinner party, I was in such a fever of excitement, that I tried in vain to sleep. I heard every hour strike on the little clock in our bedroom. Tyndale and Tyndale had given us a couple of empty offices on our being turned out of the great house, and enough of their old-fashioned furniture to fit them up very comfortably.

One, two, three, four, five, the shrill strokes of the clock seemed to beat upon my brain. The hours seemed endless, and I sometimes thought the clock in our room and all the church clocks of Willborough had stopped simultaneously.

At last, towards six o'clock in the morning, I dropped off into a feverish troubled sleep, in which I dreamed of the forged cheque, which I still kept locked in the strongbox inside the great chest in the back office.

I dreamed that it was lost, that I went to the strongbox and found the cheque gone. The horror of the thought woke me suddenly. The broad sunshine was streaming in at the window, and the church clocks were striking nine.

I had slept much later than usual. My wife had risen, and was seated in our little sitting-room at her accustomed embroidery. She was always very quiet and subdued, and sat at her work several hours every day.

My first impulse, on waking, was to look under my pillow for my watch, and a black ribbon, to which was attached the key of the strongbox. The key of the chest hung on a nail in the office, as nothing of any consequence was kept in that. My watch and the key were perfectly safe.

My mind was relieved, but I was in a fever of excitement all day.

'I will not take the cheque out of its hiding place till the last moment,' I said; 'not till the moment before I put on my hat to go to the dinner party.'

My wife dressed me carefully in a grave snuff-coloured suit, which I generally wore on Sundays; she plaited my ruffles, and arranged my lawn cravat with its lace ends. I looked an old man already, though I was little more than thirty-three years of age; and Christopher Weldon was handsomer than ever.

At four o'clock in the afternoon the courtyard was all astir with sedan-chairs and powdered footmen. My wife stood in the window, looking at the company alighting from their chairs at the great door opposite.

'You had better go, I think, Samuel,' she said; 'the Tyndales have just arrived. Ah! there is my lady Belinda at the window. How handsome she is! How magnificent she is, in powder and diamonds, and an amber-satin sacque!'

'You've a better right to wear amber satin and diamonds than she,' I said.

'I, Samuel!'

'Yes. Because you're the wife of an honest man. She is not.'

I thought for love of him she would have fired up and contradicted me; but she only turned her face away and sighed.

'You will be late, Samuel,' she said.

'I have something to fetch out of the back office, and then I shall be ready,' I answered.

The fiend himself must be in the work. It was gone – gone, every trace of it. At first, in my blind, mad fury, I blasphemed aloud. Afterwards, I fell on my knees over the open chest, and wept – wept bitter tears of rage and anguish. It was gone!

I had a brain fever after this, which confined me for nine weeks to my bed.

Christopher Weldon lived and thrived, a prosperous and successful merchant – honoured, courted, admired, and beloved.

My wife and I, childless and poor, used to sit at our windows in the dusk, and watch his children at play in the courtyard beneath us, and hear the innocent voices echoing through the great house opposite.

Thirteen years and five months after our wedding day, Lucy died in my arms; her last words to me were these:

'Samuel, I have done my best to do my duty, but life for me has never been very happy. Once only since our marriage have I deceived you. I saved you, by that action, from doing a great wrong to a man who had never knowingly wronged you. One night, Samuel, you talked in your sleep, and I learned from your disjointed sentences the story of Christopher Weldon's crime. I learned, too, your purpose in possessing yourself of the only evidence of the forgery. I learned the place in which you kept that evidence; and, while you slept, I took the key from under your pillow, and opened the strongbox. The cheque is here.'

She took it from a little black silk bag which hung by a ribbon round her neck, and put it into my hand. 'Samuel, husband, we have read the Gospel together every Sunday evening through thirteen years. Will you use it now?'

'No, Lucy, no – angel – darling – no. You have saved him from disgrace – me from sin.'

Every clerk in the house of Tyndale and Tyndale attended my wife's funeral. Not only were the clerks present; but, pale, mournful, and handsome, in his long black cloak, Christopher Weldon stood amidst the circle round the grave.

As we left the churchyard he came up to me, and shook hands.

'Let us be better friends for the future, Samuel,' he said.

'My wife, when she died, bade me give you this,' I answered, as I put the forged cheque into his hand.

LUCY ELLMANN

Pass the Parcel

When I began to find my own farts funny, I knew something was up. And on repetition, they seemed to be getting funnier.

Farting worked in quite well with my job as a traffic warden. There's a lot of solitary walking and suppressed contempt for the populace. Farting gave me a bit of extra propulsion as well as a subtle form of revenge. I'd listen to people's pathetic excuses, followed by their life stories and perhaps some threats or jibes. Then I'd move off down the street, gently pfut-pfutting.

Some bloke in Paris once made a living on the stage with his knack for musical flatulence. But I wasn't in his league. I didn't use my gases at all creatively. I was eating baked beans, Jerusalem artichokes, brown rice, digestive biscuits and fruit cake, to keep them coming. May the force be with you, was the general idea.

My mother had recently died, and there I was, trying to get a laugh out of a fart. She'd been an invalid for twenty years. She went from walking with a stick, to walking with a three-pronged stick, then a four-pronged one, to being in a wheelchair and only walking to the bathroom, to using a walking-frame and needing help getting on and off the loo, to being bedridden, to being hospitalized, suppposedly for constipation, to having enemas and external manual prodding of her stools, to being told she was full of cancer and having the sense to die of a stroke at that point.

Looking at it now, I can see the progression, but at the time I just thought she'd eaten too much white bread. At breakfast and lunch, though sometimes only half-eaten. I used to go home for lunch then.

After Mum died, I didn't have to any more, so I took to eating in parks. One day, in between the soup that was too cold and the sandwich which was a bit warm, I got yelled at. From some distance at first. A drunken woman stood in an aggressive posture and yelled at me.

'You fucking bastard! Fucking coward. You don't beat women, you coward. You don't beat me and get away with it. I'm going to tell the police. Call yourself a man!?' And so on.

Well, I don't call myself a man. I'm a thirty-five-year-old woman, unmarried, no prospects. I really didn't feel I deserved her criticisms, and I was beginning to get a bit angry, as well as scared. She came closer and closer. I put down my sandwich, ready to defend myself.

And then she passed me right by, still yelling. She ended up confronting a tramp several benches along. He was the fucking coward apparently, not me. But to have geared myself up and then not had a chance to vindicate myself was unsettling. I didn't find a single traffic violation for the rest of the day, my heart just wasn't in it.

In my spare time, I was sorting through my mother's things. All the letters from friends had to go. I don't know why she kept them, and now they meant nothing to anybody alive. Each generation flushes the toilet for the last.

I took the better clothes to Oxfam – they're getting very snooty about what they'll accept these days, but I told them those size 18 navy-blue Marks and Sparks trousers would serve some poor old devil in Africa very well. They took a few blouses too.

They gave me a black plastic bag of her effects at the hospital. It was half-empty but so heavy I wondered if they'd included a severed limb or two. Or some organs meant for transplant and then rejected. How was I supposed to know what was left of her in that tiny coffin? She was so submerged in satin that only her hands, clasping each other, appeared, and her face still smudged with tomato soup from her last meal. They were cheap undertakers.

I didn't open the black rubbish bag for months. In it were her shoes and a cardigan, as it turned out.

There was something else more worrying in the flat. I felt it clinging to me as soon as they told me she'd died in the night. When I got home, I imagined kicking it under my armchair in the sitting-room and left it there. It was a small package, carefully wrapped in layer after layer of white packaging paper so the blood wouldn't ooze out, and tied with raw twine.

'We should never have had a child, your father and I. You were bound to be fat.'

'Oh, so I'm so fat I don't deserve to exist?'

'I didn't mean that,' she said, pained.

But my mother loved me when I was small. I remember her plaiting my hair and fussing about hats and scarves before I left for school in the mornings, and I distinctly recall her face lighting up sometimes on my return. When she was going out in the evening, I would sit on her bed and watch her put on the dreaded perfume and high heels, both signs that she would leave me, however much I pleaded. I tried on the high heels too. At the front door, she would always say, 'Now make sure I haven't left anything burning.' And after the door closed I would run around the flat, my mission to find and destroy all rogue sizzling cigarettes and to check the cooker was off. A task that softened the transition from mother-love to abandonment.

That was one of the last things she said to me, in a drugged daze as she fingered the blanket: 'Check I haven't left anything burning.'

The cat was fading fast too. It had become a cat-disc, a sleeping snail-shell spiral of a cat, getting ever flatter. I took her to the vet, full of determination not to have her put down. A bird flew in with us and was fluttering all over the waiting-room. The receptionist did nothing, hardly even looked up.

'That bird must want to see the vet,' I commented. No reply.

'It seems to be sick,' I mentioned. Nothing.

When a lame bird presents itself at a veterinary establishment and displays its need for medical treatment all round the waiting-room, you'd expect and appreciate some response from the people soon to be engaged in taking the rectal temperature of your cat. That was apparently asking too much.

The vet said the cat's kidneys had shrivelled up, and that she didn't have long to live. When I got out into the waiting-room, I had an urge to enquire about the bird again. The bird, I was told, was now by the receptionist's feet, behind a waste-bin, still fluttering to and fro, ignored.

Since Mum's death, I'd taken up an old secret habit again. When I was a child I used to wrap up my favourite dolls and dolls' furniture into tiny parcels, put them in boxes and wrap them some more. Then I would unwrap them, pretending to be a different person at each layer and disappointed by finding nothing. Finally I would be the lucky one, and take the useful toy out of the debris.

Now I started going to toy shops and buying small dolls and dolls' furniture, and sent the packages off into the void, to addresses in the phone book. A few doll limbs and a doll settee for instance, or just a doll's head and a miniature lampshade rattling around in a box. I envied the people who received these curious products of my generosity, that were somehow keeping me in contact with the outside world. I placed them on the Post Office scales with pride and wished somebody would send *me* one.

One day I was sitting in the park, beside a pond. The sun was shining hard on the water. Suddenly the water began to bubble, a slow simmer. Big glops rose to the surface in astonishment at being disturbed. I decided to save what was left of my sandwich and include it in a parcel, as symbolic of that interesting disturbance. I thought it might be nice if the package arrived with mould filling the sad empty spaces around the objects. And so the packages developed.

Friends and neighbours were always coming over to see how I was doing now without my mother. Wild parties and all. They cried and said they missed her. They waited for an echo from me of similar sentiments. Sadness and badness were what they were after. They thought I ought to feel pretty guilty about being the only one left in the flat alive. Even the cat had kicked the bucket by then. And there I was, surviving. Alive and well and able to fart. I would sit with them, surrounded by pale blue kitchen cupboards, just concentrating on controlling my rectum for however long it took them to get out of my flat.

In an old writing box I found a bunch of ancient letters from the only man my mother had ever loved, somebody she knew before my father. The love of her life was an artist. He used to come into the café where she worked. She didn't tell me much except that it took him a long time to tell her he was already engaged to some rich girl whose father had made a lot of money out of parking meters. In fact he'd been knighted for bringing the parking meter over from America.

The creep's pictures were probably lousy and he needed the money. After he got married he still carried on seeing my mother until she decided it was immoral and gave him the old heave-ho.

The letters were all excuses, how he couldn't make it that day because he was so busy painting or something. Wishy-washy, vaguely affectionate letters.

Reading them, I noticed I was beginning to seethe. The flatulence had travelled upwards and turned into steam. My forehead was hot and my mouth was dry. The steam must have been coming out of my ears. I sat cross-legged on the floor, thinking of my mother's painterly paramour. She hadn't heard a peep out of him in years. He lived nearby but hadn't visited her since her first stroke. And it would have made her so happy. Her last years. The cad. The fucker. The ubiquitous shit smell down-under disappeared as I felt something harden within me. It was resolve.

I prepared a package for him. I peeled grapes for eyeballs, poured in some tinned spaghetti for brains, and stuffed some thin young Cindy doll legs into the mess, and sent it. This time I put my address on it. I hoped his conscience might be stirred.

Within days, there was a letter in his familiar handwriting. The cad. He liked it. He thought my package was some kind of Performance Art. He said he'd known my mother. What an understatement. The fucker.

We met for lunch at a fancy restaurant of his choice, presumably paid for by the fucking wife. I ordered poached salmon, my mother's favourite treat, and so did he, the fucking deserter, who'd poached and run. And we talked about my mother. Nice wishy-washy vaguely affectionate things. I noticed he was rather handsome as he gobbled that salmon a little too fast. My mother had good taste.

'A good woman,' he was saying, patronizingly.

'But not the one for you.'

This surprised him.

'Not good enough for you, was she? Especially when she got sick.'

'Now, look, your mother and I had broken up long before that, in fact before I got married of course.'

'Because she wasn't good enough, she wasn't a painter or a parking meter.'

'Grrrargh,' was his reply, as he'd just choked on a fish bone. He then went pink and didn't breathe. He looked at me with big eyes, his body heaving and not breathing. The restaurant was noisy and nobody noticed. It was a nice moment. But then I got worried. He was so good-looking, and what if he never painted again? Perhaps it would be a loss to the world. Who knows? Even a shit like that might be worth something somewhere.

So I got up and walked behind his chair, clasped my hands in front of his chest and gave him a good strong squeeze. He issued a loud heave and a big fish bone landed on top of my salmon. In his relief, he thanked me profusely in between glugs of water. We parted quite amicably.

He came to see me once more after that. No longer because he thought I was a great Performance Artist, but just to say 'thank you' again. He brought me red roses, as if we were lovers or something. And he looked over the flat, as if he'd been there before. He was studying the family photos on the wall as he passed me. I was in my armchair. So I touched his leg. I liked him. He stood still then, so I continued with both hands, running them up his legs. He pulled me up by my arms and looked straight in my eyes, and said jovially, 'Your eyelids are fluttering just like your mother's used to. Amazing. All that fluttering and the mouth puckered up ready for my little offerings to the shrine. No man could have given that woman enough.'

I remembered the feeling of my fists in his stomach and wanted it again. But I missed and he laughed. He was expert at defending himself. I punched and even kicked, and got nowhere, not a single strike.

He shoved me back into the armchair and adjusted his clothes a bit. A vain man.

'I was hoping you might show me some of those letters you found, actually,' he said as if we were two civilized people.

The letters that I'd already burnt, a voodoo rite before I'd even met him. I didn't say anything. I felt like farting and I wanted him out of there.

'I'd like you to go.'

'Yes, that does sound an appealing idea. Never liked this depressing little place.'

At the door, I had another idea. 'Oh, the letters!' I said, running into the sitting-room. I reached under the armchair and it was still there.

'Here you are,' I said to him sweetly, and then slammed the door on him. Let him have it, the guilt package, filled with warm intestines, still warm from the kill. Wrapped so neatly in layer after layer of white paper. Wait till he opens that. Which I was never able to do.

I went into the kitchen and switched on the gas cooker without lighting it. I lay down on the floor, feeling purged. I'd done my duty by my mother. At last I could get on with my own life.

CHARLOTTE RIDDELL

A Terrible Vengeance

Chapter 1
Very Strange

Round Dockett Point and over Dumsey Deep the water-lilies were blooming as luxuriantly as though the silver Thames had been the blue Mummel Lake.

It was the time for them. The hawthorn had long ceased to scent the air; the wild roses had shed their delicate leaves; the buttercups and cardamoms and dog-daisies that had dotted the meadows were garnered into hay. The world in early August needed a fresh and special beauty, and here it was floating in its matchless green bark on the bosom of the waters.

If those fair flowers, like their German sisters, ever at nightfall assumed mortal form, who was there to tell of such vagaries? Even when the moon is at her full there are few who care to cross Chertsey Mead, or face the lonely Stabbery.

Hard would it be, indeed, so near life, railways, civilization, and London, to find a more lonely stretch of country, when twilight visits the landscape and darkness comes brooding down over the Surrey and Middlesex shores, than the path which winds along the river from Shepperton Lock to Chertsey Bridge. At high noon for months together it is desolate beyond description – silent, save for the rippling and sobbing of the currents, the wash of the stream, the swaying of the osiers, the trembling of an aspen, the rustle of the withies, or the noise made by a bird, or rat, or stoat, startled by the sound of unwonted footsteps. In the warm summer nights also, when tired holiday-makers are sleeping soundly, when men stretched on the green sward outside their white tents are smoking, and talking, and planning excursions for the morrow; when in country houses young people are playing and singing, dancing or walking up and down terraces over-looking well-kept lawns, where the evening air is laden with delicious perfumes – there falls on that almost uninhabited mile or two of riverside a stillness which may be felt, which the belated traveller is loth to disturb even by the dip of his oars as he drifts down with the current past objects that seem to him unreal as fragments of a dream.

It had been a wet summer – a bad summer for the hotels. There had been some fine days, but not many together. The weather could not be depended upon. It was not a season in which young ladies were to be met about the reaches of the Upper Thames, disporting themselves in marvellous dresses, and more marvellous headgear, unfurling brilliant parasols, canoeing in appropriate attire, giving life and colour to the streets of old-world villages, and causing many of their inhabitants to consider what a very strange sort of town it must be in which such extraordinarily-robed persons habitually reside.

Nothing of the sort was to be seen that summer, even as high as Hampton. Excursions were limited to one day; there were few tents, few people camping-out, not many staying at the hotels; yet it was, perhaps for that reason, an enjoyable summer to those who were not afraid of a little, or rather a great deal, of rain, who liked a village inn all the better for not being crowded, and who were not heartbroken because their women-folk for once found it impossible to accompany them.

Unless a man boldly decides to outrage the proprieties and decencies of life, and go off by himself to take his pleasure selfishly alone, there is in a fine summer no door of escape open to him. There was a time – a happy time – when a husband was not expected to sign away his holidays in the marriage articles. But what boots it to talk of that remote past now? Everything is against the father of a family at present. Unless the weather help him, what friend has he? and the weather does not often in these latter days prove a friend.

In that summer, however, with which this story deals, the stars in their courses fought for many an oppressed paterfamilias. Any curious inquirer might then have walked ankle-deep in mud from Penton Hook to East Molesey, and not met a man, harnessed like a beast of burden, towing all his belongings up stream, or beheld him rowing against wind and tide as though he were a galley-slave chained to the oar, striving all the while to look as though enjoying the fun.

Materfamilias found it too wet to patronize the Thames. Her dear little children also were conspicuous by their absence. Charming young ladies were rarely to be seen – indeed, the skies were so treacherous that it would have been a mere tempting of Providence to risk a pretty dress on the water; for which sufficient reasons furnished houses remained unlet, and lodgings were left empty; taverns and hotels welcomed visitors instead of treating them scurvily; and the river, with its green banks and its leafy aits, its white swans, its water-lilies, its purple loosestrife, its reeds, its rushes, its weeping willows, its quiet backwaters, was delightful.

One evening two men stood just outside the door of the Ship, Lower

Halliford, looking idly at the water, as it flowed by more rapidly than is usually the case in August. Both were dressed in suits of serviceable dark grey tweed; both wore round hats; both evidently belonged to that class which resembles the flowers of the field but in the one respect that it toils not, neither does it spin; both looked intensely bored; both were of rather a good appearance.

The elder, who was about thirty, had dark hair, sleepy brown eyes, and a straight capable nose; a heavy moustache almost concealed his mouth, but his chin was firm and well cut. About him there was an indescribable something calculated to excite attention, but nothing in his expression to attract or repel. No one looking at him could have said offhand, 'I think that is a pleasant fellow,' or 'I am sure that man could make himself confoundedly disagreeable.'

His face revealed as little as the covers of a book. It might contain interesting matter, or there might be nothing underneath save the merest commonplace. So far as it conveyed an idea at all, it was that of indolence. Every movement of his body suggested laziness; but it would have been extremely hard to say how far that laziness went. Mental energy and physical inactivity walk oftener hand in hand than the world suspects, and mental energy can on occasion make an indolent man active, while mere brute strength can never confer intellect on one who lacks brains.

In every respect the younger stranger was the opposite of his companion. Fair, blue-eyed, light-haired, with soft moustache and tenderly cared-for whiskers, he looked exactly what he was — a very shallow, kindly, good fellow, who did not trouble himself with searching into the depths of things, who took the world as it was, who did not go out to meet trouble, who loved his species, women included, in an honest way; who liked amusement, athletic sports of all sorts — dancing, riding, rowing, shooting; who had not one regret, save that hours in a Government office were so confoundedly long, 'eating the best part out of a day, by Jove;' no cause for discontent, save that he had very little money, and into whose mind it had on the afternoon in question been forcibly borne that his friend was a trifle heavy — 'carries too many guns,' he considered — and not exactly the man to enjoy a modest dinner at Lower Halliford.

For which cause, perhaps, he felt rather relieved when his friend refused to partake of any meal.

'I wish you could have stayed,' said the younger, with that earnest and not quite insincere hospitality people always assume when they feel a departing guest is not to be overpersuaded to stay.

'So do I,' replied the other. 'I should have liked to stop with *you*, and I should have liked to stay here. There is a sleepy dullness about the place which exactly suits my present mood, but I must get back to town. I promised Travers to look in at his chambers this evening, and tomorrow as I told you, I am due in Norfolk.'

'What will you do, then, till train-time? There is nothing up from here till nearly seven. Come on the river for an hour with me.'

'Thank you, no. I think I will walk over to Staines.'

'Staines! Why Staines in heaven's name?'

'Because I am in the humour for a walk – a long, lonely walk; because a demon has taken possession of me I wish to exorcise; because there are plenty of trains from Staines; because I am weary of the Thames Valley line, and any other reason you like. I can give you none better than I have done.'

'At least let me row you part of the way.'

'Again thank you, no. The eccentricities of the Thames are not new to me. With the best intentions, you would land me at Laleham when I should be on my (rail) way to London. My dear Dick, step into that boat your soul has been hankering after for the past half-hour, and leave me to return to town according to my own fancy.'

'I don't half like this,' said genial Dick. 'Ah! here comes a pretty girl – look.'

Thus entreated, the elder man turned his head and saw a young girl, accompanied by a young man, coming along the road, which leads from Walton Lane to Shepperton.

She was very pretty, of the sparkling order of beauty, with dark eyes, rather heavy eyebrows, dark thick hair, a ravishing fringe, a delicious hat, a coquettish dress, and shoes which by pretty gestures she seemed to be explaining to her companion were many – very many – sizes too large for her. Spite of her beauty, spite of her dress, spite of her shoes so much too large for her, it needed but a glance from one conversant with subtle social distinctions to tell that she was not quite her 'young man's' equal.

For, in the parlance of Betsy Jane, as her 'young man' she evidently regarded him, and as her young man he regarded himself. There could be no doubt about the matter. He was over head and ears in love with her; he was ready to quarrel – indeed, had quarrelled with father, mother, sister, brother on her account. He loved her unreasonably – he loved her miserably, distractedly; except at odd intervals, he was not in the least happy with her. She flouted, she tormented, she maddened him; but then, after having nearly driven him to the verge of distraction, she would repent sweetly, and make up for all previous shortcomings by a few brief minutes of tender affection. If quarrelling be really the renewal of love, theirs had been renewed once a day at all events, and frequently much oftener.

Yes, she was a pretty girl, a bewitching girl, an arrant flirt, a scarcely well-behaved coquette; for as she passed the two friends she threw a glance at them, one arch, piquant, inviting glance, of which many would instantly have availed themselves, venturing the consequences certain to be dealt out by her companion, who, catching the look, drew closer to her side, not too well pleased, apparently. Spite of a little opposition, he drew her hand through his arm, and walked on with an air of possession infinitely amusing to onlookers, and plainly distasteful to his lady-love.

'A clear case of spoons,' remarked the younger of the two visitors, looking after the pair.

'Poor devil!' said the other compassionately.

His friend laughed, and observed mockingly paraphrasing a very different speech,

'But for the grace of God, there goes Paul Murray.'

'You may strike out the "but,"' replied the person so addressed, 'for that is the very road Paul Murray is going, and soon.'

'You are not serious!' asked the other doubtfully.

'Am I not? I am though, though not with such a vixen as I dare swear that little baggage is. I told you I was due tomorrow in Norfolk. But see, they are turning back; let us go inside.'

'All right,' agreed the other, following his companion into the hall. 'This is a great surprise to me, Murray: I never imagined you were engaged.'

'I am not engaged yet, though no doubt I shall soon be,' answered the reluctant lover. 'My grandmother and the lady's father have arranged the match. The lady does not object, I believe, and who am I, Savill, that I should refuse good looks, a good fortune, and a good temper?'

'You do not speak as though you liked the proposed bride, nevertheless,' said Mr Savill dubiously.

'I do not dislike her, I only hate having to marry her. Can't you understand that a man wants to pick a wife for himself – that the one girl he fancies seems worth ten thousand of a girl anybody else fancies? But I am so situated – Hang it, Dick! what are you staring at that dark-eyed witch for?'

'Because it is so funny. She is making him take a boat at the steps, and he does not want to do it. Kindly observe his face.'

'What is his face to me?' retorted Mr Murray savagely.

'Not much, I daresay, but it is a good deal to him. It is black as thunder, and hers is not much lighter. What a neat ankle, and how you like to show it, my dear. Well, there is no harm in a pretty ankle or a pretty foot either, and you have both. One would not wish one's wife to have a hoof like an elephant. What sort of feet has your destined maiden, Paul?'

'I never noticed.'

'That looks deucedly bad,' said the younger man, shaking his head.

'I know, however, she has a pure, sweet face,' observed Mr Murray gloomily.

'No one could truthfully make the same statement about our young friend's little lady,' remarked Mr Savill, still gazing at the girl, who was seating herself in the stern. 'A termagant, I'll be bound, if ever there was one. Wishes to go up stream, no doubt because he wishes to go down. Any caprice about the Norfolk "fair"?'

'Not much, I think. She is good, Dick – too good for me,' replied the other, sauntering out again.

'That is what we always say about the things we do not know. And so your grandmother has made up the match?'

'Yes: there is money, and the old lady loves money. She says she wants to see me settled – talks of buying me an estate. She will have to do something, because I am sure the stern parent on the other side would not allow his daughter to marry on expectations. The one drop of comfort in the arrangement is that my aged relative will have to come down, and pretty smartly too. I would wed Hecate, to end this state of bondage, which I have not courage to flee from myself. Dick, how I envy you who have no dead person's shoes to wait for!'

'You need not envy me,' returned Dick, with conviction, 'a poor unlucky devil chained to a desk. There is scarce a day of my life I fail to curse the service, the office, and Fate – '

'Curse no more, then,' said the other; 'rather go down on your knees and thank Heaven you have, without any merit of your own, a provision for life. I wish Fate or anybody had coached me into the Civil Service – apprenticed me to a trade – sent me to sea – made me enlist, instead of leaving me at the mercy of an old lady who knows neither justice nor reason – who won't let me do anything for myself, and won't do anything for me – who ought to have been dead long ago, but who never means to die – '

'And who often gives you in one cheque as much as the whole of my annual salary,' added the other quietly.

'But you know you will have your yearly salary as long as you live. I never know whether I shall have another cheque.'

'It won't do, my friend,' answered Dick Savill; 'you feel quite certain you can get money when you want it.'

'I feel certain of no such thing,' was the reply. 'If I once offended her – ' he stopped, and then went on: 'And perhaps when I have spent twenty years in trying to humour such caprices as surely woman never had before, I shall wake one morning to find she has left every penny to the Asylum for Idiots.'

'Why do you not pluck up courage, and strike out some line for yourself?'

'Too late, Dick, too late. Ten years ago I might have tried to make a fortune for myself, but I can't do that now. As I have waited so long, I must wait a little longer. At thirty a man can't take pick in hand and try to clear a road to fortune.'

'Then you had better marry the Norfolk young lady.'

'I am steadily determined to do so. I am going down with the firm intention of asking her.'

'And do you think she will have you?'

'I think so. I feel sure she will. And she is a nice girl – the sort I would like for a wife, if she had not been thrust upon me.'

Mr Savill stood silent for a moment, with his hands plunged deep in his pockets.

'Then when I see you next?' he said tentatively.

'I shall be engaged, most likely – possibly even married,' finished the other, with as much hurry as his manner was capable of. 'And now jump into your boat, and I will go on my way to – Staines – '

'I wish you would change your mind, and have some dinner.'

'I can't; it is impossible. You see I have so many things to do and to think of. Goodbye, Dick. Don't upset yourself – go down stream, and don't get into mischief with those dark eyes you admired so much just now.'

'Make your mind easy about that,' returned the other, colouring, however, a little as he spoke. 'Goodbye, Murray. I wish you well through the campaign.' And so, after a hearty handshake, they parted, one to walk away from Halliford, and past Shepperton Church, and across Shepperton Range, and the other, of course, to row up stream, through Shepperton Lock, and on past Dockett Point.

In the grey of the summer's dawn, Mr Murray awoke next morning from a terrible dream. He had kept his appointment with Mr Travers and a select party, played heavily, drank deeply, and reached home between one and two, not much the better for his trip to Lower Halliford, his walk, and his carouse.

Champagne, followed by neat brandy, is not perhaps the best thing to insure a quiet night's rest; but Mr Murray had often enjoyed sound repose after similar libations; and it was, therefore, all the more unpleasant that in the grey dawn he should wake suddenly from a dream, in which he thought some one was trying to crush his head with a heavy weight.

Even when he had struggled from sleep, it seemed to him that a wet dead hand lay across his eyes, and pressed them so hard he could not move the lids. Under the weight he lay powerless, while a damp, ice-cold hand felt burning into his brain, if such a contradictory expression may be permitted.

The perspiration was pouring from him; he felt the drops falling on his throat, and trickling down his neck; he might have been lying in a bath, instead of on his own bed, and it was with a cry of horror he at last flung the hand aside, and, sitting up, looked around the room, into which the twilight of morning was mysteriously stealing.

Then, trembling in every limb, he lay down again, and fell into another sleep, from which he did not awake till aroused by broad daylight and his valet.

145

'You told me to call you in good time, sir,' said the man.

'Ah, yes, so I did,' yawned Mr Murray. 'What a bore! I will get up directly. You can go, Davis. I will ring if I want you.'

Davis was standing, as his master spoke, looking down at the floor.

'Yes, sir,' he answered, after the fashion of a man who has something on his mind – and went.

He had not, however, got to the bottom of the first flight when peal after peal summoned him back.

Mr Murray was out of bed, and in the middle of the room, the ghastly pallor of his face brought into full prominence by the crimson dressing-gown he had thrown round him on rising.

'What is that?' he asked. 'What in the world is that, Davis?' and he pointed to the carpet, which was covered, Mrs Murray being an old-fashioned lady, with strips of white drugget.

'I am sure I do not know, sir,' answered Davis. 'I noticed it the moment I came into the room. Looks as if some one with wet feet had been walking round and round the bed.'

It certainly did. Round and round, to and fro, backwards and forwards, the feet seemed to have gone and come, leaving a distinct mark wherever they pressed.

'The print is that of a rare small foot, too,' observed Davis, who really seemed half stupefied with astonishment.

'But who would have dared – ' began Mr Murray.

'No one in this house,' declared Davis stoutly. 'It is not the mark of a boy or woman inside these doors;' and then the master and the man looked at each other for an instant with grave suspicion.

But for that second they kept their eyes thus occupied; then, as by common consent, they dropped their glances to the floor. 'My God!' exclaimed Davis. 'Where have the footprints gone?'

He might well ask. The drugget, but a moment before wet and stained by the passage and repassage of those small restless feet, was now smooth and white, as when first sent forth from the bleach-green. On its polished surface there could not be discerned a speck or mark.

Chapter 2

Where is Lucy?

In the valley of the Thames early hours are the rule. There the days have an unaccountable way of lengthening themselves out which makes it prudent, as well as pleasant, to utilize all the night in preparing for a longer morrow.

For this reason, when eleven o'clock p.m. strikes, it usually finds Church

Street, Walton, as quiet as its adjacent graveyard, which lies still and solemn under the shadow of the old grey tower hard by that ancient vicarage which contains so beautiful a staircase.

About the time when Mr Travers' friends were beginning their evening, when talk had abated and play was suggested, the silence of Church Street was broken and many a sleeper aroused by a continuous knocking at the door of a house as venerable as any in that part of Walton. Rap – rap – rap – rap awoke the echoes of the old-world village street, and at length brought to the window a young man, who, flinging up the sash, inquired,

'Who is there?'

'Where is Lucy? What have you done with my girl?' answered a strained woman's voice from out the darkness of that summer night.

'Lucy?' repeated the young man; 'is not she at home?'

'No; I have never set eyes on her since you went out together.'

'Why, we parted hours ago. Wait a moment, Mrs Heath; I will be down directly.'

No need to tell the poor woman to 'wait.' She stood on the step, crying softly and wringing her hands till the door opened, and the same young fellow who with the pretty girl had taken boat opposite the Ship Hotel bade her 'Come in.'

Awakened from some pleasant dream, spite of all the trouble and hurry of that unexpected summons, there still shone the light of a reflected sunshine in his eyes and the flush of happy sleep on his cheek. He scarcely understood yet what had happened, but when he saw Mrs Heath's tear-stained face, comprehension came to him, and he said abruptly,

'Do you mean that she has never returned home?'

'Never!'

They were in the parlour by this time, and looking at each other by the light of one poor candle which he had set down on the table.

'Why, I left her,' he said, 'I left her long before seven.'

'Where?'

'Just beyond Dockett Point. She would not let me row her back. I do not know what was the matter with her, but nothing I did seemed right.'

'Had you any quarrel?' asked Mrs Heath anxiously.

'Yes, we had; we were quarrelling all the time – at least she was with me; and at last she made me put her ashore, which I did sorely against my will.'

'What had you done to my girl, then?'

'I prayed of her to marry me – no great insult, surely, but she took it as one. I would rather not talk of what she answered. Where can she be? Do you think she can have gone to her aunt's?'

'If so, she will be back by the last train. Let us get home as fast as possible. I never thought of that. Poor child! she will go out of her mind if she finds nobody to let her in. You will come with me. O, if she is not there, what shall I do – what ever shall I do?'

The young man had taken his hat, and was holding the door open for Mrs Heath to pass out.

'You must try not to fret yourself,' he said gently, yet with a strange repression in his voice. 'Very likely she may stay at her aunt's all night.'

'And leave me in misery, not knowing where she is? Oh, Mr Grantley, I could never believe that.'

Mr Grantley's heart was very hot within him; but he could not tell the poor mother he believed that when Lucy's temper was up she would think of no human being but herself.

'Won't you take my arm, Mrs Heath?' he asked with tender pity. After all, though everything was over between him and Lucy, her mother could not be held accountable for their quarrel; and he had loved the girl with all the romantic fervour of love's young dream.

'I can walk faster without it, thank you,' Mrs Heath answered. 'But Mr Grantley, whatever you and Lucy fell out over, you'll forget it, won't you? It isn't in you to be hard on anybody, and she's only a spoiled child. I never had but the one, and I humoured her too much; and if she is wayward, it is all my own fault – all my own.'

'In case she does not return by this train,' said the young man, wisely ignoring Mrs Heath's inquiry, 'had I not better telegraph to her aunt directly the office opens?'

'I will be on my way to London long before that,' was the reply. 'But what makes you think she won't come? Surely you don't imagine she has done anything rash?'

'What do you mean by rash?' he asked evasively.

'Made away with herself.'

'*That!*' he exclaimed. 'No, I feel very sure she has done nothing of the sort.'

'But she might have felt sorry when you left her – vexed for having angered you – heartbroken when she saw you leave her.'

'Believe me, she was not vexed or sorry or heartbroken; she was only glad to know she had done with me,' he answered bitterly.

'What has come to you, Mr Grantley?' said Mrs Heath, in wonder. 'I never heard you speak the same before.'

'Perhaps not; I never felt the same before. It is best to be plain with you,' he went on. 'All is at an end between us; and that is what your daughter has long been trying for.'

'How can you say that, and she so fond of you?'

'She has not been fond of me for many a day. The man she wants to marry is not a poor fellow like myself, but one who can give her carriages and horses, and a fine house, and as much dress as she cares to buy.'

'But where could she ever find a husband able to do that?'

'I do not know, Mrs Heath. All I do know is that she considers I am no match for her; and now my eyes are opened, I see she was not a wife for me. We should never have known a day's happiness.'

It was too dark to see his face, but his changed voice and words and manner told Lucy's mother the kindly lad, who a couple of years before came courting her pretty daughter, and offended all his friends for her sake, was gone away for ever. It was a man who walked by her side – who had eaten of the fruit of the tree, and had learned to be as a god, knowing good from evil.

'Well, well,' she said brokenly, 'you are the best judge, I suppose; but O, my child, my child!'

She was so blinded with tears she stumbled, and must have fallen had he not caught and prevented her. Then he drew her hand within his arm, and said,

'I am so grieved for you. I never received anything but kindness from you.'

'And indeed,' she sobbed, 'you never were anything except good to me. I always knew we couldn't be considered your equals, and I often had my doubts whether it was right to let you come backwards and forwards as I did, parting you from all belonging to you. But I thought, when your mother saw Lucy's pretty face – for it is pretty, Mr Grantley – '

'There never was a prettier,' assented the young man, though, now his eyes were opened, he knew Lucy's beauty would scarcely have recommended her to any sensible woman.

'I hoped she might take to her, and I'd never have intruded. And I was so proud and happy, and fond of you – I was indeed; and I used to consider how, when you came down, I could have some little thing you fancied. But that's all over now. And I don't blame you; only my heart is sore and troubled about my foolish girl.'

They were on Walton Bridge by this time, and the night air blew cold and raw down the river, and made Mrs Heath shiver.

'I wonder where Lucy is,' she murmured, 'and what she'd think if she knew her mother was walking through the night in an agony about her? Where was it you said you left her?'

'Between Dockett Point and Chertsey. I shouldn't have left her had she not insisted on my doing so.'

'Isn't that the train?' asked Mrs Heath, stopping suddenly short and listening intently.

'Yes; it is just leaving Sunbury Station. Do not hurry; we have plenty of time.'

They had: they were at Lucy's home, one of the small houses situated

149

between Battlecreese Hill and the Red Lion in Lower Halliford, before a single passenger came along The Green, or out of Nannygoat Lane.

'My heart misgives me that she has not come down,' said Mrs Heath.

'Shall I go up to meet her?' asked the young man; and almost before the mother feverishly assented, he was striding through the summer night to Shepperton Station, where he found the lights extinguished and every door closed.

Chapter 3

Poor Mrs Heath

By noon the next day every one in Shepperton and Lower Halliford knew Lucy Heath was 'missing.'

Her mother had been up to Putney, but Lucy was not with her aunt, who lived not very far from the Bridge on the Fulham side, and who, having married a fruiterer and worked up a very good business, was inclined to take such bustling and practical views of life and its concerns as rather dismayed her sister-in-law, who had spent so many years in the remote country, and then so many other years in quiet Shepperton, that Mrs Pointer's talk flurried her almost as much as the noise of London, which often maddens middle-aged and elderly folk happily unaccustomed to its roar.

Girt about with a checked apron which lovingly enfolded a goodly portion of her comfortable figure, Mrs Pointer received her early visitor with the sportive remark, 'Why, it's never Martha Heath! Come along in; a sight of you is good for sore eyes.'

But Mrs Heath repelled all such humorous observations, and chilled those suggestions of hospitality the Pointers were never backward in making by asking in a low choked voice,

'Is Lucy here?'

'Lor! whatever put such a funny notion into your head?'

'Ah! I see she is,' trying to smile. 'After all, she spent the night with you.'

'Did what?' exclaimed Mrs Pointer. 'Spent the night – was that what you said? No, nor the day either, for this year nearly. Why, for the last four months she hasn't set foot across that doorstep, unless it might be to buy some cherries, or pears, or apples, or grapes, or suchlike, and then she came in with more air than any lady; and after paying her money and getting her goods went out again, just as if I hadn't been her father's sister and Pointer my husband. But there! for any sake, woman, don't look like that! Come into the parlour and tell me what is wrong. You never mean she has gone away and left you?'

Poor Mrs Heath was perfectly incapable at that moment of saying what she did mean. Seated on a stool, and holding fast by the edge of the counter for fear of falling, the shop and its contents, the early buses, the people going along the pavement, the tradesmen's carts, the private carriages, were, as in some terrible nightmare, gyrating before her eyes. She could not speak, she could scarcely think, until that wild whirligig came to a stand. For a minute or two even Mrs Pointer seemed multiplied by fifty; while her checked apron, the bananas suspended from hooks, the baskets of fruit, the pineapples, the melons, the tomatoes, and the cob-nuts appeared and disappeared, only to reappear and disappear like the riders in a maddening giddy-go-round.

'Give me a drop of water,' she said at last; and when the water was brought she drank a little and poured some on her handkerchief and dabbed her face, and finally suffered herself to be escorted into the parlour, where she told her tale, interrupted by many sobs. It would have been unchristian in Mrs Pointer to exult; but it was only human to remember she had remarked to Pointer, in that terrible spirit of prophecy bestowed for some inscrutable reason on dear friends and close relations, she knew some such trouble must befall her sister-in-law.

'You made an idol of that girl, Martha,' she went on, 'and now it is coming home to you. I am sure it was only last August as ever was that Pointer – But here he is, and he will talk to you himself.'

Which Mr Pointer did, being very fond of the sound of his own foolish voice. He stated how bad a thing it was for people to be above their station or to bring children up above that rank of life in which it had pleased God to place them. He quoted many pleasing saws uttered by his father and grandfather; remarked that as folks sowed they were bound to reap; reminded Mrs Heath they had the word of Scripture for the fact – than, which, parenthetically, no fact could be truer, as he knew – that a man might not gather grapes from thorns or even figs from thistles. Further he went on to observe generally – the observation having a particular reference to Lucy – that it did not do to judge things by their looks. Over and over again salesmen had tried to 'shove off a lot of foreign fruit on him, but he wasn't a young bird to be taken in by that chaff.' No; what he looked to was quality; it was what his customers expected from him, and what he could honestly declare his customers got. He was a plain man, and he thought honesty was the best policy. So as Mrs Heath had seen fit to come to them in her trouble he would tell her what he thought, without beating about the bush. He believed Lucy had 'gone off.'

'But where?' asked poor Mrs Heath.

'That I am not wise enough to say; but you'll find she's gone off. Girls in her station don't sport chains and bracelets and brooches for nothing – '

'But they did not cost many shillings,' interposed the mother.

'She might tell you that,' observed Mrs Pointer, with a world of meaning.

'To say nothing,' went on Mr Pointer, 'of grey gloves she could not abear to be touched. One day she walked in when I was behind the counter, and, not knowing she had been raised to the peerage, I shook hands with her as a matter of course; but when I saw the young lady look at her glove as if I had dirtied it, I said "O, I beg your pardon, miss" – jocularly, you know. "They soil so easily," she lisped.'

'I haven't patience with such ways!' interpolated Mrs Pointer, without any lisp at all. 'Yes, it's hard for you, Martha, but you may depend Pointer's right. Indeed, I expected how it would be long ago. Young women who are walking in the straight road don't dress as Lucy dressed, or dare their innocent little cousins to call them by their Christian names in the street. Since the spring, and long before, Pointer and me has been sure Lucy was up to no good.'

'And you held your tongues and never said a word to me!' retorted Mrs Heath, goaded and driven to desperation.

'Much use it would have been saying any word to you,' answered Mrs Pointer. 'When you told me about young Grantley, and I bid you be careful, how did you take my advice? Why, you blared out at me, went on as if I knew nothing and had never been anywhere. What I told you then, though, I tell you now: young Grantleys, the sons of rectors and the grandsons of colonels, don't come after farmers' daughters with any honest purpose.'

'Yet young Grantley asked her last evening to fix a day for their marriage,' said Mrs Heath, with a little triumph.

'O, I daresay!' scoffed Mrs Pointer.

'Talk is cheap,' observed Mr Pointer.

'Some folks have more of it than money,' supplemented his wife.

'They have been, as I understand, keeping company for some time now,' said the fruiterer, with what he deemed a telling and judicial calmness. 'So if he asked her to name the day, why did she not name it?'

'I do not know. I have never seen her since.'

'O, then you had only his word about the matter,' summed up Mr Pointer. 'Just as I thought – just as I thought.'

'What did you think?' inquired the poor troubled mother.

'Why, that she has gone off with this Mr Grantley.'

'Ah, you don't know Mr Grantley, or you wouldn't say such a thing.'

'It is true,' observed Mr Pointer, 'that I do not know the gentleman, and, I may add, I do not want to know him; but speaking as a person acquainted with the world – '

'I'll be getting home,' interrupted Mrs Heath. 'Most likely my girl is there waiting for me, and a fine laugh she will have against her poor old mother for being in such a taking. Yes, Lucy will have the breakfast ready. No, thank you; I'll not wait to take anything. There will be a train back presently; and besides, to tell you the truth, food would choke me till I sit down again with my girl, and then I won't be able to eat for joy.'

Husband and wife looked at each other as Mrs Heath spoke, and for the moment a deep pity pierced the hard crust of their worldly egotism.

'Wait a minute,' cried Mrs Pointer, 'and I'll put on my bonnet and go with you.'

'No,' interrupted Mr Pointer, instantly seizing his wife's idea, and appropriating it as his own. 'I am the proper person to see this affair out. There is not much doing, and if there were, I would leave everything to obtain justice for your niece. After all, however wrong she may have gone, she is your niece, Maria.'

With which exceedingly nasty remark, which held a whole volume of unpleasant meaning as to what Mrs Pointer might expect from that relationship in the future, Mr Pointer took Mrs Heath by the arm, and piloted her out into the street, and finally to Lower Halliford, where the missing Lucy was not, and where no tidings of her had come.

Chapter 4

Mr Gage on Portents

About the time when poor distraught Mrs Heath, having managed to elude the vigilance of that cleverest of men, Maria Pointer's husband, had run out of her small house, and was enlisting the sympathies of gossip-loving Shepperton in Lucy's disappearance, Mr Paul Murray arrived at Liverpool Street Station, where his luggage and his valet awaited him.

'Get tickets, Davis,' he said; 'I have run it rather close;' and he walked towards Smith's stall, while his man went into the booking-office.

As he was about to descend the stairs, Davis became aware of a very singular fact. Looking down the steps, he saw precisely the same marks that had amazed him so short a time previously, being printed hurriedly off by a pair of invisible feet, which ran to the bottom and then flew as if in the wildest haste to the spot where Mr Murray stood.

'I am not dreaming, am I?' thought the man; and he shut his eyes and opened them again.

The footprints were all gone!

At that moment his master turned from the bookstall and proceeded towards the train. A porter opened the door of a smoking carriage, but Murray shook his head and passed on. Mr Davis, once more looking to the ground, saw that those feet belonging to no mortal body were still following. There were not very many passengers, and it was quite plain to him that wherever his master went, the quick, wet prints went too. Even on

153

the step of the compartment Mr Murray eventually selected the man beheld a mark, as though some one had sprung in after him. He secured the door, and then walked away, to find a place for himself, marvelling in a dazed state of mind what it all meant; indeed, he felt so much dazed that, after he had found a seat to his mind, he did not immediately notice an old acquaintance in the opposite corner, who affably inquired,

'And how is Mr Davis?'

Thus addressed, Mr Davis started from his reverie, and exclaimed,

'Why, bless my soul, Gage, who'd have thought of seeing you here?' after which exchange of courtesies the pair shook hands gravely and settled down to converse.

Mr Davis explained that he was going down with his governor to Norwich; and Mr Gage stated that he and the old General had been staying at Thorpe, and were on their way to Lowestoft. Mr Gage and his old General had also just returned from paying a round of visits in the West of England. 'Pleasant enough, but slow,' finished the gentleman's gentleman. 'After all, in the season or out of it, there is no place like London.'

With this opinion Mr Davis quite agreed, and said he only wished he had never to leave it, adding,

'We have not been away before for a long time; and we should not be going where we are now bound if we had not to humour some fancy of our grandmother's.'

'Deuced rough on a man having to humour a grandmother's fancy,' remarked Mr Gage.

'No female ought to be left the control of money,' said Mr Davis with conviction. 'See what the consequences have been in this case – Mrs Murray outlived her son, who had to ask her for every shilling he wanted, and she is so tough she may see the last of her grandson.'

'That is very likely,' agreed the other. 'He looks awfully bad.'

'You saw him just now, I suppose?'

'No; but I saw him last night at Chertsey Station, and I could but notice the change in his appearance.'

For a minute Mr Davis remained silent. 'Chertsey Station!' What could his master have been doing at Chertsey? That was a question he would have to put to himself again, and answer for himself at some convenient time; meanwhile he only answered,

'Yes, I observe an alteration in him myself. Anything fresh in the paper?'

'No,' answered Mr Gage, handing his friend the *Daily News* – the print he affected: 'everything is as dull as ditchwater.'

For many a mile Davis read or affected to read; then he laid the paper aside, and after passing his case, well filled with a tithe levied on Mr Murray's finest cigars, to Gage, began solemnly,

'I am going to ask you a curious question, Robert, as from man to man.'

'Ask on,' said Mr Gage, striking a match.

'Do you believe in warnings?'

The old General's gentleman burst out laughing. He was so tickled that he let his match drop from his fingers unapplied.

'I am afraid most of us have to believe in them, whether we like it or not,' he answered, when he could speak. 'Has there been some little difference between you and your governor, then?'

'You mistake,' was the reply. 'I did not mean warnings in the sense of notice, but warnings as warnings, you understand.'

'Bother me if I do! Yes, now I take you. Do I believe in "coming events casting shadows before," as some one puts it? Has any shadow of a coming event been cast across you?'

'No, nor across anybody, so far as I know; but I've been thinking the matter over lately, and wondering if there can be any truth in such notions.'

'What notions?'

'Why, that there are signs and suchlike sent when trouble is coming to any one.'

'You may depend it is right enough that signs and tokens are sent. Almost every good family has its special warning: one has its mouse, another its black dog, a third its white bird, a fourth its drummer-boy, and so on. There is no getting over facts, even if you don't understand them.'

'Well, it is very hard to believe.'

'There wouldn't be much merit in believing if everything were as plain as a pikestaff. You know what the Scotch minister said to his boy: "The very devils believe and tremble." You wouldn't be worse than a devil, would you?'

'Has any sign ever appeared to you?' asked Davis.

'Not exactly; but lots of people have told me they have to them; for instance, old Seal, who drove the Dowager Countess of Ongar till the day of her death, used to make our hair stand on end talking about phantom carriages that drove away one after another from the door of Hainault House, and wakened every soul on the premises, night after night till the old Earl died. It took twelve clergymen to lay the spirit.'

'I wonder one wasn't enough!' ejaculated Davis.

'There may have been twelve spirits, for all I know,' returned Gage, rather puzzled by this view of the question; 'but anyhow, there were twelve clergymen, with the bishop in his lawn sleeves chief among them. And I once lived with a young lady's-maid, who told me when she was a girl she made her home with her father's parents. On a winter's night, after everybody else had gone to bed, she sat up to make some girdle-bread – that is a sort of bread the people in Ireland, where she came from, bake over the fire on a round iron plate; with plenty of butter it is not bad eating. Well, as I was saying, she was quite alone; she had taken all the bread off, and was setting it up on edge to cool, supporting one piece against the other, two and two, when on the table where she was putting the cakes she saw one drop of blood fall, and then another, and then another, like the beginning of a shower.

'She looked to the ceiling, but could see nothing, and still the drops kept on falling slowly, slowly; and then she knew something had gone wrong with one dear to her; and she put a shawl over her head, and without saying a word to anybody, went through the loneliness and darkness of night all by herself to her father's.'

'She must have been a courageous girl,' remarked Mr Davis.

'She was, and I liked her well. But to the point. When she reached her destination she found her youngest brother dead. Now what do you make of that?'

'It's strange, but I suppose he would have died all the same if she had not seen the blood-drops, and I can't see any good seeing them did her. If she had reached her father's in time to bid brother goodbye, there would have been some sense in such a sign. As it is, it seems to me a lot of trouble thrown away.'

Mr Gage shook his head.

'What a sceptic you are, Davis! But there! London makes sceptics of the best of us. If you had spent a winter, as I did once, in the Highlands of Scotland, or heard the banshee wailing for the General's nephew in the county of Mayo, you wouldn't have asked what was the use of second sight or banshees. You would just have stood and trembled as I did many and many a time.'

'I might,' said Davis doubtfully, wondering what his friend would have thought of those wet little footprints. 'Hillo, here's Peterborough! Hadn't we better stretch our legs? and a glass of something would be acceptable.'

Of that glass, however, Mr Davis was not destined to partake.

'If one of you is Murray's man,' said the guard as they jumped out, 'he wants you.'

'I'll be back in a minute,' observed Mr Murray's man to his friend, and hastened off.

But he was not back in a minute; on the contrary, he never returned at all.

Chapter 5
Kiss Me

The first glance in his master's face filled Davis with a vague alarm. Gage's talk had produced an effect quite out of proportion to its merit, and a cold terror struck to the valet's heart as he thought there might, spite of his lofty scepticism, be something after all in the mouse, and the bird, and the drummer-boy, in the black dog, and the phantom carriages, and the spirits it required the united exertions of twelve clergymen (with the bishop in lawn sleeves among them) to lay; in Highland second sight and Irish banshees; and in little feet paddling round and about a man's bed and following wherever he went. What awful disaster could those footprints portend? Would the train be smashed up? Did any river lie before them? and if so, was the sign vouchsafed as a warning that they were likely to die by drowning? All these thoughts, and many more, passed through Davis' mind as he stood looking at his master's pallid face and waiting for him to speak.

'I wish you to come in here,' said Mr Murray after a pause, and with a manifest effort. 'I am not quite well.'

'Can I get you anything, sir?' asked the valet. 'Will you not wait and go by another train?'

'No; I shall be better presently; only I do not like being alone.'

Davis opened the door and entered the compartment. As he did so, he could not refrain from glancing at the floor, to see if those strange footsteps had been running races there.

'What are you looking for?' asked Mr Murray irritably. 'Have you dropped anything?'

'No, sir; O, no! I was only considering where I should be most out of the way.'

'There,' answered his master, indicating a seat next the window, and at the same time moving to one on the further side of the carriage. 'Let no one get in; say I am ill – mad; that I have scarlet fever – the plague – what you please.' And with this wide permission Mr Murray laid his legs across the opposite cushion, wrapped one rug round his shoulders and another round his body, turned his head aside, and went to sleep or seemed to do so.

'If he is going to die, I hope it will be considered in my wages, but I am afraid it won't. Perhaps it is the old lady; but that would be too good fortune,' reflected Davis; and then he fell 'a-thinkynge, a-thinkynge,' principally of Gage's many suggestions and those mysterious footprints, for which he kept at intervals furtively looking. But they did not appear; and at last the valet, worn out with vain conjections, dropped into a pleasant doze, from which he did not awake till they were nearing Norwich.

'We will go to an hotel till I find out what Mrs Murray's plans are,' said that lady's grandson when he found himself on the platform; and as if they had been only waiting this piece of information, two small invisible feet instantly skipped out of the compartment they had just vacated, and walked after Mr Murray, leaving visible marks at every step.

'Great heavens! what is the meaning of this?' mentally asked Davis, surprised by fright after twenty prayerless and scheming years into an exclamation which almost did duty for a prayer. For a moment he felt sick with terror; then clutching his courage with the energy of desperation, he remembered that though wet footprints might mean death and destruction to the Murrays, his own ancestral annals held no record of such a portent.

Neither did the Murrays', so far as he was aware, but then he was aware of very little about that family. If the Irish girl Gage spoke of was informed by drops of blood that her brother lay dead, why should not Mr Murray be made aware, through the token of these pattering footsteps, that he would very soon succeed to a large fortune?

Then any little extra attention Mr Davis showed his master *now* would be remembered in his wages.

It was certainly unpleasant to know these damp feet had come down from London, and were going to the hotel with them; but 'needs must' with a certain driver, and if portents and signs and warnings were made worth his while, Mr Davis conceived there might be advantages connected with them.

Accordingly, when addressing Mr Murray, his valet's voice assumed a more deferential tone than ever, and his manner became so respectfully tender, that onlookers rashly imagined the ideal master and the faithful servant of fiction had at last come in the flesh to Norwich. Davis' conduct was, indeed, perfect: devoted without being intrusive, he smoothed away all obstacles which could be smoothed, and even, by dint of a judicious two minutes alone with the doctor for whom he sent, managed the introduction of a useful sedative in some medicine, which the label stated was to be taken every four hours.

He saw to Mr Murray's rooms and Mr Murray's light repast, and then he waited on Mr Murray's grandmother, and managed that lady so adroitly, she at length forgave the offender for having caught a chill.

'Your master is always doing foolish things,' she said. 'It would have been much better had he remained even for a day or two in London rather than risk being laid up. However, you must nurse him carefully, and try to get him well enough to dine at Losdale Court on Monday. Fortunately tomorrow is Sunday, and he can take complete rest. Now Davis, remember I trust to you.'

'I will do my best, ma'am,' Davis said humbly, and went back to tell his master the interview had gone off without any disaster.

Then, after partaking of some mild refreshment, he repaired to bed in a dressing-room opening off Mr Murray's apartment, so that he might be within call and close at hand to administer those doses which were to be taken at intervals of four hours.

'I feel better tonight,' said Mr Murray last thing.

'It is this beautiful air, sir,' answered Davis, who knew it was the sedative. 'I hope you will be quite well in the morning.'

But in spite of the air, in the grey dawn Mr Murray had again a dreadful dream – a worse dream than that which laid its heavy hand on him in London. He thought he was by the riverside beyond Dockett Point – beyond where the water-lilies grow. To his right was a little grove of old and twisted willows guarding a dell strewed in dry seasons with the leaves of many autumns, but, in his dream, wet and sodden by reason of heavy rain. There in June wild roses bloomed; there in winter hips and haws shone ruddy against the snow. To his left flowed a turbid river – turbid with floods that had troubled its peace. On the other bank lay a stagnant length of Surrey, while close at hand the Middlesex portion of Chertsey Mead stretched in a hopeless flat on to the bridge, just visible in the early twilight of a summer's evening that had followed after a dull lowering day.

From out of the gathering gloom there advanced, walking perilously near to Dumsey Deep, a solitary female figure, who, when they met, said, 'So you've come at last;' after which night seemed to close around him, silence for a space to lay its hands upon him.

About the same time Davis was seeing visions also. He had lain long awake, trying to evolve order out of the day's chaos, but in vain. The stillness fretted him; the idea that even then those mysterious feet might in the darkness be printing their impress about his master's bed irritated his brain. Twice he got up to give that medicine ordered to be taken every four hours, but finding on each occasion Mr Murray sleeping quietly, he forbore to arouse him.

He heard hour after hour chime, and it was not till the first hint of dawn that he fell into a deep slumber. Then he dreamt about the subject nearest his heart – a public house.

He thought he had saved or gained enough to buy a roadside inn on which he had long cast eyes of affectionate regard – not in London, but not too far out: a delightful inn, where holiday-makers always stopped for refreshment, and sometimes for the day; an inn with a pretty old-fashioned garden filled with fruit trees and vegetables, with a grass-plot around which were erected little arbours, where people could have tea or stronger stimulants; a skittle-ground, where men could soon make themselves very thirsty; and many other advantages tedious to mention. He had the purchase-money in his pocket, and, having paid a deposit, was proceeding to settle the affair, merely diverging from his way to call on a young widow he meant to make Mrs Davis – a charming woman, who, having stood behind a bar before, seemed the very person to make the Wheatsheaf a triumphant success. He was talking to her sensibly, when suddenly she amazed him by saying, in a sharp, hurried voice, 'Kiss me, kiss me, kiss me!' three times over.

The request seemed so strange that he stood astounded, and then awoke to hear the same words repeated.

'Kiss me, kiss me, kiss me!' some one said distinctly in Mr Murray's room, the door of which stood open, and then all was quiet.

Only half awake, Davis sprang from his bed and walked across the floor, conceiving, so far as his brain was in a state to conceive anything, that his senses were playing him some trick.

'You won't?' said the voice again, in a tone which rooted him to the spot where he stood; 'and yet, as we are never to meet again, you might *kiss me once*,' the voice added caressingly, '*only once more.*'

'Who the deuce has he got with him now?' thought Davis; but almost before the question was shaped in his mind there came a choked, gasping cry of 'Unloose me, tigress, devil!' followed by a sound of desperate wrestling for life.

In a second, Davis was in the room. Through the white blinds light enough penetrated to show Mr Murray in the grip apparently of some invisible antagonist, who seemed to be strangling him.

To and fro from side to side the man and the unseen phantom went swaying in that awful struggle. Short and fast came Mr Murray's breath, while, making one supreme effort, he flung his opponent from him and sank back across the bed exhausted.

Wiping the moisture from his forehead, Davis, trembling in every limb, advanced to where his master lay, and found *he was fast asleep!*

Mr Murray's eyes were wide open, and he did not stir hand or foot while the man covered him up as well as he was able, and then looked timidly around, dreading to see the second actor in the scene just ended.

'I can't stand much more of this,' Davis exclaimed, and the sound of his own voice made him start.

There was brandy in the room which had been left over-night, and the man poured himself out and swallowed a glass of the liquor. He ventured to lift the blind and look at the floor, which was wet, as though buckets of water had been thrown over it, while the prints of little feet were everywhere.

Mr Davis took another glass of brandy. *That* had not been watered.

'Well, this is a start!' he said in his own simple phraseology. 'I wonder what the governor has been up to?'

For it was now borne in upon the valet's understanding that this warning was no shadow of any event to come, but the tell-tale ghost of some tragedy which could never be undone.

Chapter 6

Found Drowned

After such a dreadful experience it might have been imagined that Mr Murray would be very ill indeed; but what we expect rarely comes to pass, and though during the whole of Sunday and Monday Davis felt, as he expressed the matter, 'awfully shaky,' his master appeared well and in fair spirits.

He went to the Cathedral, and no attendant footsteps dogged him. On Monday he accompanied his grandmother to Losdale Court, where he behaved so admirably as to please even the lady on whose favour his income depended. He removed to a furnished house Mrs Murray had taken, and prepared to carry out her wishes. Day succeeded day and night to night, but neither by day nor night did Davis hear the sound of any ghostly voices or trace the print of any phantom foot.

Could it be that nothing more was to come of it – that the mystery was never to be elucidated but fade away as the marks of dainty feet had vanished from floor, pavement, steps, and platform?

The valet did not believe it; behind those signs made by nothing human lay some secret well worth knowing, but it had never been possible to know much about Mr Murray.

'He was so little of a gentleman' that he had no pleasant, careless ways. He did not leave his letters lying loose for all the world to read. He did not tear up papers, and toss them into a waste-paper basket. He had the nastiest practice of locking up and burning; and though it was Mr Davis' commendable custom to collect and preserve unconsidered odds and ends as his master occasionally left in his pockets, these, after all, were trifles light as air.

Nevertheless, as a straw shows how the wind blows, so that chance remark anent Chertsey Station made by Gage promised to provide a string on which to thread various little beads in Davis' possession.

The man took them out and looked at them: a woman's fall – white tulle, with black spots, smelling strongly of tobacco-smoke and musk; a receipt for a bracelet, purchased from an obscure jeweller; a Chertsey Lock ticket; and the return half of a first-class ticket from Shepperton to Waterloo, stamped with the date of the day before they left London.

At these treasures Davis looked long and earnestly.

'We shall see,' he remarked as he put them up again; 'there I think the scent lies hot.'

It could not escape the notice of so astute a servant that his master was unduly anxious for a sight of the London papers, and that he glanced through them eagerly for something he apparently failed to find – more, that he always laid the print aside with a sigh of relief. Politics did not seem to trouble him, or any public burning question.

'He has some burning question of his own,' thought the valet, though he mentally phrased his notion in different words.

Matters went on thus for a whole week. The doctor came and went and wrote prescriptions, for Mr Murray either was still ailing or chose to appear so. Davis caught a word or two which had reference to the patient's heart, and some shock. Then he considered that awful night, and wondered how he, who 'was in his sober senses, and wide awake, and staring,' had lived through it.

'My heart, and a good many other things, will have to be considered,' he said to himself. 'No wages could pay for what has been put upon me this week past. I wonder whether I ought to speak to Mr Murray now?'

Undecided on this point, he was still considering it when he called his master on the following Sunday morning. The first glance at the stained and polished floor decided him. Literally it was interlaced with footprints. The man's hand shook as he drew up the blind, but he kept his eyes turned on Mr Murray while he waited for orders, and walked out of the room when dismissed as though such marks had been matters of customary occurrence in a nineteenth-century bedroom.

No bell summoned him back on this occasion. Instead of asking for information, Mr Murray dropped into a chair and nerved himself to defy the inevitable.

Once again there came a pause. For three days nothing occurred; but on the fourth a newspaper and a letter arrived, both of which Davis inspected curiously. They were addressed in Mr Savill's handwriting, and they bore the postmark 'SHEPPERTON.'

The newspaper was enclosed in an ungummed wrapper, tied round with a piece of string. After a moment's reflection Davis cut that string, spread out the print, and beheld a column marked at top with three blue crosses, containing the account of an inquest held at the King's Head on a body found on the previous Sunday morning, close by the 'Tumbling Bay.'

It was that of a young lady who had been missing since the previous Friday week, and could only be identified by the clothes.

Her mother, who, in giving evidence, frequently broke down, told how her daughter on the evening in question went out for a walk and never returned. She did not wish to go, because her boots were being mended, and her shoes were too large. No doubt they had dropped off. She had very small feet, and it was not always possible to get shoes to fit them. She was engaged to be married to the gentleman with whom she went out. He told her they had quarrelled. She did not believe he could have anything to do with her child's death; but she did not know what to think. It had been said her girl was keeping company with somebody else, but that could not be true. Her girl was a good girl.

Yes; she had found a bracelet hidden away among her girl's clothes, and she could not say how she got the seven golden sovereigns that were in the purse, or the locket taken off the body; but her girl was a good girl, and she did not know whatever she would do without her, for Lucy was all she had.

Walter Grantley was next examined, after being warned that anything he said might be used against him.

Though evidently much affected, he gave his evidence in a clear and straightforward manner. He was a clerk in the War Office. He had, against the wishes of all his friends, engaged himself to the deceased, who, after having some time professed much affection, had latterly treated him with great coldness. On the evening in question she reluctantly came out with him for a walk; but after they passed the Ship she insisted he should take a boat. They turned and got into a boat. He wanted to go down the river, because there was no lock before Sunbury. She declared if he would not row her up the river, she would go home.

They went up the river, quarrelling all the way. There had been so much of this sort of thing that after they passed through Shepperton Lock he tried to bring matters to a conclusion, and asked her to name a day for their marriage. She scoffed at him and asked if he thought she meant to marry a man on such a trumpery salary. Then she insisted he should land her; and after a good deal of argument he did land her; and rowed back alone to Halliford. He knew no more.

Richard Savill deposed he took a boat at Lower Halliford directly after the last witness, with whom he was not acquainted, and rowed up towards Chertsey, passing Mr Grantley and Miss Heath, who were evidently quarrelling. He went as far as Dumsey Deep, where, finding the stream most heavily against him, he turned, and on his way back saw the young lady walking slowly along the bank. At Shepperton Lock he and Mr Grantley exchanged a few words, and rowed down to Halliford almost side by side. They bade each other good evening, and Mr Grantley walked off in the direction of Walton where it was proved by other witnesses he arrived at eight o'clock, and did not go out again till ten, when he went to bed.

All efforts to trace what had become of the unfortunate girl proved unavailing, till a young man named Lemson discovered the body on the previous Sunday morning close by the Tumbling Bay. The coroner wished to adjourn the inquest, in hopes some further light might be thrown on such a mysterious occurrence; but the jury protested so strongly against any proceeding of the sort, that they were directed to return an open verdict.

No one could dispute that the girl had been 'found drowned,' or that there was 'no evidence to explain how she came to be drowned.'

At the close of the proceedings, said the local paper, an affecting incident occurred. The mother wished the seven pounds to be given to the man 'who brought her child home,' but the man refused to accept a penny. The mother said she would never touch it, when a relation stepped forward and offered to take charge of it for her.

The local paper contained also a leader on the tragedy, in the course of which it remarked how exceedingly fortunate it was that Mr Savill chanced to be staying at the Ship Hotel, so well known to boating-men, and that he happened to go up the river and see the poor young lady after Mr Grantley left her, as otherwise the latter gentleman might have found himself in a most unpleasant position. He was much to be pitied, and the leader-writer felt confident that every one who read the evidence would sympathize with him. It was evident the inquiry had failed to solve the mystery connected with Miss Heath's untimely fate, but it was still competent to pursue the matter if any fresh facts transpired.

'I must get to know more about all this,' thought Davis as he refolded and tied up the paper.

Chapter 7

Davis Speaks

If there be any truth in old saws, Mr Murray's wooing was a very happy one. Certainly it was very speedy. By the end of October he and Miss Ketterick were engaged, and before Christmas the family lawyers had their hands full drawing settlements and preparing deeds. Mrs Murray disliked letting any money slip out of her own control, but she had gone too far to recede, and Mr Ketterick was not a man who would have tolerated any proceeding of the sort.

Perfectly straightforward himself, he compelled straightforwardness in others, and Mrs Murray was obliged to adhere to the terms proposed when nothing seemed to her less probable than that the marriage she wished ever would take place. As for the bridegroom, he won golden opinions from Mr Ketterick. Beyond the income to be insured to his wife and himself, he asked for nothing. Further he objected to nothing. Never before, surely, had man been so easily satisfied.

'All I have ever wanted,' he said, 'was some settled income, so that I might not feel completely dependent on my grandmother. That will now be secured, and I am quite satisfied.'

He deferred to Mr Ketterick's opinions and wishes. He made no stipulations.

'You are giving me a great prize,' he told the delighted father, 'of which I am not worthy, but I will try to make her happy.'

And the gentle girl was happy: no tenderer or more devoted lover could the proudest beauty have desired. With truth he told her he 'counted the days till she should be his.' For he felt secure when by her side. The footsteps had never followed him to Losdale Court. Just in the place that of all others he would have expected them to come, he failed to see that tiny print. There were times when he even forgot it for a season; when he did remember it, he believed, with the faith born of hope, that he should never see it again.

'I wonder he has the conscience,' muttered Mr Davis one morning, as he looked after the engaged pair. The valet had the strictest ideas concerning the rule conscience should hold over the doings of other folks, and some pleasingly lax notions about the sacrifices conscience had a right to demand from himself. 'I suppose he thinks he is safe now that those feet are snugly tucked up in holy ground,' proceeded Davis, who, being superstitious, faithfully subscribed to all the old formulæ. 'Ah! he doesn't know what I know – yet;' which last word, uttered with much gusto, indicated a most unpleasant quarter of an hour in store at some future period for Mr Murray.

It came one evening a week before his marriage. He was in London, in his grandmother's house, writing to the girl he had grown to love with the great, entire, remorseful love of his life, when Davis, respectful as ever, appeared, and asked if he might speak a word. Mr Murray involuntarily put his letter beneath some blotting-paper, and, folding his hands over both, answered, unconscious of what was to follow, 'Certainly.'

Davis had come up with his statement at full-cock, and fired at once.

'I have been a faithful servant to you, sir.'

Mr Murray lifted his eyes and looked at him. Then he knew what was coming. 'I have never found fault with you, Davis,' he said, after an almost imperceptible pause.

'No, sir, you have been a good master – a master I am sure no servant who knew his place could find a fault with.'

If he had owned an easy mind and the smallest sense of humour – neither of which possessions then belonged to Mr Murray – he might have felt enchanted with such a complete turning of the tables; but as matters stood, he could only answer, 'Good master as I have been, I suppose you wish to leave my service. Am I right, Davis?'

'Well, sir, you are right and you are wrong. I do not want to leave your service just yet. It may not be quite convenient to you for me to go now; only I want to come to an understanding.'

'About what?' Mr Murray asked, quite calmly, though he could feel his heart thumping hard against his ribs, and that peculiar choking sensation which is the warning of what in such cases must come some day.

'Will you cast your mind back, sir, to a morning in last August, when you called my attention to some extraordinary footprints on the floor of your room?'

'I remember the morning,' said Mr Murray, that choking sensation seeming to suffocate him. 'Pray go on.'

If Davis had not been master of the position, this indifference would have daunted him; as it was, he again touched the trigger, and fired this: '*I know all!*'

Mr Murray's answer did not come so quick this time. The waters had gone over his head, and for a minute he felt as a man might if suddenly flung into a raging sea, and battling for his life. He was battling for his life with a wildly leaping heart. The noise of a hundred billows seemed dashing on his brain. Then the tempest lulled, the roaring torrent was stayed, and then he said interrogatively, 'Yes?'

The prints of those phantom feet had not amazed Davis more than did his master's coolness.

'You might ha' knocked me down with a feather,' he stated, when subsequently relating this interview. 'I always knew he was a queer customer, but I never knew how queer till then.'

'Yes?' said Mr Murray, which reply quite disconcerted his valet.

'I wouldn't have seen what I have seen, sir,' he remarked, 'not for a king's ransom.'

'No?'

'No, sir, and that is the truth. What we both saw has been with me at bed and at board, as the saying is, ever since. When I shut my eyes I still feel those wet feet dabbling about the room; and in the bright sunshine I can't help shuddering, because there seems to be a cold mist creeping over me.'

'Are you not a little imaginative, Davis?' asked his master, himself repressing a shudder.

'No, sir, I am not; no man can be that about which his own eyes have seen and his own ears have heard; and I have heard and seen what I can never forget, and what nothing could pay me for going through.'

'Nevertheless?' suggested Mr Murray.

'I don't know whether I am doing right in holding my tongue, in being so faithful, sir; but I can't help it. I took to you from the first, and I wouldn't bring harm on you if any act of mine could keep it from you. When one made the remark to me awhile ago it was a strange thing to see a gentleman attended by a pair of wet footprints, I said they were a sign in your family that some great event was about to happen.'

'Did you say so?'

'I did, sir, Lord forgive me!' answered Davis, with unblushing mendacity. 'I have gone through more than will ever be known over this affair, which has shook me, Mr Murray. I am not the man I was before ghosts took to following me, and getting into trains without paying any fare, and waking me in the middle of the night, and rousing me out of my warm bed to see sights I would not have believed I could have seen if anybody had sworn it to me. I have aged twenty-five years since last August – my nerves are destroyed; and so, sir, before you got married, I thought I would make bold to ask what I am to do with a constitition broken in your service and hardly a penny put by;' and, almost out of breath with his pathetic statement, Davis stopped and waited for an answer.

With a curiously hunted expression in them, Mr Murray raised his eyes and looked at Davis.

'You have thought over all this,' he said. 'How much do you assess them at?'

'I scarcely comprehend, sir – assess what at?'

'Your broken constitution and the five-and-twenty years you say you have aged.'

His master's face was so gravely serious that Davis could take the question neither as a jest nor a sneer. It was a request to fix a price, and he did so.

'Well, sir,' he answered, 'I have thought it all over. In the nightwatches, when I could get no rest, I lay and reflected what I ought to do. I want to act fair. I have no wish to drive a hard bargain with you, and, on the other hand, I don't think I would be doing justice by a man that has worked hard if I let myself be sold for nothing. So, sir, to cut a long story short, I am willing to take two thousand pounds.'

'And where do you imagine I am to get two thousand pounds?'

Mr Davis modestly intimated he knew his place better than to presume to have any notion, but no doubt Mr Murray could raise that sum easily enough.

'If I could raise such a sum for you, do you not think I should have raised it for myself long ago?'

Davis answered that he did; but, if he might make free to say so, times were changed.

'They are, they are indeed,' said Mr Murray bitterly; and then there was silence.

Davis knocked the conversational ball the next time.

'I am in no particular hurry, sir,' he said. 'So long as we understand one another I can wait till you come back from Italy, and have got the handling of some cash of your own. I daresay even then you won't be able to pay me off all at once; but if you would insure your life – '

'I can't insure my life: I have tried, and been refused.'

Again there ensued a silence, which Davis broke once more.

'Well, sir,' he began, 'I'll chance that. If you will give me a line of writing about what you owe me, and make a sort of a will, saying I am to get two thousand, I'll hold my tongue about what's gone and past. And I would not be fretting, sir, if I was you: things are quiet now, and, please God, you might never have any more trouble.'

Mr Davis, in view of his two thousand pounds, his widow, and his wayside public, felt disposed to take an optimistic view of even his master's position; but Mr Murray's thoughts were of a different hue. 'If I do have any more,' he considered, 'I shall go mad;' a conclusion which seemed likely enough to follow upon even the memory of those phantom feet coming dabbling out of an unseen world to follow him with their accursed print in this.

Davis was not going abroad with the happy pair. For sufficient reason Mr Murray had decided to leave him behind, and Mrs Murray, ever alive to her own convenience, instantly engaged him to stay on with her as butler, her own being under notice to leave.

Thus, in a semi-official capacity, Davis witnessed the wedding, which people considered a splendid affair.

What Davis thought of it can never be known, because when he left Losdale Church his face was whiter than the bride's dress; and after the newly-wedded couple started on the first stage of their life-journey he went to his room, and stayed in it till his services were required.

'There is no money would pay me for what I've seen,' he remarked to himself. 'I went too cheap. But when once I handle the cash I'll try never to come anigh him or them again.'

What was he referring to? Just this. As the bridal group moved to the vestry he saw, if no one else did, those wet, wet feet softly and swiftly threading their way round the bridesmaids and the groomsman, in front of the relations, before Mrs Murray herself, and hurry on to keep step with the just wed pair.

For the last time the young wife signed her maiden name. Friends crowded around, uttering congratulations, and still through the throng those unnoticed feet kept walking in and out, round and round, backward and forward, as a dog threads its way through the people at a fair. Down the aisle, under the sweeping dresses of the ladies, past courtly gentlemen, Davis saw those awful feet running gleefully till they came up with bride and bridegroom.

'She is going abroad with them,' thought the man; and then for a moment he felt as if could endure the ghastly vision no longer, but must faint dead away. 'It is a vile shame,' he reflected, 'to drag an innocent girl into such a whirlpool;' and all the time over the church step the feet were dancing merrily.

The clerk and the verger noticed them at last.

'I wonder who has been here with wet feet?' said the clerk; and the verger wonderingly answered he did not know.

Davis could have told him, had he been willing to speak or capable of speech.

Conclusion

He'd Have Seen Me Righted

It was August once again – August, fine, warm, and sunshiny – just one year after that damp afternoon on which Paul Murray and his friend stood in front of the Ship at Lower Halliford. No lack of visitors that season. Hotels were full, and furnished houses at a premium. The hearts of lodging-house keepers were glad. Ladies arrayed in rainbow hues flashed about the quiet village streets; boatmen reaped a golden harvest; all sorts of crafts swarmed on the river. Men in flannels gallantly towed their feminine belongings up against a languidly flowing stream. Pater and materfamilias, and all the olive branches, big and little, were to be met on the Thames, and on the banks of Thames, from Richmond to Staines, and even higher still. The lilies growing around Dockett Point floated with their pure cups wide open to the sun; no close folding of the white wax-leaves around the golden centre that season. Beside the water purple loosestrife grew in great clumps of brilliant colour dazzling to the sight. It was, in fact, a glorious August, in which pleasure-seekers could idle and sun themselves and get tanned to an almost perfect brown without the slightest trouble.

During the past twelvemonth local tradition had tried hard to add another ghost at Dumsey Deep to that already established in the adjoining Stabbery; but the unshrinking brightness of that glorious summer checked belief in it for the time. No doubt when the dull autumn days came again, and the long winter nights, full of awful possibilities, folded water and land in fog and darkness, a figure dressed in grey silk and black velvet fichu, with a natty grey hat trimmed with black and white feathers on its phantom head, with small feet covered by the thinnest of openwork stockings, from which the shoes, so much too large, had dropped long ago, would reappear once more, to the terror of all who heard, but for the time being, snugly tucked up in holy ground, the girl whose heart had rejoiced in her beauty, her youth, her admirers, and her finery, was lying quite still and quiet, with closed eyes, and ears that heard neither the church bells nor the splash of oars nor the murmur of human voices.

Others, too, were missing from – though not missed by – Shepperton (the Thames villages miss no human being so long as other human beings, with plenty of money, come down by rail, boat, or carriage to supply his place). Paul Murray, Dick Savill, and Walter Grantley were absent. Mrs Heath, too, had gone, a tottering, heartbroken woman, to Mr Pointer's, where she was most miserable, but where she and her small possessions were taken remarkably good care of.

'Only a year agone,' she said one day, 'my girl was with me. In the morning she wore her pretty cambric with pink spots; and in the afternoon, that grey silk in which she was buried – for we durst not change a thread, but just wrapped a winding-sheet round what was left. O! Lucy, Lucy, Lucy! to think I bore you for that!' and then she wept softly, and nobody heeded or tried to console her, for 'what,' as Mrs Pointer wisely said, 'was the use of fretting over a daughter dead a twelvemonth, and never much of a comfort neither?'

Mr Richard Savill was still 'grinding away,' to quote his expression. Walter Grantley had departed, so reported his friends, for the diamond-fields; his enemies improved on this by carelessly answering,

'Grantley! O, he's gone to the devil;' which latter statement could not have been quite true, since he has been back in England for a long time, and is now quite well to do and reconciled to his family.

As for Paul Murray, there had been all sorts of rumours floating about concerning him.

The honeymoon had been unduly protracted; from place to place the married pair wandered – never resting, never staying; alas! for him there was no rest – there could be none here.

It mattered not where he went – east, west, south, or north – those noiseless wet feet followed; no train was swift enough to outstrip them; no boat could cut the water fast enough to leave them behind; they tracked him with dogged persistence; they were with him sleeping, walking, eating, drinking, praying – for Paul Murray in those days often prayed after a desperate heathenish fashion – and yet the plague was not stayed; the accursed thing still dogged him like a Fate.

After a while people began to be shy of him, because the footsteps were no more intermittent; they were always where he was. Did he enter a cathedral, they accompanied him; did he walk solitary through the woods or pace the lake-side, or wander by the sea, they were ever and always with the unhappy man.

They were worse than any evil conscience, because conscience often sleeps, and they from the day of his marriage never did. They had waited for that – waited till he should raise the cup of happiness to his lips, in order to fill it with gall – waited till his wife's dream of bliss was perfect, and then wake her to the knowledge of some horror more agonizing than death.

There were times when he left his young wife for days and days, and went, like those possessed of old, into the wilderness, seeking rest and finding none; for no legion of demons could have cursed a man's life more than those wet feet, which printed marks on Paul Murray's heart that might have been branded by red-hot irons.

All that had gone before was as nothing to the trouble of having involved another in the horrible mystery of his own life – and that other a gentle, innocent, loving creature he might just as well have killed as married.

He did not know what to do. His brain was on fire; he had lost all hold upon himself, all grip over his mind. On the sea of life he tossed like a ship without a rudder, one minute taking a resolve to shoot himself, the next turning his steps to seek some priest, and confess the whole matter fully and freely, and, before he had walked a dozen yards, determining to go away into some savage and desolate land, where those horrible feet might, if they pleased, follow him to his grave.

By degrees this was the plan which took firm root in his dazed brain; and accordingly one morning he started for England, leaving a note in which he asked his wife to follow him. He never meant to see her sweet face again, and he never did. He had determined to go to his father-in-law and confess to him; and accordingly, on the anniversary of Lucy's death, he found himself at Losdale Court, where vague rumours of some unaccountable trouble had preceded him.

Mr Ketterick was brooding over these rumours in his library, when, as if in answer to his thoughts, the servant announced Mr Murray.

'Good God!' exclaimed the older man, shocked by the white, haggard face before him, 'what is wrong?'

'I have been ill,' was the reply.

'Where is your wife?'

'She is following me. She will be here in a day or so.'

'Why did you not travel together?'

'That is what I have come to tell you.'

Then he suddenly stopped and put his hand to his heart. He had voluntarily come up for execution, and now his courage failed him. His manhood was gone, his nerves unstrung. He was but a poor, weak, wasted creature, worn out by the ceaseless torment of those haunting feet, which, however, since he turned his steps to England had never followed him. Why had he travelled to Losdale Court? Might he not have crossed the ocean and effaced himself in the Far West, without telling his story at all?

Just as he had laid down the revolver, just as he had turned from the

171

priest's door, so now he felt he could not say that which he had come determined to say.

'I have walked too far,' he said, after a pause. 'I cannot talk just yet. Will you leave me for half an hour? No; I don't want anything, thank you – except to be quiet.' Quiet! – ah, heavens!

After a little he rose and passed out on to the terrace. Around there was beauty and peace and sunshine. He – he – was the only jarring element, and even on him there seemed falling a numbed sensation which for the time being simulated rest.

He left the terrace and crossed the lawn till he came to a great cedar tree, under which there was a seat, where he could sit a short time before leaving the Court.

Yes, he would go away and make no sign. Dreamily he thought of the wild lone lands beyond the sea, where there would be none to ask whence he came or marvel about the curse which followed him. Over the boundless prairie, up the mountain heights, let those feet pursue him if they would. Away from his fellows he could bear his burden. He would confess to no man – only to God, who knew his sin and sorrow; only to his Maker, who might have pity on the work of his hands, and some day bid that relentless avenger be still.

No, he would take no man into his confidence; and even as he so decided, the brightness of the day seemed to be clouded over, warmth was exchanged for a deadly chill, a horror of darkness seemed thrown like a pall over him, and a rushing sound as of many waters filled his ears.

An hour later, when Mr Ketterick sought his son-in-law, he found him lying on the ground, which was wet and trampled, as though by hundreds of little feet.

His shouts brought help, and Paul Murray was carried into the house, where they laid him on a couch and piled rugs and blankets over his shivering body.

'Fetch a doctor at once,' said Mr Ketterick.

'And a clergyman,' added the housekeeper.

'No, a magistrate,' cried the sick man, in a loud voice.

They had thought him insensible, and, startled, looked at each other. After that he spoke no more, but turned his head away from them and lay quiet.

The doctor was the first to arrive. With quick alertness he stepped across the room, pulled aside the covering, and took the patient's hand; then after gently moving the averted face, he said solemnly, like a man whose occupation has gone,

'I can do nothing here; he is dead.'

It was true. Whatever his secret, Paul Murray carried it with him to a country further distant than the lone land where he had thought to hide his misery.

'It is of no use talking to me,' said Davis, when subsequently telling his story. 'If Mr Murray had been a gentleman as was a gentleman, he'd have seen me righted, dead or not. *She* was able to come back – at least, her feet were; and he could have done the same if he'd liked. It was as bad as swindling not making a fresh will after he was married. How was I to know that will would turn out so much waste paper? And then when I asked for my own, Mrs Murray dismissed me without a character, and Mr Ketterick's lawyers won't give me anything either; so a lot I've made by being a faithful servant, and I'd have all servants take warning by me.'

Mr Davis is his own servant now, and a very bad master he finds himself.

JOANNA BRISCOE

Revenge

When Michaela was old enough and wise enough, she formulated an idea for revenge. She played with it like a sweet ball, moulded it and tossed it from hand to hand. She sent it springing to new heights and watched its giddy flight with the thrill of daring.

'Girls are sly little things,' Michaela's mother Lily had mused long ago. 'Boys can be rough, but they do play fair.'

And women are devious bitches, and not to be trusted.

Lily held her baby, cherub pink, and he was wide-eyed and uproarious, and her daugher Michaela bit her lip and burrowed underground. Since she was of the nasty breed, she thought, she would act out her destiny with consummate duplicity.

Lily did not know, quite, what to make of Michaela. She was a gawky web of sensitivities, whereas her toddling boy was demanding and uncomplicated. He was beautiful, her bundle, bad-tempered and long-lashed. His eyes would be a glassy dark blue, still wet with the tears of his temper, when he'd break into a toothless beam and she would pluck him into her lap, her rough naughty boy who loved her with all the abandon of physical need and a milky devotion beyond.

Michaela's awkwardness was spiny and overt. She sat at the table and a piece of her fringe curved up and bounced out of line. Her failed attempt to plaster it down with water was there for all to see.

'Would you like me to take you to the hairdresser's again?'

Michaela's hand shot to her fringe. 'Oh no, it's all right,' she said.

'Your hair will sort itself out one day, Michaela. So will your teeth, you know. Sooner or later your face will grow into them.'

Michaela pressed her tongue against her front teeth and wondered what she meant.

'We must make sure your features don't become fat, though. Double chins are easily come by on girls as they grow older.'

Michaela looked puzzled.

'I only tell you these things to help you help yourself, darling,' said Lily.

Michaela kept silent. She cleaned the table and curled up against her father, and Lily felt a stab of irritation that he was oblivious to her games.

Michaela was grateful for her privileges. She clung to a talismanic belief in atonement. For all her pretty dresses, she worked hard at school and helped in the house; for all the holidays and hamsters, she created elaborate birthday gifts. Her expiations increased with every incitement to guilt.

She tried harder to be good. She held herself so that she was physically smaller and could move through her own invented world with ease, and would fit into her dresses for longer. She glanced at Lily when her head was turned, but Lily sensed the hints and twitches of secret knowledge behind her blank gaze.

'Don't you want any pudding?'

Michaela looked up as if surprised. 'Oh,' she said, and hovered by the table, unfocused and hesitating, and Lily roared inside, the act so obvious she wanted to lift that skinny body up and thump it back into a chair. Poor little martyr. Poor bloody deprived orphan. All guile.

Michaela dropped her gaze, and all the while she was waiting, suspended in exquisite cold fury, to run to the haven of her room where she could, oh delicious, cram her sheets into her mouth and make herself choke with crying at the image of her baby brother tucking into his yoghurt and bananas, and then, through the dry film of her tears, lie under the bedclothes and fantasize in florid dream sequences, a soap opera that grew new arms and legs of invention every day. She plotted fresh episodes in the saga that involved a boy who was mentally retarded and a mother who patrolled his bedroom like a matron stalking the wards issuing appropriate punishment. The matron became a half-demented tyrant; the boy wet himself and was whipped; armed with the insurance of a hasty prayer that people would not die as a result of her misappropriations, Michaela masterminded ever more daring scenarios.

Later, it dawned upon Michaela that her mother was, frankly, offended by femininity. As she grew up, and sweet child smells were sharpened by sweat, and breasts were embarrassed protuberances beneath a jumper, she wanted to fling it in her mother's face. Condense to its very essence all that offended and slap it in her eyes, nose, mouth. Leave caked sanitary towels on the stairs, the bath full of pubic curls, lactate in front of her and soil her clothes. She had a compulsion to open her legs wide, show puckered cellulite and stretch marks, and sit there on display.

And then, looking back, she'd tease out the evidence of distaste. Pursed lips and venomous references to sluts and hoydens, self-effacement and nervous hints about inappropriate filial intimacy. Lily cut new wounds with smiles. She'd lodge doubts like drops of poison. She'd flirt with fledgling fears, but subtly, subtly, couched in anxious concern.

But it had all changed. Michaela ignored the battalion of Mum roll-ons that appeared in the bathroom. She no longer concealed her offence; she flaunted it. She sat in the kitchen with her friends, and the room was warm and smelly, high with female voices.

Lily came in. Michaela suppressed a sigh and darted a conspiratorial glance at her friends as they abandoned their discussion and sat in a flush of subdued hilarity.

'Hey, Mum. Who'd you think's tastier, the man, what's his name, at the news stand, or the wanker in the basement?'

Lily smiled tolerantly. The friends giggled. They returned to their discussion and ignored her.

Michaela shot a look at the others. 'I'm as randy as a swine,' she said, loud enough for Lily to hear.

There was silence.

Lily looked at the healthy bosom. 'Why do you persistently stuff yourself with such rubbish?' she said as Michaela delved into a family size packet of crisps.

Michaela stretched her legs under the table, and looked Lily up and down over her mug and said, 'Mother dear, I feel you're hardly in a position to air your opinions on the effects of healthy eating.'

Lily pursed her lips. Silence. She made tea. The overhead light began to buzz. Michaela looked across the table and smirked, a surreptitious hiss of laughter through her nose as the ruptured calm drifted and re-settled. Lily caught her eye. She tightened her lips against a clump of tears and walked out.

Michaela had strayed beyond her to her own world of contempt. She and her friends wore casual clothes. They were weepy and emotional: they gathered in the kitchen and giggled and hugged and cried without restraint. They talked about their menstrual cycles and aired their intimate desires with almost defiant ease.

The Michaela who had concealed herself behind dresses hung out of skimpy strips of lycra and sat like a man on train seats. She was voluptuous and earthy. Lily, embarrassed, shrank from her.

'Calm down,' said Penny. 'What's the problem?' She laughed.

Lily's old friend Penny was blasé and outspoken. Lily was by turns affronted and amused by her. She looked at her and smiled uneasily. She suspected her of unwittingly inciting Michaela to greater displays of irreverence. Michaela had always avoided Lily's friends, but now she found that a new empathy had sprung up between herself and Penny, and they laughed and confided and talked about men.

Lily was compelled by a prurient curiosity to face the sweaty ranks of boys who appeared in the house. They padded through the kitchen in their socks and left tea bags on the draining board. Michaela's furious flirtations made her cringe.

'If she throws herself at them, they'll simply take advantage of her,' she said to Penny.

'Who? Me?' said Michaela, overhearing. 'What's wrong with my friends?'

'Oh.' Lily shrugged. 'Nothing.'

'But I thought you liked boys,' said Michaela, simply, and the corners of her mouth curved into a smile.

Lily would have welcomed a son-in-law to the family. He was already sculpted in vague form in her mind, manly in baggy cords with a wallet full of keys, a little older, dark and assured. A ready-made son-in-law without the interim chaos of Adam's apples and hangdog expressions of lust. Lily felt stirrings of affection for her picture of Michaela with husband.

The usual crowd had taken over the kitchen. Michaela's shrieks leaked through the door. The room prickled with mockery.

Her body tensed with awareness as Lily walked in. She watched her move silently to the kettle, and felt the ease of her own legs stretched out on the table, emanated the smug secret of new-found sex.

Penny was there, smoking by the window. Lily felt vaguely hurt and excluded. The boys were teasing her, but with uncustomary deference. She drew on her cigarette and talked back, and Lily darkened with disapproval. Penny had always been loose, she ruminated; she had ceased to keep track of the men in her life.

She looked at Penny's figure-hugging attire and turned to Michaela. 'Your skirt's riding up,' she half mouthed, half hissed, nodding violently at Michaela's thighs.

'What?' said Michaela. 'Oh.' She continued her conversation with the boy beside her, her elbows propped on his shoulder, and leant over him when she laughed.

'Jesus,' said Lily.

Michaela froze inside and rested her head momentarily against his neck. The memory of pursed lips, of hints and murmurs heavy with disapproval, floated in front of her.

'What?' she said. '*What?*'

'Oh nothing,' said Lily.

'OK.'

Lily paused. 'I mean, really.' She bit her lip. 'You really are so arrogant,

Michaela. I don't know what – what you think you are, or who you think you are.'

'God, I wish you'd stop going on and on at me.'

'How else can I get through to you? You've become so hard recently. And this unbelievable vanity . . . This flirting, it's embarrassing, you know, it really is.'

'Lily,' said Penny.

'Yes, but I wish she wouldn't try her clever-clever stuff on me.'

'You bloody bitch.' Fear beaded her gut. The terror of earlier years was now transformed into hysterical daring. She no longer dreamed under the bedclothes; she pushed herself to new levels. 'Just because you're a dried up withered old hag who hates herself, I make you *sick*.' She tossed her hair back, felt her smooth plump skin.

'Get out,' said Lily.

Michaela sat there and looked at her. The old tight lips. She wanted to choke her with sex, with juices, with vibrant life.

'You should go and get yourself fucked some time,' said Michaela.

'You slut,' said Lily slowly. 'You slag, you've never been anything but a little slut. Even your own father!' Her voice rose to a hysterical whine. 'Your behaviour with him always made me *disgusted*, flinging yourself at him and kissing him, and parading through the house in that tart's bikini. And now you're a full-time slut, can't get enough of it, can you, men, men, men, spotty youths, throwing yourself at them.'

Michaela lifted an eyebrow, trembling.

Lily's voice was a low yowl. 'A born slut. Look at you. Just look at yourself, spilling out everywhere, you great big lump. You just can't stop yourself, can you, can't get enough, dirty little whore.'

Michaela was filled with a strangely detached serenity. Vengeance was her own to play with: it bubbled through her veins. She floated through the days.

When Lily returned to the house one night, a low amber light seeped from the front room. She opened the door and blinked dark floaters until she was accustomed to the shadow. She saw two figures in the corner of the room. Backs gleamed dully in the light, a twist of limbs; with a sudden clarity, she made out her daughter copulating on the sofa. She jolted backwards. The figures swam in front of her, then with a surge the details rearranged themselves in a sickening configuration, and she saw stomachs and breasts pale in the lamplight, and Michaela stared at her through Penny's hair.

ANNE ENRIGHT

The Portable Virgin

Dare to be dowdy! that's my motto, because it comes to us all – the dirty acrylic jumpers and the genteel trickle of piss down our support tights. It will come to her too.

She was one of those women who hold their skin like a smile, as if she was afraid her face might fall off if the tension went out of her eyes.

I knew that when Ben made love to her, the thought that she might break pushed him harder. I, by comparison, am like an old sofa, welcoming, familiar, well-designed.

This is the usual betrayal story, as you have already guessed – the word 'sofa' gave it away. The word 'sofa' opened up rooms of sleeping children and old wedding photographs, ironic glances at crystal wine glasses, BBC mini series where Judi Dench plays the deserted furniture and has a little sad fun.

It is not a story about hand-jobs in toilets, at parties where everyone is in the van rental business. It is not a story where Satan turns around like a lawyer in a swivel chair. There are no doves, no prostitutes, no railway stations, no marks on the skin.

So there I was knitting a bolero jacket when I dropped a stitch. Bother. And there was Ben with a gin and tonic crossing his legs tenderly by the phone.

'Thoroughly fucked?' I asked and he spilt his drink.

Ben has been infected by me over the years. He has my habit of irony, or perhaps I have his. Our inflections coincide in bed, and sometimes he startles me in the shops, by hopping out of my mouth.

'Thoroughly,' he said, brushing the wet on his trousers and flicking drops of gin from his fingertips.

*

179

There was an inappropriate desire in the room and a strange dance of description as I uncovered her brittle blonde hair, her wide strained mouth. A woman replete with modified adjectives, damaged by men, her body whittled into thinness so unnatural you could nearly see the marks of the knife. Intelligent? No. Funny? No. Rich, with a big laugh and sharp heels? No. Happy? Definitely not. Except when he was there. Ben makes me too sad for words. I finished the row, put away my needles and went to bed.

Judi Dench came out of the wardrobe and decided that it was time she had an affair herself. She would start a small business in the gardening shed and leave her twinsets behind. And just when she realised that *she* was a human being *too* – attractive, generous and witty (albeit in a sofa kind of way), some nice man would come along and agree with her.

Mrs Rochester punched a hole in the ceiling and looked at Ben where he sat at the end of the bed, maimed and blind. She whispered a long and very sensible monologue with an urgency that made the mattress smoulder, and we both had a good laugh about that.

Karen . . . Sharon . . . Teresa . . . all good names for women who dye their hair. Suzy . . . Jacintha . . . Patti . . .

'What's her name?' I asked.

'Mary,' he said.

My poor maimed husband is having sex in the back of our car with a poor maimed woman who has a law degree and a tendency to overdress. She works for a van rental firm. You would think at least she could get them something with a bigger back seat.

My poor maimed husband is seriously in danger of damaging his health with the fillip this fact has given to our love life. And while he bounces on top of his well-loved sofa, Satan turns around in the corner, like a lawyer in a swivel chair, saying 'Go on, go on, you'll wake the children.' (Or is that me?)

She is the silence at the other end of the phone. She is the smile he starts but does not finish. She is the woman standing at the top of the road, with cheap nail polish and punctured ears. She is the girl at the front of the class, with ringlets and white knees and red eyes.

The phone calls are more frequent. It is either getting serious or going sour. He used to head straight for the bathroom when he came home, in order to put his dick in the sink. Then he stopped doing it by accident and started going to her flat instead, with its (naturally) highly scented soap. Should I tell her the next time she rings? Should we get chatty about Pears, fall in love over Palmolive? We could ring up an agency and do an advert, complete wilth split screen. 'Mary's soap is all whiffy, but *Mary* uses X –

so mild her husband will never leave.' Of course we have the same name, it is part of Ben's sense of irony, and we all know where he got that from.

So Ben is tired of love. Ben wants sad sex in the back of cars. Ben wants to desire the broken cunt of a woman who will never make it to being real.

'But I thought it *meant* something!' screams the wife, throwing their crystal honeymoon wine glasses from Seville against the Magnolia matt wall.

I am not that old after all. Revenge is not out of the question. There is money in my purse and an abandoned adolescence that never got under way.

I sit in a chair in the most expensive hairdresser in Grafton Street and a young man I can't see pulls my head back into the sink and anoints (I'm sorry) my head with shampoo. It is interesting to be touched like this; hairdressers, like doctors, are getting younger by the day. My 'stylist' is called Alison and she checks my shoes beneath the blue nylon cape, looking for a clue.

'I want a really neat bob,' I say, 'but I don't know what to do with this bit.'

'I know,' she says, 'it's driving you mad. That's why it's so thin, you just keep brushing it out of your eyes.'

I am a woman whose hair is falling out, my stuffing is coming loose.

'But look, we're nearly there,' and she starts to wave the scissors (like a blessing) over my head.

'How long is it since you had it cut last?'

'About ten weeks.'

'Exactly,' she says, 'because we're not going to get any length with all these split ends, are we?'

'I want to go blonde,' says the wet and naked figure in the mirror and the scissors pause mid-swoop.

'It's very thin . . .'

'I know, I want it to break. I want it blonde.'

'Well . . .' My stylist is shocked. I have finally managed to say something really obscene.

The filthy metamorphosis is effected by another young man whose hair is the same length as the stubble on his chin. He has remarkable, sexual blue eyes, which come with the price. 'We' start with a rubber cap which he punctures with a vicious crochet hook, then drags my poor thin hair through the holes. I look 'a fright'. All the women around me look 'a fright'. Mary is sitting to my left and to my right. She is blue from the neck down, she is reading a magazine, her hair stinks, her skin is pulled into a smile by the rubber tonsure on her head. There is a handbag at her feet, the inside of which is coated with blusher that came loose. Inside the bags are bills, pens, sweetpapers, diaphragms, address books full of people she doesn't know any more. I know this because I stole one as I left the shop.

I am sitting on Dollymount Strand going through Mary's handbag, using her little mirror, applying her 'Wine Rose and Gentlelight Colourize Powder Shadow Trio', her Plumsilk lipstick, her Venetian Brocade blusher and her Tearproof (thank God) mascara.

I will be bored soon. I will drown her slowly in a pool and let the police peg out the tatters to dry when they pick up the bag on the beach. It affords me some satisfaction to think of her washed up in the hairdresser's, out of her nylon shift and newly shriven, without the means to pay.

My revenge looks back at me, out of the mirror. The new fake me looks twice as real as the old. Underneath my clothes my breasts have become blind, my iliac crests mottle and bruise. Strung out between my legs is a triangle of air that pulls away from sex, while my hands clutch. It used to be the other way around.

I root through the bag, looking for a past. At the bottom, discoloured by Wine Rose and Gentlelight, I find a small portable Virgin. She is made of transparent plastic, except for her cloak, which is coloured blue. 'A present from Lourdes' is written on the globe at her feet, underneath her heel and the serpent. Mary is full of surprises. Her little blue crown is a screw-off top, and her body is filled with holy water, which I drink.

Down by the water's edge I set her sailing on her back, off to Ben, who is sentimental that way. Then I follow her into his story, with its doves and prostitutes, railway stations and marks on the skin. I have nowhere else to go. I love that man.

MURIEL SPARK

The Portobello Road

One day in my young youth at high summer, lolling with my lovely companions upon a haystack I found a needle. Already and privately for some years I have been guessing that I was set apart from the common run, but this of the needle attested the fact to my whole public, George, Kathleen, and Skinny. I sucked my thumb, for when I had thrust my idle hand deep into the hay, the thumb was where the needle had stuck.

When everyone had recovered George said, 'She put in her thumb and pulled out a plum.' Then away we were into our merciless hacking-hecking laughter again.

The needle had gone fairly deep into the thumby cushion and a small red river flowed and spread from this tiny puncture. So that nothing of our joy should lag, George put in quickly,

'Mind your bloody thumb on my shirt.'

Then hac-hec-hoo, we shrieked into the hot Borderland afternoon. Really I should not care to be so young of heart again. That is my thought every time I turn over my old papers and come across the photograph. Skinny, Kathleen, and myself are in the photo atop the haystack. Skinny had just finished analysing the inwards of my find.

'It couldn't have been done by brains. You haven't much brains but you're a lucky wee thing.'

Everyone agreed that the needle betokened extraordinary luck. As it was becoming a serious conversation, George said,

'I'll take a photo.'

I wrapped my hanky round my thumb and got myself organized. George pointed up from his camera and shouted,

'Look, there's a mouse!'

Kathleen screamed and I screamed although I think we knew there was no mouse. But this gave us an extra session of squalling hee-hoo's. Finally we three composed ourselves for George's picture. We look lovely and it was a great day at the time, but I would not care for it all over again. From that day I was known as Needle.

One Saturday in recent years I was mooching down the Portobello Road, threading among the crowds of marketers on the narrow pavement when I saw a woman. She had a haggard careworn wealthy look, thin but for the breasts forced-up high like a pigeon's. I had not seen her for nearly five years. How changed she was! But I recognized Kathleen, my friend; her features had already begun to sink and protrude in the way that mouths and noses do in people destined always to be old for their years. When I had last seen her, nearly five years ago, Kathleen, barely thirty, had said,

'I've lost all my looks, it's in the family. All the women are handsome as girls, but we go off early, we go brown and nosey.'

I stood silently among the people, watching. As you will see, I wasn't in a position to speak to Kathleen. I saw her shoving in her avid manner from stall to stall. She was always fond of antique jewellery and of bargains. I wondered that I had not seen her before in the Portobello Road on my Saturday-morning ambles. Her long stiff-crooked fingers pounced to select a jade ring from amongst the jumble of brooches and pendants, onyx, moonstone, and gold, set out on the stall.

'What d'you think of this?' she said.

I saw then who was with her. I had been half-conscious of the huge man following several paces behind her, and now I noticed him.

'It looks all right,' he said. 'How much is it?'

'How much is it?' Kathleen asked the vendor.

I took a good look at this man accompanying Kathleen. It was her husband. The beard was unfamiliar, but I recognized beneath it his enormous mouth, the bright sensuous lips, the large brown eyes forever brimming with pathos.

It was not for me to speak to Kathleen, but I had a sudden inspiration which caused me to say quietly,

'Hallo, George.'

The giant of a man turned round to face the direction of my voice. There were so many people – but at length he saw me.

'Hallo, George,' I said again.

Kathleen had started to haggle with the stall-owner, in her old way, over the price of the jade ring. George continued to stare at me, his big mouth slightly parted so I could see a wide slit of red lips and white teeth between the fair grassy growths of beard and moustache.

'My God!' he said.

'What's the matter?' said Kathleen.

'Hallo, George!' I said again, quite loud this time, and cheerfully.

'Look!' said George. 'Look who's there, over beside the fruit stall.'

Kathleen looked but didn't see.

'Who is it?' she said impatiently.

'It's Needle,' he said. 'She said "Hallo, George".'

'*Needle*,' said Kathleen. 'Who do you mean? You don't mean our old friend *Needle* who — '

'Yes. There she is. My God!'

He looked very ill, although when I had said 'Hallo, George' I had spoken friendly enough.

'I don't see anyone faintly resembling poor Needle,' said Kathleen, looking at him. She was worried.

George pointed straight at me. 'Look *there*. I tell you that is Needle.'

'You're ill, George. Heavens, you must be seeing things. Come on home. Needle isn't there. You know as well as I do, Needle is dead.'

I must explain that I departed this life nearly five years ago. But I did not altogether depart this world. There were those odd things still to be done which one's executors can never do properly. Papers to be looked over, even after the executors have torn them up. Lots of business except, of course, on Sundays and Holidays of Obligation, plenty to take an interest in for the time being. I take my recreation on Saturday mornings. If it is a wet Saturday I wander up and down the substantial lanes of Woolworth's as I did when I was young and visible. There is a pleasurable spread of objects on the counters which I now perceive and exploit with a certain detachment, since it suits with my condition of life. Creams, toothpastes, combs, and hankies, cotton gloves, flimsy flowering scarves, writing-paper, and crayons, ice-cream cones and orangeade, screwdrivers, boxes of tacks, tins of paint, of glue, of marmalade; I always liked them but far more now that I have no need of any. When Saturdays are fine I go instead to the Portobello Road where formerly I would jaunt with Kathleen in our grown-up days. The barrow-loads do not change much, of apples and rayon vests in common blues and low-taste mauve, of silver plate, trays, and teapots long since changed hands from the bygone citizens to dealers, from shops to the new flats and breakable homes, and then over to the barrow-stalls and the dealers again: Georgian spoons, rings, ear-rings of turquoise and opal set in the butterfly pattern of true-lovers' knot, patch-boxes with miniature paintings of ladies on ivory, snuff-boxes of silver with Scotch pebbles inset.

Sometimes as occasion arises on a Saturday morning, my friend Kathleen, who is a Catholic, has a Mass said for my soul, and then I am in attendance as it were at the church. But most Saturdays I take my delight among the solemn crowds with their aimless purposes, their eternal life not far away, who push past the counters and stalls, who handle, buy, steal, touch, desire, and ogle the merchandise. I hear the tinkling tills, I hear the jangle of loose change and tongues and children wanting to hold and have.

That is how I came to be in the Portobello Road that Saturday morning when I saw George and Kathleen. I would not have spoken had I not been inspired to it. Indeed it's one of the things I can't do now – to speak out, unless inspired. And most extraordinary, on that morning as I spoke, a degree of visibility set in. I suppose from poor George's point of view it was like seeing a ghost when he saw me standing by the fruit barrow repeating in so friendly a manner, 'Hallo, George!'

We were bound for the south. When our education, what we would get of it from the north, was thought to be finished, one by one we were sent or sent for to London. John Skinner whom we called Skinny went to study more archaeology, George to join his uncle's tobacco farm, Kathleen to stay with her rich connections and to potter intermittently in the Mayfair hat-shop which one of them owned. A little later I also went to London to see life, for it was my ambition to write about life, which first I had to see.

'We four must stick together,' George said very often in that yearning way of his. He was always desperately afraid of neglect. We four looked likely to shift off in different directions and George did not trust the other three of us not to forget all about him. More and more as the time came for him to depart for his uncle's tobacco farm in Africa he said,

'We four must keep in touch.'

And before he left he told each of us anxiously,

'I'll write regularly, once a month. We must keep together for the sake of the old times.' He had three prints taken from the negative of that photo on the haystack, wrote on the back of them, 'George took this the day that Needle found the needle' and gave us a copy each. I think we all wished he could become a bit more callous.

During my lifetime I was a drifter, nothing organized. It was difficult for my friends to follow the logic of my life. By the normal reckonings I should have come to starvation and ruin, which I never did. Of course, I did not live to write about life as I wanted to do. Possibly that is why I am inspired to do so now in these peculiar circumstances.

I taught in a private school in Kensington, for almost three months, very small children. I didn't know what to do with them but I was kept fairly busy escorting incontinent little boys to the lavatory and telling the little girls to use their handkerchiefs. After that I lived a winter holiday in London on my small capital, and when that had run out I found a diamond bracelet in the cinema for which I received a reward of fifty pounds. When it was used up I got a job with a publicity man, writing speeches for absorbed industrialists, in which the dictionary of quotations came in very useful. So it went on. I got engaged to Skinny, but shortly after that I was left a small legacy, enough to keep me for six months. This somehow decided me that I didn't love Skinny so I gave him back the ring.

But it was through Skinny that I went to Africa. He was engaged with a party of researchers to investigate King Solomon's mines, that series of ancient workings ranging from the ancient port of Ophir, now called Beira, across Portuguese East Africa and Southern Rhodesia to the mighty jungle-city of Zimbabwe whose temple walls still stand by the approach to an ancient and sacred mountain, where the rubble of that civilization scatters itself over the surrounding Rhodesian waste. I accompanied the party as a sort of secretary. Skinny vouched for me, he paid my fare, he sympathized by his action with my inconsequential life although when he spoke of it he disapproved. A life like mine annoys most people; they go to their jobs every day, attend to things, give orders, pummel typewriters, and get two or three weeks off every year, and it vexes them to see someone else not bothering to do these things and yet getting away with it, not starving, being lucky as they call it. Skinny, when I had broken off our engagement, lectured me about this, but still he took me to Africa knowing I should probably leave his unit within a few months.

We were there a few weeks before we began inquiring for George, who was farming about four hundred miles away to the north. We had not told him of our plans.

'If we tell George to expect us in his part of the world he'll come rushing to pester us the first week. After all, we're going on business,' Skinny had said.

Before we left Kathleen told us, 'Give George my love and tell him not to send frantic cables every time I don't answer his letters right away. Tell him I'm busy in the hat-shop and being presented. You would think he hadn't another friend in the world the way he carries on.'

We had settled first at Fort Victoria, our nearest place of access to the Zimbabwe ruins. There we made inquiries about George. It was clear he hadn't many friends. The older settlers were the most tolerant about the half-caste woman he was living with, as we found, but they were furious about his methods of raising tobacco which we learned were most unprofessional and in some mysterious way disloyal to whites. We could never discover how it was that George's style of tobacco farming gave the blacks opinions about themselves, but that's what the older settlers claimed. The newer immigrants thought he was unsociable and, of course, his living with that nig made visiting impossible.

I must say I was myself a bit off-put by this news about the brown woman. I was brought up in a university town to which came Indian, African, and Asiatic students in a variety of tints and hues. I was brought up to avoid them for reasons connected with local reputation and God's ordinances. You cannot easily go against what you were brought up to do unless you are a rebel by nature.

Anyhow, we visited George eventually, taking advantage of the offer of transport from some people bound north in search of game. He had heard of our arrival in Rhodesia and though he was glad, almost relieved, to see us he pursued a policy of sullenness for the first hour.

'We wanted to give you a surprise, George.'

'How were we to know that you'd get to hear of our arrival, George? News here must travel faster than light, George.'

'We did hope to give you a surprise, George.'

We flattered and 'Georged' him until at last he said, 'Well, I must say it's good to see you. All we need now is Kathleen. We four simply must stick together. You find when you're in a place like this, there's nothing like old friends.'

He showed us his drying sheds. He showed us a paddock where he was experimenting with a horse and a zebra mare, attempting to mate them. They were frolicking happily, but not together. They passed each other in their private playtime and again, but without acknowledgement and without resentment.

'It's been done before,' George said. 'It makes a fine strong beast, more intelligent than a mule and sturdier than a horse. But I'm not having any success with this pair, they won't look at each other.'

After a while, he said, 'Come in for a drink and meet Matilda.'

She was dark brown, with a subservient hollow chest and round shoulders, a gawky woman, very snappy with the houseboys. We said pleasant things as we drank on the stoep before dinner, but we found George difficult. For some reason he began to rail at me for breaking off my engagement to Skinny, saying what a dirty trick it was after all those good times in the old days. I diverted attention to Matilda. I supposed, I said, she knew this part of the country well?

'No,' she said, 'I been a-shellitered my life. I not put out to working. Me nothing to go from place to place is allowed like dirty girls does.' In her speech she gave every syllable equal stress.

George explained, 'Her father was a white magistrate in Natal. She had a sheltered upbringing, different from the other coloureds, you realize.'

'Man, me no black-eyed Susan,' said Matilda, 'no, no.'

On the whole, George treated her as a servant. She was about four months advanced in pregnancy, but he made her get up and fetch for him, many times. Soap: that was one of the things Matilda had to fetch. George made his own bath soap, showed it proudly, gave us the receipt which I did not trouble to remember; I was fond of nice soaps during my lifetime and George's smelt of brilliantine and looked likely to soil one's skin.

'D'you brahn?' Matilda asked me.

George said, 'She is asking if you go brown in the sun.'

'No, I go freckled.'

'I got sister-in-law go feckles.'

She never spoke another word to Skinny nor to me, and we never saw her again.

Some months later I said to Skinny,

'I'm fed up with being a camp-follower.'

He was not surprised that I was leaving his unit, but he hated my way of expressing it. He gave me a Presbyterian look.

'Don't talk like that. Are you going back to England or staying?'

'Staying, for a while.'

'Well, don't wander too far off.'

I was able to live on the fee I got for writing a gossip column in a local weekly, which wasn't my idea of writing about life, of course. I made friends, more than I could cope with, after I left Skinny's exclusive little band of archaeologists. I had the attractions of being newly out from England and of wanting to see life. Of the countless young men and go-ahead families who purred me along the Rhodesian roads, hundred after hundred miles, I only kept up with one family when I returned to my native land. I think that was because they were the most representative, they stood for all the rest: people in those parts are very typical of each other, as one group of standing stones in that wilderness is like the next.

I met George once more in a hotel in Bulawayo. We drank highballs and spoke of war. Skinny's party were just then deciding whether to remain in the country or return home. They had reached an exciting part of their research, and whenever I got a chance to visit Zimbabwe he would take me for a moonlight walk in the ruined temple and try to make me see phantom Phoenicians flitting ahead of us, or along the walls. I had half a mind to marry Skinny; perhaps, I thought, when his studies were finished. The impending war was in our bones: so I remarked to George as we sat drinking highballs on the hotel stoep in the hard bright sunny July winter of that year.

George was inquisitive about my relations with Skinny. He tried to pump me for about half an hour and when at last I said, 'You are becoming aggressive, George,' he stopped. He became quite pathetic. He said, 'War or no war I'm clearing out of this.'

'It's the heat does it,' I said.

'I'm clearing out in any case. I've lost a fortune in tobacco. My uncle is making a fuss. It's the other bloody planters; once you get the wrong side of them you're finished in this wide land.'

'What about Matilda?' I asked.

He said, 'She'll be all right. She's got hundreds of relatives.'

I had already heard about the baby girl. Coal black, by repute, with George's features. And another on the way, they said.

'What about the child?'

He didn't say anything to that. He ordered more highballs and when they arrived he swizzled his for a long time with a stick. 'Why didn't you ask me to your twenty-first?' he said then.

'I didn't have anything special, no party, George. We had a quiet drink among ourselves, George, just Skinny and the old professors and two of the wives and me, George.'

'You didn't ask me to your twenty-first,' he said. 'Kathleen writes to me regularly.'

This wasn't true. Kathleen sent me letters fairly often in which she said, 'Don't tell George I wrote to you as he will be expecting word from me and I can't be bothered actually.'

'But you,' said George, 'don't seem to have any sense of old friendships, you and Skinny.'

'Oh, George!' I said.

'Remember the times we had,' George said. 'We used to have times.' His large brown eyes began to water.

'I'll have to be getting along,' I said.

'Please don't go. Don't leave me just yet. I've something to tell you.'

'Something nice?' I laid on an eager smile. All responses to George had to be overdone.

'You don't know how lucky you are,' George said.

'How?' I said. Sometimes I got tired of being called lucky by everybody. There were times when, privately practising my writings about life, I knew the bitter side of my fortune. When I failed again and again to reproduce life in some satisfactory and perfect form, I was the more imprisoned, for all my carefree living, within my craving for this satisfaction. Sometimes, in my impotence and need I secreted a venom which infected all my life for days on end and which spurted out indiscriminately on Skinny or on anyone who crossed my path.

'You aren't bound by anyone,' George said. 'You come and go as you please. Something always turns up for you. You're free, and you don't know your luck.'

'You're a damn sight more free than I am,' I said sharply. 'You've got your rich uncle.'

'He's losing interest in me,' George said. 'He's had enough.'

'Oh well, you're young yet. What was it you wanted to tell me?'

'A secret,' George said. 'Remember we used to have those secrets.'

'Oh, yes we did.'

'Did you ever tell any of mine?'

'Oh no, George.' In reality, I couldn't remember any particular secret out of the dozens we must have exchanged from our schooldays onwards.

'Well, this is a secret, mind. Promise not to tell.'

'Promise.'

'I'm married.'

'Married, George! Oh, who to?'

'Matilda.'

'How dreadful!' I spoke before I could think, but he agreed with me.

'Yes, it's awful, but what could I do?'

'You might have asked my advice,' I said pompously.

'I'm two years older than you are. I don't ask advice from you, Needle, little beast.'

'Don't ask for sympathy then.'

'A nice friend you are,' he said, 'I must say after all these years.'

'Poor George!' I said.

'There are three white men to one white woman in this country,' said George. 'An isolated planter doesn't see a white woman and if he sees one she doesn't see him. What could I do? I needed the woman.'

I was nearly sick. One, because of my Scottish upbringing. Two, because of my horror of corny phrases like 'I needed the woman,' which George repeated twice again.

'And Matilda got tough,' said George, 'after you and Skinny came to visit us. She had some friends at the Mission, and she packed up and went to them.'

'You should have let her go,' I said.

'I went after her,' George said. 'She insisted on being married, so I married her.'

'That's not a proper secret, then,' I said. 'The news of a mixed marriage soon gets about.'

'I took care of that,' George said. 'Crazy as I was, I took her to the Congo and married her there. She promised to keep quiet about it.'

'Well, you can't clear off and leave her now, surely,' I said.

'I'm going to get out of this place. I can't stand the woman and I can't stand the country. I didn't realize what it would be like. Two years of the country and three months of my wife has been enough.'

'Will you get a divorce?'

'No, Matilda's Catholic. She won't divorce.'

George was fairly getting through the highballs, and I wasn't far behind him. His brown eyes floated shiny and liquid as he told me how he had written to tell his uncle of his plight, 'Except, of course, I didn't say we were married, that would have been too much for him. He's a prejudiced hardened old Colonial. I only said I'd had a child by a coloured woman and was expecting another, and he perfectly understood. He came at once

191

by plane a few weeks ago. He's made a settlement on her, providing she keeps her mouth shut about her association with me.'

'Will she do that?'

'Oh, yes, or she won't get the money.'

'But as your wife she has a claim on you, in any case.'

'If she claimed as my wife she'd get far less. Matilda knows what she's doing, greedy bitch she is. She'll keep her mouth shut.'

'Only, you won't be able to marry again, will you, George?'

'Not unless she dies,' he said. 'And she's as strong as a trek ox.'

'Well, I'm sorry, George,' I said.

'Good of you to say so,' he said. 'But I can see by your chin that you disapprove of me. Even my old uncle understood.'

'Oh, George, I quite understand. You were lonely, I suppose.'

'You didn't even ask me to your twenty-first. If you and Skinny had been nicer to me, I would never have lost my head and married the woman, never.'

'You didn't ask me to your wedding,' I said.

'You're a catty bissom, Needle, not like what you were in the old times when you used to tell us your wee stories.'

'I'll have to be getting along,' I said.

'Mind you keep the secret,' George said.

'Can't I tell Skinny? He would be very sorry for you, George.'

'You mustn't tell anyone. Keep it a secret. Promise.'

'Promise,' I said. I understood that he wished to enforce some sort of bond between us with this secret, and I thought, 'Oh well, I suppose he's lonely. Keeping his secret won't do any harm.'

I returned to England with Skinny's party just before the war.

I did not see George again till just before my death, five years ago.

After the war Skinny returned to his studies. He had two more exams, over a period of eighteen months, and I thought I might marry him when the exams were over.

'You might do worse than Skinny,' Kathleen used to say to me on our Saturday morning excursions to the antique shops and the junk stalls.

She too was getting on in years. The remainder of our families in Scotland were hinting that it was time we settled down with husbands. Kathleen was a little younger than me, but looked much older. She knew her chances were diminishing but at that time I did not think she cared very much. As for myself, the main attraction of marrying Skinny was his prospective expeditions to Mesopotamia. My desire to marry him had to be stimulated by the continual reading of books about Babylon and Assyria; perhaps Skinny felt this, because he supplied the books and even started instructing me in the art of deciphering cuneiform tablets.

Kathleen was more interested in marriage than I thought. Like me, she had racketed around a good deal during the war; she had actually been engaged to an officer in the US navy, who was killed. Now she kept an antique shop near Lambeth, was doing very nicely, lived in a Chelsea square, but for all that she must have wanted to be married and have children. She would stop and look into all the prams which the mothers had left outside shops or area gates.

'The poet Swinburne used to do that,' I told her once.

'Really? Did he want children of his own?'

'I shouldn't think so. He simply liked babies.'

Before Skinny's final exam he fell ill and was sent to a sanatorium in Switzerland.

'You're fortunate after all not to be married to him,' Kathleen said. 'You might have caught TB.'

I was fortunate, I was lucky . . . so everyone kept telling me on different occasions. Although it annoyed me to hear, I knew they were right, but in a way that was different from what they meant. It took me very small effort to make a living; book reviews, odd jobs for Kathleen, a few months with the publicity man again, still getting up speeches about literature, art, and life for industrial tycoons. I was waiting to write about life and it seemed to me that the good fortune lay in this, whenever it should be. And until then I was assured of my charmed life, the necessities of existence always coming my way and I with far more leisure than anyone else. I thought of my type of luck after I became a Catholic and was being confirmed. The Bishop touches the candidate on the cheek, a symbolic reminder of the sufferings a Christian is supposed to undertake. I thought, how lucky, what a feathery symbol to stand for the hellish violence of its true meaning.

I visited Skinny twice in the two years that he was in the sanatorium. He was almost cured, and expected to be home within a few months. I told Kathleen after my last visit.

'Maybe I'll marry Skinny when he's well again.'

'Make it definite, Needle, and not so much of the maybe. You don't know when you're well off,' she said.

This was five years ago, in the last year of my life. Kathleen and I had become very close friends. We met several times each week, and after our Saturday-morning excursions in the Portobello Road very often I would accompany Kathleen to her aunt's house in Kent for a long weekend.

One day in the June of that year I met Kathleen specially for lunch because she had phoned me to say she had news.

'Guess who came into the shop this afternoon,' she said.

'Who?'

'George.'

We had half imagined George was dead. We had received no letters in the past ten years. Early in the war we had heard rumours of his keeping a nightclub in Durban, but nothing after that. We could have made inquiries if we had felt moved to do so.

At one time, when we discussed him, Kathleen had said,

'I ought to get in touch with poor George. But then I think he would write back. He would demand a regular correspondence again.'

'We four must stick together,' I mimicked.

'I can visualize his reproachful limpid orbs,' Kathleen said.

Skinny said, 'He's probably gone native. With his coffee concubine and a dozen mahogany kids.'

'Perhaps he's dead,' Kathleen said.

I did not speak of George's marriage, nor of any of his confidences in the hotel at Bulawayo. As the years passed we ceased to mention him except in passing, as someone more or less dead so far as we were concerned.

Kathleen was excited about George's turning up. She had forgotten her impatience with him in former days; she said,

'It was so wonderful to see old George. He seems to need a friend, feels neglected, out of touch with things.'

'He needs mothering, I suppose.'

Kathleen didn't notice the malice. She declared, 'That's exactly the case with George. It always has been, I can see it now.'

She seemed ready to come to any rapid new and happy conclusion about George. In the course of the morning he had told her of his wartime nightclub in Durban, his game-shooting expeditions since. It was clear he had not mentioned Matilda. He had put on weight, Kathleen told me, but he could carry it.

I was curious to see this version of George, but I was leaving for Scotland next day and did not see him till September of that year just before my death.

While I was in Scotland I gathered from Kathleen's letters that she was seeing George very frequently, finding enjoyable company in him, looking after him. 'You'll be surprised to see how he has developed.' Apparently he would hang round Kathleen in her shop most days, 'it makes him feel useful' as she maternally expressed it. He had an old relative in Kent whom he visited at week-ends; this old lady lived a few miles from Kathleen's aunt, which made it easy for them to travel down together on Saturdays, and go for long country walks.

'You'll see such a difference in George,' Kathleen said on my return to London in September. I was to meet him that night, a Saturday. Kathleen's aunt was abroad, the maid on holiday, and I was to keep Kathleen company in the empty house.

George had left London for Kent a few days earlier. 'He's actually helping with the harvest down there!' Kathleen told me lovingly.

Kathleen and I planned to travel down together, but on that Saturday she was unexpectedly delayed in London on some business. It was arranged that I should go ahead of her in the early afternoon to see to the provisions for our party; Kathleen had invited George to dinner at her aunt's house that night.

'I should be with you by seven,' she said. 'Sure you won't mind the empty house? I hate arriving at empty houses, myself.'

I said no, I liked an empty house.

So I did, when I got there. I had never found the house more likeable. A large Georgian vicarage in about eight acres, most of the rooms shut and sheeted, there being only one servant. I discovered that I wouldn't need to go shopping, Kathleen's aunt had left many and delicate supplies with notes attached to them: 'Eat this up please do, see also fridge' and 'A treat for three hungry people see also 2 bttles beaune for yr party on black kn table.' It was like a treasure hunt as I followed clue after clue through the cool silent domestic quarters. A house in which there are no people – but with all the signs of tenancy – can be a most tranquil good place. People take up space in a house out of proportion to their size. On my previous visits I had seen the rooms overflowing, as it seemed, with Kathleen, her aunt, and the little fat maidservant; they were always on the move. As I wandered through that part of the house which was in use, opening windows to let in the pale yellow air of September, I was not conscious that I, Needle, was taking up any space at all, I might have been a ghost.

The only thing to be fetched was the milk. I waited till after four when the milking should be done, then set off for the farm which lay across two fields at the back of the orchard. There, when the byreman was handing me the bottle, I saw George.

'Hallo, George,' I said.

'Needle! What are you doing here?' he said.

'Fetching milk,' I said.

'So am I. Well, it's good to see you, I must say.'

As we paid the farm-hand, George said, 'I'll walk back with you part of the way. But I mustn't stop, my old cousin's without any milk for her tea. How's Kathleen?'

'She was kept in London. She's coming on later, about seven, she expects.'

We had reached the end of the first field. George's way led to the left and on to the main road.

'We'll see you tonight, then?' I said.

'Yes, and talk about old times.'

'Grand,' I said.

But George got over the stile with me.

'Look here,' he said. 'I'd like to talk to you, Needle.'

'We'll talk tonight, George. Better not keep your cousin waiting for the milk.' I found myself speaking to him almost as if he were a child.

'No, I want to talk to you alone. This is a good opportunity.'

We began to cross the second field. I had been hoping to have the house to myself for a couple more hours and I was rather petulant.

'See,' he said suddenly, 'that haystack.'

'Yes,' I said absently.

'Let's sit there and talk. I'd like to see you up on a haystack again. I still keep that photo. Remember that time when – '

'I found the needle,' I said very quickly, to get it over.

But I was glad to rest. The stack had been broken up, but we managed to find a nest in it. I buried my bottle of milk in the hay for coolness. George placed his carefully at the foot of the stack.

'My old cousin is terribly vague, poor soul. A bit hazy in her head. She hasn't the least sense of time. If I tell her I've only been gone ten minutes she'll believe it.'

I giggled, and looked at him. His face had grown much larger, his lips full, wide, and with a ripe colour that is strange in a man. His brown eyes were abounding as before with some inarticulate plea.

'So you're going to marry Skinny after all these years?'

'I really don't know, George.'

'You played him up properly.'

'It isn't for you to judge. I have my own reasons for what I do.'

'Don't get sharp,' he said, 'I was only funning.' To prove it, he lifted a tuft of hay and brushed my face with it.

'D'you know,' he said next, 'I didn't think you and Skinny treated me very decently in Rhodesia.'

'Well, we were busy, George. And we were younger then, we had a lot to do and see. After all, we could see you any other time, George.'

'A touch of selfishness,' he said.

'I'll have to be getting along, George.' I made to get down from the stack.

He pulled me back. 'Wait, I've got something to tell you.'

'OK, George, tell me.'

'First promise not to tell Kathleen. She wants it kept a secret so that she can tell you herself.'

'All right. Promise.'

'I'm going to marry Kathleen.'

'But you're already married.'

Sometimes I heard news of Matilda from the one Rhodesian family with whom I still kept up. They referred to her as 'George's Dark Lady' and of course they did not know he was married to her. She had apparently made a good thing out of George, they said, for she minced around all tarted up, never did a stroke of work, and was always unsettling the respectable coloured girls in their neighbourhood. According to accounts, she was a living example of the folly of behaving as George did.

'I married Matilda in the Congo,' George was saying.

'It would still be bigamy,' I said.

He was furious when I used that word bigamy. He lifted a handful of hay as if he would throw it in my face, but controlling himself meanwhile he fanned it at me playfully.

'I'm not sure that the Congo marriage was valid,' he continued. 'Anyway, as far as I'm concerned, it isn't.'

'You can't do a thing like that,' I said.

'I need Kathleen. She's been decent to me. I think we were always meant for each other, me and Kathleen.'

'I'll have to be going,' I said.

But he put his knee over my ankles, so that I couldn't move. I sat still and gazed into space.

He tickled my face with a wisp of hay.

'Smile up, Needle,' he said; 'let's talk like old times.'

'Well?'

'No one knows about my marriage to Matilda except you and me.'

'And Matilda,' I said.

'She'll hold her tongue so long as she gets her payments. My uncle left an annuity for the purpose, his lawyers see to it.'

'Let me go, George.'

'You promised to keep it a secret,' he said, 'you promised.'

'Yes, I promised.'

'And now that you're going to marry Skinny, we'll be properly coupled off as we should have been years ago. We should have been – but youth! – our youth got in the way, didn't it?'

'Life got in the way,' I said.

'But everything's going to be all right now. You'll keep my secret, won't you? You promised.' He had released my feet. I edged a little farther from him.

I said, 'If Kathleen intends to marry you, I shall tell her that you're already married.'

'You wouldn't do a dirty trick like that, Needle? You're going to be happy with Skinny, you wouldn't stand in the way of my – '

'I must, Kathleen's my best friend,' I said swiftly.

He looked as if he would murder me and he did, he stuffed hay into my mouth until it could hold no more, kneeling on my body to keep it still, holding both my wrists tight in his huge left hand. I saw the red full lines of his mouth and the white slit of his teeth last thing on earth. Not another soul passed by as he pressed my body into the stack, as he made a deep nest for me, tearing up the hay to make a groove the length of my corpse, and finally pulling the warm dry stuff in a mound over this concealment, so natural-looking in a broken haystack. Then George climbed down, took up his bottle of milk, and went his way. I suppose that was why he looked so unwell when I stood, nearly five years later, by the barrow in the Portobello Road and said in easy tones, 'Hallo, George!'

The Haystack Murder was one of the notorious crimes of that year.

My friends said, 'A girl who had everything to live for.'

After a search that lasted twenty hours, when my body was found, the evening papers said, '"Needle" is found: in haystack!'

Kathleen, speaking from that Catholic point of view which takes some getting used to, said, 'She was at Confession only the day before she died – wasn't she lucky?'

The poor byre-hand who sold us the milk was grilled for hour after hour by the local police, and later by Scotland Yard. So was George. He admitted walking as far as the haystack with me, but he denied lingering there.

'You hadn't seen your friend for ten years?' the Inspector asked him.

'That's right,' said George.

'And you didn't stop to have a chat?'

'No. We'd arranged to meet later at dinner. My cousin was waiting for the milk, I couldn't stop.'

The old soul, his cousin, swore that he hadn't been gone more than ten minutes in all, and she believed it to the day of her death a few months later. There was the microscopic evidence of hay on George's jacket, of course, but the same evidence was on every man's jacket in the district that fine harvest year. Unfortunately, the byreman's hands were even brawnier and mightier than George's. The marks on my wrists had been done by such hands, so the laboratory charts indicated when my post-mortem was all completed. But the wrist-marks weren't enough to pin down the crime to either man. If I hadn't been wearing my long-sleeved cardigan, it was said, the bruises might have matched up properly with someone's fingers.

Kathleen, to prove that George had absolutely no motive, told the police that she was engaged to him. George thought this a little foolish. They checked up on his life in Africa, right back to his living with Matilda. But the marriage didn't come out – who would think of looking up registers in the Congo? Not that this would have proved any motive for murder. All the same, George was relieved when the inquiries were over without the marriage to Matilda being disclosed. He was able to have his nervous breakdown at the same time as Kathleen had hers, and they recovered together and got married, long after the police had shifted their inquiries to an Air Force camp five miles from Kathleen's aunt's home. Only a lot of excitement and drinks came of those investigations. The Haystack Murder was one of the unsolved crimes that year.

Shortly afterwards the byre-hand emigrated to Canada to start afresh, with the help of Skinny, who felt sorry for him.

After seeing George taken away home by Kathleen that Saturday in the Portobello Road, I thought that perhaps I might be seeing more of him in similar circumstances. The next Saturday I looked out for him, and at last there he was, without Kathleen, half-worried, half-hopeful.

I dashed his hopes. I said, 'Hallo, George!'

He looked in my direction, rooted in the midst of the flowing market-mongers in that convivial street. I thought to myself, 'He looks as if he had a mouthful of hay.' It was the new bristly maize-coloured beard and moustache surrounding his great mouth suggested the thought, gay and lyrical as life.

'Hallo, George!' I said again.

I might have been inspired to say more on that agreeable morning, but he didn't wait. He was away down a side-street and along another street and down one more, zig-zag, as far and as devious as he could take himself from the Portobello Road.

Nevertheless he was back again next week. Poor Kathleen had brought him in her car. She left it at the top of the street, and got out with him, holding him tight by the arm. It grieved me to see Kathleen ignoring the spread of scintillations on the stalls. I had myself seen a charming Battersea box quite to her taste, also a pair of enamelled silver ear-rings. But she took no notice of these wares, clinging close to George, and, poor Kathleen – I hate to say how she looked.

And George was haggard. His eyes seemed to have got smaller as if he had been recently in pain. He advanced up the road with Kathleen on his arm, letting himself lurch from side to side with his wife bobbing beside him, as the crowds asserted their rights of way.

'Oh, George!' I said. 'You don't look at all well, George.'

'Look!' said George. 'Over there by the hardware barrow. That's Needle.'

Kathleen was crying. 'Come back home, dear,' she said.

'Oh, you don't look well, George!' I said.

They took him to a nursing home. He was fairly quiet, except on Saturday mornings when they had a hard time of it to keep him indoors and away from the Portobello Road.

But a couple of months later he did escape. It was a Monday.

They searched for him in the Portobello Road, but actually he had gone off to Kent to the village near the scene of the Haystack Murder. There he went to the police and gave himself up, but they could tell from the way he was talking that there was something wrong with the man.

'I saw Needle in the Portobello Road three Saturdays running,' he explained, 'and they put me in a private ward but I got away while the nurses were seeing to the new patient. You remember the murder of Needle – well, I did it. Now you know the truth, and that will keep bloody Needle's mouth shut.'

Dozens of poor mad fellows confess to every murder. The police obtained an ambulance to take him back to the nursing home. He wasn't there long. Kathleen gave up her shop and devoted herself to looking after him at home. But she found that the Saturday mornings were a strain. He insisted on going to see me in the Portobello Road and would come back to insist that he'd murdered Needle. Once he tried to tell her something about Matilda, but Kathleen was so kind and solicitous, I don't think he had the courage to remember what he had to say.

Skinny had always been rather reserved with George since the murder. But he was kind to Kathleen. It was he who persuaded them to emigrate to Canada so that George should be well out of reach of the Portobello Road.

George has recovered somewhat in Canada but of course he will never be the old George again, as Kathleen writes to Skinny. 'That Haystack tragedy did for George,' she writes. 'I feel sorrier for George sometimes than I am for poor Needle. But I do often have Masses said for Needle's soul.'

I doubt if George will ever see me again in the Portobello Road. He broods much over the crumpled snapshot he took of us on the haystack. Kathleen does not like the photograph, I don't wonder. For my part, I consider it quite a jolly snap, but I don't think we were any of us so lovely as we look in it, gazing blatantly over the ripe cornfields, Skinny with his humorous expression, I secure in my difference from the rest, Kathleen with her head prettily perched on her hand, each reflecting fearlessly in the face of George's camera the glory of the world, as if it would never pass.

ELLEN GILCHRIST

Revenge

It was the summer of the Broad Jump Pit.

The Broad Jump Pit, how shall I describe it! It was a bright orange rectangle in the middle of a green pasture. It was three feet deep, filled with river sand and sawdust. A real cinder track led up to it, ending where tall poles for pole-vaulting rose forever in the still Delta air.

I am looking through the old binoculars. I am watching Bunky coming at a run down the cinder path, pausing expertly at the jump-off line, then rising into the air, heels stretched far out in front of him, landing in the sawdust. Before the dust has settled Saint John comes running with the tape, calling out measurements in his high, excitable voice.

Next comes my thirteen-year-old brother, Dudley, coming at a brisk jog down the track, the pole-vaulting pole held lightly in his delicate hands, then vaulting, high into the sky. His skinny tanned legs make a last, desperate surge, and he is clear and over.

Think how it looked from my lonely exile atop the chicken house. I was ten years old, the only girl in a house full of cousins. There were six of us, shipped to the Delta for the summer, dumped on my grandmother right in the middle of a world war.

They built this wonder in answer to a V-Mail letter from my father in Europe. The war was going well, my father wrote, within a year the Allies would triumph over the forces of evil, the world would be at peace, and the Olympic torch would again be brought down from its mountain and carried to Zurich or Amsterdam or London or Mexico City, wherever free men lived and worshipped sports. My father had been a participant in an Olympic event when he was young.

Therefore, the letter continued, Dudley and Bunky and Philip and Saint John and Oliver were to begin training. The United States would need athletes now, not soldiers.

201

They were to train for broad jumping and pole-vaulting and discus throwing, for fifty-, one-hundred-, and four-hundred-yard dashes, for high and low hurdles. The letter included instructions for building the pit, for making pole-vaulting poles out of cane, and for converting ordinary saw-horses into hurdles. It ended with a page of tips for proper eating and admonished Dudley to take good care of me as I was my father's own dear sweet little girl.

The letter came one afternoon. Early the next morning they began construction. Around noon I wandered out to the pasture to see how they were coming along. I picked up a shovel.

'Put that down, Rhoda,' Dudley said. 'Don't bother us now. We're working.'

'I know it,' I said. 'I'm going to help.'

'No, you're not,' Bunky said. 'This is the Broad Jump Pit. We're starting our training.'

'I'm going to do it too,' I said. 'I'm going to be in training.'

'Get out of here now,' Dudley said. 'This is only for boys, Rhoda. This isn't a game.'

'I'm going to dig it if I want to,' I said, picking up a shovelful of dirt and throwing it on Philip. On second thought I picked up another shovelful and threw it on Bunky.

'Get out of here, Ratface,' Philip yelled at me. 'You German spy.' He was referring to the initials on my Girl Scout uniform.

'You goddamn niggers,' I yelled. 'You niggers. I'm digging this if I want to and you can't stop me, you nasty niggers, you Japs, you Jews.' I was throwing dirt on everyone now. Dudley grabbed the shovel and wrestled me to the ground. He held my arms down in the coarse grass and peered into my face.

'Rhoda, you're not having anything to do with this Broad Jump Pit. And if you set foot inside this pasture or come around here and touch anything we will break your legs and drown you in the bayou with a crowbar around your neck.' He was twisting my leg until it creaked at the joints. 'Do you get it, Rhoda? Do you understand me?'

'Let me up,' I was screaming, my rage threatening to split open my skull. 'Let me up, you goddamn nigger, you Jap, you spy. I'm telling Grannie and you're going to get the worst whipping of your life. And you better quit digging this hole for the horses to fall in. Let me up, let me up. Let me go.'

'You've been ruining everything we've thought up all summer,' Dudley said. 'And you're not setting foot inside this pasture.'

In the end they dragged me back to the house, and I ran screaming into the kitchen where Grannie and Calvin, the black man who did the cooking, tried to comfort me, feeding me pound cake and offering to let me help with the mayonnaise.

'You be a sweet girl, Rhoda,' my grandmother said, 'and this afternoon we'll go over to Eisenglas Plantation to play with Miss Ann Wentzel.'

'I don't want to play with Miss Ann Wentzel,' I screamed. 'I hate Miss Ann Wentzel. She's fat and she calls me a Yankee. She said my socks were ugly.'

'Why, Rhoda,' my grandmother said. 'I'm surprised at you. Miss Ann Wentzel is your own sweet friend. Her momma was your momma's roommate at All Saints'. How can you talk like that?'

'She's a nigger,' I screamed. 'She's a goddamned nigger German spy.'

'Now it's coming. Here comes the temper,' Calvin said, rolling his eyes back in their sockets to make me madder. I threw my second fit of the morning, beating my fists into a door frame. My grandmother seized me in soft arms. She led me to a bedroom where I sobbed myself to sleep in a sea of down pillows.

The construction went on for several weeks. As soon as they finished breakfast every morning they started out for the pasture. Wood had to be burned to make cinders, sawdust brought from the sawmill, sand hauled up from the riverbank by wheelbarrow.

When the pit was finished the savage training began. From my several vantage points I watched them. Up and down, up and down they ran, dove, flew, sprinted. Drenched with sweat they wrestled each other to the ground in bitter feuds over distances and times and fractions of inches.

Dudley was their self-appointed leader. He drove them like a demon. They began each morning by running around the edge of the pasture several times, then practising their hurdles and dashes, then on to discus throwing and callisthenics. Then on to the Broad Jump Pit with its endless challenges.

They even pressed the old mare into service. Saint John was from New Orleans and knew the British ambassador and was thinking of being a polo player. Up and down the pasture he drove the poor old creature, leaning far out of the saddle, swatting a basketball with my grandaddy's cane.

I spied on them from the swing that went out over the bayou, and from the roof of the chicken house, and sometimes from the pasture fence itself, calling out insults or attempts to make them jealous.

'Guess what,' I would yell, 'I'm going to town to the Chinaman's store.' 'Guess what, I'm getting to go to the beauty parlour.' 'Doctor Biggs says you're adopted.'

They ignored me. At meals they sat together at one end of the table, making jokes about my temper and my red hair, opening their mouths so I could see their half-chewed food, burping loudly in my direction.

At night they pulled their cots together on the sleeping porch, plotting against me while I slept beneath my grandmother's window, listening to the soft assurance of her snoring.

I began to pray the Japs would win the war, would come marching into Issaquena County and take them prisoners, starving and torturing them, sticking bamboo splinters under their fingernails. I saw myself in the Japanese colonel's office, turning them in, writing their names down, myself being treated like an honoured guest, drinking tea from tiny blue cups like the ones the Chinaman had in his store.

They would be outside, tied up with wire. There would be Dudley, begging for mercy. What good to him now his loyal gang, his photographic memory, his trick magnet dogs, his perfect pitch, his camp shorts, his Baby Brownie Camera?

I prayed they would get polio, would be consigned forever to iron lungs. I put myself to sleep at night imagining their laboured breathing, their five little wheelchairs lined up by the store as I drove by in my father's Packard, my arm around the jacket of his blue uniform, on my way to Hollywood for my screen test.

Meanwhile, I practised dancing. My grandmother had a black housekeeper named Baby Doll who was a wonderful dancer. In the mornings I followed her around while she dusted, begging for dancing lessons. She was a big woman, as tall as a man, and gave off a dark rich smell, an unforgettable incense, a combination of Evening in Paris and the sweet perfume of the cabins.

Baby Doll wore bright skirts and on her blouses a pin that said REMEMBER, then a real pearl, then HARBOR. She was engaged to a sailor and was going to California to be rich as soon as the war was over.

I would put a stack of heavy, scratched records on the record player, and Baby Doll and I would dance through the parlours to the music of Glenn Miller or Guy Lombardo or Tommy Dorsey.

Sometimes I stood on a stool in front of the fire-place and made up lyrics while Baby Doll acted them out, moving lightly across the old dark rugs, turning and swooping and shaking and gliding.

Outside the summer sun beat down on the Delta, beating down a million volts a minute, feeding the soybeans and cotton and clover, sucking Steele's Bayou up into the clouds, beating down on the road and the store, on the pecans and elms and magnolias, on the men at work in the fields, on the athletes at work in the pasture.

Inside Baby Doll and I would be dancing. Or Guy Lombardo would be playing 'Begin the Beguine' and I would be belting out lyrics.

> 'Oh, let them begin . . . we won't care,
> America all . . . ways does its share,

We'll be there with plenty of ammo,
Allies . . . don't ever despair . . .'

Baby Doll thought I was a genius. If I was having an especially creative morning she would go running out to the kitchen and bring anyone she could find to hear me.

'Oh, let them begin any warrr . . .' I would be singing, tapping one foot against the fire-place tiles, waving my arms around like a conductor.

'Uncle Sam will fight
for the underrr . . . doggg.
Never fear, Allies, never fear.'

A new record would drop. Baby Doll would swoop me into her fragrant arms, and we would break into an improvisation on Tommy Dorsey's 'Boogie-Woogie.'

But the Broad Jump Pit would not go away. It loomed in my dreams. If I walked to the store I had to pass the pasture. If I stood on the porch or looked out my grandmother's window, there it was, shimmering in the sunlight, constantly guarded by one of the Olympians.

Things went from bad to worse between me and Dudley. If we so much as passed each other in the hall a fight began. He would hold up his fists and dance around, trying to look like a fighter. When I came flailing at him he would reach underneath my arms and punch me in the stomach.

I considered poisoning him. There was a box of white powder in the toolshed with a skull and crossbones over the label. Several times I took it down and held it in my hands, shuddering at the power it gave me. Only the thought of the electric chair kept me from using it.

Every day Dudley gathered his troops and headed out for the pasture. Every day my hatred grew and festered. Then, just about the time I could stand it no longer, a diversion occurred.

One afternoon about four o'clock an official-looking sedan clattered across the bridge and came roaring down the road to the house.

It was my cousin, Lauralee Manning, wearing her WAVE uniform and smoking Camels in an ivory holder. Lauralee had been widowed at the beginning of the war when her young husband crashed his Navy training plane into the Pacific.

Lauralee dried her tears, joined the WAVES, and went off to avenge his death. I had not seen this paragon since I was a small child, but I had memorized the photograph Miss Onnie Maud, who was Lauralee's mother, kept on her dresser. It was a photograph of Lauralee leaning against the rail of a destroyer.

Not that Lauralee ever went to sea on a destroyer. She was spending the war in Pensacola, Florida, being secretary to an admiral.

Now, out of a clear blue sky, here was Lauralee, home on leave with a two-carat diamond ring and the news that she was getting married.

'You might have called and given some warning,' Miss Onnie Maud said, turning Lauralee into a mass of wrinkles with her embraces. 'You could have softened the blow with a letter.'

'Who's the groom?' my grandmother said. 'I only hope he's not a pilot.'

'Is he an admiral?' I said, 'or a colonel or a major or a commander?'

'My fiancé's not in uniform, honey,' Lauralee said. 'He's in real estate. He runs the war-bond effort for the whole state of Florida. Last year he collected half a million dollars.'

'In real estate!' Miss Onnie Maud said, gasping. 'What religion is he?'

'He's Unitarian,' she said. 'His name is Donald Marcus. He's best friends with Admiral Semmes, that's how I met him. And he's coming a week from Saturday, and that's all the time we have to get ready for the wedding.'

'Unitarian!' Miss Onnie Maud said. 'I don't think I've ever met a Unitarian.'

'Why isn't he in uniform?' I insisted.

'He has flat feet,' Lauralee said gaily. 'But you'll love him when you see him.'

Later that afternoon Lauralee took me off by myself for a ride in the sedan.

'Your mother is my favourite cousin,' she said, touching my face with gentle fingers. 'You'll look just like her when you grow up and get your figure.'

I moved closer, admiring the brass buttons on her starched uniform and the brisk way she shifted and braked and put in the clutch and accelerated.

We drove down the river road and out to the bootlegger's shack where Lauralee bought a pint of Jack Daniel's and two Cokes. She poured out half of her Coke, filled it with whiskey, and we roared off down the road with the radio playing.

We drove along in the lengthening day. Lauralee was chain-smoking, lighting one Camel after another, tossing the butts out the window, taking sips from her bourbon and Coke. I sat beside her, pretending to smoke a piece of rolled-up paper, making little noises into the mouth of my Coke bottle.

We drove up to a picnic spot on the levee and sat under a tree to look out at the river.

'I miss this old river,' she said. 'When I'm sad I dream about it licking the tops of the levees.'

I didn't know what to say to that. To tell the truth I was afraid to say much of anything to Lauralee. She seemed so splendid. It was enough to be allowed to sit by her on the levee.

'Now, Rhoda,' she said, 'your mother was matron of honour in my wedding to Buddy, and I want you, her own little daughter, to be maid of honour in my second wedding.'

I could hardly believe my ears! While I was trying to think of something to say to this wonderful news I saw that Lauralee was crying, great tears were forming in her blue eyes.

'Under this very tree is where Buddy and I got engaged,' she said. Now the tears were really starting to roll, falling all over the front of her uniform. 'He gave me my ring right where we're sitting.'

'The maid of honour?' I said, patting her on the shoulder, trying to be of some comfort. 'You really mean the maid of honour?'

'Now he's gone from the world,' she continued, 'and I'm marrying a wonderful man, but that doesn't make it any easier. Oh, Rhoda, they never even found his body, never even found his body.'

I was patting her on the head now, afraid she would forget her offer in the midst of her sorrow.

'You mean I get to be the real maid of honour?'

'Oh, yes, Rhoda, honey,' she said. 'The maid of honour, my only attendant.' She blew her nose on a lace-trimmed handkerchief and sat up straighter, taking a drink from the Coke bottle.

'Not only that, but I have decided to let you pick out your own dress. We'll go to Greenville and you can try on every dress at Nell's and Blum's and you can have the one you like the most.'

I threw my arms around her, burning with happiness, smelling her whiskey and Camels and the dark Tabu perfume that was her signature. Over her shoulder and through the low branches of the trees the afternoon sun was going down in an orgy of reds and blues and purples and violets, falling from sight, going all the way to China.

Let them keep their nasty Broad Jump Pit, I thought. Wait till they hear about this. Wait till they find out I'm maid of honour in a military wedding.

Finding the dress was another matter. Early the next morning Miss Onnie Maud and my grandmother and Lauralee and I set out for Greenville.

As we passed the pasture I hung out the back window making faces at the athletes. This time they only pretended to ignore me. They couldn't ignore this wedding. It was going to be in the parlour instead of the church so they wouldn't even get to be altar boys. They wouldn't get to light a candle.

'I don't know why you care what's going on in that pasture,' my grandmother said. 'Even if they let you play with them all it would do is make you a lot of ugly muscles.'

'Then you'd have big old ugly arms like Weegie Toler,' Miss Onnie Maud said. 'Lauralee, you remember Weegie Toler, that was a swimmer. Her arms got so big no one would take her to a dance, much less marry her.'

'Well, I don't want to get married anyway,' I said. 'I'm never getting married. I'm going to New York City and be a lawyer.'

'Where does she get those ideas?' Miss Onnie Maud said.

'When you get older you'll want to get married,' Lauralee said. 'Look at how much fun you're having being in my wedding.'

'Well, I'm never getting married,' I said. 'And I'm never having any children. I'm going to New York and be a lawyer and save people from the electric chair.'

'It's the movies,' Miss Onnie Maud said. 'They let her watch anything she likes in Indiana.'

We walked into Nell's and Blum's Department Store and took up the largest dressing-room. My grandmother and Miss Onnie Maud were seated on brocade chairs and every saleslady in the store came crowding around trying to get in on the wedding.

I refused to even consider the dresses they brought from the 'girls" department.

'I told her she could wear whatever she wanted,' Lauralee said, 'and I'm keeping my promise.'

'Well, she's not wearing green satin or I'm not coming,' my grandmother said, indicating the dress I had found on a rack and was clutching against me.

'At least let her try it on,' Lauralee said. 'Let her see for herself.' She zipped me into the green satin. It came down to my ankles and fit around my midsection like a girdle, making my waist seem smaller than my stomach. I admired myself in the mirror. It was almost perfect. I looked exactly like a nightclub singer.

'This one's fine,' I said. 'This is the one I want.'

'It looks marvellous, Rhoda,' Lauralee said, 'but it's the wrong colour for the wedding. Remember I'm wearing blue.'

'I believe the child's colour-blind,' Miss Onnie Maud said. 'It runs in her father's family.'

'I am not colour-blind,' I said, reaching behind me and unzipping the dress. 'I have twenty-twenty vision.'

'Let her try on some more,' Lauralee said. 'Let her try on everything in the store.'

I proceeded to do just that, with the salesladies getting grumpier and grumpier. I tried on a gold gabardine dress with a rhinestone-studded cummerbund, I tried on a pink ballerina-length formal and a lavender voile tea dress and several silk suits. Somehow nothing looked right.

'Maybe we'll have to make her something,' my grandmother said.

'But there's no time,' Miss Onnie Maud said. 'Besides first we'd have to find out what she wants. Rhoda, please tell us what you're looking for.'

Their faces all turned to mine, waiting for an answer. But I didn't know the answer.

The dress I wanted was a secret. The dress I wanted was dark and tall and thin as a reed. There was a word for what I wanted, a word I had seen in magazines. But what was that word? I could not remember.

'I want something dark,' I said at last. 'Something dark and silky.'

'Wait right there,' the saleslady said. 'Wait just a minute.' Then, from out of a pre-war storage closet she brought a black-watch plaid recital dress with spaghetti straps and a white piqué jacket. It was made of taffeta and rustled when I touched it. There was a label sewn into the collar of the jacket. *Little Miss Sophisticate*, it said. *Sophisticate*, that was the word I was seeking.

I put on the dress and stood triumphant in a sea of ladies and dresses and hangers.

'This is the dress,' I said. 'This is the dress I'm wearing.'

'It's perfect,' Lauralee said. 'Start hemming it up. She'll be the prettiest maid of honour in the whole world.'

All the way home I held the box on my lap thinking about how I would look in the dress. Wait till they see me like this, I was thinking. Wait till they see what I really look like.

I fell in love with the groom. The moment I laid eyes on him I forgot he was flat-footed. He arrived bearing gifts of music and perfume and candy, a warm dark-skinned man with eyes the colour of walnuts.

He laughed out loud when he saw me, standing on the porch with my hands on my hips.

'This must be Rhoda,' he exclaimed, 'the famous red-haired maid of honour.' He came running up the steps, gave me a slow, exciting hug, and presented me with a whole album of Xavier Cugat records. I had never owned a record of my own, much less an album.

Before the evening was over I put on a red formal I found in a trunk and did a South American dance for him to Xavier Cugat's 'Poinciana'. He said he had never seen anything like it in his whole life.

The wedding itself was a disappointment. No one came but the immediate family and there was no aisle to march down and the only music was Onnie Maud playing 'Liebstraum'.

Dudley and Philip and Saint John and Oliver and Bunky were dressed in long pants and white shirts and ties. They had fresh military crew cuts and looked like a nest of new birds, huddled together on the blue velvet sofa, trying to keep their hands to themselves, trying to figure out how to act at a wedding.

The elderly Episcopal priest read out the ceremony in a gravelly smoker's voice, ruining all the good parts by coughing. He was in a bad mood because Lauralee and Mr Marcus hadn't found time to come to him for marriage instruction.

Still, I got to hold the bride's flowers while he gave her the ring and stood so close to her during the ceremony I could hear her breathing.

The reception was better. People came from all over the Delta. There were tables with candles set up around the porches and sprays of greenery in every corner. There were gentlemen sweating in linen suits and the record player playing every minute. In the back hall Calvin had set up a real professional bar with tall, permanently frosted glasses and ice and mint and lemons and every kind of whiskey and liqueur in the world.

I stood in the receiving line getting compliments on my dress, then wandered around the rooms eating cake and letting people hug me. After a while I got bored with that and went out to the back hall and began to fix myself a drink at the bar.

I took one of the frosted glasses and began filling it from different bottles, tasting as I went along. I used plenty of crème de menthe and soon had something that tasted heavenly. I filled the glass with crushed ice, added three straws, and went out to sit on the back steps and cool off.

I was feeling wonderful. A full moon was caught like a kite in the pecan trees across the river. I sipped along on my drink. Then, without planning it, I did something I had never dreamed of doing. I left the porch alone at night. Usually I was in terror of the dark. My grandmother had told me that alligators come out of the bayou to eat children who wander alone at night.

I walked out across the yard, the huge moon giving so much light I almost cast a shadow. When I was nearly to the water's edge I turned and looked back toward the house. It shimmered in the moonlight like a jukebox alive in a meadow, seemed to pulsate with music and laughter and people, beautiful and foreign, not a part of me.

I looked out at the water, then down the road to the pasture. The Broad Jump Pit! There it was, perfect and unguarded. Why had I never thought of doing this before?

I began to run toward the road. I ran as fast as my Mary Jane pumps would allow me. I pulled my dress up around my waist and climbed the fence in one motion, dropping lightly down on the other side. I was sweating heavily, alone with the moon and my wonderful courage.

I knew exactly what to do first. I picked up the pole and hoisted it over my head. It felt solid and balanced and alive. I hoisted it up and down a few times as I had seen Dudley do, getting the feel of it.

Then I laid it ceremoniously down on the ground, reached behind me, and unhooked the plaid formal. I left it lying in a heap on the ground. There I stood, in my cotton underpants, ready to take up pole-vaulting.

I lifted the pole and carried it back to the end of the cinder path. I ran slowly down the path, stuck the pole in the wooden cup, and attempted throwing my body into the air, using it as a lever.

Something was wrong. It was more difficult than it appeared from a distance. I tried again. Nothing happened. I sat down with the pole across my legs to think things over.

Then I remembered something I had watched Dudley doing through the binoculars. He measured down from the end of the pole with his fingers spread wide. That was it, I had to hold it closer to the end.

I tried it again. This time the pole lifted me several feet off the ground. My body sailed across the grass in a neat arc and I landed on my toes. I was a natural!

I do not know how long I was out there, running up and down the cinder path, thrusting my body further and further through space, tossing myself into the pit like a mussel shell thrown across the bayou.

At last I decided I was ready for the real test. I had to vault over a cane barrier. I examined the pegs on the wooden poles and chose one that came up to my shoulder.

I put the barrier pole in place, spit over my left shoulder, and marched back to the end of the path. Suck up your guts, I told myself. It's only a pole. It won't get stuck in your stomach and tear out your insides. It won't kill you.

I stood at the end of the path eyeballing the barrier. Then, above the incessant racket of the crickets, I heard my name being called. Rhoda . . . the voices were calling. Rhoda . . . Rhoda . . . Rhoda . . . Rhoda.

I turned toward the house and saw them coming. Mr Marcus and Dudley and Bunky and Calvin and Lauralee and what looked like half the wedding. They were climbing the fence, calling my name, and coming to get me. Rhoda . . . they called out. Where on earth have you been? What on earth are you doing?

I hoisted the pole up to my shoulders and began to run down the path, running into the light from the moon. I picked up speed, thrust the pole into the cup, and threw myself into the sky, into the still Delta night. I sailed up and was clear and over the barrier.

I let go of the pole and began my fall, which seemed to last a long, long time. It was like falling through clear water. I dropped into the sawdust and lay very still, waiting for them to reach me.

Sometimes I think whatever has happened since has been of no real interest to me.

EMMA TENNANT

Rigor Beach

Friday. 6 p.m.

Ingrid did the last things, awaiting this unknown man, to ensure his comfort, even his surprise. Little fronds of jasmine sprouted in a glass. On the round table were bottles of wine and champagne. I LOVE YOU she had lipsticked on the mirror, which shone, now evening had come and the lights outside in the boulevard were lit, like neon in a room otherwise comfortable and dusty. This is it, she said aloud, for she regretted her age and that there had been so many. And, This will be a holiday to remember, she added. A pâté the size of a fist was laid out ready. Toast when he had come. She went to the window and looked out suddenly tired at the strolling crowds and the shops in the arcades like bright boxes and the strip of static sea beyond. The bell sounded. As much as she could do, after the energy and expectation of the day, to go and pull it open.

7 p.m.

And so I grew up in Paris, Ingrid explained to the stranger. That's why I love the Coast. We came here for our holidays always. And you?

The man, who was fair-haired – and this was a secret disappointment to Ingrid – smiled and nodded and held out his glass for more. Constraint remained between them although the bottle of champagne was nearly emptied and the gold paper at its neck frayed, showing the wire beneath. He was handsome certainly, but spoke little. A toast crumb clung to the smooth skin above his upper lip. There was no violence in him – Ingrid had seldom felt so unafraid. She had become more of a man in his presence perhaps for when he failed to answer she strode about the room half-dancing and would laugh at the sound of carnival music in the street, wishing, although she would not wish herself anywhere else on earth, for a moment the wearer of a monstrous nose or Humpty Dumpty head. She

212

must alert him somehow. And he had seen the lipsticked mirror and stayed quiet. He sat a little too forward yet his legs, crossed in green velvet trousers, were elegant. She paused, pretending for the first time to observe his hands.

8 p.m.

The man and Ingrid sat together on the settee. Which faced the open French windows, a smell of cheap scent and salt air blowing in. Because of the nearness of the sea the upholstery in the apartment was sticky and clung for longer than was normal to bare flesh. Ingrid's legs were glued there, the man's hands playing over them like moths; as if the furniture had trapped her and made her quiet at last and the man still free to come and go as he pleased. Now he was so close, signs of fatigue were visible about his eyes, which were blue and slanted and hung suspended like flies in the surrounding spiders' webs of vein and tissue.

Are we falling in love? Ingrid asked him. She felt all at once sad, and imagined this must be the cause. The man smiled, as if resigned to her talk.

9 p.m.

In the bedroom, two doors down the grey-painted landing, Ingrid and the man stripped to the skin and climbed between sheets which were cold and dank. In the dark pool they lay for a moment stunned, then swam for each other. Ingrid knew her own smell and fought to recognise his, but it was nothing she had known yet, it was faint, might even be repulsive, and there was a lotion on the hair which made her see, suddenly in the blackness ringed with magenta circles from her eyes, a day at the seaside long ago when her father had carried her across rocks to a hidden beach. The skin of his face was fine, like sand running through an hourglass when it touched hers. The chest was concave and hesitant, the hips narrow. There was no desire yet – outrage even from his body that it should burn and rise up and exhaust itself.

10 p.m.

Ingrid's tongue probed the man's penis and it shrank and floated away at first like a sea anemone under the water before thickening and beginning to throb. He turned to lie on her again, for in the intervening hour he had lain spreadeagled on her twice; each time retreating cold at the entrance to what she saw now as a monstrous cave, hot and overhung with lichens, filled with an inner sea. Then he was there, uncertain. Ingrid saw there were slippery steps descending, and he was afraid to miss the handrail and plunge perilously. He came and went, going always as if he might never return. The hair tore a little, giving way. She lay entranced, on her own clock of these things time passed slowly. Deep under water, she felt the hulls of great boats as they went above her on the surface, obscuring the sun. She lost something of herself, joined to his body, and when she came it was with a sense of loss, seeing their white bones, long forgotten, scattered on the ocean bed. The man slept. Only to wake and find her hands cupping him, curving round his penis like hands protecting a candle from the wind.

Saturday. 1 a.m.

Ingrid rode astride the man, her head higher than it could usually be and the wall in front of her like a dim screen where patterns from her eyes flickered and faint moving shadows of light from the street outside. She galloped across a marsh. There was no breath in the air, the man lay still under her. Bunches of reed poked up out of the wet clay. He shrank, but not before sending a shower of red stars up into her. Triumphant, Ingrid said: We'll go to the beach tomorrow. What a holiday we'll have! Already, as she climbed down from him, she planned with swift strokes the picnic box and the checkered tablecloth spread out over the sand. The man's sand-coloured hair she would garland with the wild lilies that grew there. She breathed in deeply, expecting salt and the stench of seaweed which bobbed like knotted fingers in the pools. But he smelled of wet flannel, and she told him, although she knew he would laugh at her for this, that she felt she might grow a crop of mustard and cress on his body. She lay beside him, caressing his shoulders. He turned his head to one side and slept.

Saturday. 8 a.m.

When the man made to go, Ingrid held him down and stared intensely into his face. Her mother was there, loveless. The tides receded, leaving an empty expanse where the pale, half-cloudy sky was reflected. Her entrails went, and she saw herself in the bare day ahead as square and white as the walls of her apartment. Nothing was contained in her. He was tired, for he sighed as she held him and made only a slight move of resistance. She rose with a leap, went to the cupboard and pulled out bright scarves and straw hats in her search. The room was soon littered with holiday wear, as if something exciting were about to happen and the silks and red cottons must be agitated by the preparations. The butt of the pistol came hard into her hand. The man looked only a little surprised, his eyebrows going up in semicircles, like a clown. The bullet hole in the side of his head was perfectly small and round.

Saturday. 12 p.m.

Ingrid ransacked the apartment, pulling from the backs of musty shelves the plastic cocktail sticks and frilly serviettes and miniature Japanese umbrellas with which she had adorned her previous parties. She went in to the man, he was stiff now, and she knelt beside him, she on the floor so that her eyes were level with his body. With wads of face tissue she propped up his penis, stiff too though she felt no regret. Jewelled hatpins, imitation rubies, made eyes at the top of the phallus, like the beam of light from a watch tower sweeping the sea. Along the smooth plain of his chest and abdomen, where a few hairs grew, bent double as if flattened by the wind, she planted her holiday resort: the gay paper umbrellas shading little tables and chairs of red and blue plastic; a lacy napkin laid out as picnic cloth. Armpits and arms were undulating dunes and these she filled and covered with shells, which were dry and brittle, long since removed from the beach. His face she painted blue from her pot of eye shadow, and made foam-specked waves of cold cream along the ridges of cheekbone and jaw. So that the neck, a thin peninsula of golden sand, ran to an unmoving, glistening sea. She had no idea of his name, but she wished to name him. J, she scratched with nail scissors along a thigh as biscuit-coloured and striated as a cliff. The initial she had chosen stood out a pale red, like lettering on seaside rock, and she put her mouth there, sucking at the flesh.

Sunday. 6 p.m.

It had been hot all day, and Ingrid had paced the apartment, going every few minutes to the French windows to look out at the crowd of holiday-makers below. Down the landing, in the room where the sun never penetrated, the body had begun to bloat and leak. At first she had shored it up, pressing face tissue and beach towels against the oozing apertures. But she was tired now, and went less often to kiss the legs and arms, kneel by the beach with her eyes, like pools of trapped water, just beyond the sand dunes. It was growing dark and she threw on her shawl, went to promenade with the rest in the crowded arcades. She knew, by the time she returned, there would be the smell of the sea in the apartment, and rotting weed.

KATE SAUNDERS

Jim's Angel

'We travel along time in a straight line, like a spider making thread.' Clara addressed Ursula's massive, tweedy bottom, which was on a level with her face. 'I certainly don't believe that the thread ever loops back on itself, so that past and present mingle.'

'There are some things you can't leave behind. They're like photographs.' Ursula's voice was tight with the strain of bending down. 'They recur along the line, until something happens to erase them.'

Clara sighed, and turned her sad, misted gaze outwards across the churchyard. The vast Norfolk sky made the black trees on the horizon look like the pattern on the rim of a bowl. 'I don't understand. You've been so strange and cross, ever since we came back.'

'And you were the one who was supposed to be upset by it,' said Ursula. 'Upstaging you, am I?'

'What are you talking about? What? Have I done something?' Clara, her back resting comfortably against a gravestone, spoke with tremulous sorrow. She was wrapped in a soft jacket of pale blue wool, with a grey cashmere jersey underneath and lace-trimmed thermals under that. Slender and elegant, she swooned into the stone like a Victorian lady on a chaise-longue. Her white hair was rolled into an immaculate pleat, fastened by combs of real tortoiseshell. Her great languid eyes were grey, tinged with lavender. She was a brittle, fine-boned beauty, with an impalpable air of tragic sweetness, which made everything around her seem coarse and obvious. At the age of sixty-two, she was reinventing old age, investing it with dignified grace. Whereas Ursula, just turned sixty, looked simply terrible.

But people had always remarked on the difference between the two Shottery sisters. Ursula was fat, weatherbeaten and loudly jolly. The Mediterranean sun, under which they had lived for the past thirty-five

years, had melted her jowls so that they ran down her face like icecream.
She liked hard, bright colours and knobbly ceramic jewellery. The bosom
of her fiercely orange jersey was studded with cigarette burns, and she had
found her shapeless green tweed suit at the village jumble sale on their first
Saturday back. She always tried not to spend too much of her sister's
money, as if Clara could have done without her.

Clara remembered someone – who? – remarking that Ursula had inner
qualities of true beauty, and that her reverential worship of Clara was the
most beautiful one of all. The worship had always been there, warm as a
blanket, when they were the two Shottery girls, the pretty and the plain. If
it had not been for her, Clara would never have survived the trauma of her
brief life as young Mrs Vibart. She shivered.

'It's dreadfully frosty, isn't it?' She waited for Ursula to apologise for the
cold, and take her home. Ursula went on working, as if she had not heard.
She was crouched beside the grave, pulling at the weeds, her face turned
away.

Eventually, she said: 'I call it a bloody disgrace. Just look at the state of
Jim's angel.' The cracked concrete angel lay sprawled on its side in the
brown grass, bound and gagged with sinewy ropes of ivy. Ursula began to
snap these away, a scimitar of ash drooping from the end of her cigarette.
'Every single year we were away, I sent that verger five pounds for the
upkeep of the grave. Unless he puts that angel back on its little plinth, I
shall take him to the county court.'

Clara glanced at the back of the angel's head, without interest. 'I never
did care for your angel. It looks like Shirley Temple.'

'It was all the mason had in the yard,' snapped Ursula. 'If we hadn't been
in such a rush to leave, I could have ordered a better one.'

'I was so very ill.' Clara said this in a reminiscent tone, but she meant it
as a rebuke. Ursula only grunted, and she tried again. 'Is the writing still
there?'

'Oh, yes.' Ursula snatched at the frost-patched curtain of bindweed, and
pulled it aside before Clara could avoid reading:

> JAMES GEORGE VIBART
> TILL THE DAY BREAKS AND
> THE SHADOWS FLEE AWAY

Ursula turned to frown at her. 'Nothing can take away that writing.'

'No,' she agreed. She felt a disagreeable twinge of fear, and suddenly
remembered that it had been Jim who remarked upon Ursula's inner
beauty, in the early days of their marriage. They had both depended on her
so. 'Ursula, do let's go home!'

Straightening, with her broad hand in the small of her back, Ursula
shouted angrily at the sky: 'Burn and sink that verger, he's done damn all!'

*

Later, in the cavernous, stone-flagged kitchen of the Yellow House, Ursula brought up the subject again. Over the past five days, Clara had learned to dread it. 'I once asked Jim if he thought people ever came back.'

'Did you?' with a papery, delicate hand, Clara shook out her pills. The bottles were lined up on an old lacquered tray, and she washed them down in Evian, sipped from a crystal wine glass. Ursula's misshapen pottery mug, half-filled with slops of instant coffee, offended her. She pushed it away. 'What did he say?'

'He said nothing could keep him away from you.'

Three of the little violet pellets scattered on the tray. 'Are you suggesting he's still here somewhere?'

'It's coming up to the anniversary. How like him, if he came back to explain.'

'Explain what?' demanded Clara, with unusual irritation, 'Why do you keep trying to frighten me?' She wished she could get a look at Ursula's face, but she was at the Aga, stirring a stew made of hunks of muddy local vegetables. The smell of cayenne pepper and tomato puree mingled with the mildewed breath of the Yellow House, once Clara's bridal home.

'Naturally, when it happened, you were so ill I didn't have time to think about anything else,' Ursula said. 'But afterwards, I did wonder why he never left a note. He was very much given to notes, was Jim.'

Clumsily, Clara chased the last slippery pill round the tray, and put it on her tongue with a shaking hand. She was remembering the notes Jim had left around the place for her. They had an unpleasant immediacy, unsoftened by the long lapse of time. 'Yes,' she said.

Ursula was chatty, but it was possible to detect a gleam of menace. 'Wasn't it odd of him? And rather endearing. Like those people with cleft palates, who agonise one by telling long stories.'

'Why do you keep talking about Jim?' Clara asked despairingly.

'I feel like it.'

'You haven't mentioned him for years – and you know how ill it makes me.'

'But Clara dear, you have to face it sometime. Especially now we've come back.'

Clara found a more graceful position, and focused her mind on her tragedy, until she found the underground seam of poignancy and self-pity that had sustained her all these years.

'Perhaps you're right. I was so happy, so very much in love. And then in one afternoon, it was all over.'

'Fuck,' Ursula said distinctly.

Clara was amazed. 'What?'

'Dropped the knife in the casserole.'

'Oh. Yes, well . . . naturally, I think of him. This frosty weather reminds me . . . we were only together for one year and seven months. But perhaps I should be grateful. Some people never experience a love like mine.'

Ursula, stirring her stew, muttered something which seemed to end with 'cow-shit', which Clara decided not to understand. She wondered if Ursula was going senile.

'I remember it so clearly,' she continued. 'He was whistling when he came in, just as he always did. There were ignorant people who thought he was a bit simple, but I used to tell them, look how happy he is. And not simple, I used to say, unless you mean the sancta simplicitas of saints and children. Oh yes, he came in whistling. I never could have guessed anything was wrong.'

'Why'd you run out after him, then?' asked Ursula.

'Why?' echoed Clara blankly.

'You wouldn't explain it. You were too ill.'

'Well, I was taking him out some sandwiches.'

'What was in them?'

'Well – ' Clara's breathing had become rapid and shallow, 'I don't recall – cheese – '

'Can't have been cheese, dear. He couldn't stand cheese.'

'No, no he couldn't – I'd forgotten.'

'You must have known something was wrong, to go dashing out into the woods like that.'

'It was all blown out of my mind when I found his body,' Clara said heatedly. 'How do you expect me to remember? He was lying on the snow, and it had gone all pink around him, like a sunset. And everything was blank until I woke up and you were here. They found me lying across him, my dress all drenched with his blood, begging him to wake up. And he sacrificed himself for me, because he was afraid he would become a burden. Oh poor, poor Jim, as if I would have minded – '

'What happened to the sandwiches?'

'Ursula, what has got into you? Why are you being so funny? Please don't talk about him any more. He's dead, and the dead can't come back.'

'They can,' said Ursula, 'Not all ghosts wear trunk-hose and carry their heads under their arms. But don't look so horrified, dear – you told me you'd give every penny of Jim's money, for one more glimpse of him. You should be glad.'

That night, Clara dreamt that she had killed an angel, just as Tootles shot down the Wendy-bird in *Peter Pan*. It lay gasping and dying on the patch of lawn outside the dining room window, its ghastly white wings twitching, like a poor wounded swan. She woke in terror, and called for Ursula. She called again. A board creaked in the next room. Nobody came.

*

Ursula was sitting up in bed, dropping tears and cigarette ash into the bundle of yellowed exercise paper scattered across the eiderdown. For thirty-five years, Clara's least whisper of pain had cut into her own soul, and the dream had died so recently that part of her still longed to soothe and comfort. But the woman was a liar and a murderess and a complete bitch, and leaving her to whimper alone in the dark was only a fragment of the punishment she deserved. Ever since she had found the box of Jim's letters, shoved hastily among the speckled corpses of old pillows in the wardrobe, she had been rewriting history. The truth brought him back.

When Ursula came down from Cambridge, the Vibarts of Canehurst House had employed her five mornings a week as Jim's tutor. 'Tutoring' had been a polite euphemism for teaching him to read and write. The family had been rich landowners since the Conquest, and each generation had turned up a dimwit or two. Jim had come into a handsome legacy of this congenital fogginess, and if he had not also been the heir to the Vibart acres, he would probably have ended up in a special school, happily making baskets and blanket-stitching dishcloths. By the time he was twenty-two, he was unmistakably backward.

Ursula had hated Clara for talking about sancta simplicitas, but it was absolutely true. Jim's feeble mind had been irradiated by a miraculous sweetness. Ideas, even basic ones, could find no foothold in his memory, but he retained affections like marble. Never discouraged by his lack of progress, he sat with Ursula in the Canehurst library, hour after hour, his fair hair falling across his flushed face as he tried to decipher the simplest words. Tiers of books, collected by his ancestors, towered around him, and he could barely stumble through the headlines in *The Sporting life*. Ursula grew very fond of him, and she encouraged his passion for writing. Jim felt that a sentiment put down on paper had a kind of mystical legality, and he littered the house with a trail of loving notes.

His parents roared over the spelling of these letters, but they made Ursula want to cry – they expressed such perfect trust and assurance. Once read, they were carefully gathered up. Jim hoarded them proudly in boxes, written proof of his intellectual achievements. As soon as she had read her way through the box she found at the Yellow House, Ursula wondered how she could have been such a fool.

This was the romantic scenario she had carried around for all these years: Act One. A Forest Glade. Jim (tenor) is introduced simultaneously to Clara (soprano) and the notion of sexual love. Overcoming parental opposition, aided and abetted by Ursula (contralto), the young couple settle in the dower house on the edge of the Canehurst woods. Interlude: married bliss. Act Two. Love illuminates Jim's mind to such an extent that he is made aware of his own state. A doctor (basso profundo) tells him what he might become, and warns him against having children. To save Clara from the future while she is still young, he goes out to the woods with his rabbiting gun, shoots himself rather inexpertly in the heart and bleeds to death. Clara goes mad with grief, and is removed by her adoring sister, to live in a permanently precarious mental state in the South of France. Heart and mind broken, she sings of her eternal grief. Curtain.

In the abstract, it was still a pretty tale. Ursula might have believed it forever, if the lease had not expired in France, and brought them home. Now, she looked back at Clara's long illness, and saw not pastel-hued grief, but hideous guilt. Only guilt could have made her keep the letter, instead of putting on the boiler. And what a letter it was – it must have taken poor Jim ages. Despair had elevated his spelling to new heights of absurdity. Even now, Ursula remembered most of the names, and marvelled over them. 'Mik Yug' was Mick Young, the baker's roundsman. 'Husmen' was obviously Douglas Houseman, the married solicitor who had lived at The Pines in Dawn Lane. 'Berd' could only mean John Beard, the organist at St Stephen's. Jim had known about them, and that last day, the famous day when he came in whistling, he had caught her at it. Clara had destroyed him with the simplest cruelty. She had murdered the innocent. Ursula crammed the back of her hand into her mouth, to muffle her sobs. Faithless. And all that time, she had kept the faith so well.

Clara found the first note on her dressing table, impaled on the bristles of her silver-backed hairbrush. It was an aged scrap of paper torn from an exercise book, decorated with a row of staggering pot-hooks: 'I will cum bak'. Smelling blood on her dress, she screamed, and retreated clumsily against the bed, her hand on her demented, racing heart.

In the passage outside, she heard Ursula's heavy tread. Clara's hand shook so violently that she could hardly pick up the note. She caught up with her on the stairs.

'What does this mean?'

'It means I will come back,' Ursula said promptly. 'Fairly obvious, I should say.'

Furious, Clara grabbed the back of her dressing-gown. 'You – you put it there – what are you trying to do to me?'

'I don't know what you're talking about.'

'It's from Jim – it's one of his bloody letters – '

'Is it?' Ursula shook away her hand. 'You'd better take one of your white pills.'

Clara was left on the landing, weeping and trembling in her lawn nightgown. 'Where are they?' she wailed after her sister. 'I don't know where they are!'

She found the second one while she was searching for her pills in the kitchen cupboard. It was neatly fastened to the zip of one of Ursula's suede boots, which were drying on the hotplate of the Aga. 'Gon out but cumming bak soon'.

'I don't want you back, you idiot!' shrieked Clara. 'Lie there and bleed, and see if I care! What the hell does she know? She didn't have to marry you!' She hurled the boots into the boiler, and Ursula finally came in to see what the dreadful smell was. She found Clara huddled on the kitchen floor, with two long trails of snot oozing from her nose like pieces of elastic.

Ursula called the doctor, and asked him if he could make any sense of Clara's ramblings about letters. He was a local man, and he knew the story of the Yellow House. Drinking coffee together at the kitchen table, while Clara slept upstairs, they both agreed that it was very sad.

'I feel responsible,' sighed Ursula, 'I should never have allowed her to come back. Do you take sugar?'

Clara became afraid to leave her room. She was haunted by the dread of finding another of Jim's old notes. Sometimes, they were rolled in the neck of a pill bottle; sometimes, they were in her underwear drawer, or lying in her saucer, or pinned to the lavatory chain. She was often alone. Ursula had embarked on a brisk social life in the village, and she left Clara in the empty house, listening for noises, and often convinced that she heard someone whistling as they came to her door.

'Do you know what day it is?' asked Ursula, one afternoon. Clara wrapped her hands around her teacup. Her eyes and lips had sunk, and she wore one of Ursula's violent mauve jerseys to warm her scraggy, ungainly bundle of bones. Her long white hair snaked down her back in two matted plaits.

Ursula continued chattily, as if everything was normal: 'You've been barmy exactly thirty-five years today.'

'Tell him to go away,' croaked Clara.

'This time thirty-five years ago, poor Jim still had an hour or two to live. I suppose just about now, you would have heard him whistling as he came in. And then you would have made those famous sandwiches. What did you say was in them?'

'What sandwiches? Give me my pills.'

'Here they are, dear.' Ursula set the lacquered tray in front of her. Clara yelped and threw the teacup at the wall.

'Take it away! Take it away! It wasn't my fault!'

'You really should read this one,' Ursula said. 'It's the last, and the best. The end crowns all.' She picked up the piece of paper on the tray, and offered it to Clara.

Clara read 'Fatheless', and a dribble of saliva glistened on her chin. 'I cant liv wen you don lov me. Yo ar not inersent I am inersent I am not mad yo ar fatheless'

'Faithless,' said Ursula. 'Faithless murderess. The butcher, the baker, the candlestick-maker, the organist and Mr Houseman from The Pines – you read it, you evil woman – you – you killed him!'

Clara, on tottering matchstick legs, ran out of the Yellow House into the dying sun.

'Whiteways seems to be a pleasant enough place,' Ursula told the Vicar, as they strolled out of church after morning service. 'Not that she notices her surroundings much these days. Ever since I found her, gibbering over that poor smashed angel, and trying to wipe its heart with the hem of her dress, she's hardly spoken a word of sense. But she's been unbalanced for years. It was only a matter of time.'

'You'll be lonely at the Yellow House without her,' the Vicar said. 'If there's anything we can do –'

They halted beside the grave, where Jim's angel had been cemented back on its little plinth.

'I shall keep busy,' said Ursula, staunchly brave.

The Vicar watched as she tenderly arranged her bunch of early primroses, and thought what a splendid woman she was.

ALICE WALKER

The Revenge of Hannah Kemhuff

In grateful memory of Zora Neale Hurston

Two weeks after I became Tante Rosie's apprentice we were visited by a very old woman who was wrapped and contained, almost smothered, in a half-dozen skirts and shawls. Tante Rosie (pronounced Ro'*zee*) told the woman she could see her name, Hannah Kemhuff, written in the air. She told the woman further that she belonged to the Order of the Eastern Star.

The woman was amazed. (And I was, too! Though I learned later that Tante Rosie held extensive files on almost everybody in the country, which she kept in long cardboard boxes under her bed.) Mrs Kemhuff quickly asked what else Tante Rosie could tell her.

Tante Rosie had a huge tank of water on a table in front of her, like an aquarium for fish, except there were no fish in it. There was nothing but water and I never was able to see anything in it. Tante Rosie, of course, could. While the woman waited Tante Rosie peered deep into the tank of water. Soon she said the water spoke to her and told her that although the woman looked old, she was not. Mrs Kemhuff said that this was true, and wondered if Tante Rosie knew the reason she looked so old. Tante Rosie said she did not and asked if she would mind telling us about it. (At first Mrs Kemhuff didn't seem to want me there, but Tante Rosie told her I was trying to learn the rootworking trade and she nodded that she understood and didn't mind. I scrooched down as small as I could at the corner of Tante Rosie's table, smiling at her so she wouldn't feel embarrassed or afraid.)

'It was during the Depression,' she began, shifting in her seat and adjusting the shawls. She wore so many her back appeared to be humped!

'Of course,' said Tante Rosie, 'and you were young and pretty.'

'How do you know that?' exclaimed Mrs Kemhuff. 'That is true. I had been married already five years and had four small children and a husband with a wandering eye. But since I married young – '

224

'Why, you were little more than a child,' said Tante Rosie.

'Yes,' said Mrs Kemhuff. 'I were not quite twenty years old. And it was hard times everywhere, all over the country and, I suspect, all over the world. Of course, no one had television in those days, so we didn't know. I don't even know if it was invented. We had a radio before the Depression which my husband won in a poker game, but we sold it somewhere along the line to buy a meal. Anyway, we lived for as long as we could on the money I brought in as a cook in a sawmill. I cooked cabbage and cornpone for twenty men for two dollars a week. But then the mill closed down, and my husband had already been out of work for some time. We were on the point of starvation. We was so hungry, and the children were getting so weak, that after I had crapped off the last leaves from the collard stalks I couldn't wait for new leaves to grow back. I dug up the collards, roots and all. After we ate that there was nothing else.

'As I said, there was no way of knowing whether hard times was existing around the world because we did not then have a television set. And we had sold the radio. However, as it happened, hard times hit everybody we knew in Cherokee County. And for that reason the government sent food stamps which you could get if you could prove you were starving. With a few of them stamps you could go into town to a place they had and get so much and so much fat back, so much and so much of corn meal, and so much and so much of (I think it was) red beans. As I say, we was, by then, desperate. And my husband prevailed on me for us to go. I never wanted to do it, on account of I have always been proud. My father, you know, used to be one of the biggest colored peanut growers in Cherokee County and we never had to ask nobody for nothing.

'Well, what had happened in the meantime was this: My sister, Carrie Mae – '

'A tough girl, if I remember right,' said Tante Rosie.

'Yes,' said Mrs Kemhuff, 'bright, full of spunk. Well, she were at that time living in the North. In Chicago. And she were working for some good white people that give her they old clothes to send back down here. And I tell you they were good things. And I was glad to get them. So, as it was gitting to be real cold, I dressed myself and my husband and the children up in them clothes. For see, they was made up North to be worn up there where there's snow at and they were warm as toast.'

'Wasn't Carrie Mae later killed by a gangster?' asked Tante Rosie.

'Yes, she were,' said the woman, anxious to go on with her story. 'He were her husband.'

'Oh,' said Tante Rosie quietly.

'Now, so I dresses us all up in our new finery and with our stomachs growling all together we goes marching off to ask for what the government said was due us as proud as ever we knew how to be. For even my husband,

225

when he had on the right clothes, could show some pride, and me, whenever I remembered how fine my daddy's peanut crops had provided us, why there was nobody with stiffer backbone.'

'I see a pale and evil shadow looming ahead of you in this journey,' said Tante Rosie, looking into the water as if she'd lost a penny while we weren't looking.

'That shadow was sure pale and evil all right,' said Mrs Kemhuff. 'When we got to the place there was a long line, and we saw all of our friends in this line. On one side of the big pile of food was the white line – and some rich peoples was in that line too – and on the other side there was the black line. I later heard, by the by, that the white folks in the white line got bacon and grits, as well as meal, but that is neither here nor there. What happened was this. As soon as our friends saw us all dressed up in our nice warm clothes, though used and castoff they were, they began saying how crazy we was to have worn them. And that's when I began to notice that all the people in the black line had dressed themselves in tatters. Even people what had good things at home, and I knew some of them did. What does this mean? I asked my husband. But he didn't know. He was too busy strutting about to even pay much attention. But I began to be terribly afraid. The baby had begun to cry and the other little ones, knowing I was nervous, commenced to whine and gag. I had a time with them.

'Now, at this time my husband had been looking around at other women and I was scared to death I was going to lose him. He already made fun of me and said I was arrogant and proud. I said that was the way to be and that he should try to be that way. The last thing I wanted to happen was for him to see me embarrassed and made small in front of a lot of people because I knew if that happened he would quit me.

'So I was standing there hoping that the white folks what give out the food wouldn't notice that I was dressed nice and that if they did they would see how hungry the babies was and how pitiful we all was. I could see my husband over talking to the woman he was going with on the sly. She was dressed like a flysweep! Not only was she raggedy, she was dirty! Filthy dirty, and with her filthy slip showing. She looked so awful she disgusted me. And yet there was my husband hanging over her while I stood in the line holding on to all four of our children. I guess he knew as well as I did what that woman had in the line of clothes at home. She was always much better dressed than me and much better dressed than many of the white peoples. That was because, they say she was a whore and took money. Seems like people want that and will pay for it even in a depression!'

There was a pause while Mrs Kemhuff drew a deep breath. Then she continued.

'So soon I was next to get something from the young lady at the counter. All around her I could smell them red beans and my mouth was watering for a taste of fresh-water cornpone. I was proud, but I wasn't fancy. I just wanted something for me and the children. Well, there I was, with the children hanging to my dresstails, and I drew myself up as best I could and made the oldest boy stand up straight, for I had come to ask for what was mine, not to beg. So I wasn't going to be acting like a beggar. Well, I want you to know that that little slip of a woman, all big blue eyes and yellow hair, that little *girl*, took my stamps and then took one long look at me and my children and across at my husband – all of us dressed to kill I guess she thought – and she took my stamps in her hand and looked at them like they was dirty, and then she give them to an old gambler who was next in line behind me! "You don't need nothing to eat from the way you all dressed up, Hannah Lou," she said to me. "But Miss Sadler," I said, "my children is hungry." "They don't look hungry," she said to me. "Move along now, somebody here may really need our help!" The whole line behind me began to laugh and snigger, and that little white moppet sort of grinned behind her hands. She give the old gambler double what he would have got otherwise. And there me and my children about to keel over from want.

'When my husband and his woman saw and heard what happened they commenced to laugh, too, and he reached down and got her stuff, piles and piles of it, it seemed to me then, and helped her put it in somebody's car and they drove off together. And that was about the last I seen of him. Or her.'

'Weren't they swept off a bridge together in the flood that wiped out Tunica City?' asked Tante Rosie.

'Yes,' said Mrs Kemhuff. 'Somebody like you might have helped me then, too, though looks like I didn't need it.'

'So –'

'So after that looks like my spirit just wilted. Me and my children got a ride home with somebody and I tottered around like a drunken woman and put them to bed. They was sweet children and not much trouble, although they was about to go out of their minds with hunger.'

Now a deep sadness crept into her face, which until she reached this point had been still and impassive.

'First one then the other of them took sick and died. Though the old gambler came by the house three or four days later and divided what he had left with us. He had been on his way to gambling it all away. The Lord called him to have pity on us and since he knew us and knew my husband had deserted me he said he were right glad to help out. But it was mighty late in the day when he thought about helping out and the children were far gone. Nothing could save them except the Lord and he seemed to have other things on his mind, like the wedding that spring of the mean little moppet.'

Mrs Kemhuff now spoke through clenched teeth.

'My spirit never recovered from that insult, just like my heart never recovered from my husband's desertion, just like my body never recovered from being almost starved to death. I started to wither in that winter and each year found me more hacked and worn down than the year before. Somewhere along them years my pride just up and left altogether and I worked for a time in a whorehouse just to make some money, just like my husband's woman. Then I took to drinking to forget what I was doing, and soon I just broke down and got old all at once, just like you see me now. And I started about five years ago to going to church. I was converted again, 'cause I felt the first time had done got worn off. But I am not restful. I dream and have nightmares still about the little moppet, and always I feel the moment when my spirit was trampled down within me while they all stood and laughed and she stood there grinning behind her hands.'

'Well,' said Tante Rosie. 'There are ways that the spirit can be mended just as there are ways that the spirit can be broken. But one such as I am cannot do both. If I am to take away the burden of shame which is upon you I must in some way inflict it on someone else.'

'I do not care to be cured,' said Mrs Kemhuff. 'It is enough that I have endured my shame all these years and that my children and my husband were taken from me by one who knew nothing about us. I can survive as long as I need with the bitterness that has laid every day in my soul. But I could die easier if I knew something, after all these years, had been done to the little moppet. God cannot be let to make her happy all these years and me miserable. What kind of justice would that be? It would be monstrous!'

'Don't worry about it, my sister,' said Tante Rosie with gentleness. 'By the grace of the Man-God I have use of many powers. Powers given me by the Great One Herself. If you can no longer bear the eyes of the enemy that you see in your dreams the Man-God, who speaks to me from the Great Mother of Us All, will see that those eyes are eaten away. If the hands of your enemy have struck you they can be made useless.' Tante Rosie held up a small piece of what was once lustrous pewter. Now it was pock-marked and blackened and deteriorating.

'Do you see this metal?' she asked.

'Yes, I see it,' said Mrs Kemhuff with interest. She took it in her hands and rubbed it.

'The part of the moppet you want destroyed will rot in the same fashion.'

Mrs Kemhuff relinquished the piece of metal to Tante Rosie.

'You are a true sister,' she said.

'Is it enough?' Tante Rosie asked.

'I would give anything to stop her grinning behind her hands,' said the woman, drawing out a tattered billfold.

'Her hands or the grinning mouth?' asked Tante Rosie.

'The mouth grinned and the hands hid it,' said Mrs Kemhuff.

'Ten dollars for one area, twenty for two,' said Tante Rosie.

'Make it the mouth,' said Mrs Kemhuff. 'That is what I see most vividly in my dreams.' She laid a ten-dollar bill in the lap of Tante Rosie.

'Let me explain what we will do,' said Tante Rosie, coming near the woman and speaking softly to her, as a doctor would speak to a patient. 'First we will make a potion that has a long history of use in our profession. It is a mixture of hair and nail parings of the person in question, a bit of their water and faeces, a piece of their clothing heavy with their own scents, and I think in this case we might as well add a pinch of goober dust; that is, dust from the graveyard. This woman will not outlive you by more than six months.'

I had thought the two women had forgotten about me, but now Tante Rosie turned to me and said, 'You will have to go out to Mrs Kemhuff's house. She will have to be instructed in the recitation of the curse-prayer. You will show her how to dress the black candles and how to pay Death for his interception in her behalf.'

Then she moved over to the shelf that held her numerous supplies: oils of Bad and Good Luck Essence, dried herbs, creams, powders, and candles. She took two large black candles and placed them in Mrs Kemhuff's hands. She also gave her a small bag of powder and told her to burn it on her table (as an altar) while she was praying the curse-prayer. I was to show Mrs Kemhuff how to 'dress' the candles in vinegar so they would be purified for her purpose.

She told Mrs Kemhuff that each morning and evening for nine days she was to light the candles, burn the powder, recite the curse-prayer from her knees and concentrate all her powers on getting her message through to Death and the Man-God. As far as the Supreme Mother of Us All was concerned, She could only be moved by the pleas of the Man-God. Tante Rosie herself would recite the curse-prayer at the same time that Mrs Kemhuff did, and together she thought the two prayers, prayed with respect, could not help but move the Man-God, who, in turn, would unchain Death, who would already be eager to come down on the little moppet. But her death would be slow in coming because first the Man-God had to hear all of the prayers.

'We will take those parts of herself that we collect, the faeces, water, nail parings, etcetera, and plant them where they will bring for you the best results. Within a year's time the earth will be rid of the woman herself, even as almost immediately you will be rid of her grin. Do you want something else for only two dollars that will make you feel happy even today?' asked Tante Rosie.

But Mrs Kemhuff shook her head. 'I'm carefree enough already, knowing that her end will be before another year. As for happiness, it is something that deserts you once you know it can be bought and sold. I will not live to see the end result of your work, Tante Rosie, but my grave will fit nicer, having someone proud again who has righted a wrong and by so doing lies straight and proud throughout eternity.'

And Mrs Kemhuff turned and left, bearing herself grandly out of the room. It was as if she had regained her youth; her shawls were like a stately toga, her white hair seemed to sparkle.

2

To the Man-God: O great One, I have been sorely tried by my enemies and have been blasphemed and lied against. My good thoughts and my honest actions have been turned to bad actions and dishonest ideas. My home has been disrespected, my children have been cursed and ill-treated. My dear ones have been backbitten and their virtue questioned. O Man-God, I beg that this that I ask for my enemies shall come to pass:

That the South wind shall scorch their bodies and make them wither and shall not be tempered to them. That the North wind shall freeze their blood and numb their muscles and that it shall not be tempered to them. That the West wind shall blow away their life's breath and will not leave their hair grow, and that their fingernails shall fall off and their bones shall crumble. That the East wind shall make their minds grow dark, their sight shall fail and their seed dry up so that they shall not multiply.

I ask that their fathers and mothers from their furtherest generation will not intercede for them before the great throne, and the wombs of their women shall not bear fruit except for strangers, and that they shall become extinct. I pray that the children who may come shall be weak of mind and paralyzed of limb and that they themselves shall curse them in their turn for ever turning the breath of life into their bodies. I pray that disease and death shall be forever with them and that their worldly goods shall not prosper, and that their crops shall not multiply and that their cows, their sheep, and their hogs and all their living beasts shall die of starvation and thirst. I pray that their house shall be unroofed and that the rain, the thunder and lightning shall find the innermost recesses of their home and that the foundation shall crumble and the floods tear it asunder. I pray that the sun shall not shed its rays on them in benevolence, but instead it shall beat down on them and burn them and destroy them. I pray that the moon shall not give them peace, but instead shall deride them and decry them and cause their minds to shrivel. I pray that their friends shall betray them and cause them loss of power, of gold and of silver, and that their enemies shall smite them until they beg for mercy which shall not be given them. I pray that their tongues shall forget how to speak in sweet words, and that it shall be paralyzed and that all about them will be desolation, pestilence and death. O Man-God, I ask you for all these things because they have dragged me in the dust and destroyed my good name; broken my heart and caused me to curse the day that I was born. So be it.

This curse-prayer was regularly used and taught by rootworkers, but since I did not know it by heart, as Tante Rosie did, I recited it straight from Zora Neale Hurston's book, *Mules and Men*, and Mrs Kemhuff and I learned it on our knees together. We were soon dressing the candles in vinegar, lighting them, kneeling and praying – intoning the words rhythmically – as if we had been doing it this way for years. I was moved by the fervor with which Mrs Kemhuff prayed. Often she would clench her fists before her closed eyes and bite the insides of her wrists as the women do in Greece.

3

According to courthouse records Sarah Marie Sadler, 'the little moppet,' was born in 1910. She was in her early twenties during the Depression. In 1932 she married Ben Jonathan Holley, who later inherited a small chain of grocery stores and owned a plantation and an impressive stand of timber. In the spring of 1963, Mrs Holley was fifty-three years old. She was the mother of three children, a boy and two girls; the boy a floundering clothes salesman, the girls married and oblivious, mothers themselves.

The elder Holleys lived six miles out in the country, their house was large, and Mrs Holley's hobbies were shopping for antiques, gossiping with colored women, discussing her husband's health and her children's babies, and making spoon bread. I was able to glean this much from the drunken ramblings of the Holleys' cook, a malevolent nanny with gout, who had raised, in her prime, at least one tan Holley, a preacher whom the Holleys had sent to Morehouse.

'I bet I could get the nanny to give us all the information and nail parings we would ever use,' I said to Tante Rosie. For the grumpy woman drank muscatel like a sow and clearly hated Mrs Holley. However, it was hard to get her tipsy enough for truly revealing talk and we were quickly running out of funds.

'That's not the way,' Tante Rosie said one evening as she sat in her car and watched me lead the nanny out of the dreary but secret-evoking recesses of the Six Forks Bar. We had already spent six dollars on muscatel.

'You can't trust gossips or drunks,' said Tante Rosie. 'You let the woman we are working on give you everything you need, and from her own lips.'

'But that is the craziest thing I have ever heard,' I said. 'How can I talk to her about putting a fix on her without making her mad, or maybe even scaring her to death?'

Tante Rosie merely grunted.

'Rule number one. OBSERVATION OF SUBJECT. Write that down among your crumpled notes.'

'In other words – ?'

'Be direct, but not blunt.'

On my way to the Holley plantation I came up with the idea of pretending to be searching for a fictitious person. Then I had an even better idea. I parked Tante Rosie's Bonneville at the edge of the spacious yard, which was dotted with mimosas and camellias. Tante Rosie had insisted I wear a brilliant orange robe and as I walked it swished and blew about my legs. Mrs Holley was on the back patio steps, engaged in conversation with a young and beautiful black girl. They stared in amazement at the length and brilliance of my attire.

'Mrs Holley, I think it's time for me to go,' said the girl.

'Don't be silly,' said the matronly Mrs Holley. 'She is probably just a light-skinned African who is on her way somewhere and got lost.' She nudged the black girl in the ribs and they both broke into giggles.

'How do you do?' I asked.

'Just fine, how you?' said Mrs Holley, while the black girl looked on askance. They had been talking with their heads close together and stood up together when I spoke.

'I am looking for a Josiah Henson' – a runaway slave and the original Uncle Tom in Harriet Beecher Stowe's novel, I might have added. 'Could you tell me if he lives on your place?'

'That name sounds awful familiar,' said the black girl.

'Are you *the* Mrs Holley?' I asked gratuitously, while Mrs Holley was distracted. She was sure she had never heard the name.

'Of course,' she said, and smiled, pleating the side of her dress. She was a grayish blonde with an ashen untanned face, and her hands were five blunt and pampered fingers each. 'And this is my ... ah ... my friend, Caroline Williams.'

Caroline nodded curtly.

'Somebody told me old Josiah might be out this way ...'

'Well, we hadn't seen him,' said Mrs Holley. 'We were just here shelling some peas, enjoying this nice sunshine.'

'Are you a light African?' asked Caroline.

'No,' I said. 'I work with Tante Rosie, the rootworker. I'm learning the profession.'

'Whatever *for*?' asked Mrs Holley. 'I would have thought a nice-looking girl like yourself could find a better way to spend her time. I been hearing about Tante Rosie since I was a little bitty child, but everybody always said that rootworking was just a whole lot of n—, I mean colored foolishness. Of course we don't believe in that kind of thing, do we, Caroline?'

'Naw.'

The younger woman put a hand on the older woman's arm, possessively, as if to say 'You get away from here, bending my white folks' ear with your crazy mess!' From the kitchen window a dark remorseful face worked itself into various messages of 'Go away!' It was the drunken nanny.

'I wonder if you would care to prove you do not believe in rootworking?'

'Prove?' said the white woman indignantly.

'Prove?' asked the black woman with scorn.

'That is the word,' I said.

'Why, not that I'm afraid of any of this nigger magic!' said Mrs Holley staunchly, placing a reassuring hand on Caroline's shoulder. *I* was the nigger, not she.

'In that case won't you show us how much you don't have fear of it.' With the word *us* I placed Caroline in the same nigger category with me. Let her smolder! Now Mrs Holley stood alone, the great white innovator and scientific scourge, forced to man the Christian fort against heathen nigger paganism.

'Of course, if you like,' she said immediately, drawing herself up in the best English manner. Stiff upper lip, what? and all that. She had been grinning throughout. Now she covered her teeth with her scant two lips and her face became flat and resolute. Like so many white women in sections of the country where the race was still 'pure' her mouth could have been formed by the minute slash of a thin sword.

'Do you know a Mrs Hannah Lou Kemhuff?' I asked.

'No I do not.'

'She is not white, Mrs Holley, she is black.'

'Hannah Lou, Hannah Lou . . . do we know a Hannah Lou?' she asked, turning to Caroline.

'No, ma'am, we don't!' said Caroline.

'Well, she knows you. Says she met you on the bread lines during the Depression and that because she was dressed up you wouldn't give her any corn meal. Or red beans. Or something like that.'

'Bread lines, Depression, dressed up, corn meal . . . ? I don't know what you're talking about!' No shaft of remembrance probed the depths of what she had done to colored people more than twenty years ago.

'It doesn't really matter, since you don't believe . . . but she says you did her wrong, and being a good Christian, she believes all wrongs are eventually righted in the Lord's good time. She came to us for help only when she began to feel the Lord's good time might be too far away. Because we do not deal in the work of unmerited destruction, Tante Rosie and I did not see how we could take the case.' I said this humbly, with as much pious intonation as I could muster.

'Well, I'm glad,' said Mrs Holley, who had been running through the back years on her fingers.

'But,' I said, 'we told her what she could do to bring about restitution of peaceful spirit, which she claimed you robbed her of in a moment during which, as is now evident, you were not concerned. You were getting married the following spring.'

'That was '32,' said Mrs Holley. 'Hannah *Lou?*'

'The same.'

'How black *was* she? Sometimes I can recall colored faces that way.'

'That is not relevant,' I said, 'since you do not believe . . .'

'Well of *course* I don't believe!' said Mrs Holley.

'I am nothing in this feud between you,' I said. 'Neither is Tante Rosie. Neither of us had any idea until after Mrs Kemhuff left that you were the woman she spoke of. We are familiar with the deep and sincere interest you take in the poor colored children at Christmastime each year. We know you have gone out of your way to hire needy people to work on your farm. We know you have been an example of Christian charity and a beacon force of brotherly love. And right before my eyes I can see it is true you have Negro friends.'

'Just what is you want?' asked Mrs Holley.

'What *Mrs Kemhuff* wants are some nail parings, not many, just a few; some hair (that from a comb will do), some water and some faeces – and if you don't feel like doing either number one or number two, I will wait – and a bit of clothing, something that you have worn in the last year. Something with some of your odor on it.'

'What!' Mrs Holley screeched.

'They say this combination, with the right prayers, can eat away part of a person just like the disease that ruins so much fine antique pewter.'

Mrs Holley blanched. With a motherly fluttering of hands Caroline helped her into a patio chair.

'Go get my medicine,' said Mrs Holley, and Caroline started from the spot like a gazelle.

'Git away from here! Git away!'

I spun around just in time to save my head from a whack with a gigantic dust mop. It was the drunken nanny, drunk no more, flying to the defense of her mistress.

'She just a tramp and a phony!' she reassured Mrs Holley, who was caught up in an authentic faint.

Not long after I saw Mrs Holley, Hannah Kemhuff was buried. Tante Rosie and I followed the casket to the cemetery, Tante Rosie most elegant in black. Then we made our way through briers and grass to the highway. Mrs Kemhuff rested in a tangly grove, off to herself, though reasonably near her husband and babies. Few people came to the funeral, which made the faces of Mrs Holley's nanny and husband stand out all the more plainly. They had come to verify the fact that this dead person was indeed *the*

Hannah Lou Kemhuff whom Mr Holley had initiated a search for, having the entire country militia at his disposal.

Several months later we read in the paper that Sarah Marie Sadler Holley had also passed away. The paper spoke of her former beauty and vivacity, as a young woman, and of her concern for those less fortunate than herself as a married woman and pillar of the community and her church. It spoke briefly of her harsh and lengthy illness. It said all who knew her were sure her soul would find peace in heaven, just as her shrunken body had endured so much pain and heartache here on earth.

Caroline had kept us up to date on the decline of Mrs Holley. After my visit, relations between them became strained and Mrs Holley eventually became too frightened of Caroline's darkness to allow her close to her. A week after I'd talked to them Mrs Holley began having her meals in her bedroom upstairs. Then she started doing everything else there as well. She collected stray hairs from her head and comb with the greatest attention and consistency, not to say desperation. She ate her fingernails. But the most bizarre of all was her response to Mrs Kemhuff's petition for a specimen of faeces and water. Not trusting any longer the earthen secrecy of the water mains, she no longer flushed. Together with the nanny Mrs Holley preferred to store those relics of what she ate (which became almost nothing and then nothing, the nanny had told Caroline) and they kept it all in barrels and plastic bags in the upstairs closets. In a few weeks it became impossible for anyone to endure the smell of the house, even Mrs Holley's husband, who loved her but during the weeks before her death slept in a spare room of the nanny's house.

The mouth that had grinned behind the hands grinned no more. The constant anxiety lest a stray strand of hair be lost and the foul odor of the house soon brought to the hands a constant seeking motion, to the eyes a glazed and vacant stare, and to the mouth a tightly puckered frown, one which only death might smooth.

MAUREEN FREELY

Delia and the Avengers

It did not take long for us to work out a routine. I would arrive at our rendezvous spot in downtown El Paso exactly ten minutes late. I would find her in the crowd, check to make sure there were no border patrol trucks parked around the plaza, and then manoeuvre my car towards the kerb as delicately as if it were an eggshell. Delia would step forward without appearing to notice me. Without appearing to notice her, I would unlock the car doors.

As she settled herself and her carrier bags in the passenger seat, I would say, *Como esta, Delia?* She would give me a weak smile and say, *Bien, señora. Muy bien.* And sigh, to indicate that she was exaggerating.

With a pounding heart, I would begin to think of rejoining the traffic. (I had only just learned how to drive.) As my eyes darted from mirror to mirror, Delia would calmly rearrange herself, clasp her hands around her ample stomach, and listen in polite silence while the Japanese voice machine told her over and over to put on her seat belt. *Ay Chihuahua*, she would say when we were sitting safely in front of our first red light. That woman has such a strange voice. Like a *mona*.

I would agree, and then she would ask me how I was. I would tell her I was fine, and then she would ask me how my husband was. I would say he was teaching or playing golf.

She would ask after my son. I would say he was in school. She would ask me if Emma had slept through the night. I would say no, that she had woken up five times again. She would shake her head and say, *Ay, pobrecita!*

Then she would sigh again, and say how nice it was to be back in El Paso. This was the cue for me to ask her how things were on the other side

236

of the border. She would sigh tragically and say, *Ay, señora*! You will scarcely believe what I have to tell you today!

But I always did.

Delia was a good woman who had had the misfortune of marrying a bad man. He was a taxidriver who also did work on the side for the son of one of the richest men in Juarez. This may have involved smuggling. Because he had a steady job, he and his family were all eligible for passports that allowed them to shop within the El Paso city limits. This was why Delia could come to work through the official checkpoint, instead of doing what most maids had to do, which was to wade across the Rio Grande. She considered herself lucky to have retained her shopping passport in spite of the fact that she and the bad man were now divorced.

She wanted me to know that it had not been a love match. You could not follow your heart when it came to marriage – that's what her mother had told her. That's why she had sent away her childhood sweetheart, the pale, thoughtful and destitute Fernando, and opted instead for this fierce, handsome taxidriver named Eduardo who would come cruising past her house, his black eyes piercing the gauze curtains for a glimpse of Delia demurely rolling out flour tortillas for the evening meal. Fernando had a good heart, Delia's mother told her, but Eduardo had a car, and that was more important.

As Delia soon discovered, it was not enough. Already, on the first morning after the wedding, he came home with lipstick on his collar. As she laboured to remove the stain, she cried bitter tears for Fernando to come and rescue her, but he had already disappeared from the *colonia* the better to hide his broken heart. She went to her mother to cry on her shoulder. Her mother responded with a bitter and knowing laugh. Such things were to be expected, the older woman told Delia. All true men went to prostitutes, and the day would come when Delia would thank them for attending to her husband's insatiable needs. 'Everything has its place,' Delia's mother told her, and with that she returned her daughter back to hers.

And so Delia had made the best of it. Over the next fifteen years, she had given the bad man seven children. Two of them had died in early infancy – one from the heat, she told me, and one from the cold. The remaining five had thrived against all odds. Despite the crippling effect of the constant beatings to which the bad man subjected her, Delia had managed to hold her head high throughout the years of broken bones and black eyes. She had kept her surviving children well-fed, clean and neatly dressed. They had returned the favour by doing well in school. They were even regular churchgoers in spite of the fact that Delia had decided against baptizing her three youngest.

When I met Delia, only these last three were still living at home. Her eldest, the saintly Ramon, was a primary teacher. He taught in an Indian school in the mountains between Juarez and Chihuahua City. Her second eldest, Cheche, worked as a mechanic in Los Angeles. Patricia, who lived at home, was studying accounting at the university and doing well in spite of having sustained grave injuries in a car accident – in Delia's ancient and now perhaps irreparably damaged Ford Mustang. They would not know for sure if it was salvageable until they were in a position to bribe the traffic police, who had impounded it. Patricia had been working nights as a dentist's receptionist to raise the money.

Marta, the fourth child, did not have her elder siblings' air of seriousness, but she was, with her ribbons and her interest in movie stars and pretty clothes, a delightful presence. Delia's plan was to keep her in school for three more years and then marry her off to a good man. She had higher hopes for little Charlie, who was a star in the classroom and on the baseball diamond. If she played her cards right, she was sure she could turn him into an elecrician.

Three long years had passed, she told me, since the bad man had left her for the woman called La Rubia. He still returned from time to time to taunt her, but she was no longer afraid of him. She no longer let him in if he had lipstick on his collar or tequila on his breath. She did not want to remarry. She was through with men, and content with her house, her friends, her jobs and her children.

Just look at Señora Winny, she would say during the early days of our association. (Winny was a rich lady, a native El Pasoan, who was Delia's primary employer.) All that money, all those private jets and swimming pools bigger than all of Southfork, and she was enduring the same sorrows as Delia on account of having the misfortune of marrying a bad man. At the time, Winny was in the middle of divorce proceedings made messier than necessary on account of Winny having decided to use a lawyer whose most important client was her husband. But that's another story, albeit one that Delia and I discussed at length on our bi-weekly trips up the monotonous strip that was Coronado Highway – until that hot October day when she got into the car and announced to me that an amazing coincidence had occurred the previous evening on her way home from work.

To get to her neighbourhood from the border checkpoint, Delia had to take three buses. She had been waiting for the second when a handsome traffic policeman came up to the bus stop on a motorcycle. It was rush hour. He was waiting with everyone else for the lights to change, and this alone was remarkable. Traffic policemen in Juarez were a law unto themselves. The spectacle of a traffic policeman obeying the very regulations they enforced on others was enough to attract the interest of the entire bus queue. But when Delia looked into his eyes, a shudder of recognition passed first through her, and then, when he returned her gaze, through him.

'*Delia!*' he cried in a quivering voice. '*Delia! Eres tu?*'

To which she replied,

'*Fernando, eres tu?*'

Because yes, it was none other than her childhood sweetheart, the once sickly, idealistic and destitute Fernando, now a handsome traffic policeman with a mustache and a motorcycle.

He invited her to join him for a coffee. She accepted and climbed onto his motorcycle. Off they went to a place where he was so well known he didn't have to pay. Here, over the best coffee to be had in the entire city of Juarez, he told her his sad story: he, too, had married but had recently divorced his wife because she had not been able to give him any children – this was, Delia did not have to remind me, the greatest shame that could ever befall a Mexican man.

'Do you have children, Delia?' he asked. His voice was rich and deep.

She nodded modestly. 'Yes, I have five.' She proceeded to tell him her sad story. It brought tears to his eyes. 'How could any man act in such a way towards a woman of your worth?' he murmured in a cracking voice.

He asked her out to dinner. She demurred, saying that she was needed at home. He took her there on his motorcycle, causing a sensation in the neighbourhood. The next day he was back to tell her that he had found her impounded Ford Mustang and arranged for it to be taken to a garage where a trusted associate would make it as good as new. And *he* was as good as his word. No less than a week later, it was standing in front of Delia's house, surrounded by neighbours admiring its shiny new red paint job.

Fernando began to take her out to all the finest restaurants in the city on a regular basis. Once he even turned up unannounced at her son Charlie's baseball game. It was the custom for the school to give free dinners to the winning team. Charlie was therefore doubly distressed when his team lost, but Fernando saved the day by taking him out for the best meal of the boy's life.

Inevitably, Delia's bad ex-husband did not take long to find out about Fernando's reappearance. He was not pleased, but neither was he about to tangle with a traffic policeman. So he bided his time, the tequila bottle his only companion, because by now even La Rubia had grown tired of leaving lipstick on his collar.

Then came the holiday season. Fernando went to Mexico City to visit his ailing mother, while Delia was rejoined by her saintly eldest son Ramon, who was on leave from his Indian school in the mountains. They were able to celebrate a joyous Christmas, the only regretted absent family member being Cheche, the Los Angeles car mechanic. He could not travel on account of being an illegal.

The day after Christmas, another family crisis erupted. Delia's youngest sister, who lived in the *colonia* right across the river from my husband's university, and who had five children under the age of five, was abandoned by her husband, another bad man. The word was he was going to make his fortune in a cannery in the Imperial Valley. It was with this poor, abandoned woman that Delia spent New Year's Eve. Her saintly eldest son Ramon had been urging her to accompany him to a bona fide party, but she had insisted that he enjoy an evening out away from family responsibilities.

Patricia did not go out – her broken bones had not yet mended. Marta, of course, was too young for such matters. The two girls stayed up until midnight, embraced each other dutifully, and went to bed.

They were awakened at five in the morning by a hammering on the door. Patricia got up, still half asleep, and went to open it.

It was her father. He was in a drunken rage. 'Where is your mother?' he roared. She told him the truth, but he didn't believe her. 'She's out whoring with the traffic policeman, isn't she?' With that he hurled the poor girl first against the wall and then across the floor.

Out came Marta to find out what was happening. When she tried to protect her sister, her father beat her to a pulp.

They were both still unconscious when Ramon, the saintly elder brother, returned to the house.

Hours later, as he stood in the emergency room of Juarez General Hospital waiting to take his sisters and their newly broken bones home, he vowed that never again would he allow such an outrage to happen.

Delia never would have had the nerve to press charges. It was Kiki who insisted. The bad father did his best to use his powerful connections, but Ramon drew even greater power than money or privilege could buy on account of being in the right. By the time Ramon returned to his Indian school in the mountains, the bad man was behind bars with a three month sentence, and with the warning that if he repeated the offence after his release, he would return to prison for a minimum of two years.

Here followed a period of tranquility. In mid-January, my husband went to live on a beach on the Pacific coast of Mexico to work on a book. I took over his job and arranged to have Delia stay over two nights a week to help me with the children. We became closer than ever.

Fernando returned to Juarez. The romance resumed with an offer of marriage and a catch – Fernando was soon to be transferred to Mexico City. Would she follow him there? She asked for time to think – she had her children's schooling to consider. And of course he said, Delia, you have all the time in the world because you mean the world to me.

Meanwhile, her two daughters stayed at home and nursed each other back to health. Once a week, the bad father sent his laundry to the house in a taxi. Delia refused to touch it, but the daughters washed and ironed it faithfully. With the passage of time, Patricia was able to resume her accounting course. Marta was another matter. Always an indifferent student, she had now lost interest altogether. She began to play hookey and used the free time to get up to no good. There were indications of an unsuitable involvement. There was an unexplained influx of money and fripperies. Delia became worried. She went to Marta's school and discovered that Marta had not made a single appearance since the new year.

Here followed a heated domestic argument. Delia put Marta under a benign form of house arrest. Marta began to pine away even further. Suddenly it was not just school she wanted out of – it was the city of Juarez. She wanted to go live with her brother in Los Angeles.

Delia said absolutely not. There would be no one to supervise her. She would have no papers. She would end up on the streets. But the more Delia objected, the more her daughter longed to escape.

Such was the state of affairs when the bad man got out of prison in early spring.

The first thing he did was look into the Fernando problem. When he found out that the romance was still flowering, he vowed that he would not sit still until he had found a way to make his ex-wife pay. It did not take him long to figure out the perfect plan. A week after he got out of prison, he turned up at the family home with a one-way ticket to Los Angeles for his daughter Marta.

He knew exactly what he was doing. He was sending his daughter to a shameful fate, but he told Delia he didn't care. It would be a pleasure to watch Delia suffer with worry about her daughter. Delia had ruined his life. It was time for him to return the compliment.

Delia was distraught. She called her eldest son, the saintly Ramon, down from the mountains. He, too, tried to reason with Marta but to no avail. In the end, the best he could do was agree to accompany her to Los Angeles and help her settle in over the Easter holiday. That way there would be a chance of finding a responsible woman to keep an eye on her.

The bad man watched these developments and gloated from a distance. Then, two nights before Marta was due to leave, it suddenly struck him that it was not just Delia who was losing a daughter.

He was overcome by grief.

Delia was out with Fernando when the bad man turned up at the house at ten o'clock that evening. The two daughters were sitting in the kitchen listening to the radio. The first thing their father did was turn it off. 'Do you call that music?' he said. 'Is this the way your mother shows her love for you, by leaving you to your own devices on the penultimate day of your

241

blessed childhood? *I* am the one who loves you, Marta. I want you to remember that always.' With that, he threw open the front door. There, standing in the street, was an entire mariachi band, waiting to sing her a farewell song.

Mariachi bands are large and charge by the song. At the time, the rate was $25. The musicians had not escaped the notice of the neighbourhood. Everyone came outside to hear the song that Marta would choose.

'Any song you like, my daughter,' said the bad man, making sweeping gestures for the benefit of his burgeoning audience.

And Marta named a song about hope and doves, which the mariachis sang with all their heartstrings.

When it was over, his other daughter asked if she could have a song. The bad man looked alarmed. He had not counted on this extra expense. 'Of course,' said Patricia, speaking loud enough for all the neighbours to hear her, 'If it's too expensive . . .'

The bad man looked at the crowd in the street, at the scores and scores of curious heads poking out windows. 'No expense is too great for my daughters,' he said. And so Patricia requested a song about blood and tears and betrayal.

Then Marta asked for a third song, this one about an incorrigible rake. Patricia asked for a fourth about a vendetta in the desert.

They continued in this way all night, listening to love song after love song, until they were certain they had ruined their father financially.

When Delia returned at the crack of dawn, the mariachis were still singing, and the daughters still radiant with the echoes of love songs, while the bad man was slumped on the kitchen table, a broken and tearful man.

She told me it was the most magnificent moment of her life. She could not begin to describe the music, or the musicians' finery, or the expressions on the neighbours' faces, or the proud posture of her beautiful daughters, or the sight of a bad man agonizing over which to choose, financial ruination or public loss of face . . .

Two days later, Delia's saintly eldest son went with Marta to El Paso International Airport. He returned alone the following Sunday with weak assurances. It was at about this same time that my husband returned from Mexico and decided to take me and the children off to Europe for an openended holiday. I must have known that we were unlikely to return, but for some reason I felt compelled to tell Delia that I would use every opportunity to talk my husband into bringing us back to El Paso. She promised that when we returned, she would drop everything and come back to work for us.

She helped me pack. I gave her everything I didn't need – everything, that is, that my husband did not sell at the garage sale. This was attended mostly by shoppers from the other side of the border. The woman who bought our television set was a notorious evangelist whom Delia recognized from her neighbourhood. She kept interrupting the bargaining by saying she had to ask God for guidance. I remember Delia calling me over to one of the three windows in our six-bedroom condominium so that I could see the evangelist talking to the Lord in her Cadillac.

The day before we were due to leave, Delia drove over for the first time in her own car so that she could take away all the things I was giving her, things which either upset or exposed the uneasy balance of our friendship. I was only getting odd details of the saga now. Marta was 'fine', Patricia doing 'better'. The saintly Ramon was back in the mountains. Charlie was still playing baseball. The amorous Fernando was still waiting for Delia to decide on his fate.

There were some packages of books I had to send off before the post office closed. I also wanted to register to vote so that I could send in my absentee ballot against Reagan. Delia offered me the use of her car.

It was only as I was driving it out of the condominium complex that I realized this was not the Ford Mustang she had been describing to me. It wasn't even red.

It was black and its brakes hardly worked. I had to drive down the hill at fifteen miles per hour. Because the car had Juarez plates, all the other drivers on the road assumed that was where I came from too. That was how and when I discovered what it was like to be a Mexican in Texas.

When Delia left that afternoon, she even took our sour milk, saying that her sister needed it. We promised to keep in touch and for a while we did. My letters were full of cheerful lies about what a wonderful time we were having in Europe. Her replies were gloomy, with few references to her children and none to Fernando. She told me that life was harder than ever as she had not been able to find new work. When were we coming back? she kept asking. The gaps between my letters grew greater as it got harder and harder to lie to her. I think she caught on because eventually her letters stopped coming. Or was I the one who forgot to write to her? I can't remember. My own life was now taking all my attention. When my husband took the children back to Texas for a visit after our divorce, he tried to get in touch with Delia, but he couldn't find a single person who remembered her name.

ELIZABETH BOWEN

Making Arrangements

Six days after Margery's departure, a letter from her came for Hewson Blair. That surprised him; he had not expected her to write: surely the next move should be his? Assuming this, he had deliberated comfortably – there was time, it had appeared, for sustained deliberation – and now Margery had pounced back upon him suddenly. It was like being spoken to when he was settling down to a stiff book in the evening; Margery had often done this.

He remembered as he scrutinized the postmark that the last time she had written to him was from Switzerland, last Christmas. She always said she found him difficult to write to – why write now, then, when she might be better occupied? Hewson never sneered; his face lacked the finer mobility and his voice the finer inflections: he turned over the unopened letter, felt that it was compact and fat, and pinched the corners thoughtfully.

He found the name of a riverside hotel printed on the flap of the envelope, and re-read this several times with amazement, unable to conceive how a young woman who had gone away with somebody else to a riverside hotel – with white railings, Hewson imagined, and geraniums swinging in baskets, and a perpetual, even rushing past of the water – could spare some hours of her time there writing to her husband. Unless, of course, she simply wanted to tell him about Leslie.

Of course, she must have a considerable amount to say about Leslie after having lived with him under necessarily restricted conditions for the last six days. She had always told Hewson about her many friends, at great length, and as he was not interested in these people the information went in at one ear and out at the other. He imagined that Leslie was the one with the cello, though he might have been the one with the golf handicap – he could not say.

If she wanted to come back – he was slitting open the envelope carefully,

244

and this made him pause a moment – if she wanted to come back he must write briefly and say he was sorry, he could not have her, he had made other arrangements. His sister was coming to keep house for him tomorrow, and the servants were even now getting ready the spare room.

Hewson had just come in, having got away a little earlier than usual from the office, where people were beginning to know, and to speak to him awkwardly with scared faces. He had not, of course, been near the club. In stories, people who were treated as Margery had treated him threw up everything and went abroad; but Hewson did not care for travelling, and it would be difficult to leave his business just at present. He had never seen very much of Margery, his wheels went round without her; all this, if one could regard it rationally, came down to a few readjustments in one's menage and a slight social awkwardness which one would soon outgrow.

Parkins had just made up the library fire; she was drawing the curtains noiselessly across the windows. Hewson wondered what she had thought of Margery's letter as she enisled it, lonely, gleaming and defiant, on the silver salver on to which Margery had so often flung her gloves. Margery would fling her gloves on to the salver and her furs across the oak chest and swing humming into the library to read her letters by the fire. She would settle down over them like a cat over a saucer of milk, bend and smile and murmur over each, rustling the paper; and one by one drop them, crumpled, into the grate. Margery was a person who dealt summarily with her husks; bit through direct to the milk kernel of things and crunched delectably.

Tonight the grate was very tidy. Hewson watched Parkins' back and felt the room unbearably crowded.

'That's all right,' he said. 'That will do. Thank you, Parkins.'

He stood with his back to the fire, watching Parkins narrowly until she had left the room. Then he let Margery out of the envelope.

'It does seem funny to be writing to you again,' Margery wrote. 'I haven't for such ages – that note I left on the mantelpiece doesn't count, of course. Wasn't it dramatic, leaving a note like that! I couldn't help laughing; it just shows how true novels really are.

'Dear Hewson, there are several things, quite a lot, that I want sent after me at once. As I expect you saw, I didn't take more than my dressing-case. I know you will make all arrangements – you are so awfully good at that sort of thing. I suppose there are rather a lot of arrangements – I mean, like getting the divorce and sending my clothes on and writing to tell people; and I expect you would rather give away the dogs.

'We don't quite know how long a divorce takes or how one gets it, but as I told Leslie, who often gets rather depressed about all this fuss, you will be able to arrange it all beautifully. We are going abroad till it is all over;

Leslie is so fearfully sensitive. We want to go quite soon, so I should be so much obliged if you could send those clothes off to me at once. I enclose a list.

'Leslie says he thinks I am perfectly wonderful, the way I think of everything, and I suppose it really is rather wonderful, isn't it, considering you always made all the arrangements. It just shows what one can do if one is put to it. Leslie would like to send a message; he feels he can't very well send his love, but he asks me to say how sorry he is for any inconvenience this will cause you, but that he is sure you cannot fail to feel, as we do, that it is all for the best. Leslie is fearfully considerate.

'Dear Hewson, I think you are too sweet, and you know I have always liked you. I feel quite homesick sometimes in this horrid hotel, but it's no good being sentimental, is it? We never suited each other a bit, and I never quite knew what you wanted me for. I expect you will be fearfully happy now and settle down again and marry some fearfully nice girl and get the rock-garden really nice without my horrid dogs to come and scratch it up. Now, about the clothes . . .'

Directions followed.

As Hewson read this letter he remembered Leslie (though he still could not say whether he was the one with the cello or the golf handicap), a young man with a very fair short moustache and flickering lashes, who liked his port. It seemed quite right that such a fair young man should admire Margery, who was dark. Many people had, indeed, admired Margery, which gratified Hewson who had married her. Many more people praised her clothes, which still further gratified Hewson who had paid for them. When he married Margery he stamped himself as a man of taste (and a man of charm, too, to have secured her), and he rose still higher in the estimation of his friends; while even men who had thought him a dull dog in the army or at Oxford began coming to the house again.

It was all very nice, and Hewson often found himself arrested in a trance of self-congratulation; when he came in in the evenings, for instance, and found firelight flooding and ebbing in the white-panelled hall and more cards on the table, and heard Parkins moving about in the dining room, where through the slit of the door the glass and silver on the table sparkled under the low inverted corolla of the shade. Sometimes he would have to put his hand before his mouth, and pass for yawning, to conceal the slow smile that crept irresistibly across his face; as when he stood beside the really good gramophone and changed the records of thudding music for Margery and her friends to dance to. She danced beautifully with her slim, balanced partners; they moved like moths, almost soundlessly, their feet hiss-hissing faintly on the parquet. Hewson's hand brushed across the switchboard, lights would spring up dazzlingly against the ceiling and pour down opulently on to the amber floor to play and melt among the shadows of feet. This had all been very satisfactory.

Hewson never conceived or imagined, but he intended; and his home had been all that he had intended. He had a sense of fitness and never made an error in taste. He was not amusing, he did not intend to be an amusing man; but he had always intended to marry an amusing wife, a pretty little thing with charm. He considered that Margery was becoming to him, which indeed she was. He had a fine fair impassive face with the jaw in evidence and owl's eyebrows; he stood for dark oak and white panelling, good wine and billiard-tables. Margery stood for watercolours, gramophones, and rosy chintz. They had made a home together with all this; none of these elements was lacking, and thus their home had, rightly, the finality of completeness.

Tonight he dined early, and, though eating abstractedly, ate well. He knew the importance of this. They had taken out all the leaves, the table had shrunk to its smallest. Margery had often been away or out, and this evening was in no way different from many others. They brought his coffee to the table, and after coffee he went upstairs, slowly, turning out all but one of the hall lights behind him. He carried Margery's letter, and paused on the landing to look through the list again, because he had decided to get the things packed up tonight and sent off early tomorrow. As he did not wish to give Emily or Parkins Margery's letter (the list being punctuated by irrelevancies), he proposed to get the shoes and dresses out himself and leave them on the bed for Emily or Parkins to pack.

Yes, Margery was not unperceptive; he really did like making arrangements. The sense of efficiency intoxicated him, like dancing. He liked going for a thing methodically and getting it done; jotting down lists on pieces of paper and clipping the papers together and putting them away in the one inevitable drawer.

'You can't think what Hewson's like!' Margery would exult to their friends, waving a glass dessertspoon at him from her end of the table. 'He does everything and finds everything and puts everything away and sends everything off. He's absolutely amazing!'

At this, all the way down the table the shirt-fronts and pink quarter-faces veered intently toward Margery would veer round, guffawing, toward Hewson, and become three-quarter faces, twinkling over with mirth, while the ladies, tittering deprecatingly, swayed toward Hewson, their mirth drawn out into a sigh. 'You must forgive us, Mr Blair,' they implied; 'but your wife is really so amusing!' And Hewson sat on solidly and kept the wine going.

Margery's room sprang into light nakedly; the servants had taken away the pink shades. The curtains were undrawn, and Emily, with a housemaid's one cannot say how conscious sense of the dramatic, had dropped a sheet over the mirror and swathed the dressing-table: bowls and bottles here and there projected, glacial, through the folds. The room was very cold and Hewson thought of ordering a fire, then recoiled in shyness from the imagined face of Emily or Parkins. He had not entered Margery's room since her departure – he preferred to think of it as a departure rather than a flight, an ignominious scurrying-forth unworthy of the home and husband that she left. He preferred to feel that if his wife sinned, she would sin like a lady.

Margery's directions were minute, though perhaps a trifle incoherent. Hewson sat down on the sofa along the end of the bed to study the list in the light of imminent activity. He must revise it systematically, making it out into headings: 'Contents of wardrobe, contents of chest by window, contents of dressing-table drawers.' Something caught his eye; he started. Margery's pink slippers, overlooked by Emily, peeped out at him from under the valance of the bed.

From the slippers, connections of ideas brought round his eyes to the fireplace again; he had never seen it black on a chilly evening; Margery had had everything, this was a really good room. She would never have a room like this again; Leslie would not be able to give it to her. What could have been the attraction? . . . Well, that was a blind alley; it was no good wandering down there.

She had written: 'I never quite know what you wanted me for.'

That statement amazed Hewson; it simply amazed him. He got up and walked round the room, staring at the shining furniture, challenging the pictures, thinking of the library fire, the dancing-floor under the downpour of light, the oval table in the dining room compassed about for him always with an imaginary crowd of faces. Surely the sense of inclusion in all this should have justified Margery's existence to her. It was not as if he had ever bothered her to give him anything. He had assumed quite naturally that this sense of being cognate parts of a whole should suffice for both of them. He still could not understand where this had failed her.

He could not conceive what Leslie had held out to her, and what she had run to grasp.

Hewson advanced toward his reflection in the wardrobe mirror, and they stood eyeing one another sternly; then their faces softened. 'Lonely fellow,' Hewson condescended. The ghost of one of his old happy trances returned to his reflection; he saw the slow smile spread across its face, its fine face. That she should have fallen short of this . . .

He tugged at the handle of the wardrobe door, and his reflection swung toward him, flashed in the light and vanished. From the dusk within, cedar-scented and cavernous, Margery leaped out to him again as she had leaped up out of the envelope. There were so many Margerys in there, phalanx on phalanx, and the scent of her rushed out to fill this room, depose the bleak regency of Emily, and make the pictures, the chairs, the chintzes, the shadows in the alcove, suddenly significant. He drew out his fountain pen, detached a leaf from his notebook and headed it: ' Contents of Wardrobe.'

If he had been a different type of man Margery's chameleon quality would, he knew, have irritated him; the way she took colour from everything she put on, and not only took colour but became it, while shadowing behind all her changes an immutable, untouched, and careless self. Now the black dress – Hewson took it down and carried it over to the bed, and its long draperies swept the carpet, clinging to the pile, and seemed to follow him reluctantly – you would have said the black dress was the very essence, the expression of the innermost of her, till you met her in the flame-colour.

He took down the flame-colour next, and could hardly help caressing it as it lay across his arms, languishing and passive. The shimmer and rustle of it, the swinging of its pendent draperies round his feet, filled him with a sharp nostalgia, though they stood to him for nothing in particular – there had been that evening in the billiard-room. He laid the dress down reverently on the bed, like a corpse, and folded its gauzy sleeves across its bosom.

He was less tender with the one that followed, a creamy, slithery thing with a metallic brilliance that slipped down into his hands with a horrible wanton willingness. He had always felt an animosity toward it since they drove together to that dance. It slid and shone round Margery's limbs as though she were dressed in quicksilver; more beautiful than all the rest, more costly also, as Hewson knew. He let it drip down from his arms on to the bed and creep across the counterpane like a river.

He was summary, too, with the velvety things that followed, weighed down by their heavy fur hems. They were evenings at home to him, *tête-à-têtes* with their faint, discomfortable challenge; Margery tilting back her chin to yawn, or lolling sideways out of her chair to tickle her dog in the stomach, or shuffling illustrated papers. She would say: 'Talk to me, Hewson. Hewson, do talk . . .' And later: 'Hewson, I suppose evenings at home are good for one. I'm so sleepy. That does show, doesn't it, how I need sleep?'

He worked more quickly after this, carrying the dresses one by one across the room, laying them on the bed, and pausing after each to compare his list with Margery's. Sometimes the name of a colour, the description of a stuff, would puzzle him, and he pored above the two lists with bent brows, unable to make them tally. Reluctantly he would inscribe a question mark. He heard ten strike, and began working even faster. He had still to make arrangements with the chauffeur: he liked to be in bed himself by half-past eleven, and he didn't approve of keeping the servants late.

Then, leaning deep into the cupboard, he saw the red dress, melting away into the shadows of the cedar-wood. It hung alone in one corner with an air of withdrawal. Hewson reached out, twitched it down; it hung limp from his hands, unrustling, exhaling its own perfume of chiffon. He stepped back; it resisted for an infinitesimal second, then, before he could release the tension on it, tore with a long soft sound.

It came out into the light of the room hanging jagged and lamentable, the long hem trailing. Hewson had torn it, torn the red dress; of all her dresses. He looked at it in fear and a kind of defiant anger. He assured himself the stuff was rotten; she had not worn it for so long. Had, indeed, Margery's avoidance of the red dress been deliberate?

With what motive, Hewson wondered, had this unique presentation of herself been so definitely eschewed? Did it make her shy – was she then conscious that it stood for something to be forgotten? He could never have believed this of Margery; he was startled to find that he himself should suspect it. Yet he returned to this: she had never worn the red dress since *that* occasion. He had watched for it speechlessly those ensuing weeks, evening after evening, but it had never appeared again. And here he had found it, hanging in the deepest shadow, trying to be forgotten.

Margery had put the red dress down on her list; she had underlined it. It was one of the dresses she wanted to take away to Leslie. Now it was torn, irreparably torn; she would never be able to wear it.

Hewson wondered whether Margery would be angry. He quailed a little, feeling the quick storm of her wrath about him; windy little buffets of derision and a fine sting of irony. She would certainly be angry when she knew, and go sobbing with rage to Leslie: Hewson wondered whether Leslie would be adequate. He debated whether he should pack the dress. Well, since it had admittedly stood for that to Margery as well as to himself, let her have it as it was! Hewson's wits stirred – this should be his comment. Why should he let her go to Leslie with that dress, the dress in which Hewson had most nearly won her? It had been pacific, their relationship; neither of them would have admitted a crescendo, a climax, a decrescendo; but there had been a climax, and the red dress shone in both their memories to mark it. He did not think he would let the Margery who lived for Leslie wear the red dress of his own irreclaimable Margery.

Smiling and frowning a little with concentration, he eyed the thing, then gripped the folds in both hands and tore the dress effortlessly from throat to hem, refolded it, and tore again. A fine dust of silk crimsoned the air for a moment, assailed his nostrils, made him sneeze. He laid the dead dress gently down among the other dresses and stood away, looking down at them all.

These were all his, his like the room and the house. Without these dresses the inner Margery, unfostered, would never have become perceptible to the world. She would have been like a page of music written never to be played.

All her delightfulness to her friends had been in this expansion of herself into forms and colours. Hewson had fostered this expansion, as it now appeared, that Leslie might ultimately be delighted. From the hotel by the river the disembodied ghost of Margery was crying thinly to him for her body, her innumerable lovely bodies. Hewson expressed this to himself concisely and heavily, as a man should, as he stood looking down at the bed, half smiling, and said, 'She has commited suicide.'

From boyhood, Hewson had never cared for any thoughts of revenge. Revenge was a very wild kind of justice, and Hewson was a civilized man. He believed in the Good, in the balance of things, and in an eventual, tremendous pay-day. At once, the very evening Margery had left him, he had felt the matter to be out of his hands, and, wondering quite impartially how much she would be punished, had sat down almost at once to write and make arrangements with his sister. He had not, these last few days, felt sorrowful, venomous, or angry, because he had not felt at all; the making of these and other arrangements had too fully occupied him. He had always very lucidly and reasonably contended that the importance of mere feeling in determining a man's line of action is greatly overrated.

Now, looking down, he watched the dresses, tense with readiness to fall upon them if they stirred and pin them down and crush and crush and crush them. If he could unswervingly and unsparingly hold them in his eyes, he would be able to detect their movements, the irrepressible palpitation of that vitality she had infused into them. They lay there dormant; only the crimson dress was dead. He bent, and touched the creamy trickle of the ball-dress; his finger dinted it and a metallic brightness spurted down the dint, filling it like a tide. He drew back his finger, cold yet curiously vibrant from the contact. The folds were cool; and yet he had expected, had expected . . . He brought down his outspread hands slowly; they paused, then closed on handfuls of the creamy stuff that trickled icily away, between his fingers. The dress lay stretched out and provocative and did not resist him, and Hewson with dilated eyes stared down at it and did not dare to breathe.

He turned and crossed the room on tiptoe, peered out into the darkness of the trees, then drew the blinds down. He glanced round secretly and stealthily at the pictures; then he went over to the door and peered out, listening intently, on to the landing. Silence there and silence through the house. Shutting the door carefully behind him, he returned to the bedside.

It seemed to him, as he softly, inexorably approached them, that the swirls, rivers, and luxuriance of silk and silver, fur and lace and velvet, shuddered as he came. His shadow drained the colour from them as he bent over the bed.

*

Half an hour later, Hewson once more crossed the landing and went up to the box-room to look for Margery's trunk. He was intent and flushed, and paused for a moment under the light to brush some shreds of silver from his sleeve. He seemed unconscious that a wraith of flame-coloured chiffon drifted away from his shoulder as he walked, hung in the air, and settled on the carpet behind him. He came down again from the box-room breathing hard, bent beneath the trunk, and as he re-entered the bedroom something black and snake-like lying across the threshold wound round his feet and nearly entangled him. Approaching the bed, his steps were once more impeded; sometimes he was walking ankle-deep.

He pitched the trunk down in a clear space, propped it open and began to pack. Many of the fragments, torn too fine, were elusive; he stooped with the action of a gleaner to gather them in armfuls, then thrust them down into the trunk. The silks – they seemed still sentient – quivered under his touch; the velvets lay there sullenly, and sometimes, when he heaped them in, dripped out over the edge of the box again. Here and there an end of fur ruffled into deeper shadows under his excited breath. When he had amassed everything, Hewson beat with the flat of his hands upon the pile to make it level, spread tissue over it, and locked the trunk. Then he rang for Parkins and sat down to wait. He re-read Margery's list once again, folded it, and put it away in his pocket-book.

That night, Lippit the chauffeur received his instructions. He was to take Mrs Blair's box to the station at half-past eight the following morning, and despatch it to the given address per luggage in advance, having taken to the same station a ticket to be afterwards destroyed. This extravagance Hewson deplored, but the exigencies of the railway company demanded it. The trunk was strapped and corded and placed in the back hall in readiness for its early departure, and Hewson, seated comfortably at his table by the library fire, printed out two labels in neat black characters, then himself affixed them to the handles of the trunk.

'Would there be anything more, sir?' inquired Parkins, standing at attention.

'No, not tonight,' said Hewson courteously. 'I am sorry to have kept you late, Parkins: you had better go to bed.'

'Thank you, sir.'

'And oh, Parkins!'

'Sir?'

'You had better ask Emily to sweep out Mrs Blair's room again tonight. The carpet needs sweeping; she should pay particular attention to the carpet.'

Hearing the hall clock strike eleven, Hewson turned the lights out, quenched the astonished face of Parkins and went upstairs to bed.

RUTH RENDELL

A Glowing Future

'Six should be enough,' he said. 'We'll say six tea chests, then, and one trunk. If you'll deliver them tomorrow, I'll get the stuff all packed and maybe your people could pick them up Wednesday.' He made a note on a bit of paper. 'Fine,' he said. 'Round about lunchtime tomorrow.'

She hadn't moved. She was still sitting in the big oak-armed chair at the far end of the room. He made himself look at her and he managed a kind of grin, pretending all was well.

'No trouble,' he said. 'They're very efficient.'

'I couldn't believe,' she said, 'that you'd really do it. Not until I heard you on the phone. I wouldn't have thought it possible. You'll really pack up all those things and have them sent off to her.'

They were going to have to go over it all again. Of course they were. It wouldn't stop until he'd got the things out and himself out, away from London and her for good. And he wasn't going to argue or make long defensive speeches. He lit a cigarette and waited for her to begin, thinking that the pubs would be opening in an hour's time and he could go out then and get a drink.

'I don't understand why you came here at all,' she said.

He didn't answer. He was still holding the cigarette box, and now he closed its lid, feeling the coolness of the onyx on his fingertips.

She had gone white. 'Just to get your things? Maurice, did you come back just for that?'

'They are my things,' he said evenly.

'You could have sent someone else. Even if you'd written to me and asked me to do it – '

'I never write letters,' he said.

She moved then. She made a little fluttering with her hand in front of her mouth. 'As if I didn't know!' She gasped, and making a great effort she steadied her voice. 'You were in Australia for a year, a whole year, and you never wrote to me once.'

'I phoned.'

'Yes, twice. The first time to say you loved me and missed me and were longing to come back to me and would I wait for you and there wasn't anyone else was there? And the second time, a week ago, to say you'd be here by Saturday and could I – could I put you up. My God, I'd lived with you for two years, we were practically married, and then you phone and ask if I could put you up!'

'Words,' he said. 'How would you have put it?'

'For one thing, I'd have mentioned Patricia. Oh, yes, I'd have mentioned her. I'd have had the decency, the common humanity, for that. D'you know what I thought when you said you were coming? I ought to know by now how peculiar he is, I thought, how detached, not writing or phoning or anything. But that's Maurice, that's the man I love, and he's coming back to me and we'll get married and I'm so happy!'

'I did tell you about Patricia.'

'Not until after you'd made love to me first.'

He winced. It had been a mistake, that. Of course he hadn't meant to touch her beyond the requisite greeting kiss. But she was very attractive and he was used to her and she seemed to expect it – and oh, what the hell. Women never could understand about men and sex. And there was only one bed, wasn't there? A hell of a scene there'd have been that first night if he'd suggested sleeping on the sofa in here.

'You made love to me,' she said. 'You were so passionate, it was just like it used to be, and then the next morning you told me. You'd got a resident's permit to stay in Australia, you'd got a job all fixed up, you'd met a girl you wanted to marry. Just like that you told me, over breakfast. Have you ever been smashed in the face, Maurice? Have you ever had your dreams trodden on?'

'Would you rather I'd waited longer? As for being smashed in the face – ' he rubbed his cheekbone ' – that's quite a punch you pack.'

She shuddered. She got up and began slowly and stiffly to pace the room. 'I hardly touched you. I wish I'd killed you!' By a small table she stopped. There was a china figurine on it, a bronze paperknife, an onyx pen jar that matched the ashtray. 'All those things,' she said. 'I looked after them for you. I treasured them. And now you're going to have them all shipped out to her. The things we lived with. I used to look at them and think, Maurice bought that when we went to – oh God, I can't believe it. Sent to her!'

He nodded, staring at her. 'You can keep the big stuff,' he said. 'You're specially welcome to the sofa. I've tried sleeping on it for two nights and I never want to see the bloody thing again.'

She picked up the china figurine and hurled it at him. It didn't hit him

254

because he ducked and let it smash against the wall, just missing a framed drawing. 'Mind the Lowry,' he said laconically, 'I paid a lot of money for that.'

She flung herself onto the sofa and burst into sobs. She thrashed about, hammering the cushions with her fists. He wasn't going to be moved by that – he wasn't going to be moved at all. Once he'd packed those things, he'd be off to spend the next three months touring Europe. A free man, free for the sights and the fun and the girls, for a last fling of wild oats. After that, back to Patricia and a home and a job and responsibility. It was a glowing future which this hysterical woman wasn't going to mess up.

'Shut up, Betsy, for God's sake,' he said. He shook her roughly by the shoulder, and then he went out because it was now eleven and he could get a drink.

Betsy made herself some coffee and washed her swollen eyes. She walked about, looking at the ornaments and the books, the glasses and vases and lamps, which he would take from her tomorrow. It wasn't that she much minded losing them, the things themselves, but the barrenness which would be left, and the knowing that they would all be Patricia's.

In the night she had got up, found his wallet, taken out the photographs of Patricia, and torn them up. But she remembered the face, pretty and hard and greedy, and she thought of those bright eyes widening as Patricia unpacked the tea chests, the predatory hands scrabbling for more treasures in the trunk. Doing it all perhaps before Maurice himself got there, arranging the lamps and the glasses and the ornaments in their home for his delight when at last he came.

He would marry her, of course. I suppose she thinks he's faithful to her, Betsy thought, the way I once thought he was faithful to me. I know better now. Poor stupid fool, she doesn't know what he did the first moment he was alone with her, or what he would do in France and Italy. That would be a nice wedding present to give her, wouldn't it, along with all the pretty bric-a-brac in the trunk?

Well, why not? Why not rock their marriage before it had even begun? A letter. A letter to be concealed in, say, that blue-and-white ginger jar. She sat down to write. Dear Patricia – what a stupid way to begin, the way you had to begin a letter even to your enemy.

Dear Patricia: I don't know what Maurice has told you about me, but we have been living here as lovers ever since he arrived. To be more explicit, I mean we have made love, have slept together. Maurice is incapable of being faithful to anyone. If you don't believe me, ask yourself why, if he didn't want me, he didn't stay in a hotel. That's all. Yours – and she signed her name and felt a little better, well enough and steady enough to take a bath and get herself some lunch.

Six tea chests and a trunk arrived on the following day. The chests smelled of tea and had drifts of tea leaves lying in the bottom of them. The trunk was made of silver-coloured metal and had clasps of gold-coloured metal. It was rather a beautiful object, five feet long, three feet high, two feet wide, and the lid fitted so securely it seemed a hermetic sealing.

Maurice began to pack at two o'clock. He used tissue paper and newspapers. He filled the tea chests with kitchen equipment and cups and plates and cutlery, with books, with those clothes of his he had left behind him a year before. Studiously, and with a certain grim pleasure, he avoided everything Betsy might have insisted was hers – the poor cheap things, the stainless steel spoons and forks, the Woolworth pottery, the awful coloured sheets, red and orange and olive, that he had always loathed. He and Patricia would sleep in white linen.

Betsy didn't help him. She watched, chain-smoking. He nailed the lids on the chests and on each lid he wrote in white paint his address in Australia. But he didn't paint in the letters of his own name. He painted Patricia's. This wasn't done to needle Betsy but he was glad to see it was needling her.

He hadn't come back to the flat till one that morning, and of course he didn't have a key. Betsy had refused to let him in, had left him down there in the street, and he had to sit in the car he'd hired till seven. She looked as if she hadn't slept either. Miss Patricia Gordon, he wrote, painting fast and skilfully.

'Don't forget your ginger jar.' said Betsy. 'I don't want it.'

'That's for the trunk.' Miss Patricia Gordon, 23 Burwood Park Avenue, Kew, Victoria, Australia 3101. 'All the pretty things are going in the trunk. I intend it as a special present for Patricia.'

The Lowry came down and was carefully padded and wrapped. He wrapped the onyx ashtray and the pen jar, the alabaster bowl, the bronze paperknife, the tiny Chinese cups, the tall hock glasses. The china figurine, alas . . . he opened the lid of the trunk.

'I hope the customs open it!' Betsy shouted at him. 'I hope they confiscate things and break things! I'll pray every night for it to go to the bottom of the sea before it gets there!'

'The sea,' he said, 'is a risk I must take. As for the customs – ' He smiled. 'Patricia works for them, she's a customs officer – didn't I tell you? I very much doubt if they'll even glance inside.' He wrote a label and pasted it on the side of the trunk. Miss Patricia Gordon, 23 Burwood Park Avenue, Kew . . . 'And now I'll have to go out and get a padlock. Keys, please. If you try to keep me out this time, I'll call the police. I'm still the legal tenant of this flat remember.'

She gave him the keys. When he had gone she put her letter in the ginger jar. She hoped he would close the trunk at once, but he didn't. He left it open, the lid thrown back, the new padlock dangling from the gold-coloured clasp.

'Is there anything to eat?' he said.

'Go and find your own bloody food! Go and find some other woman to feed you!'

He liked her to be angry and fierce; it was her love he feared. He came back at midnight to find the flat in darkness, and he lay down on the sofa with the tea chests standing about him like defences, like barricades, the white paint showing faintly in the dark. Miss Patricia Gordon . . .

Presently Betsy came in. She didn't put on the light. She wound her way between the chests, carrying a candle in a saucer which she set down on the trunk. In the candlelight, wearing a long white nightgown, she looked like a ghost, like some wandering madwoman, a Mrs Rochester, a Woman in White.

'Maurice.'

'Go away, Betsy, I'm tired.'

'Maurice, please. I'm sorry I said all those things. I'm sorry I locked you out.'

'OK, I'm sorry too. It's a mess, and maybe I shouldn't have done it the way I did. But the best way is for me just to go and my things to go and make a clean split. Right? And now will you please be a good girl and go away and let me get some sleep?'

What happened next he hadn't bargained for. It hadn't crossed his mind. Men don't understand about women and sex. She threw herself on him, clumsily, hungrily. She pulled his shirt open and began kissing his neck and his chest, holding his head, crushing her mouth to his mouth, lying on top of him and gripping his legs with her knees.

He gave her a savage push. He kicked her away, and she fell and struck her head on the side of the trunk. The candle fell off, flared and died in a pool of wax. In the darkness he cursed floridly. He put on the light and she got up, holding her head where there was a little blood.

'Oh, get out, for God's sake,' he said, and he manhandled her out, slamming the door after her.

In the morning, when she came into the room, a blue bruise on her forehead, he was asleep, fully clothed, spreadeagled on his back. She shuddered at the sight of him. She began to get breakfast but she couldn't eat anything. The coffee made her gag and a great nauseous shiver went through her. When she went back to him he was sitting up on the sofa, looking at his plane ticket to Paris.

'The men are coming for the stuff at ten,' he said as if nothing had happened, 'and they'd better not be late. I have to be at the airport at noon.'

She shrugged. She had been to the depths and she thought he couldn't hurt her any more.

'You'd better close the trunk,' she said absent-mindedly.

'All in good time.' His eyes gleamed. 'I've got a letter to put in yet.'

Her head bowed, the place where it was bruised sore and swollen, she looked loweringly at him. 'You never write letters.'

'Just a note. One can't send a present without a note to accompany it, can one?'

He pulled the ginger jar out of the trunk, screwed up her letter without even glancing at it, and threw it on the floor. Rapidly yet ostentatiously and making sure that Betsy could see, he scrawled across a sheet of paper: *All this is for you, darling Patricia, for ever and ever.*

'How I hate you,' she said.

'You could have fooled me.' He took a large angle lamp out of the trunk and set it on the floor. He slipped the note into the ginger jar, rewrapped it, tucked the jar in between the towels and cushions which padded the fragile objects. 'Hatred isn't the word I'd use to describe the way you came after me last night.'

She made no answer. Perhaps he should have put a heavy object like that lamp in one of the chests, perhaps he should open up one of the chests now. He turned round for the lamp. It wasn't there. She was holding it in both hands.

'I want that, please.'

'Have you ever been smashed in the face, Maurice?' she said breathlessly, and she raised the lamp and struck him with it full on the forehead. He staggered and she struck him again, and again and again, raining blows on his face and his head. He screamed. He sagged, covering his face with bloody hands. Then with all her strength she gave him a great swinging blow and he fell to his knees, rolled over and at last was stilled and silenced.

There was quite a lot of blood, though it quickly stopped flowing. She stood there looking at him and she was sobbing. Had she been sobbing all the time? She was covered with blood. She tore off her clothes and dropped them in a heap around her. For a moment she knelt beside him, naked and weeping, rocking backwards and forwards, speaking his name, biting her fingers that were sticky with his blood.

But self-preservation is the primal instinct, more powerful than love or sorrow, hatred or regret. The time was nine o'clock, and in an hour those men would come. Betsy fetched water in a bucket, detergent, cloths and a sponge. The hard work, the great cleansing, stopped her tears, quieted her heart and dulled her thoughts. She thought of nothing, working frenziedly, her mind a blank.

When bucket after bucket of reddish water had been poured down the sink and the carpet was soaked but clean, the lamp washed and dried and polished, she threw her clothes into the basket in the bathroom and had a bath. She dressed carefully and brushed her hair. Eight minutes to ten.

Everything was clean and she had opened the window, but the dead thing still lay there on a pile of reddened newspapers.

'I loved him,' she said aloud, and she clenched her fists. 'I hated him.'

The men were punctual. They came at ten sharp. They carried the six tea chests and the silver-coloured trunk with the gold-coloured clasps downstairs.

When they had gone and their van had driven away, Betsy sat down on the sofa. She looked at the angle lamp, the onyx pen jar and ashtray, the ginger jar, the alabaster bowls, the hock glasses, the bronze paperknife, the little Chinese cups, and the Lowry that was back on the wall. She was quite calm now and she didn't really need the brandy she had poured for herself.

Of the past she thought not at all and the present seemed to exist only as a palpable nothingness, a thick silence that lay around her. She thought of the future, of three months hence, and into the silence she let forth a steady, rather toneless peal of laughter. Miss Patricia Gordon, 23 Burwood Park Avenue, Kew, Victoria, Australia 3101. The pretty, greedy, hard face, the hands so eager to undo that padlock and prise open those golden clasps to find the treasure within . . .

And how interesting that treasure would be in three months' time, like nothing Miss Patricia Gordon had seen in all her life! It was as well, so that she would recognize it, that it carried on top of it a note in a familiar hand: *All this is for you, darling Patricia, for ever and ever.*

Notes on the Authors

LOUISA MAY ALCOTT was born in 1832, in Germantown, Philadelphia. Her father was the philosopher Bronson Alcott, a friend of Emerson and Thoreau. The education he gave Louisa and her three sisters was liberal and unorthodox, but his extreme unworldliness kept the family on the brink of poverty. Louisa earned her living by sewing, teaching and a miserable spell in domestic service – all described in her autobiographical novel *Work* (1873). From the age of nineteen, she wrote 'sensation' stories for popular magazines, including 'Pauline's Passion and Punishment'. In 1868, she produced her masterpiece, *Little Women*, which together with its sequels *Good Wives*, *Little Men* and *Jo's Boys*, became one of the enduring bestsellers of the nineteenth century. A staunch campaigner for black rights and women's suffrage, she died in Boston in 1888.

ELIZABETH BOWEN was born in Dublin in 1899, the only child of an Anglo-Irish lawyer and landowner. After her marriage in 1923, she divided her time between London, Oxford and Bowen's Court, her ancestral home in County Cork. Her novels include *The Hotel* (1927), *The Death of the Heart*, (1938) *The Little Girls* (1964) and *Eva Trout* (1969). A writer of great poetic elegance, she was mistress of the art of the short story. 'Making Arrangements' was first published in *Eve* magazine in 1925. Elizabeth Bowen died in 1973.

MARY ELIZABETH BRADDON, born in 1835, created a sensation when her novel *Lady Audley's Secret*, a classic melodrama concerning a bigamous marriage, appeared in 1862. Following this with *Aurora Floyd* (1863), she established herself as one of the most popular women writers of the nineteenth century. Her private life was no less sensational. She lived out of wedlock with her publisher, John Maxwell, and bore him seven children. They eventually married when his first wife died in a lunatic asylum. Despite producing books at a tremendous rate her work was always stylish and powerful, and she was very much admired by her literary contemporaries up to her death in 1915. 'Samuel Lowgood's Revenge' is taken from *Ralph the Bailiff and Other Tales*, which was first published in 1862.

JOANNA BRISCOE was born in London in 1963. She grew up in Devon, and read English at University College, London. She has published one non-fiction book and two short stories, and is currently writing a novel and working as a journalist.

LUCY ELLMANN was born in America in 1956, and moved to Britain in 1970. After studying Art, she went to Essex University and the Courtauld Institute. She has written articles and reviews for the *Guardian*, the *Observer* and the *New Statesman and Society*. Her novel *Sweet Desserts* won the 1988 Guardian Fiction Prize. She lives in London with her daughter Emily.

ANNE ENRIGHT lives in Dublin, where she was born in 1962. Her first short story was published in *Faber Introductions 10*, and her first collection of stories will appear in 1991. She works as a television producer and director for RTE in Ireland.

MARY FLANAGAN was born in 1943 in New England, USA, and read History of Art at Brandyce University. In 1984, she published *Bad Girls*, her acclaimed collection of short stories. Her first novel, *Trust*, appeared in 1987. She has just completed a second, *Rose Reason*. She lives in North London.

MAUREEN FREELY was born in New Jersey, USA, spent her childhood in Turkey, and finished her education at Harvard. Her first novel, *Mother's Helper*, was published in 1979. Her second, *The Life of the Party*, appeared in 1985. She has recently completed a third novel, *The Stork Club*, part of which has been published in *Soho Square*. She has two children, and works as a journalist and critic.

ELIZABETH GASKELL was born Elizabeth Stevenson in 1810, daughter of a Unitarian minister. Much of her childhood was spent with her aunt in Knutsford, Chesire, the original of *Cranford* – the much-loved humorous novel for which she is best remembered today. In 1832, she married William Gaskell, a Unitarian minister in Manchester. The sufferings of the industrial poor, among whom she worked, inspired her magnificent first novel *Mary Barton*, published in 1848. Instantly a literary celebrity, she was asked by Charles Dickens to contribute to his magazine *Household Words*, and her 1855 novel *North and South* first appeared in its pages. Besides her novels, which include *Ruth*, *Wives and Daughters* and *Sylvia's Lovers*, Mrs Gaskell wrote many short stories, and produced a classic biography of her friend, Charlotte Brontë. 'The Doom of the Griffiths' first appeared in *Harper's* magazine in 1858. Elizabeth Gaskell died in 1865.

ELLEN GILCHRIST was born in 1935, in the Mississippi Delta, and now lives in New Orleans. She has published two collections of short stories, *In the Land of Dreamy Dreams* (1981), from which 'Revenge' is taken, and *Victory Over Japan* (1985). Her novel *The Annunciation* was published in 1983.

WINIFRED HOLTBY was born in Yorkshire in 1898. After serving in the Women's Auxiliary Army Corps during the First World War, she attended Somerville College, Oxford. Throughout the 1920s and 1930s she was a successful journalist, and she published five novels. Her most famous, *South Riding*, appeared posthumously in 1936, after her tragically early death at the age of thirty-seven.

261

SHENA MACKAY was born in Edinburgh in 1944. Her first novel, *Dust Falls on Eugene Schlumburger/Toddler on the Run*, which she wrote at the age of seventeen, was published in 1964, to instant critical acclaim. This was followed by *Music Upstairs* (1965), *Old Crow* (1967), *An Advent Calendar* (1971) and *A Bowl of Cherries* (1984). *Redhill Rococo*, which appeared in 1986, was awarded the Fawcett Society prize. Her latest book, *Dunedin*, will appear in 1990. She has also published two collections of short stories – *Babies in Rhinestones* and *Dreams of Dead Women's Handbags*. Shena Mackay also works as a journalist and critic, and lives in London.

CANDIA McWILLIAM was born in Edinburgh in 1955. After leaving Cambridge with a first, she worked for *Vogue* magazine, and later as an advertising copywriter. Her first novel, *A Case Of Knives*, was joint winner of the 1988 Betty Trask Award. Her second, *A Little Stranger*, was published in 1989, and she is the author of numerous short stories. Candia McWilliam lives in Oxford.

RUTH RENDELL is often described as 'The Queen of Crime'. Her award-winning detective novels, which include *From Doon With Death*, *A Judgement in Stone* and *A Guilty Thing Surprised*, have redefined crime fiction by examining the psychology of the murderer. Writing as Barbara Vine, she has further extended the conventional barriers with a series of brilliant, complex novels – such as *A Fatal Inversion* and *A Dark-Adapted Eye* – which focus on the problem of human evil. Rendell is one of Britain's finest and most popular writers.

MRS J. H. RIDDELL was born Charlotte Cowan, in Carrickfergus, Ireland. In 1855, she arrived in London, and set about supporting herself and her invalid mother with her pen. These early struggles are described in her novel *A Struggle for Fame* (1883). In 1857, she married an engineer, J. H. Riddell, and his work provided her with the background for her most successful novel, *George Geith of Fen Court* (1864), the tale of a clergyman who abandons his failed marriage for a city career. Mrs Riddell was highly regarded for her ghost stories – a genre in which Victorian women writers excelled. 'A Terrible Vengeance' appeared in *Princess Sunshine and Other Stories* in 1889. Mrs Riddell died in 1906.

KATE SAUNDERS was born in London in 1960. After ten years as a professional actor, she published her first novel, *The Prodigal Father*, in 1986. Her second novel, *Storm in the Citadel*, appeared in 1989. She now works as a freelance journalist and book reviewer.

MURIEL SPARK was born in Scotland in 1918. Her Edinburgh education became the background for her most celebrated novel, *The Prime of Miss Jean Brodie*. During the war, she worked in the Political Intelligence Department of the Foreign Office. Her first novel, *The Comforters*, published in 1957, instantly established her as one of the most original and brilliant writers of the century. Later novels include *Memento Mori*, *The Ballad of Peckham Rye* and *The Girls of Slender Means*. Her latest book, *A Far Cry From Kensington*, was published in 1988. 'The Portobello Road' first appeared in 1958, in *The Go-Away Bird*, a collection of stories which drew on her experiences in Central Africa in the 1940s. In 1954, she was received into the Roman Catholic Church, and she now lives in Italy.

Notes on the Authors

EMMA TENNANT was born in London, and grew up during the war in Scottish border country – the work of fellow-borderer James Hogg inspired her novel *The Bad Sister*. Her work is imaginative and experimental, ranging from eighteenth-century pastiche to psychological horror. It includes *Hotel de Dream*, *The Adventures of Robina* and two volumes of a projected cycle, *The House of Hospitalities* (1987) and *A Wedding of Cousins* (1988). *Two Women of London*, her feminist reworking of Stevenson's *Dr Jekyll and Mr Hyde*, was published in 1989. 'Rigor Beach' first appeared in *Bananas*, a literary magazine founded and edited by Emma Tennant, in 1975. She now lives in West London.

LISA ST AUBIN DE TERÁN was born in London in 1953, daughter of a Jersey mother and a South American father. At sixteen, she married a Venezuelan landowner, and spent two years wandering around Italy. After seven years in the Andes, managing her husband's sugar plantation, she returned to England with her daughter. In 1982, she published her first novel, *The Keepers of the House*. This was followed by *Slow Train to Milan* (1983), *The Tiger* (1984), *The Bay of Silence* (1986) and *Black Idol* (1987). She has also produced a volume of poetry, *The High Place*, a collection of short stories, *The Marble Mountain*, and an autobiography, *Off the Rails: Memoirs of a Train Addict*, which appeared in 1988. Her sixth novel *Joanna*, was published by Virago in 1990. Now married to the painter Robbie Duff-Scott, Lisa St Aubin de Terán lives in Italy.

ALICE WALKER is one of the most powerful voices in modern American fiction. Born in Georgia, she now lives in San Francisco. She has published poetry, critical essays, and three novels, including *The Color Purple* (1983), which won a Pulitzer Prize. 'The Revenge of Hannah Kemhuff' is taken from her 1984 collection of short stories, *In Love and Trouble*.

263